Praise for

Murder by Misrule was selected as one of Kirkus Review's Best Indie Books of 2014.

"Castle's characters brim with zest and real feeling... Though the plot keeps the pages turning, the characters, major and minor, and the well-wrought historical details will make readers want to linger in the 16th century. A laugh-out loud mystery that will delight fans of the genre." — Kirkus, starred review

"*Murder by Misrule* is a delightful debut with characters that leap off the page, especially the brilliant if unwilling detective Francis Bacon and his street smart man Tom Clarady. Elizabeth Tudor rules, but Anna Castle triumphs." — Karen Harper, NY Times best-selling author of *The Queen's Governess*

"Well-researched... *Murder by Misrule* is also enormously entertaining; a mystery shot through with a series of misadventures, misunderstandings, and mendacity worthy of a Shakespearian comedy." — M. Louisa Locke, author of the Victorian San Francisco Mystery Series

"Castle's period research is thorough but unobtrusive, and her delight in the clashing personalities of her crime-fighting duo is palpable: this is the winning fictional odd couple of the year, with Bacon's near-omniscience being effectively grounded by Clarady's street smarts. The book builds effectively to its climax, and a last-minute revelation that is particularly well-handled, but readers will most appreciate the wry humor. An extremely promising debut." — Steve Donoghue, Historical Novel Society

"Historical mystery readers take note: *Murder by Misrule* is a wonderful example of Elizabethan times brought to life...a blend of Sherlock Holmes and history." — D. Donovan, eBook Reviewer, Midwest Book Review

"I love when I love a book! *Murder by Misrule* by Anna Castle was a fantastic read. Overall, I really liked this story and highly recommend it." — Book Nerds

Praise for Anna Castle's *Death by Disputation*

Death by Disputation won the 2015 Chaucer Awards First In Category Award for the Elizabethan/Tudor period.

"Castle's style shines ... as she weaves a complex web of scenarios and firmly centers them in Elizabethan culture and times." — D. Donovan, eBook Reviewer, Midwest Book Review

" I would recommend *Death by Disputation* to any fan of historical mysteries, or to anyone interested in what went on in Elizabethan England outside the royal court." — E. Stephenson, Historical Novel Society

"Accurate historical details, page turning plot, bodacious, lovable and believable characters, gorgeous depictions and bewitching use of language will transfer you through time and space back to Elizabethan England." — Edi's Book Lighthouse

"This second book in the Francis Bacon mystery series is as strong as the first. At times bawdy and rowdy, at times thought-provoking ... Castle weaves religious-political intrigue, murder mystery, and Tom's colorful friendships and love life into a tightly-paced plot." — Amber Foxx, Indies Who Publish Everywhere

Praise for Anna Castle's *The Widows Guild*

"As in Castle's earlier book, Murder by Misrule, she brings the Elizabethan world wonderfully to life, and if Francis Bacon himself seems a bit overshadowed at times in this novel, it's because the great, fun creation of the Widow's Guild itself easily steals the spotlight.

Strongly recommended." -- Editor's Choice, Historical Novel Society.

"Fans of historical mysteries will find this book just as captivating and well-done as the rest in a highly recommended read brimming with action and captivating scenarios." -- D. Donovan, Senior Book Reviewer, Midwest Book Review.

Praise for Anna Castle's *Publish and Perish*

Won an Honorable Mention for Mysteries in Library Journal's 2017 Indie Ebook Awards!

"In this aptly titled fourth book in the Francis Bacon series, Castle combines her impressive knowledge of English religion and politics during the period with masterly creativity. The result is a lively, clever story that will leave mystery fans delighted.—Emilie Hancock, Mount Pleasant Regional Lib., SC, for Library Journal.

Also by Anna Castle

The Francis Bacon Mystery Series
Murder by Misrule
Death by Disputation
The Widow's Guild
Publish and Perish

The Professor & Mrs. Moriarty Mystery Series
Moriarty Meets His Match
Moriarty Takes His Medicine
Moriarty Brings Down the House

The Lost Hat, Texas Mystery Series
Black & White & Dead All Over
Flash Memory

A Francis Bacon Mystery — #4

Publish and Perish

Anna Castle

Publish and Perish
A Francis Bacon Mystery — #4

Print Edition | June 2017
Discover more works by Anna Castle at www.annacastle.com

Copyright © 2017 by Anna Castle
Cover design by Jennifer Quinlan
Editorial services by Jennifer Quinlan, Historical Editorial

ISBN-10: 1-945382-09-0
ISBN-13: 978-1-945382-09-3
Produced in the United States of America

ONE

Francis Bacon sat at his desk, the windows opened wide in a futile effort to relieve the fustiness of his chambers. In late July, the buildings surrounding the central yard at Gray's Inn trapped the breeze, freighting it with the smell of sunbaked horse dung before allowing a few meager breaths to rise up to the first floor. He longed to go lie down in his bedchamber, where the fresh wind blew in from flower-dappled fields, but he didn't want his clerk to catch him napping after dinner.

He picked up his pen to continue working on his latest advice letter, *An Advertisement Touching the Controversies of the Church of England*. His theme could hardly be more timely. The whole country was embroiled in a battle of pamphleteers, hurling scathing broadsides at one another over the proper constitution of the Church. That such a topic could become the dominant form of entertainment in the great city of London boggled the mind, but there it was.

One side was led by an anonymous zealot who styled himself Martin Marprelate. The clever name stated his purpose right from the title page. He meant to mar public opinion of the prelates of the established church, from the Archbishop of Canterbury on down. He'd published four fat pamphlets since last November while evading the archbishop's pursuivants. He'd fallen silent in April, around the time that a chorus of anti-Martins had raised their voices, issuing volleys of scurrilous ballads, mocking plays, and satirical commentaries. They'd succeeded in drawing Martin back into the fray with a new work.

Francis glanced at the door and picked up Martin's latest to read a little further. This one, titled *Theses Martinianae,* had ostensibly been written by one Martin Junior. He made a great play of wondering where his father had got to — a question that vexed even the Privy Council. The body of the work consisted of one hundred and ten demands for the complete reformation of the English church. Dry stuff on the whole, but framed by an introduction and conclusion peppered with the provocative raillery that won the applause of the masses. The demands crowded the border of treason, but the humorous passages were far more dangerous because they made the work so entertaining.

He read another passage and chuckled. *Outrageous! But what wit!*

A perfunctory knock on the door heralded the clerk's return. Francis stuffed Martin's pamphlet under a book, dipped his quill in the inkpot, and turned his face toward his letter.

Thomas Clarady strode in with his customary bounce and took up his stool, struggling, as always, to fit his long legs under his desk. Francis's previous clerk had been a mousy fellow of modest stature. Tom, a shade over six feet tall, grumbled daily at the confinement, when not quibbling over the tasks set for him.

Something had lifted his spirits this afternoon. His handsome features were alight with merriment — a welcome change. Tom was one of those men who grew handsomer with age. His blue eyes had depths now, and ruddy tints burnished his fair curls and short beard. He kept himself in top condition with fencing and dancing, like other young Inns of Court gentlemen, and made an impressive representative when Francis needed to send a confidential message. If only he would put away the absurd yellow pearl that dangled from his left ear. But no; his late father had brought it back from his round-the-world journey with Sir Francis Drake, and no amount of argument or cajolery could induce him to remove it.

Tom waved a battered quarto. "Martin's back! I snagged this copy from a fellow reading it in the jakes."

Francis wished he would keep such details to himself, but he welcomed the rare good cheer. Tom's temper, once as mild as a summer morning, had grown peevish since his father died and his estate was turned over to a guardian, who happened to be Francis's aunt, Lady Elizabeth Russell. She'd reduced Tom's allowance to a fraction of its former bounty, paying his fixed expenses, like his fees at Gray's Inn, directly. She'd set him to work as Francis's clerk in exchange for tutoring in the common law. She even paid his tailor's bills herself, wisely recognizing that any coins given to Tom would swiftly find their way into the hands of lightskirts and tavern keepers.

Tom had endured this regimen with equanimity until the day he turned twenty-one. He had foolishly believed his estates would revert to him on his birthday by some inevitable natural process in spite of Francis's warnings. According to the law, a ward must sue for the livery of his estate on reaching his majority. Until then, everything remained under his guardian's control.

Furious, Tom had run wild, practically living in his favorite brothel, racking up mountainous charges for drink and other services and brazenly sending the bills to Lady Russell. She paid the first one, then had him arrested for lewdness, letting him stew in Bridewell for a few nights to reconsider his priorities. He'd returned to Gray's beaten but unbowed. He now devoted his leisure to studying the laws of wardship and devising ways to earn the money he needed to pay for his suit.

Francis sympathized. He had undergone a similar outburst of delayed grief after his father's equally unexpected death ten years ago. Nothing could replace the loss of a father's loving hand guiding one through the rocky shoals of youth into the safe harbor of a profession suited to one's talents and station. Nothing.

Having five older brothers, Francis suffered from a lack of property rather than lack of control over a substantial inheritance, but the results were similar. While his mother fruitlessly battled his stepbrothers in the courts, he'd sunk into a state of complete rebellion, locking himself in his chambers at Gray's for a weeks-long orgy of Roman satirical plays. He still blushed to remember that period of intellectual debauchery.

In time, he'd joined the other members of Gray's Inn in the purposeful life of legal men, ordered by the annual calendar of the courts and given structure by the daily rhythm of prayers, meals, legal exercises, and administrative meetings. He found satisfaction — if little pecuniary reward — writing his letters of counsel for Her Majesty and members of the Privy Council. In time, Tom would settle into his destined role as well.

Tom slapped the pamphlet he was reading. "You'd think Martin would have the sense to stay hidden. I suppose he couldn't resist stabbing back at the anti-Martinists. Who could blame him? *Martin's Mirror Mar'd* was pure genius, starting with the subtitle: *A Poultice for a Poke-Prelate.* That would raise my hackles!" He twisted around to take another foolscap quarto from the shelf behind his desk and held it toward Francis. "Have you seen that one?"

Francis regarded it as if it were a cold bowl of greasy pottage. "You shouldn't be wasting your time on that rubbish."

"At least it's legal — unlike that copy of Martin Junior you've been sneaking peeks at all morning."

"I can't offer useful advice to counter Martin's influence without knowledge of Martin's works. My bookseller finds them for me. I don't ask where."

Tom smirked. "Well, you should take a peek at *Martin's Mirror* as well. He seems to know who Martin is, or at least *where* he is."

"Impossible. No one knows either of those things."

"He knows something, this Pasquill Caviliero, whoever that is. He's got a battle between the knight of the ants of the north and the king of the south. Ants of the north; that's Northants — Northamptonshire. Get it?"

Francis groaned. Such was the state of English literature in 1589.

Tom laughed, heartily entertained by both the lame wit and his master's reaction. "A knight of Northamptonshire. That's fairly specific. I don't know about the king of the south though. He can't mean Spain, can he?"

"Hardly. Martin's a Presbyterian, not a Catholic." Francis sniffed to show his disdain, but the wordplay had caught his attention. "He could mean Surrey. 'Sur' is Spanish for south and 'rey' means king."

"Good catch!" Tom snapped his fingers. "But does that mean Martin is north or south?"

"It's nonsense. It doesn't mean anything."

"It's better than that endless list of nattering *theses* you find so fascinating."

"These 'nattering theses' amount to an explicit plan to demolish the established church!"

Tom cocked his head and pressed a thoughtful finger to his cheek. "Do you need a plan to accomplish a demolition? You could just get a catapult and start firing away."

"Of course you need a plan. Taking buildings apart is more delicate work than you, apparently, can imagine. For one thing, there may be many salvageable timbers —" Francis broke off as Tom's toothy smile told him he'd fallen into a trap.

Well, he wasn't about to allow himself to be bested in a rhetorical contest by a testy clerk. He was composing a sally that expanded on the metaphor established by the catapult when the door flew open and his fifteen-year-old servant popped in.

"More dignity, Pinnock, if you please!" Francis scolded.

The impertinent boy winked at Tom and slowed to a solemn march for the remaining few yards. He handed Francis a sealed letter, then folded his hands behind his back to wait for a reply.

Francis slit the seal with his knife and read the brief note. Then he waved it at Tom. This might well cheer them both up. "My lord uncle has a sensitive matter he wants us to look into."

"Both of us?"

"Both of us. He doesn't say what it is, of course." One didn't put such things in writing. "But if he wants you as well as me, it must be more than another advice letter." Francis jotted a note agreeing to present himself as soon as possible, then he sanded, folded, and sealed it, handing the small square to Pinnock. "Run this down to Burghley House, quick as a bunny, then come straight home."

After the door closed behind him, Francis picked up Martin's *Theses* and read nearly a page before Tom burst out, "Aren't you going?"

Francis allowed him a wry smile. "I wouldn't want my uncle to think I'm just sitting here twiddling my thumbs."

"Ah."

Francis finished reading the whole pamphlet. For all he knew, it had something to do with his uncle's request. Then he took a pair of pristine wrist ruffs and got up to let Tom fasten them. He went into his bedchamber to choose a hat, then returned to the front chamber and raised his eyebrows for his clerk's approval.

Tom shrugged one shoulder. "It makes your point." He tucked his tongue in his cheek, plainly wanting to add something.

"Yes?" Francis prompted.

"I know His Lordship won't come right out and offer you payment. But if you could find a way to hint or suggest it, I personally would prefer cash to honors this time. I need money, lots of it, if I'm ever going to win back my estate."

"I'll do what I can, but remember that your guardian is his sister-in-law as well as my aunt."

"How could I ever forget that?"

Francis left without further ado but had to pause on the landing to chuckle to himself. His uncle, the Lord Treasurer, was also the Master of the Court of Wards. Any sums he paid Tom for services rendered would soon find their way right back into his coffers.

TWO

As soon as the door closed, Tom jumped up and sprinted into the bedchamber to look out the window on the south side of the house. He watched Bacon walk around the corner and disappear into the passageway leading to Holborn Road.

Good. He'd be gone for at least an hour. Possibly two. Lord Burghley never admitted anyone the minute he arrived; it would look like he had nothing else to do. Bacon hadn't invented that little ploy. No, the Lord Treasurer would let his nephew cool his heels in the portico for at least half an hour. They'd talk for half an hour — Bacon would be sure they did. Every minute standing near the seat of power counted.

Tom returned to his desk, unearthed a folded square of paper, and slipped it into his sleeve. Then he jogged down the stairs to his room at the back of the house, which he had moved into at the end of Trinity term when his former chambermate went home to get married. Lady Russell paid the excessive rent from Tom's estate. Heaven forbid that so much as a stray groat should fall into Tom's misruly hands!

Never mind. Where there was a will, there was a way. He'd found a means of earning a few shillings — enough to visit his favorite doxy every other week and treat his friends to a jug or two at the tavern once in a while. A man must enjoy some pleasures, or what's it all for?

He pulled off his legal robes and changed into his city shoes — passable, but sturdy and easily cleaned. He changed his plain black hat for one with a wide brim and a flouncy feather that somewhat hid his face. Lady Russell might require him to dress in black — her favorite color — from head to toe, but she had an eye for quality. His doublet and round hose, while soberly trimmed, were made of finest broadcloth and fitted him to perfection. She considered him her representative as well as Bacon's. He doubted either would be much pleased with his next assignation.

Walking was faster than waiting for a wherry these days. Tom took the shortest route to St. Paul's Cathedral, glad for the chance to stretch his long legs. He entered through the great south doors and shouldered through the crowd of lightskirts, coney-catchers, pick-pockets, and masterless men working the ever-flowing stream of fresh prey, newly arrived from wherever such innocents were grown. In these hallowed halls of vice and thievery, Tom was almost glad to have an empty purse.

He took up his station on the far side of Duke Humphrey's tomb and hadn't long to wait before his best customer, a draper's apprentice with a passion for a mercer's daughter, sidled up.

"Do you have it?"

"I do." Tom drew the paper square from his sleeve and unfolded it. He exhibited the page in his flawless script, then cleared his throat and read aloud. "To my darling Lettice, captor of my heart and queen of my desires, I humbly beg you receive with a kind and pitiful regard this fervent cry from within the very depths of my soul."

"That's beautiful," the apprentice moaned, clasping his hands to his chest. "Won't you read the verse too, Mr. Veritas? You always add a little flourish. I do my best to imitate it."

Tom signed his poems "Valentine Veritas" in honor of his father, who had the same first name. "Tush! It's nothing." Tom set one fist on his hip and held up the page with the other hand, though of course he knew the verse by heart. He lowered his pitch so his voice would carry through the dull roar of noise inside the cathedral.

"Oh, fair sweet face! Oh, eyes, celestial bright,
Twin stars in heaven that now beguile my sight!
Oh, fruitful lips, where cherries ever grow,
And damask cheeks, like peaches, soft as snow!
I beg of you, my fairest Lettice,
That never, ever you forget us,
And grant me this, one honeyed kiss,
To hold me in undying bliss."

The apprentice gaped at Tom in thunderstricken admiration. Tom never got tired of this part. Even better, the youth added sixpence to the usual fee of six shillings. "Mere money seems so inadequate." He sighed. "Could you do me another one next week? Same time?"

"I shall summon the muse." Tom undid a hook in his doublet to add the coins to his purse and tucked it well out of sight again. A man could not be too careful in this place. "Will it still be Lettice, d'ye think?"

"Of course! She's the light of my life." The apprentice paused, then added, "If it isn't, I'll send you a note." He touched the brim of his cap and skipped off to pitch his woo.

Tom wished him luck. He also wished the man would fall in love with a woman whose name was easier to rhyme, like Grace or Mary.

"Clarady, Clarady! Selling wretched verses to apprentices? How are the mighty fallen!" The mocking voice came from behind Duke Humphrey's tomb. "'I beg of you, my fairest Lettice, that never, ever you forget us'? I should charge you six shillings for the damage to my ears."

"What?" Tom turned on his heel and met the impish grin of his sometime friend from Cambridge University, Thomas Nashe. The scrawny poet looked newly prosperous in a green doublet that almost fit and a matching hat whose crown had not yet been broken. His straw-blond hair still needed trimming, and he hadn't managed to sprout any on his chin, though he was only a month younger than Tom. The lack of that manly ornament gave Nashe a perpetually boyish air, belied by the shrewdness of his sand-colored eyes.

"Nashey!" Tom cried gladly, clapping him on the shoulders. "What brings you to London?"

"I am now an inhabitant of this fair city, soon to become one of its most renowned quillsmen. I came down from Cambridge in May, choosing to avoid the crush of those tiresome graduation ceremonies."

"No master's degree?"

"I am my own master, that's sufficient degree for me. But what's new with you? Where's the dashing lad in the green hose and the yellow stockings? You look like you're on your way to a funeral. Who died?"

"My father."

Nashe's mocking laughter died at once. "I am truly sorry. I know how much you loved him. How did it happen?"

Tom's answer was cut off by a staggering oaf, who must have weighed fifteen stone, roaring curses at another of his tribe, drowning out all hope of conversation. Tom cocked his head toward the north doors. They made their way out and walked over to a timeworn tomb standing under an ancient yew tree. Moss grew in the dank dirt around its base, and birds had made free with its roughened surface.

A couple of wastrels leaned against it. Tom shooed them away. Nashe hopped up and made himself comfortable, heedless of his clothes. Tom pulled out a large handkerchief and spread it over the spotted surface before gingerly setting himself down.

"Fastidious, aren't you?"

Tom shrugged. "I'm not walking about the city with bird shit speckling my arse."

"A fair point." Nashe shot Tom a sidelong glance and said, "Tell me about your father. Did he fall in the battle against the Spanish Armada?"

Tom's father had been a privateer, captain of his own ship and more successful than most. He'd relieved the Spanish of many a rich cargo and had the sense to invest his takings in land, building an estate worth six hundred per annum, not counting his widow's portion. He'd been determined to hoist his only son into the ranks of the gentry, getting him into Gray's Inn by finding a member of the governing board with a burden of debt and paying it off. That member happened to be Francis Bacon.

"He survived the battles," Tom said, "with his ship intact and most of his crew as well. He came to London for a week last September in hopes of finding some supplies. There wasn't much, but I got to see him. Then he sailed to France in search of shot and powder, planning to sail out to harass the Spanish fleet on their way home. He found enough to fill his hold. Somehow it caught fire and blew his ship into the skies, killing him and his quartermaster. Fortunately, no one else was aboard."

"He was a hero," Nashe said. "He died in defense of our queen and our liberty, the same as if he'd been facing a Spanish galleon in the German Sea."

Tom nodded. They sat in silence for a few minutes, enjoying the shade. Sparrows twittered overhead and people's voices sounded all around them, from shoppers visiting the bookstalls lining the north wall of the cathedral.

"What will you do now?" Nashe asked. "Will you stay on at Gray's Inn and become a barrister? You're your own man now, like me."

"I'll stay the course my father set for me. I would anyway, but I have no choice. I'm not my own man. I belong to Lady Elizabeth Russell as surely as if she'd bought me at an auction."

"How's that?"

"My father's father bought manors that once belonged to Tarrant Abbey, not far from our house in Dorset. A wise purchase, but little did we know that any lands that once belonged to the old Church still owe knight service to the Crown. That duty sticks to the land like burrs in a rough cloak."

"Knight service? That sounds like something you'd like, galloping around the countryside rescuing damsels. Although I expect these days they just extract a healthy fine and send you on your merry way — the damsels, I mean." Nashe couldn't stay rational for too long at a stretch.

"If I had gained my majority before my father lost his life. I missed it by three months. Since a minor can't perform knight's service, however ceremonial, I became a ward of the queen, and my estate fell under the jurisdiction of the Court of Wards."

"That doesn't sound good."

"It isn't, trust me. The market in wardships is hotter than the Spanish Main in August. Anyone with cash in the house and an eye for a good investment sends a messenger galloping to Westminster to place their bid. Especially for an estate as large as mine."

Nashe whistled. "Remind me to ask you for a loan next time I come up short. Speaking of which—"

"You don't think I get any of it, do you? I'm the infant, as the legal documents describe us wards. No one gives money to an infant. Anyway, there are people watching out for news of rich wards, and the bidding starts early. My master, Francis Bacon—"

"I remember him. He's the one who wrote all those pithy letters while you were up at Cambridge."

"The same. We were together when I got the news. His uncle is the Master of the Court of the Wards and he knows the sorts of people most likely to win the prize. He did his best, I do believe, going straight to his aunt, Lady Russell, so she could get her bid in first. Since she's Lord Burghley's sister-in-law, she had the advantage."

Nashe held up a hand and pretended to calculate a sum on his fingers. "Let me get this straight. Your master, Francis Bacon, is the nephew of your guardian, Lady Russell, who is the aunt—"

"Sister-in-law," Tom corrected, "of the Master of Wards, who is also Mr. Bacon's uncle and also, to cap it all, the Lord Treasurer and the queen's right hand."

"Phew!" Nashe pulled off his hat and fanned himself with it, crimping the brim in his sweaty palm. "You *have* risen into exalted circles! I'd be afraid to sit next to you if I didn't have the tomb of this poor churl to raise me up a bit."

"I think it's Aethelred."

"Who is who?"

"The knave inside the tomb. I think it's Aethelred the Unready."

Nashe twisted around, lifting up half his arse in an attempt to read the worn lettering. "More likely Aethelflaed the Unwilling. She died of shame after hearing her name rhymed with 'red,' 'mad,' and 'trod' in the same verse."

Tom laughed. Leave it to Thomas Nashe to turn a serious moment into foolery.

Nashe grinned, pleased with the effect of his balm. "But your guardian is a lady, is she not? Of the feminine variety? I should think you'd have her in your palm by now."

"Not she!" The idea of cajoling Lady Russell with his usual light flirtations made Tom clutch his belly in dismay. "She's made entirely of hammered steel."

"Still, you don't look like you're going hungry."

"I get no allowance whatsoever." Tom's complaints began to sound petty, even to himself. He was plainly living in greater comfort and security than Nashe ever had.

"What's more, she and Mr. Bacon agree that I have loose tendencies best curbed by limiting my free time to the barest minimum. When I'm not studying or participating in legal exercises, I'm expected to work as Mr. Bacon's clerk. Luckily, he attends upon the royal court and takes a lot of naps —"

He broke off at Nashe's sputtering laughter. "Not both together! Anyway, I sneak out when I can. I came up with this idea to earn some money. I can earn twelve shillings a week in a good week. Half for pleasure, half to support my suit of liberty."

"I believe the word is 'livery.' Delivery from wardship, I suppose." Nashe might play the fool, but he'd been a good scholar.

"I like it my way better. I have to sue for *livery* of my estate from my guardian, and you know how lawsuits work. A line of prothonotaries, assessors, and feodaries from here to Westminster Abbey, each with his hand out for a fee. Every document has to be copied out three times. Do you know they actually charge by the foot for every parchment scroll? You have to watch them like a hawk to keep them from repeating sections just to make the vile thing longer."

"I wish I could make my vile thing longer," Nashe said somberly.

It took Tom's mind a moment to catch up, then he surrendered to the pure Nashery of it all and laughed, long and loudly.

"You have my deepest sympathies, my friend." Nashe patted him on the shoulder. "Mine and Queen Aethelflaed's. So now you're as poor as me in spite of your elegant garb." He studied Tom with a twisted smile. "Well, you might still be able to help. I have a ticklish sort of problem."

"Ticklish in what way?"

"Not the fun way." Nashe grimaced and hunched his thin shoulders. "To put it bluntly, someone is trying to kill me."

"What? Who would want to kill *you?*"

Nashe bristled. "I'll have you know I've offended many important persons over the years, especially recently." Then he shrugged and added, "Most of them masters at Cambridge, who are now dancing galliards in their classrooms in joy at my departure. I can see processions with boys in spring colors tossing flowers and singing —"

"Wake me when you get to the part about your putative assassin." Tom closed his eyes and snored.

"All right, all right. But I have to start in June, when it all began, so bear with me."

Tom flicked his fingers. "Let's have it, *camarade.*"

"That's when I came down to London. I had my first tender masterpiece, *An Anatomie of Absurdity* —"

"That sounds very Nashean."

"It's the epitome of Nashery, I assure you. Alas, my being a nobody of negative importance, no publisher would have it. There I was, alone and friendless —"

"What about Kit? He's in London. He would take you in." Christopher Marlowe had been Tom's Latin tutor for a few months at Cambridge. He'd taught him very little Latin, but quite a bit about spycraft. Tom had only seen him once or twice since then. They moved in different circles now.

"Ah, Marlowe, master of the mighty line! Strider across continents, king — nay, caesar — of the English stage! Handsome Kit, witty Kit, French-speaking Kit, sought after by every nobleman with a confidential message to be delivered abroad." Nashe grinned to leach the bitterness from his words. "He's too busy for me. And seldom in town in the summer. 'Tis the season for spies, you know."

"I didn't. Then where are you living? You don't look so terribly ill-used to me."

"I am not, and thank you for noticing. I found a like-minded spirit, a colleague, a guide . . . a guardian, if you will. Robert Greene. You've heard of *him,* I presume."

Everyone who understood the English language had heard of Robert Greene. "That's lucky," Tom said, not quite making it a question.

"Very lucky, although we do have a bond, a natural affinity. We met in a tavern favored by the inky tribe and fell into conversation. Two university men in a sea of self-educated lackwits. He took me under his wing and granted me the great favor of allowing me to write the introduction to his latest work, *Menaphon.* Have you read it?"

Tom shook his head. "I read law books and copy Bacon's legal maxims. And sneak in a little anti-Martin humor when I get the chance." He laughed at the reminder. "Have you read *Martin's Mirror Mar'd?* It's the funniest thing I've seen this year, unless you count some of Martin's own stuff."

"Seen it, my good man? I wrote it." Nashe grinned broadly, showing his gag-tooth.

"You?" That was twice he'd caught Tom off guard. He'd missed his calling. Nashe ought to be arguing cases in a court of law.

"Yours truly." Nashe doffed his hat. The poor object wouldn't survive long in his ownership. "Allow me to introduce myself: I am none other than Pasquill, the Caviliero."

"*The* Caviliero? I am honored, sir!" Tom swept off his floppy hat and bowed his head. "How did that come about? And does it pay?"

"Greene brought me in. And it does." He lowered his voice to a whisper. "Our paymaster is none other than Canon Bancroft."

Tom gaped at him, then snapped his mouth shut, glancing from side to side. Nobody was paying them the least attention. "Don't whisper, it's more suspicious than talking in a low voice. Marlowe taught me that. So you and Robert Greene are trying to lure out Martin Marprelate?"

"In addition to making a public mockery of him, which is almost too much fun to accept payment. Almost. I haven't identified the pomposticating Puritan yet, but I've caught his scent. He's somewhere in Northamptonshire, I think."

"I caught that!" Tom stabbed a finger at him. "Mr. Bacon thought it was pure nonsense, but it was a real hint, wasn't it? And now I'm putting these pieces together. If Martin thought you were getting too close, he might try to stop you. Hence the attempted assassinations."

"Hence." Nashe shifted on the tomb to face Tom but let his eyes wander as if he were watching the passersby. "There are three of us in the canon's employ: me, Robert Greene, and John Lyly. You know him, of course."

"By reputation." Lyly had been the darling of the royal court for the past decade, but he was no lowly scribbler. His father was certainly a gentleman.

"A week ago Monday, a pamphleteer named Edgar Stokes was strangled outside the house I had vacated the day before. Stokes, for his sins, was about my size and also beardless."

Tom frowned, judging it. "Could be a coincidence."

"It could. But then on Friday, also late at night, another man was strangled in Norton Folgate on his way past the house where I now live with Robert Greene. Another pamphleteer, whose name happened to be John Little."

"That sounds like less of a coincidence."

"I'm inclined to agree."

"Stop the writing," Tom advised. "Leave Martin to the authorities. Find another way to buy your next hat."

"Alas, I need more than hats. I need bread and a bed, every day if I can get them. The only tool I know how to use is a quill, so I'm following in Greene's footsteps and dedicating myself to the art of the pamphleteer."

"Can you make a living at that?" Tom fully intended to get back to the main point, but money was a present topic of concern.

"Not a great one. Not a large one. Not one that runs to brass buttons and silk linings." Nashe pointed his chin at Tom's doublet. "But enough to keep body and soul more or less together. A good pamphlet can pay as much as two pounds. If I could sell ten a year, I'd be comfortable. But I'm hoping—"

"Two pounds!" Tom had no idea that writing could earn such a sum. "I only get six shillings for my sonnets."

"Ah yes. Well, er . . ." Nashe offered another one of his contorted grimaces. "As for your poetry — and I say this as one who loves you like the brother you never had . . ."

Tom leveled a look at him. "My poetry sells like hot buns in February."

Nashe's lips formed an O. "That's brisk! Very brisk! But let's be grateful that your guardian sustains you on the path to a profession more suited to your native talents. And then let's leave it at that."

"Fair enough. My apologies for the digression. I know your life is more important than my tavern bills. How did you find out Martin's in Northamptonshire? No one else has caught so much as a whisper."

"There are whispers, if you listen for them. I've become the anti-Martinists' intelligencer, so to speak. All expenses paid by the Church of England, if you can believe that."

"Sometimes the world is very strange." Tom grinned.

"Mmm." Nashe nodded. "My job is to gad about the countryside sniffing out rumors of strangers with ink on their clothes who don't like to mingle. Carts arriving with a heavy load at the local manor house, where the master is known to be the hottest sort of nonconformist. The parish church will tend toward the Puritan as well in such cases, since the lord of the manor doubtless appointed the vicar. I've learned more than I expected, to tell you the truth. Something about me makes folks tell me things they wouldn't tell their own mothers."

"I'm not surprised," Tom said. "You've got that waifish quality and you make people laugh, which makes them trust you for some reason."

"Waifish." Nashe worked his mouth as if tasting the word. "I'll take it. My job is to scour up tidbits for we three Mar-Martins, as we call ourselves, to use in our pamphlets. Raillery laced with enough facts to give Martin a chill. Let him think we're closing in."

"And now you've struck too near the mark, and Martin is striking back. But what do you want me to do about it? Walk you home from the tavern every night? I'm on a short leash, remember."

"I want you to find the killer. You've a knack for this sort of thing. Even Kit says so, and you know how hard it is to impress him."

"High praise, but my hours are fully accounted for."

"If I know you, you'll have ways of getting around that." Nashe waggled his pale eyebrows. "I can pay you."

Tom gave that a lip fart. "No, you can't. Money runs through your fingers like sand through a sieve."

"I have more of it now. I got half a pound for my introduction to *Menaphon*. And I'll get a whole pound for my *Countercuffe*, when it's published. I'll split it with you."

"Ten shillings? I can earn that with two sonnets without risking my neck."

"Clarady, Clarady! You disappoint me. Where's your sense of loyalty? Of adventure? Have you really grown so callous as to let your old friend, your dear friend, the friend of your youth, those halcyon days in the halls of learning —"

"Peace, enough!" Tom growled under his breath. "I'm not sure what I can do. You're asking me to catch Martin

Marprelate when the Archbishop of Canterbury and all his men haven't managed it in nine months."

"Not Martin, necessarily. Just the accomplice who's killing us poor pamphleteers."

"Oh, that makes it *much* easier. All I have to do is find a strangler lurking about the liberties after midnight who also happens to be a religious zealot who will hang if he's caught helping the most wanted traitor in England." Tom twitched his lips. "Then again, I am fond of you, after a fashion. All right. I accept your commission. But I want that whole pound. And you'll pay my expenses."

"What expenses? And how will I live, if I hand over my whole fee?"

"Don't ask how," Tom said with a knowing grin. "Ask, how long?"

THREE

"Mr. Bacon?"

The voice sounded like a summons from far away. Francis had been waiting in his uncle's marble portico for so long his mind had wandered back into the arguments he was developing for his *Advertisement*. Fresh metaphors stimulated men's minds and engaged their hearts. His sense of injury at being kept waiting had borne a small fruit — a pleasing turn of phrase. *The wound is in no way dangerous, unless we poison it with our remedies.*

He repeated the phrase under his breath. He liked it. Easy to understand, neatly balanced, and apt.

"Mr. Bacon?"

Francis blinked and returned to the present place and time. He didn't recognize the man standing a few feet away, but he recognized the style and manner of a member of Lord Burghley's staff: well-framed and well-groomed, wearing a modest but well-cut suit of clothes, an unremarkable face framed by closely trimmed brown hair and beard. The man's only distinctive features were his unusually sharp eyes. Intelligence was outweighed only by discretion in the selection of a confidential secretary.

"Yes?" Francis answered.

The man smiled. "We're sorry to have kept you waiting so long. The press of business . . . you understand."

"Of course. Is my lord uncle ready to see me now?" Francis laid a slight emphasis on the term of kinship.

The man tilted his head to acknowledge the term. "I'm afraid my Lord Burghley is unable to speak with you. He isn't feeling well. Still suffering, you know, from his terrible loss."

"A great loss for us all." Lady Burghley, Francis's mother's eldest sister, had died in April. Her death was in truth a great loss since she had been a tireless supporter of the poor. Who would take up that standard now?

"My master, Mr. Cecil, is fully apprised of the matter at hand. He is ready now to speak with you, if you would be so good as to follow me?" He leaned toward the stairs, gesturing with both hands.

Francis swallowed his pride at the substitution. He could hardly refuse to see his cousin after sitting here waiting for half an hour. It would be churlish — and childish. But he knew Robert understood the slight and would enjoy it, in a small way.

"Very well." Francis rose and followed the secretary up the marble staircase to a chamber facing the front of the house. The room was pleasant enough in terms of size and light, but far more utilitarian than Lord Burghley's exquisite study, which looked onto the orchards at the rear. Here, traffic clattering out on the Strand rose above the high stone wall and drifted in through the open windows. The view included little to rest the eye upon beyond a single oak with a stone bench at its feet.

Robert had probably chosen this room because it overlooked the gatehouse controlling access to this center of power. Although even that failed to capture his attention. He sat hunched at his desk, glancing up at the new arrival with his quill in his hand as if he'd been caught in mid-sentence, snatching the precious interval between visitors to catch up on his Sisyphean correspondence.

"Ah, Frank! There you are." Robert didn't trouble himself to rise. He preferred to meet people while seated to mask his dwarfish stature and his malformed shoulder. Besides, they were cousins. Robert was two years Francis's junior, and their mothers had been good friends as well as sisters. They'd spent many months in each other's company during their boyhood years.

Robert's late mother, Mildred, was the eldest of the renowned Cooke sisters, students in the world's first female university, which they established under their father's roof. They received a thorough education in classical literature, humanist philosophy, and Protestant theology, developing and sustaining an outlook shared by Queen Elizabeth. How not, when they had shared so many brilliant tutors?

Robert and Francis, reared by such extraordinary mothers, also had exceptional fathers. William Cecil, now Lord Burghley, had counseled the young princess when her future was uncertain. He had risen to become the most powerful man in the realm, sitting at Her Majesty's right hand. If Sir Nicholas Bacon had lived, he would undoubtedly be seated on her left. Alas, he had died when Francis was only eighteen, leaving his youngest son without an advocate at court. Now he scrambled to pick up crumbs, like invitations to write advice letters and odd commissions that could never be openly acknowledged and thus earned little tangible reward. Robert, in contrast, climbed steadily upward on the ladder of influence and power.

Francis helped himself to the best armchair in front of the cluttered desk. "I dropped my own work to answer my lord uncle's summons."

Robert turned toward the secretary. "Thank you, Mr. Hollowell. That will be all for now."

The secretary bowed his head and left, closing the door behind him.

Robert held up a finger of his left hand while scribbling a few more words. Then he set his quill in its holder and rubbed his fingers with a bit of linen. "I do apologize for the delay, Frank. My father meant to see you himself when he sent that note, but he doesn't have the stamina he once had. He was flagging. We insisted he go up to rest on his bed for a while."

"I understand. I share your concern. He works too hard; he always has. England is the better for it, but he, I fear, is the worse."

"Just so," Robert said. "I'm trying to relieve him of whatever work I can. Now that I'm married and settling into the obligations of adulthood, it's time to take up my share of the burdens of state, including his intelligence service."

Francis granted that not-so-subtle dig a tight smile. Sitting on the board of governors of the most prestigious of the Inns of Court might also be considered a sign of maturity. And what was that about taking over his father's stable of intelligencers?

He demonstrated his superior restraint by focusing on the task at hand. "My lord's note mentioned a task requiring both me and my clerk. That suggests a confidential investigatory commission along the lines of the work we did in Cambridge a year or so ago."

Robert nodded. "This would be similar, insofar as the present problem also concerns Presbyterian zealots. I assume you're familiar with Martin Marprelate and his works."

"His works, certainly, but not the man. Martin remains unidentified." Francis's stomach clenched. "Surely you don't expect me to find Martin Marprelate! I'm only one man — or two, counting Tom. What could I do that the archbishop's army of pursuivants hasn't already tried?"

Robert shook his head. "They're not particularly clever, I fear. A more subtle approach might yield better results. But no, my lord father preferred not to meddle in the archbishop's efforts, and we believed the whole uproar had started to die down."

"Until today," Francis said, "I thought Martin had abandoned the field. He had made his point, after all. He'd thumbed his nose at the Church and won the public's acclaim without getting caught. He could retire to some safe haven, and none would ever be the wiser."

"Leaving the applause ringing in the archbishop's ears. His Grace could never tolerate that. He turned the whole pursuit over to Canon Bancroft. He's the one who stirred up the anti-Martinists, hiring satirical pamphleteers to answer Martin in his own terms."

Francis gaped, unable to believe what he'd just heard. "Do you mean to say Canon Bancroft deliberately poured oil on the dying embers of Martin's incendiary tracts?"

"I'm afraid so." Robert shook his head, weary disbelief on his face as well. "His timing is dreadful. Martin is nimble, where the Church is cumbersome. It must have taken Canon Bancroft many weeks to arrive at the plan, choose his men, and give them time to compose their first ripostes. You must have heard the results all the way out at Gray's — the songs, the jeers, the obscene comedies. An utter cacophony. Much of it written by Bancroft's men, but others are jumping aboard now as well."

"I can't even visit my bookseller without some antic clown leaping across my path or some obscene broadside being shouted into my ears." Francis met his cousin's eyes. "That may be the stupidest idea I've ever heard."

Robert smiled grimly. "I suppose Bancroft meant to discredit Martin in public opinion, but he's only succeeded in drawing him back out. I assume you've seen Martin Junior's *Theses Martinianae?*"

"A copy found its way onto my desk this morning. No surprises, apart from its comprehensiveness. But now I'm wondering if drawing Martin out again wasn't Bancroft's true intention. As long as he stayed hidden, he could never be caught. The trail had gone cold."

"That's too devious for our good canon. More likely, neither he nor Archbishop Whitgift could bear to let Martin have the last word. You know His Grace and his demands for impossible oaths. He wants more than mere compliance. He wants absolute commitment. Martin's cleverness poses a greater threat to him personally than the Spanish fleet did to our sovereignty as a nation."

"That's a little overstated," Francis said. Then he granted his cousin a small chuckle. "But perhaps not by much."

They traded knowing glances, each having inherited his father's pragmatism rather than his mother's religious devotion.

Francis asked, "What do you want me to do? Attempt a 'more subtle approach' to catching Martin?"

"Leave Martin alone," Robert said. "Let Bancroft exhaust the archbishop's resources. They're stirring up more tumult than they're suppressing. And you know how my father hates tumult."

Francis nodded. He shared that view. "Better to ignore Martin than to mock him. The second blow makes the fray. What do you want me to do?"

"Have you heard about the recent murders of two pamphleteers?"

"No. Two of Bancroft's men?"

"No, but I believe his men were the intended victims."

"That sounds murky." Francis sighed. Another perplexing series of murders with tricky political ramifications. "What's our interest? These writers live precarious lives, many of them. They rove between St. Paul's churchyard and the theaters in Shoreditch snuffling up anything that pays for a little quill work, then spend it all in the nearest tavern. Those murders most likely have nothing to do with Martin Marprelate."

"We would be pleased if you returned that result, but from the little I've learned thus far, I think it's too great a coincidence. And there is a motive. These writers, especially the one calling himself Pasquill Caviliero, seem to have gotten closer to Martin than any of the official pursuivants."

"Pasquill! Don't tell me *you've* read *Martin's Mirror?*"

Robert sighed with the infinite weariness of the overburdened public servant. "I receive summaries of almost everything that's published. That's one of the chores I've lifted from my father's desk along with the rest of his intelligencing services."

"Hmm." Francis let his gaze be diverted to the gatehouse, through which an elegant coach pulled by two handsome gray horses now passed. No doubt the passenger was one of Lord Burghley's noble wards, returning from a game of tennis at Whitehall or a gallop through Richmond Park. And here sat Robert the dwarf, skimming endless mountains of chaff, searching for that one grain of wheat that needed to be ground more finely.

"You would hate it, Frank," Robert said, following his cousin's thoughts. "I must spend nine hours a day in this chair, leaving my new wife at home, meeting with everyone from my father's pampered wards to ruffians who style themselves as intelligence gatherers. Your visit is a respite for me. For a rarity, I don't have to explain everything three times."

"But there are rewards."

"Not from the intelligence work, I assure you. Even Hollowell has to double as an official in the Court of Wards to earn any kind of salary."

The Court of Wards was the most corrupt — and lucrative — institution in the realm. As master of that court, Lord Burghley had scraped enough off the top of every wardship sold and every lawsuit prosecuted to build a palace in Yorkshire that rivaled anything belonging to the Crown. Now it would seem Cousin Robert was being fitted for that office as well.

"We patch our livings together as best we can," Francis said dryly. "My job, then, is to identify the murder of two pamphleteers. My clerk will appreciate the excuse to get out and about. However, I must remind you that murders in the London streets are rarely solved."

"But you'll have a direction in which to look. If we're correct and the real targets were Bancroft's writers, you might be able to set a trap. You've done that sort of thing before, haven't you?"

"Ah." Now Francis understood why he had been favored with this impossible commission. He'd designed several masques for the Christmas revels at Gray's Inn and the court. He had also staged scenes to catch a murderer once or twice. "Very well. I will endeavor to catch your killer or frighten him off into eternal obscurity. Either way, Bancroft's pet provocateurs will be protected."

Robert chuckled at the alliteration. "This goes without saying, but I'll say it anyway: be as discreet as you can. My father wants to quiet the uproar, not increase it. And serve justice for the murdered men, of course."

"Of course. But does my lord believe Martin Marprelate had a hand in the murders?"

"Not Martin himself, who may not even know about them. It's more likely an accomplice with a growing fear of the gallows. Martin may have powerful friends, but what about the printer and his men? They may not know who Martin is either, and if they're caught and can't surrender him, they'll almost certainly hang."

"May God protect them." Francis swallowed, preparing for the most difficult question. "There is the matter of compensation . . ."

"That is a matter for my lord father to determine, and naturally it will depend on the outcome."

"Naturally. But there will be expenses. My clerk no longer has his own funds, but he'll have to visit these writers' haunts and buy drinks, perhaps pay a few small bribes."

Robert gave him a flat look. He knew all too well that Francis could not hold on to money to save his life. "Send your man to Hollowell for funds. Within reason, mind."

"Thank you." That should satisfy Tom. Francis gathered himself to leave, then thought of one last question. "Just between us, Robert — who do you think Martin is?"

"I think what everyone thinks. He's an educated gentleman, a member of Parliament, with powerful friends and possibly a family whose very name provides a shelter." His lips curved in a sly smile as he met Francis's eyes. "In short, Coz, someone very much like us."

FOUR

Lady Alice Trumpington paced clockwise around the walled garden behind Lady Russell's house in Blackfriars on Monday afternoon. This time she reversed her direction, taking the right-hand diagonal across the center and turning left on the other side. The graveled path was just wide enough for her skirts, whose obsidian blackness swung in stark contrast to the red brick walls and profusions of flowering vines. Every now and then a breeze would straggle over the walls, lift the brim of her broad straw hat, and stir up the astringent scents of sun-warmed herbs from the meticulously tended beds.

Last summer, Trumpet had worn rose pink and leaf green, which Tom said made her eyes glow like emeralds lit from beneath. This year — her year of penance — she wore black. Taffeta in summer, broadcloth in winter, trimmed with braid and lined with silk, but still black from head to toe except for the white linen at her wrists and throat. Tom, always looking for the bright side, had shrugged and said, "At least it matches your hair."

Trumpet chafed at the gloomy garb and at her straitened circumstances, living almost like a prisoner in Lady Russell's house. In fairness, she'd brought her troubles on herself last summer in her ill-fated attempt to determine her own future. She'd arranged a marriage with an elderly invalid, who would soon die a natural death and leave her a widow with full legal control over her property. Unfortunately, he had been murdered on their wedding night. She'd been caught in her chemise with Tom the next morning, shredding her reputation. Still a virgin, to add insult to injury.

Worst of all, since she'd had to prove her virginity in order to save Tom from real punishment, she couldn't even claim to be a widow. The marriage was simply voided and all her careful planning came to naught. She had to restore her reputation before she could try again, and she had much to learn about being a woman of significance. So she'd offered herself as a companion to Lady Elizabeth Russell, famously straitlaced and strong-minded. A year with her would wash Trumpet's name as clean as a new coif and give her much-needed training in the art of widowhood as well.

She came to a stop in the shade of the arbor, where her maidservant, Catalina Luna, sat sewing. Nothing could induce Catalina to sit in the sun. Born into a Gypsy tribe in southern Spain, she'd spent her early youth traveling around Italy with a troupe of street performers, where her warm olive skin had absorbed enough sun to last a lifetime.

"We should have stayed out this morning," Trumpet said, stripping off the gray kidskin gloves Catalina insisted she wear to keep her hands from turning brown. She had a music lesson with a master who lived in the Savoy on Monday mornings, one of the few times she managed to escape from this house. She'd decided to learn to play the virginals because the queen played them, and in hopes that the mere word would stimulate the desired resonance in people's minds. She'd also discovered that Lady Russell couldn't abide the sound, forcing her to go elsewhere for instruction. One measly hour of freedom.

Then she discovered that she genuinely enjoyed playing. Someday, when she and Tom finally found a way to be together, they would be terribly old, but they could beguile their sunset years making music.

"My lady wishes us home for dinner each day." Catalina set aside the cuffs she was embroidering and poured her mistress a cup of cool beer from a stone jug.

Trumpet drank it thirstily. She glanced toward the windows of the three-story house. "Three days of captivity before we can escape to my aunt's house. Then another two days before I get to see Tom again." She took another sip of beer and glared at the house. "I'm longing to escape from this cage."

"You will get a good offer soon, my lady. Then everything change."

"They'll just move me to a different cage."

Catalina shrugged in that gypsy way that meant a multitude of things. "A bigger one, with a coach. Keep your dresses more clean."

Trumpet laughed. "That would be something. And I'll have my own house in London. I can engage Tom as my legal counselor. Although my husband will have to be a very stupid man for that to work out the way I want."

"There are many stupid men, my lady."

"Better still would be a man like my father, possessed by such a lust for adventure and Spanish treasure that he rarely visits his own home." Like Tom's father. Another thing they had in common, though Tom also had a mother, two aunts, and several sisters. Trumpet had grown up in a crumbling castle by the German Sea, tended by a few loyal servants, with occasional visits from her favorite uncle. Her father's rare appearances had little impact on the smooth workings of the estate.

The sad truth was that she had received precious few offers of marriage, some of which were downright insulting. They thought she was desperate, nineteen years old with a name stained by scandal and few negotiable assets. She had a title to pass to her son, but that wasn't much inducement for men of high enough station for her advisors to consider. But she'd delayed as long as she could. She'd soon have to accept the best of her bad choices, if no new ones came.

Lady Russell's body servant appeared at the gate. She wore the standard livery of this household — black on black with more black around the edges — which made her look ordinary in stature from a distance. At close quarters, she towered over Trumpet, whose height failed to reflect her character. The servant had been chosen for her strength. Her Ladyship suffered from a malformed back which often left her helpless physically, though she remained indomitable on every other score.

Trumpet left Catalina sewing in the garden and followed the taller woman inside to the library. The interior felt cool in contrast to the garden and smelled of books and beeswax in spite of the open windows. Lady Russell sat in a thickly cushioned armchair with one hand resting on a stack of paper. Her black gown heightened the paleness of her face and the touches of color on her cheeks and in her ginger hair.

"I've finished my part. You may add your special touches before you make the fair copy. When you're finished, deliver it to our messenger."

Trumpet accepted the manuscript and took her customary seat to read it. The title, penned in Her Ladyship's flowing script, was *The Just Censure and Reproof of Martin Junior.* She'd invented an elder brother, Martin Senior, to take credit for this latest blast.

"I thought we were going to give Martin Junior another turn," Trumpet said, leafing through the pages.

"I decided to add a third voice. I want to make it clear to all that Martin is legion. He is a spirit, a force beyond the limits of one individual. They might confine the *man,*" she lifted her arched eyebrows, "but they cannot halt the march of time."

No one, from the queen on down, had ever so much as speculated that Martin Marprelate might be a woman.

34

Trumpet grinned at Her Ladyship's subtle joke. She might chafe at her restricted life, but she'd grown fond of this extraordinary woman in the past year. Nothing daunted Elizabeth Russell. Not the queen, not the Privy Council, not the Church. Not any task or challenge. She wrote poetry, she designed funerary monuments, she managed her estates with ferocity and aplomb. Gifted in the art of image-making, she presented herself as passionless and rational, but Trumpet had learned to catch the flashes of deftly aimed humor. And she'd learned what it meant to be cared for unstintingly by a woman who had all but adopted her as a true daughter.

Trumpet read the pages quickly, chuckling at several choice phrases. "Anti-Christian beasts might be a little strong, my lady."

Lady Russell shook her head. "This may be our last work, Alice. I said everything needful in my *Theses*, outlining the full program for what must be done to bring about the true, complete reformation. Martin Senior will carry our standard a few steps further. We can't allow those impudent mockers to believe they've chased us off the field."

"Never." They traded wise looks. Neither of them was the sort to quail in the face of a challenge. "But they haven't stopped, my lady. Mr. Clarady mentioned a new salvo that appeared on Saturday. Another anti-Martinist upstart calling himself Pasquill Caviliero."

"We can't address them all, my dear. And we mustn't stoop to their level." Lady Russell smiled her cat's smile. "But we may feel compelled to correct any truly egregious errors."

Trumpet murmured, "They are vanity and the work of errors." She'd learned the trick of quoting the Bible as a form of conversational punctuation from Tom, who had learned it during his months spying on Puritans in Cambridge. There seemed to be a quote for every occasion.

She had never been overly particular about religion. She attended the expected church at the appointed times because it was simpler to comply, but she would worry about the afterlife when she got there. She had enough on her plate and trusted God to understand that. He saw everything. He could surely recognize the justice in her quest for some modicum of control over her own destiny. She knew from personal observation that women prayed twice as much as men. God must know everything about their lot in life and its unreasonable constraints.

Furthermore, she had spent a year learning Calvinist doctrine at the knees of two of England's leading proponents, Lady Elizabeth Russell and her elder sister, Lady Anne Bacon. She had absorbed their rock-solid certainty that they were among the chosen, and therefore what they did was righteous.

That certainty — and her father's title— helped Trumpet hold up her head when gossips cast gleefully malicious glances in her direction. Better, she'd learned that theology, especially in its more political aspects, could be as useful to a woman as a working knowledge of property law. Religion was the only sphere in which women could wield real power, if always hidden behind another name. At this stage, Trumpet only wanted power over her own life. But if managing other people's religious activities was the only way to achieve that, she intended to be good at it

FIVE

Francis Bacon paid the wherryman at the Lambeth Stairs and walked along the trail winding through the marshy banks on the south side of the river. Morton's Gatehouse rose before him, five stories of red brick trimmed with white stone. He passed through the gate and across the courtyard toward the palace proper, considering the best approach to his upcoming audience with Archbishop Whitgift.

Although Lambeth sat nearly due south across the river from Whitehall, Francis rarely had occasion to visit and the contrast between the two palaces struck him every time. Whitehall was the main center of the English government, even when the queen was in residence elsewhere. It drew men and women from every corner of England and every country in Europe, some on matters of greatest importance, others merely to gawk at the fountains and the tournament field. Everyone wore their best clothes. Their costly garb added color to the vibrant scene.

At Lambeth Palace, most of the visitors and occupants wore somber clerical garb, the hems of their long robes dusting the ground. No vendors hawked sweet buns or bitter ale. No clusters of cheerful foreigners stood about pointing and chattering. And while the palace in no way resembled a Vatican-upon-Thames, as Martin Marprelate would have it, it did have the hushed and secretive atmosphere of a center of religious power.

Francis had readily been granted an appointment, even on such short notice. He and his brother Anthony had lived in John Whitgift's house at Cambridge University when His Grace was Master of Trinity College. The Bacon boys had been thus honorably lodged thanks to their father's position as the Lord Keeper of the Great Seal. Now Sir Nicholas had fallen, while Whitgift had risen to the highest seat a cleric could attain in England.

The archbishop sat in the tall chair on the dais in his reception chamber, wearing the sleeveless black gown of his office over billowing white sleeves, his head fully covered by a black coif topped by the square black Canterbury cap. He beckoned Francis forward with a flick of his bony fingers.

Francis bowed from the waist before saying, "Thank you for seeing me, Your Grace."

"How not, my boy? I remember, as if it were yesterday, our struggles to find something your brother could eat without distress." Whitgift smiled fondly at his former pupil.

"*Tempus fugit*, Your Grace. It seems so long ago to me." It had been fifteen years ago — more than half Francis's life — and he'd only stayed for a few terms. He'd found university boring. Aristotle, Aristotle, all day long, as if he hadn't read that dull philosopher's complete works by the age of ten. His mother was a better tutor than any Cambridge master.

"Do you hear from Anthony?" the archbishop asked.

"Not as often as I could wish. He's still in Montauban, still writing a weekly report for us, although some weeks I hear nothing from him." Also still spending far beyond his means. If Anthony ever made it home, he'd have to squeeze in with Francis at Gray's to save money.

"And your mother?"

"She is well, Your Grace. It's kind of you to ask."

"She was so pretty when she was young. Long before you knew her!" Whitgift chuckled. "You take after her, my boy. You have her eyes."

Francis smiled, noticing the papery quality of his old tutor's cheeks and the lengthening lines around his eyes. He must be nearly seventy, a trifle younger than Lady Bacon. A decade younger than Lord Burghley. The old generation was fading, aging alongside their queen. But still in her service, still holding the reins of power.

For how much longer? And who would replace them? Robert Devereux, the Earl of Essex, for one. Robert Cecil, for another. But not Francis Bacon if things continued in their present direction.

"I know why you're here," Whitgift said. "Lord Burghley asked me to give you whatever help I can. No one is more eager than I am to see that foul-mouthed Martin Marprelate caught and hanged."

That was not precisely Francis's mission, but this wasn't the time to split hairs.

"I blame him, if you want to know," Whitgift grumbled, "for making this nonsense possible. He's nothing like as moderate as the queen, though he feigns agreement."

Francis had to make a mental leap to catch up. The old man meant Lord Burghley, whose personal sympathies lay with the nonconformists, at least the more moderate ones. He liked a plain church and an emphasis on reading the Bible rather than sitting in splendor to witness an elaborate weekly ritual. Nevertheless, he had always supported Her Majesty's policies concerning religion.

Whitgift rumbled on. "I thought when Leicester passed — may God rest his soul in peace — these radicals, these change-alls, these never-satisfied zealots, would lose their chief advocate on the Privy Council. His Lordship may be gone, but his allies live on. Burghley, Cobham, Knollys. Too many!"

Lord Burghley had married Francis's mother's sister. Baron Cobham was his Aunt Elizabeth's neighbor and the father of Robert Cecil's new bride. Leicester's brother, the Earl of Warwick, had married the sister of Elizabeth's late husband, John Russell. Sir Francis Knollys's daughter Lettice was Leicester's widow and the mother of the queen's young favorite, the Earl of Essex.

The webs of kinship and common interest were densely woven among the queen's old guard. In the dangerous years of her youth, she had relied on the staunchest Protestants, choosing many close counselors whose kin had fled to Germany during the Marian years to avoid a fiery martyrdom. They married, had children, and then used their children to strengthen their bonds.

In contrast, archbishops entered the Church from a university, first making a name at Oxford or Cambridge. They might come from anywhere, from families of no importance. Whitgift's father had been a Lincolnshire merchant, for example. If such men wanted power, they had only the clerical ladder to climb and no children to help extend their reach.

Listening to the old man's grumbling, Francis recognized two things. First, the archbishop's view of the Marprelate controversy was wholly political. He saw Martin as the pawn of some powerful figure, perhaps even someone on the Privy Council. Second, he failed to understand the popularity of Presbyterian ideas among the middling sort, merchants and prosperous yeomen who had achieved literacy and wanted more say about their manner of worship. Whitgift had lectured at Cambridge, but he had never preached in a parish church. He had no sense of the common Englishman.

"The queen must replace the Earl of Leicester with a moderate man," Whitgift said. "A true friend of the true church."

"Do you have any idea who she'll choose?"

Whitgift grunted. "That whelp Robert Cecil, if his father has anything to say about it, which he will, mark my words. He's already bringing him to every meeting. I don't like it."

His gaze shifted toward the door. Francis knew his allotted time was nearly up and he hadn't asked any of his questions. "I wanted to ask Your Grace, in confidence, if you have learned anything from the men who were arrested last autumn that hasn't been generally reported."

"Arrested! Pah! We caught a few minnows and took statements from them, but the other councilors made us release them. I would have hanged them, each and every one."

"For preaching?" As far as Francis knew, the raids conducted in November and December had yielded only a few well-known hotheads, against whom Whitgift had long-standing grudges, and a few rumors of Martin-like books being written by unnamed parsons in vague locations.

"For aiding and abetting a seditious rebel!" Whitgift's long hands gripped the carven arms of his chair. "And worse, for refusing to admit it. But no, no! We were obliged to let the little fish swim back to the whale, leaving him lurking safely in his lair."

Did whales live in lairs? Francis supposed they might do. There could be whole cities under the sea, for all anyone knew. Their inhabitants were as likely to yield clues about Martin as the poor parsons that had been netted so far.

"Do you have any idea where Martin might be?" Francis asked. "Or who is helping him?"

"Martin Malcontent has support in high places, mark my words. Spurred on and cosseted, especially by women with too much education, too much money, and too little supervision. They resent the masculine power of the

Church and seek to undermine it by stealth, harboring banned preachers and writers of seditious trash."

"I'm not sure that's the —"

Whitgift either didn't hear him or couldn't stop himself. "I wish your father were still alive, my boy. He would know how to manage women like your moth —" He broke off with a cough. "How to manage such meddlers. Pah! They believe themselves to be beyond the reach of the law, but they are not. They are not! They may be women, but they can be caught, and they can be punished."

He leveled his glassy gaze, laden with meaning. Francis took it as a warning. "I am sure my lady mother understands her duty to the Church as well as the Crown. But I will speak with her, I promise."

That empty promise was met with a derisory grunt. They both knew Francis had no control over his mother, who had ruled her small fiefdom as *femme sole* for ten years.

SIX

Tom walked down to Burghley House on Tuesday morning after breakfast, already enjoying the greatest benefit of a new commission from the Lord Treasurer: release from his confinement in Francis Bacon's study chamber. The servant who admitted him into the house led him upstairs to a long gallery and left him on a bench. He didn't mind waiting. Anything was better than sitting at that undersized desk making endless copies of legal maxims.

Another liveried servant stood motionless at the end of the gallery with his arms at his sides. He stared at nothing, seemingly, doing his job by merely waiting. Tom hoped the poor fellow had an active imagination and a beautiful young wife, at least.

The gallery looked across an interior courtyard to another gallery on the other side, marked by a long bank of tall windows whose spotless glass glittered in countless diamond panes. Tom's arse reposed upon a brocaded cushion while his feet enjoyed the comfort of thick rush matting, which also muffled sounds. There weren't many. A door closed somewhere in the depths of the house with a soft thud; a coachman cried, "Yep, yep!" to horses somewhere outside. Otherwise, this gallery was quiet and cool, perfumed with rosemary to ward off plague.

Not that such a vile disease would dare to enter these exalted precincts! This house rivaled Whitehall in its appointments. Like the paneling that supported Tom's back, which he twisted around to admire. The wall was divided into rows of squares, each outlined with carved moldings to add depth. These moldings were painted in bands of scarlet, green, and yellow.

Tom pictured the painter at work, a man at the pinnacle of his craft to win a job in this house. He stood here in this gallery week upon endless week, laying down those unwavering ribbons of color. Did he do all the red lines first, working from ceiling to floor and end to end, before cleaning his brush and taking up a new color?

That seemed far more tedious than making fair copies of Bacon's maxims. And Tom would bet a pair of velvet slippers that the painter's master had never told him to hop down to Mr. Cecil's office to collect a purseful of money so he could spend a week buying drinks for an unruly lot of poets and pamphleteers.

As the fullness of that truth expanded in his mind, Tom realized that his situation could be worse. It could be a *lot* worse.

A man in a dark red doublet with longish slops leaned out of a nearby doorway. "Are you Thomas Clarady?"

Tom rose. "I am."

The man beckoned him forward. "I'm Peter Hollowell, Mr. Cecil's secretary. Do come in. I'm sorry to keep you waiting."

"I don't mind," Tom said. "It's a pleasant place to wait."

They went in to Hollowell's small office. His paneling wasn't painted, but someone kept it polished to a fare-thee-well. Tom could smell the lemony wax as he entered.

"Sit, please." Hollowell gestured at a chair as he seated himself behind his desk. "You told the gatekeeper you were here on an errand for Mr. Bacon pursuant to the conversation he had yesterday with Mr. Cecil."

"That's right."

"Mr. Cecil has placed this matter in my hands, as far as the day-to-day is concerned. He trusts me, as your master trusts you." He smiled. "Looks like you and I will be seeing each other every week or so until this matter has been resolved."

Tom returned the smile. "That'll make things simpler, Mr. Hollowell. Less fuss." He hadn't much wanted to deal with Mr. Cecil directly. Bacon didn't like him, though he never said it in so many words. But he clearly didn't trust his cousin and therefore Tom didn't either. Bacon had his flaws — which Tom could list at length, in alphabetical order — but he was a profoundly honest man. If he didn't trust someone, there must be a reason.

"I'm glad we understand each other." Hollowell ran a hand through his light brown hair as he cast a glance at the piles of paper covering his desk, letting out a weary breath. "If you're thinking you've caught me at a bad time, I'm afraid it's always like this. My master is doing everything he can to relieve my Lord Burghley's burdens, which means we secretaries have larger loads to shoulder as well. Not that I'm complaining!"

It sounded more like bragging to Tom, but he didn't hold it against him. Hollowell had probably been angling for this position for years and now must come to terms with the truth of what he'd wished for. "Mr. Bacon and I appreciate everything you do."

"As we appreciate both of you."

They beamed at each other for a moment or two, taking stock. Tom knew he presented the perfect image of a gentleman of the Inns of Court. One good thing he could say about his guardian: she had a keen eye for appearances.

Hollowell fitted his role equally well. His clothes were conservative in color and style — dark red with pale red linings and the longer slops that draped almost to the knee favored by older men. But the suit was of the best quality and liberally trimmed with silk braid and brass buttons. He wore his beard in a smoothly rounded point, a style that required regular barbering. He was shorter than average, about Mr. Bacon's size. Doubtless one of his qualifications. Most lords liked tall retainers, but shrimpish Robert Cecil must prefer ones closer to his size.

Hollowell said, "Mr. Cecil told me you'd need funds for conducting your inquiries."

"That's right. I'm kept on short rations these days, and Mr. Bacon never has — well, it wouldn't be right to expect him to pay the costs of His Lordship's commission out of his own pocket."

"Of course not." Hollowell's twinkling eyes signaled his complete understanding. "I prepared a purse." He unlocked a small box and took out a leather sack. "Small coins. Nothing larger than a shilling." He hefted it in his hand as if judging the amount by its weight. "I suppose Mr. Bacon already has a strategy planned."

"How not?" Tom chuckled as if the idea of Bacon being in any way behindhand were utterly absurd. "He'll start at the top with a visit to Archbishop Whitgift. He lived in His Grace's household at Trinity College, you know, before His Grace became archbishop, of course."

Hollowell acknowledged the impressive connection with a tilt of his head.

"My job," Tom went on, "is to go low, so to speak, and find out what I can about the victims. That will mean handing out the odd tip here and there and buying drinks to curry favor with potential witnesses." He shook his head regretfully.

"A dirty job, but someone has to do it." Hollowell laughed. "If I could escape for even an hour, I'd go with you."

Tom grinned. "They're more likely to speak freely if they're a little cup-shot. I'll wear plainer clothes when I visit the victims' lodgings and talk to the neighbors. I'm pretty good at getting people to spill their little secrets."

"I don't doubt it. My advice, which you don't seem to need, is not to offer a bribe unless it's absolutely necessary. This purse will have to last you, and you might not find that one crucial witness until you've poked around a bit. Also, and I know this doesn't have to be said — except that it always does — don't tell anyone about this commission. No chatting with your chums at Gray's, for example. They don't need to know."

"I understand," Tom said. "Not one word to anyone but Mr. Bacon."

"We have every confidence in your discretion." Hollowell gave the purse another little heft, then tossed it across the desk to Tom.

He caught it in his left hand and weighed it in his turn. "Feels like about a pound. That should be plenty." He'd pocket ten percent for himself, like any civil servant. Tom was well satisfied with this first meeting. He'd made a friend here today, or at least had started in that direction. A potentially useful friend too. "I'd better leave you to your work and get on with mine." He rose, casting a sympathetic glance at Hollowell's overloaded desk. "You know, I never thought intelligencing would demand so many documents. I reckoned that sort of information mostly went unwritten."

"Oh, you'd be surprised at what gets kept," Hollowell said. "Lord Burghley is a stickler for proper reporting, and Mr. Cecil inherited that trait. But this isn't all spy work." He shot Tom a wink. "My master wears many hats, and so, perforce, must I. That large stack there consists entirely of letters concerning suits in the Court of Wards, which have to be read and answered, with copies made, before Michaelmas term begins."

"The Court of Wards!" Tom gaped at him, then sat right back down again. This man might be a better friend than he'd imagined. "I'm about to embark on a suit in that court myself. I just received my proofs of age from my mother last night."

A nice fat scroll containing depositions from a dozen people, members of their parish who could swear that Thomas Clarady had met the world on the second of December in the year 1567. Each witness had supplied a brief account of how they were able to remember after so many years. Several seemed to have broken limbs in that same week, but such things did happen.

"Oh my!" Hollowell grimaced in a way that sent a chill down Tom's spine. "I wish you the best of luck. How did you end up in that unfortunate position?"

"My father died three months before my twenty-first birthday."

Hollowell winced. "I'm sorry on both counts. Who's your guardian?"

"Lady Elizabeth Russell. Your master's aunt, as it happens."

"Oh my!" Hollowell sat back in his chair, his expression grave. "Oh my!" He swallowed visibly, then rallied. "No, I shouldn't be so . . . She's a magnificent lady, truly magnificent, an old friend of the queen, a stalwart. She's one of our most active correspondents. We must receive a letter from her every other day, sharing her observations about this matter and that, which are often quite astute, as you can imagine given her education, her history, and her position. I feel that I know her, she expresses herself so vigorously."

The man had started babbling at the mere mention of the lady's name. That did not bode well, not well at all. Tom said, "She might loosen the purse strings a little. It is my purse, after all. But she does pay all my fees and doesn't skimp on essentials like clothing, so I suppose it could be worse."

"Oh yes. Much worse." Hollowell raised his eyebrows and grimaced. "The stories I could tell you! Well, of course,

I couldn't. Confidential matters of the court." He leaned forward a little, as if about to confide something, and asked, "How much is this estate worth, if you don't mind my asking?"

"Six hundred per annum, not counting my mother's portion."

Hollowell drew in a whistling breath. "That does complicate things."

"Whether my guardian is good or bad doesn't matter," Tom said. "I'm not a minor anymore. I want to manage my own affairs. It's unfair to make me sue for my own estate."

"Many people in England would agree with you, Mr. Clarady. Many people. I'm afraid the Court of Wards isn't popular. Between you and me, I tend to agree. It's all rather obsolete, isn't it? This whole business of knight service being attached to one parcel of land and not the one next to it. It's ancient history." Hollowell shot Tom another wink. "More work for you lawyers though, eh? Something to look forward to, with the experience you'll gain."

Tom wasn't much comforted. "Do you have any advice for me?"

"Well, let's see. You said you had your *writ de etate probanda* — your proof of age. I suppose that means you're going to sue for general livery?"

"My friend— er, my legal counsel — advised me that general livery takes longer, but I can pay the fees as I go rather than having to come up with a huge sum at once. My mother and I don't have the ready money to pay for special livery, especially not with Lady Russell soaking up my annual rents."

"Those are the two thorns of your dilemma, all right." Hollowell tugged at his left earlobe, perhaps in an unthinking reflection of Tom's pearl earring, which he would never sell at any price. "Of course, general livery isn't cheap either. There are about twenty steps to go through, from one office to another and back again, each requiring its own set of fees. All told, you should be prepared to spend about half your annual rents; in your case, then, about three hundred pounds."

Tom swallowed. Ben had estimated something closer to two hundred. "But special livery is vastly more, isn't it? And you have to pay it all at once, which I can't do. I won't allow my mother to sell any of her dower lands on my account. As far as I can tell, I have two choices: hand the court every penny I can scrape up for the next two or three years or somehow conjure a small chest of gold."

"Thorns," Hollowell said, shaking his head. "There is a third option. It's unlikely to succeed, but it can't hurt to try."

Tom scooted to the edge of his chair and clasped his hands between his knees. "I'll do anything, Mr. Hollowell. Anything at all."

"Well . . . why not ask Lady Russell to release the monies for special livery from your estate?"

Tom blinked at him. "Wait. You mean, just ask her? Go to her with my hat in my hand and beg for my livery?"

"Why not? She'd want some compensation, of course, but you might be able to pay that over time once you take possession."

"Is there any chance she'd agree?"

"Practically none, but it is a reasonable first step. You're a comely man, if you don't mind the observation. Dress your best and pay her a formal call. Present your case as clearly as you can, showing her you have the maturity and wisdom to manage your own estates."

Tom scowled. "That's the infuriating part! You see, my father was a privateer. He was rarely home for two months running. My mother and her steward manage our estates, always have, and they do a fine job of it. I would naturally leave everything in their hands until I pass the bar and establish. When I'm ready to buy a house and look about me for a wife."

Hollowell had been nodding while he listened, as if judging Tom's performance. "That makes sense to me. Very well put. But I'd leave out the part about the wife. You don't want to bring that thought to the front of your guardian's mind."

"Don't I?"

"Oh my, no. She has the right to arrange a match for you, you know, since she is responsible for your future well-being. *In loco parentis,* as we say. And I don't need to tell you how lucrative a marriage negotiation can be!" He chuckled heartily.

Tom watched him with a sort of horror. He was nowhere near ready for marriage. He would pass the bar in four or five years, during which time he was obliged to maintain his residency at Gray's Inn. What would be the point of having a wife if he couldn't live with her?

Hollowell sighed, signaling the end of their digression into Tom's personal troubles. "Let's revisit this topic next time, shall we? Try making that request to get it out of the way. Then if you want to bring me your proofs of age, I could look them over for you. I have no jurisdiction in your case, of course, but I am an officer of the court. Mr. Cecil made me a feodary in my home county of Northamptonshire. I might spot any oddities before you submit it formally."

"That would be exceedingly generous of you," Tom said with abject sincerity. "You've already given me some excellent advice."

Hollowell smiled. "What's a favor or two between us secretaries, eh? We're much alike, after all. Your Mr. Bacon and my Mr. Cecil are both highly respected counselors. One is a governor at Gray's; the other the right hand of the queen's right hand. And here's the two of us, doing our best to help them keep the ship of state afloat."

Tom noted the thick gold rings on the secretary's fingers and the lustrous silk linings peeking through the slashes in his sleeves. How much of that had been purchased with fees from the Court of Wards? They might both serve cousins, but Hollowell's post was more lucrative than Tom's. On the other hand, he couldn't be much more than thirty and he'd already reached the top of his ladder, while Tom's stretched all the way up to a judge's bench, if he could keep on climbing.

He rose again and bowed before walking out the door. No, he didn't want to trade places with Peter Hollowell. But he'd take twenty percent from the purse in his pocket. They'd wring it back out of him again anyway.

SEVEN

Tom turned east on the Strand and started walking. The spring returned to his steps as he decided the best balm for his wounded spirits would be a visit with his best friend, Trumpet. He got a wherry from the bottom of Strand Lane along Somerset Place, getting off at the Blackfriars Stairs. He walked around the Office of the Queen's Revels to enter the narrow passage that ran alongside Lady Russell's gardens. Trumpet's bedchamber looked out over those gardens at this corner of the house with another small window overlooking the alley. A thick vine with broad leaves covered most of the wall beneath her garden windows.

Tom stood beneath the alley-side window and whistled "The Sweet and Merry Month of May." Catalina's oval face appeared. "Ten minutes," she called softly down in her Spanish-flavored voice. He found one of them in their room as often as not, and there was little risk since Lady Russell spent most of the day in one of two places: her special chair in the library or in her bed with a portable writing desk.

Tom strolled back down to the Blackfriars Stairs to watch the boatmen ply their trade until he judged sufficient time had passed. Then he strode back up as if he had an errand, walking right past the house. He turned the corner and caught up with the two women, who were walking slowly toward St. Paul's. Both wore black gowns, as usual these days. Catalina had a veil draped over her head, but not covering her face. Trumpet had perched a smaller version of a man's hat on top of her black hair. It looked ridiculous; starched and saucy at the same time.

Trumpet held a book-shaped parcel wrapped in oiled cloth.

"Good morrow, my lady!" Tom swept off his hat and bowed deeply, showing a leg.

Trumpet smiled at the leg, as he knew she would. "How did you escape? I thought Bacon kept you slaving away at your tiny desk every morning."

"Not today. I had an errand, but now that's done." He fell in between the two women as they began walking at a snail's pace toward their unknown destination. Tom flicked a greeting at Catalina with his eyebrows.

"What sort of errand?" Trumpet demanded.

"Just delivering a message. Nothing interesting. You know Mr. Bacon."

"I do." Trumpet stopped and turned her heart-shaped face up to study him. "If it were an ordinary message, he'd send it with Pinnock. Therefore it was no ordinary message. What was it? Is something interesting afoot?"

"Not at all." Tom grinned, giving her the full effect of his dimple.

"Don't you dimple me!" She clicked her tongue. "Now I know you're up to something. Something ticklish, I'll wager. Something fun. Tell me."

"Can't. It's a secret."

"When did you start keeping secrets from *me?*"

Tom shrugged. "I don't tell you everything."

"You used to." Trumpet's bow-shaped lips turned downward. It didn't stop them from being adorable. Tom considered dropping a swift kiss, but apart from being on a public street, he never knew how she would take it. She'd slapped him once, to their mutual astonishment. He'd never figured out why.

"I know what it is," she said. "You and Mr. Bacon have a new commission from Lord Burghley, giving you an excuse to get out and about on your own."

Tom gaped at her. "How could you possibly know that? We just learned of it our —"

"Aha!" Trumpet's green eyes blazed with victory. "What is it this time? Murder? Sedition? A plot to assassinate the queen?" She rubbed her gloved hands together and squealed happily at Catalina. Then she grinned up at Tom. "You won't get anywhere without our help. Let's think of where and how we can meet so you can fill me in on the plan. We can climb out my window, if we can work out how to get down from the wall."

"Can't do it, *camarade*. I promised not to tell." Tom regretted that rash act. He should have come up with something vaguer and more ambiguous than "not one word."

Trumpet growled under her breath. "Don't tell me, then. I'll find out soon enough. You know I will."

"But I won't be the one who told you." He tilted his chin at her parcel. "What've you got there?"

"Nothing that concerns you."

"It looks like a book."

"There's more than one book in the world."

"What kind of an answer is that?"

She lifted one shoulder to her chin in an exaggerated shrug. "You're not the only one with secrets."

"Something to do with one of your famous marriage proposals?" That reminded him. "Hoi, did you know that on top of helping herself to my income, your friend Lady Russell has the right to arrange a marriage for me?"

"For *you?*" Trumpet stopped short. They'd gained almost two whole yards that time. "Why would anyone want to marry *you?*"

That stung. "I have my qualities."

"That's not what I meant. I mean, why should anyone be arranging marriages for you now? You're years away from passing the bar."

"That's what I think. I have no interest in marrying anyone, especially if I can't have —" He gave her a hot look, and she bit her lip, dropping her gaze. She knew how he felt about her, he was fairly certain, and she felt the same way about him, as far as he could tell. But their stations were so far apart they might as well be living on opposite sides of the globe. Nothing he did could ever raise him high enough to reach the daughter of an earl.

Trumpet sniffed, wrinkling her nose as if none of that mattered. "I'd be careful about that if I were you. Her Ladyship hasn't mentioned it. She seldom mentions you in my presence; she thinks we're too familiar as it is. But she knows more about the law than you and Ben combined, and she can be fearsomely crafty. I know this much — she treats marriage negotiations with the same strategic focus as a marshal planning a foreign campaign."

Tom blew out a noisy sigh. "Another front in the war for my liberty. They don't make it easy for us, do they?"

She didn't answer.

They walked another yard or two in silence. "Where are we going?" Tom asked.

"The bookseller's."

"So it is a book!"

Trumpet gave him a weary look from under her dark brows.

"Have you gotten any good offers lately?" Tom asked. "Speaking of arranging matches."

"None that you need to know about."

Tom sighed, surrendering. He'd offended her, leaving her out of the new commission. In truth, these two women would be very useful, especially in his part of the investigation. Catalina was the mistress of disguises, and

Trumpet could pry secrets out of an oyster. But a man's word was his bond.

They reached the printer's shop. Trumpet looked up at him, her eyes as somber as his mood. "See you on Sunday?"

He nodded, tipped his hat, and walked back the way they'd come. Things were complicated enough for them with their peculiar history, their exacting taskmasters, and their mismatched stations. Having to keep secrets from one another as well might be more than their friendship could endure.

EIGHT

"What's this? Still abed?"

Francis buried his head under his pillow at the sound of Tom's cheery voice. Three inches of best goose down failed to muffle the rattle of the bed curtains and the cacophony of bird song that told him the windows had been thrown open, admitting a blast of chilly air.

"You've got an answer from that canon. Time to go to work, Master!"

Francis pulled himself up with a groan, reaching for the cup of hot spiced ale Tom set beside his bed each morning. That warmed him enough to scramble out of bed and close the windows before scrubbing himself with the heated towels Pinnock provided for him and pulling on clean linens. He grimaced into the mirror while he rubbed the sleep from his teeth with the little cloths his mother embroidered, then combed his hair and beard. By then, Pinnock had come in to help him finish dressing.

Another day of business, running hither, thither, and yon, having sensitive conversations with pepper-nosed courtiers. He'd be lucky to steal as much as one meager hour of reading after climbing back into bed that night.

Francis waited at the Temple Stairs for a wherry to carry him across to Lambeth. Two journeys south of the river in as many days; more than he'd made in all of the previous year. A silent cleric led him up to an oak-lined closet, smaller than his study chamber at Gray's, with only one little window showing a patch of sky. The air in the room was stuffy with the faint but unmistakable odor of rank sweat.

Canon Bancroft sat behind a desk buried in paper and leather-bound books, a map partially unrolled atop the piles. He was a small, homely man of middle years, his face sallow and pinched, with a monkey's overlarge ears. But his dark eyes gleamed with intelligence.

Francis had never met him and knew little about him beyond the bare fact that he had been a preacher at Cambridge University for a few years. "I appreciate your taking the time to see me."

"I serve His Grace in every way." Bancroft remained seated, gesturing to a chair.

Francis took it. "I assume you know why I'm here."

"Yes. I suppose I should be grateful that Lord Burghley has finally seen fit to offer us some assistance in our desperate battle."

"I doubt he views a flurry of pamphlets as a matter of military concern."

"Oh, but he should!" Bancroft leaned forward with his small teeth bared, as if to bite. "Martin's aim is nothing short of revolution. Tear down the Church and the state falls with it."

Francis tucked his chin, alarmed by the man's aggressive manner. "That's a bit strong. Martin has taken pains to make clear that he respects and reveres our queen and has no quarrel with the monarchy. He would leave Her Majesty at the head of the Church, replacing only the intermediate hierarchy." Alarmed by the hostility in Bancroft's small eyes, he added, "Obviously, he must be stopped. He stirs up too much discord."

"Discord." Bancroft grunted dismissively. "What have you discovered so far?"

An abrupt shift, but a welcome one. "I only received this commission two days ago. I spoke with His Grace, as you know. I'm hoping you can tell me something about

Martin's accomplices, any small details gathered from your interrogations so far."

"We haven't caught any accomplices yet," Bancroft admitted. "I'm sorry for those men's deaths, but they won't have died in vain if you succeed in bringing one of Martin's henchmen to account. I credit my strategy of provocation with drawing the villain out, forcing him to take direct action. Now he's left a trail you can pursue."

"It has had that effect." Francis refrained from further judgment. "Did it not occur to you that setting writers on Martin's trail might place them at risk?"

"There are always casualties in war," Bancroft said. "Regrettable as that harsh fact might be. John Lyly, my first recruit, understood that fact when he agreed to participate. There should have been little risk. The identities of my anti-Martinists are a closely guarded secret."

Not closely enough since two men had been strangled to death. Bancroft had just given one name to Francis without even asking for his discretion. And Tom had warned him only yesterday that Thomas Nashe could hold a secret about as long as a toddler could hold a jug of small ale laced with hawthorn — a powerful diuretic.

Francis nodded, as if it all made sense. "Did Mr. Lyly recruit the others?"

"Of course. He chose Robert Greene as the most prolific writer of his acquaintance. We wanted someone who could respond quickly to new attacks. He chose some young university acquaintance of Greene's to go out and scour up information with which to harry Martin. I leave all that to them, provided they keep expenses within bounds. The Privy Council refused to subscribe to this plan or offer it any material support."

With good reason. The imprudent scheme had unleashed a kind of anti-Martin madness in the streets. The authorities might be forced to close the theaters to suppress the tumult, which would cause more outrage.

Bancroft had created all this turmoil in his zeal to suppress a handful of insolent pamphlets.

"I understood that you had several pursuivants searching for Martin's press."

"Only one good one," Bancroft said. "The Council won't share those resources either. A man named Anthony Munday. He comes highly recommended by Sir Richard Topcliffe. Do you know him?"

"I do," Francis said, gulping down a surge of bile. He'd served with Topcliffe on a commission last summer to question recusant Catholics in Her Majesty's prisons — an unpleasant but necessary task in the aftermath of the Spanish assault on England's coast. Topcliffe had gone out of his way to frighten and humiliate Francis, leaving him with the vilest of images etched forever in his mind. If Munday was a man of similar tastes, heaven help Martin and his poor printers!

Bancroft didn't seem to notice his visitor's distress. In fact, he seemed pleased to see recognition of his pursuivant's potential for violence or the incitement thereof. "Munday apprehended that arrant rascal Giles Wigginton."

Wigginton was a former vicar, educated at Cambridge, where he had first locked horns with John Whitgift. Outspoken and irrepressible, Wigginton had moved from parish to parish, preaching more or less Martin's message long before Martin took up his pen. He'd been a thorn in the archbishop's side for many years. Francis was surprised he hadn't been arrested immediately after Martin's first volley. "Did he supply any clues about Martin?"

Bancroft's mouth worked as if forcing down a bad grape. "Not as such. But he's a notorious troublemaker. He's spent more time in jail than he has behind a pulpit. He lied through his teeth all through his deposition. He refused to answer any question sensibly, returning each with some vulgar riposte. He denied knowing Martin and

61

scolded His Grace — the Archbishop of Canterbury! — to his face for arresting him for the mere knowledge of a book that could be found in the pockets of many lords and ladies. Why didn't he question them, the impudent churl demanded, instead of troubling only the poor and helpless?"

A dangerous question. But even if it had some justice in it, the answer was obvious. Persons of different stations were judged by different standards; that was the way of the world.

"Forgive me for my slowness," Francis said, "but I don't understand the utility of hiring pamphleteers to write counterstrikes. Martin stopped publishing in March. Things had nearly quieted down."

Bancroft's nostrils flared at the unconvincing humility. "We could never allow Martin to retire from the fray victorious. Without an answer, his words would echo in the people's ears, poisoning their faith in the established church. That could never be allowed!" His right hand curled into a hard fist, his knuckles turning white. "This isn't just a matter of a few disrespectful works. No, Mr. Bacon. We are in a battle for nothing less than the hearts and minds of the people of England. Nothing less! And now, finally, thanks to my strategic recruitment of these talented and effective writers, we are winning. You can hear it everywhere. Martin has become a laughingstock."

Francis listened to this passionate defense of a fundamentally unsound strategy with a bland expression and a silent tongue. But he noted the central flaw in the argument. Once the archbishop ceded the power to determine the structure of the Church to the people, he was fighting a battle in a war that had already been lost.

Clouds had been passing across the small patch of sky visible beyond the window, casting stripes of shadow that worked their way from one wall to its opposite. Dark ones began to predominate. The weather was changing.

Francis asked the question he now asked everyone he met. "Who do you think Martin is?"

Bancroft grunted. "That question haunts my every waking hour. A gentleman, an educated man. That much is clear from his writings. He must have connections with influence, who he expects to shield him when he is finally caught. He may be a lawyer, and I believe he is likely to be a bachelor."

"Why a bachelor?" Francis hadn't considered Martin's domestic circumstances.

"He's taking a tremendous risk in publishing such treasons. He must be prepared to flee to the Continent at any moment. He may be there now."

"But Martin Junior was just published. It refers to some of the anti-Martinists' work. That's all quite recent, this past month. He must still be in England."

"For now." Bancroft said. "I'm sure he enjoys stirring the pot and watching the dissension bubble. Martin is also likely a member of Parliament. He knows how to frame an argument. That list of theses reminds me of a bill presented in the House of Commons."

"That's an interesting observation." Francis had also been a member of that august body since 1584. "But there are over four hundred men in the House of Commons. All are educated gentlemen, and many have fathers or brothers of high standing."

A dark cloud covered the patch of window as a cold rush of wind slipped inside. Its freshness relieved the increasingly oppressive smell of Bancroft's body, but it sent a chill down Francis's neck.

Or did the chill arise from the conversation? A glitter in Bancroft's small black eyes warned him he might be on the canon's list. He was a bachelor, a lawyer, a member of Parliament. He'd gained praise for his skill with a pen, and his uncle sat in the second-highest seat in the realm. His mother's ardent Calvinism was well known in these circles.

Bancroft's lips curved, acknowledging that he'd struck his mark. "I have every confidence in Mr. Munday. He is nothing if not persistent. He will do whatever is necessary to catch that traitor and bring him to me in irons."

Francis rose. "Meanwhile, I will pursue the murderer, who may turn out to have nothing to do with Martin Marprelate."

"Not likely. I doubt Mr. Munday will have to search much farther than a day's ride from London. Martin likes to stay close, where he can get the news while it's hot. He'll be living at his ease in some great one's house. Some great lady, I suspect. One who has never been reconciled to the established church. One with a protector close to power, possibly even on the Privy Council." Bancroft laughed, three short grunts from deep in his chest. "Perhaps you should pay a call on your mother, Mr. Bacon. She knows all the hottest nonconformists, I believe."

NINE

The smell of stale beer and tobacco smoke smacked Tom in the face as he swung open the low door of the Goose and Gall tavern on Hog Lane. Thomas Nashe had sent him a note telling him this was the favorite haunt of poets, pamphleteers, and others of the inky company. Tom peered through the murk and spotted his friend at a round table near the front. He asked a wench bearing two fistfuls of empty mugs to bring two full ones when she had the chance and joined him, pushing his feet off the stool so he could sit by the window.

He opened it a couple of inches to provide a breath of — well, not fresh air, but at least air not composed chiefly of smoke. He'd tried tobacco a time or two and didn't much like it. The reek had clung to his doublet long enough for Trumpet to catch a whiff and treat him to her vividly expressed opinion of the vice.

The grimy window afforded an excellent view of the grimy wall across the lane, which couldn't be much wider than nine feet. Still, he could see anyone approaching the tavern in time to dash out the back door if he so desired. A good spot for a man with debts, like most of these poor scribblers.

"What's the word?" he asked Nashe, anticipating a nonsensical reply.

"The word," Nashe said slowly, screwing up his homely face, "is metaphysical transubstantiation."

"Ouch." Tom rubbed his ear. "That's two words, which fetched me a bruise on the way in. Don't you have a kinder one?"

"More kind, perhaps, but less germane." Nashe shook his head. "Kind, kin, germane? No. Too obscure. " He sighed. "Let's get straight to business, shall we?"

"By all means. First, tell me why I'm here. Who was murdered, where, how, and when? All you've given me so far is the why: because the murderer thought the victims were you or one of your fellow anti-Mart —"

"Hssst! No one knows who we are. Or rather, only a select few know those names. More mimicking monkeys pop up every day. That's why we need you. It's supposed to be a great secret, yet someone outside our little circle . . ."

Nashe's words turned into a leer as the wench arrived. He watched with rapt attention as she leaned forward to set the mugs on their table. She waited, hand on hip, while Tom and Nashe traded glares, silently contending which of them would pay. She tapped her foot and Tom relented. These coins came out of the government's purse, after all, not his.

After she left, Nashe took a sip as if sampling a sweet wine, then put his elbows on the table, turning toward Tom and pitching his voice low. He could not have looked more like a conspirator if he'd drawn a black hood down to his pug nose. "The first victim's name was John Little. Did I mention him? He lodged in the same house as Robert Greene. I'm in his room now, though hoping to avoid his fate."

"You told me that much before."

"Well, Greene and I are convinced that Little was killed in place of John Lyly, the third of our triad. He's scuttled off to the country for the nonce. We three — or rather those two, with me brought in by Greene to do the legwork

— were hired by our esteemed patron, the Canon of Westminster, Richard Bancroft."

"Wait." Tom gave Nashe a warning frown. This was not a subject for jesting. "You don't mean to tell me that Mar-Martin was hired by the Church of England."

"Oh, but I do." Nashe grinned, nodding, eyes twinkling. "Life in London is more filled with wonders than even I could have imagined."

"The Canon of Westminster — presumably a pious and sober knave — hired you and Robert Greene to write profane, yet jocular, pamphlets in order to quell the profane, yet jocular, pamphlets being written by a Presbyterian rogue." Tom shook his head, baffled by the absurdity.

"Don't try to understand it," Nashe advised. "Just focus on the task at hand. Poor John Little met his end in the alley around the corner from our house, not far from here."

"How was it done?"

"He was strangled with a leather cord, which we know because the murderer left it tied around poor Little's neck. That was a week ago Monday — the eighteenth — sometime between ten o'clock, when Greene staggered home drunk, as usual, according to his landlady, and six o'clock the next morning, when the sweepers found him."

"Aren't there constables in this ward?"

Nashe shrugged. "It's a liberty. It's new to me. I don't know how it's governed."

"I'll want to visit the house and talk to the landlady. Have any neighbors come forward with anything? They might have had their windows open on these warm nights."

"Not if they're afraid of corrupt airs and mischievous spirits. There wouldn't have been much to hear besides a few soft steps and low gurgle." Nashe demonstrated the sound.

"If that's all we've got, we'll never catch him."

"You'll have to go the other way round. Find out who knows who we are, we three anointed ones. Who wants to silence us?"

"Who doesn't?" Tom laughed. "In all seriousness, it's too vague. I can't ask that question without spilling the secret. What about the second one?"

"That newly minted angel is Edgar Stokes, the most inoffensive mortal ever to achieve publication in the City of London. He wrote about earthquakes, Clarady. Earthquakes and big winds and the morals that should be drawn from such notable events. His only sin lay in occupying the garret recently vacated by my humble self."

"Strangled, I suppose?"

"No cord this time. Just fingers."

"Ugh." Tom swigged that image away with beer. "But wait! The name Stokes sounds nothing like Nashe. And besides, you said you hadn't written any of Mar-Mart —" He cut off the name as Nashe touched a finger to his lips.

"I'm becoming quite a well-known figure in these parts. My future rises to greet me with open arms and a glad cry."

That future must have representatives in low places because the words no sooner left his mouth when two men ambled up to their table. Both were dressed in gentleman's attire, but one looked more prosperous than the other. He wore a scarlet doublet with yellow linings and short, round hose well-puffed over yellow stockings. He had a tall hat with a gallant feather and a fashionably pointed beard.

The other one's potbelly strained the laces holding his rusty green doublet and baggy slops together. Their linings were faded linen, and his buttons were made of wood.

"Nashe!" the potbelly man cried, gripping his target's shoulder hard enough to draw a wince. His ruddy hair stuck out around his small cloth cap, and his beard looked like he'd cut it himself with a dull knife.

"I'm real enough," Nashe said, twisting free. "No need to prove my bodily existence."

The well-dressed man slid onto the stool next to Tom with a flick of his eyebrows for a greeting. "I'm John Dando and my fat friend there is Oliver Oatmeale."

"Impossible!" Tom gaped at them in delight. "I thought you were products of some printer's imagination." These were two of Ben's favorite pamphleteers.

Oatmeale lifted his chin with mock dignity. "I assure you, my good man, we are both quite as real as your friend here." He helped himself to a stool.

"I take it you're familiar with our work," Dando said, his blue eyes twinkling. "Tell me, which did you find the most compelling? In purely literary terms, I mean. *How the Tripe Wife Tricked her Husband* or *Bank's Bay Horse in a Trance?*"

"The horse, definitely the horse. Though I'll confess I haven't kept up with your master works since my chambermate left me to take a wife. He's the one who bought your pamphlets by the pound."

"Bless him," Dando said. "May he never come to regret the exchange." His merry expression sobered as he turned toward Nashe. "Have you heard any more about your would-be assassin?"

Nashe shot Tom a sidelong glance and answered, "Nothing useful."

"You'd best tuck yourself into bed behind locked doors well before dark," Oatmeale said. "Good advice for us all since our strangler can't tell us apart."

"You'd think anyone could tell the difference between Thomas Nashe and an actual man," Dando said. So much for the sober moment!

"All cats are gray in the dark," Nashe retorted.

"Which would matter if the issue were color, not height," Oatmeale said. "If your troublesome reports on

Martin's doings are equally confused, our strangler is strangling in vain."

"Not if he's strangling for the pleasure of it," Dando said. "In that case, he's a rousing success. Or so we assume, having been mercilessly spared the sight of the said rousing."

The three men bantered on, pouring out words with more alliteration than import. Listening, Tom opened his mouth, then shut it again, twice. At last, he could hold his peace no longer. He pounded his fist on the table to get their attention. "Hold on! Isn't Pasquill, or Mar-Martin, or whoever he is -- isn't his identity supposed to be a great secret?"

All three fell silent, giving him the round-eyed, blinking stares of men caught in bed with another man's wife.

Oatmeale spoke first. "Did Nashe tell you that?"

Dando expanded the question. "Did Thomas 'the babbling brook' Nashe tell you that?"

The babbler shrugged a weak apology. "My friends, whose number does not include these two clowns, could scarcely fail to notice that writers were falling in my wake — and not in awe of my superior talents."

That drew a round of spit-spraying lip farts.

Tom regarded them with narrowed eyes, drumming his fingers on the table dramatically, as if considering strangling them himself. Then he relented. "How many know? About Mar-Martin, I mean. I suppose the stranglings are general gossip by now."

"I've written a full account," Dando bragged. "It'll be published tomorrow."

"How much?" Oatmeale demanded. "Mine won't be out till Thursday."

"Copies," Dando admitted. "But a gross of them, and I'm sure to get a penny apiece."

"You're quick," Nashe said admiringly. "I hadn't even thought about writing it up."

"You have to be quick to get ahead of the pack," Dando said with a wink at his friend. "And you have to add a moral to give it weight or the printer won't even read it. Sensation sells to the churl on the street, but printers like to pretend they have loftier aims."

Tom soaked up the information. Plain prose must be easier to write than love poetry, which had to rhyme. After his months with the Cambridge Puritans, he could moralize in his sleep. How likely was that penny apiece for one hundred and forty-four copies? It sounded like a lot. How long would it take to sell them?

That could wait. He asked his question again. "How many know about Mar-Martin and Nashe's poking around the countryside?"

"Not many," Dando answered. "The three conspirators, of course. Me and Oatmeale, maybe two or three others. We discussed it here for some time on Saturday after poor Stokes was found."

"We're all in danger," Oatmeale said. "This killer doesn't seem to care if he gets Mar-Martin or not. Most of us do a bit of roving around, sniffing out stories. Accounts of crimes and secret conspiracies sell like hotcakes at Lent, but there's a lot of competition."

"We don't all have special patrons," Dando said, cutting a sour glance at Nashe. Then he turned his cool blue eyes to Tom. "Tell us, Clarady. How do you know our friend Mr. Nashe?"

"From Cambridge." Tom noted the envious tone, but left it unremarked. "I had a hand in solving a similar problem there, which is why he asked me to poke around and see what I can find out. It might be best to start at the beginning. Do you men have any idea who Martin is?"

"Buy us another jug and we'll fill your ears," Oatmeale said. "Ideas are our stock in trade."

Tom waved at the serving wench and surrendered another tuppence. He filled all the cups and leaned back against the window frame with his own. "Let's hear it."

Dando smiled like the cat with the cream. "My favorite candidate is the ghost of the Earl of Leicester."

Tom groaned.

"No, hear me out," Dando said. "Everyone knows Leicester was the main protector of the most radical nonconformists. The queen's favorite. Who could stop him? I don't mean to say his ghost sat down on a tomb and wrote Martin's Epistle by moonlight, but His Lordship could have written those tracts anytime, or had them written to his specifications. He might have set the whole process in train before his unfortunate demise."

"That didn't end up quite as stupidly as it started," Tom said. "I don't think it was Leicester or his ghost, but you might be pointing in the right general direction. Martin doesn't seem to fear punishment. And he must have money to hire printers and move that press around the country. He must dish out bribes from time to time as well."

"Not necessarily," Nashe said. "At least not the bribes. These zealots know each other, don't forget. They gladly pass their banned books and barred preachers from house to house."

"Have to be a good-sized house," Oatmeale said, "to have room for a printing press and two or three men to run it."

"Which brings us back to a man with money," Tom said. "We'll add a good-sized house for good measure."

"But that's Martin," Dando said. "None of us think Martin Marprelate the Great is stalking scribblers through the streets. We're looking for Martin's minion, who could be anyone."

"Minion," Tom said, savoring the word. "I like it. But who is he?"

"Someone whose wits have been curdled from too much Bible study," Nashe said. His father was a vicar of the loyal variety, though a very poor one. Nashe had a special loathing for Presbyterians, Calvinists, and all other Puritanical sorts. He was a traditionalist at heart.

Dando said, "My first idea could still be right. Martin's minion might be the living servant of Leicester's ghost. Ghosts are bound to a single location, after all, like Leicester House on the Strand. He'd need a minion to mangle his manuscripts and murder —"

"Not the Strand," Oatmeale said. "Too much traffic. What ghost could rest there? He'll be in Kenilworth Castle, where's there plenty of room to stretch out."

They began to bicker again about the relative merits of a castle they had surely never seen and an equally unknown palace on the Strand. Tom rolled his eyes and turned his nose to the window for a smokeless breath of air. Lengthening shadows had darkened the narrow lane. A man wearing a dated doublet and knee-length galligaskins came into view, walking toward the tavern. He cast a furtive glance behind him, then hawked and spat as he approached the door. He paused on the threshold to give himself a little shake and square his shoulders, the way actors did before they strode onto the stage.

"No, no, no!" Oatmeale shouted, pulling Tom's attention back to the table. "You've got it all wrong! The strangler isn't Martin's minion. He wouldn't give a fart for Martin or his heresies. The motive is far baser — mere profit — and the strangler is none other than Thomas Nashe." He raised his arm to stab an accusatory finger at his candidate.

"Me!" Nashe recoiled from the finger as if from a hot poker. "I didn't even know those poor piddlers. I'm new here, in case you've forgotten."

"Precisely," Oatmeale said. "Here you are, new to London, supposedly fresh from university, but you haven't any proof apart from an unusual ability to filch from the classics. You're unknown, undistinguished, untested, and to be candid, difficult to spot given your diminutive stature."

Dando wagged his finger, nodding sagely. "Yes, I can see it. I can see it all too well. Nashe could be Martin's minion as well as Robert Greene's new puppet. Playing both sides of the coin for double fees."

Nashe tried for a shrewd look as he took a swig from his cup but lost the whole mouthful when Oatmeale clapped him on the back with a great guffaw. He righted himself, coughing and wiping his mouth with his hand while Dando and Oatmeale roared with laughter. Tom chuckled along, though he was losing patience with their foolery.

The man he'd seen outside sauntered up to their table and the laughter vanished like the light from a snuffed candle. The man smiled thinly, as if he'd attained his desired result.

"Munday," Dando said, his tone unwelcoming.

Munday greeted the other pamphleteers with a curled lip. Not a friendly sort of churl. On the short side of average with a rounded brown beard well streaked with gray, though Tom guessed he was a year or two shy of thirty. Hard years, or unhappy ones, judging by the lines already etched into his forehead.

The newcomer must be a debt collector. But Nashe patted the table in front of Tom and said, "Meet Anthony Munday, a writer acclaimed for reminding everyone that their weekly holiday is over."

"Thomas Clarady," Tom said, tilting up his chin.

Munday returned the gesture, then walked around Dando to lean against the window, blocking Tom's view. It didn't matter; he didn't need to look out. He only let his gaze wander when his nose ached for relief from the reek. But the sidelong glance Munday shot him as he settled his

74

shoulder against the jamb said the move had been deliberate.

A challenge. Small, but unwarranted. Tom's gut twinged a warning. He always heeded signals from that reliable source.

"Any news about the murders?" Munday asked.

The others shrugged. A pause developed, then Oatmeale said, "The authorities don't seem to be pursuing the matter."

"Maybe you should," Dando said. "You're a pursuivant, aren't you?"

Munday smirked at the recognition. Most pursuivants were just official messengers, but this rough semi-gentleman didn't seem that type. Another kind was sent out by Privy Councilors and court officials to track down criminals and serve warrants for their arrest. Others — the ones no one liked — roved around searching out violators of religious laws, both minor and major. Crypto-Catholics, mostly, although Martin Marprelate also qualified.

"I've done my part to serve my queen. It pays better than the drivel you wastrel lackwits piss out like stale beer." He made a sour face at the spattered tabletop. "Lucky for me, there's always some rat needs catching." Munday turned his glittering black eyes directly at Nashe, curling his lip in a knowing sneer.

Nashe blinked, his nose twitching, speechless for once.

Oatmeale broke the tense moment by raising his cup. "Here's hoping our rat gets caught before another of our brethren meets his doom. If all the pamphleteers are murdered, who'll be left to tell the tale?"

"There's always another scribbler coming out of the woodwork to scrabble at our heels," Dando said, his eyes on Tom. "Keep your heads on, brothers, and remember — crime pays, if you can hotfoot it to your publisher."

"Crime pays!" The foursome at the table cried, hoisting their cups in the air.

Anna Castle

Munday watched them, not joining in, pointedly waiting until they'd drunk their toasts before draining his own cup. "Be careful what you wish for," he said darkly, then wandered off to kill the laughter at another table.

"Dreary sort of a knave, isn't he?" Tom poured another round. "Nobody seems to like him."

"Not *seems*," Dando said. He held up a finger for a moment of silence, then intoned the words, "His seams may be straight, but his aims are crooked."

Tom chuckled at the witty phrasing, but the others didn't even bother to smile. Tough audience.

He enjoyed this company, feeling at home among these clever lads. While listening to them bandy words, he considered the possibility of joining them on an occasional basis. Not leaving Gray's — that would be stupid — but gentlemen of the lesser sort, like him, often wrote for publication, pamphlets especially. He had a university degree, like Nashe, Marlowe, and Greene. He was as qualified as anyone else.

He had no idea what he might write about and he wasn't ready to face these sharp critics, but it was something to keep in mind.

Nashe said quietly, "If we want a good candidate for Martin's minion, we need look no further." He tilted his head in the direction Munday had gone.

Tom expected that idea to be ridiculed, but the others took it seriously. "I can't believe you all agree on something," he said. "What makes you think he has anything to do with this?"

"You saw the way he looked at me," Nashe said. "He knows I'm the one that's been bringing tidbits to Mar-Martin."

"He doesn't like you, that's certain," Dando said. "Whereas most people find you irritating and endearing in equal measure."

Tom nodded at the justice in that assessment.

76

"Munday's a nasty one," Oatmeale told him. "He's a writer, like the rest of us, more prolific than anyone but Greene, but with not a thimble's worth of Greene's talent. He'll write anything for anyone, steal anything from anyone, and lay credit to things he never wrote, nor ever could."

"But why would he care?" Tom asked. "Even a mistrustful whoreson like that Munday would need a strong reason to strangle two men."

"Maybe he's Martin's minion," Nashe said. "He hates Catholics and nobody hates Catholics more than the Puritans. I believe Martin's in London somewhere or near. Munday could be the one delivering manuscripts to the printers."

Tom frowned, thinking that through. Then Dando said, "Envy, that's what it is. He thinks he's the new Robert Greene. Why wouldn't he try to get rid of the old one?"

"But he seems to be after Nashe and John Lyly," Tom pointed out.

"To start with," Dando said. "He must be furious that he wasn't chosen to be one of the elite anti-Martinists. Maybe he thinks if he removes the current crew, he'll be next on the canon's list."

"That's not bad," Tom said. "Not bad at all." He hefted the jug and found it empty. He waved it at the wench near the counter. They'd need more drink to wash down the ugly thought of a writer strangling his rivals.

After the wench came and went, Dando said, "Let's go back to Martin. Martin proper, not his minion. We don't have to look as high as the Earl of Leicester, alive or dead. He could be any gentleman of leisure and education with a safe hiding place and powerful friends. He might, for example, be a member of an Inn of Court. Someone like Francis Bacon. Have any of you simpletons ever heard of him?"

Oatmeale shook his head. Tom could sense Nashe holding his breath, waiting for him to answer first. Tom hummed and looked up at the ceiling as if searching his memory, pondering which would be worse: to reveal himself now and spoil the camaraderie or let them discover the truth later, as they inevitably would because such secrets were the devil to keep, and these two made a living sniffing out such things. They'd hate him for the deception, but in the meantime, they might share something to help him do his job.

Besides, if they learned he was a member of Gray's Inn, they'd be after him to loan them money.

He dug himself a deep hole and jumped into it. "Never heard of him."

Nashe emitted a high-pitched yap of laughter. "Inns of Court man, you say? Then he must be a wily sort of crook to hold so honorable an office."

"He's officious, that much is certain." Dando's lip curled. "He's a member of Parliament. I've heard him speak. He can argue with the best, though he doesn't spend much time in court, by all accounts. He keeps to himself, hiding in his chambers writing 'advice letters,' as he calls them. Advice to whom? The archbishop, perhaps?"

"What do you have against this gentleman?" Tom asked. He knew Bacon was innocent, but the idea of an Inns of Court man was not unreasonable. They were ostensibly supervised by the benchers — the governing board — but in practice, members' chambers were nearly inviolable. They all spent most of their time reading and writing. Nobody had the time or the inclination to oversee anyone else's work. Bacon said he was writing an advisement to cool the controversy, but he could be the one throwing faggots on the fire, for all Tom knew.

"I have nothing against him myself," Dando said. A touch of bitterness in his tone belied the mild words. "I merely present him as a plausible candidate. We say Martin has powerful friends and family. Bacon's father was the late Lord Keeper. What's more, it's widely known that his mother is one of the leading Calvinists in England."

Tom nodded. "And all those feathery fops have money to burn and leisure besides."

"And fathers and brothers and mothers and others with houses in the country with room for a press," Oatmeale said.

"And horses," Nashe added, "with stables at their inns and a ready excuse to ride out on legal business anytime they please with a satchel full of documents. They could pretend to be visiting Old Lady Clankpurse to add a codicil to her will."

That image sold the idea better than all the rest of the argument. Perhaps they should be seeking closer to home. But how could he suggest that Mr. Bacon look for someone exactly like himself?

TEN

Francis clucked his horse to a trot to catch up with Tom after they turned onto Aldersgate Street, heading north. They were riding to Gorhambury, his boyhood home and the place he loved above all others. He loved his mother too, of course, especially in small doses. After a few days, her constant stream of nagging, coddling, scolding, praise, and exhortation would exhaust his tolerance, and he would flee back to the bachelor serenity of Gray's Inn. This visit would be mercifully short. He just wanted to ask her a few questions.

They rode in silence for a while through the moist early morning. Yesterday's fitful rains had damped the dust without creating too much mud and washed the trees and fields clean. It was worth the discomfort of spending a day on horseback to clear the fug of his chambers from his body and his mind.

They stopped at the Angel in Islington for a breakfast of bread and ale and then pressed on. Francis didn't care for travel as a rule. He suffered from piles and was easily thrown out of balance by unfamiliar food, but he could enjoy an easy pace on a summer day. A fresh breeze blew from the northeast. It wouldn't get hot for hours yet. The road was not overcrowded and the fields alongside it were green with grass where horses frolicked or glimmering gold where oats ripened in the sun. Yellow loosestrife marked the edges of woods, whose trees were filled with twittering birds.

Travel had its appeal — especially in small doses. And the open road made a good place for confidential conversations.

Francis asked Tom to report on his evening at the tavern. Under his tutelage, his clerk had learned to remember key portions of conversations nearly verbatim, enhanced by his native intuition about the character of the participants.

Tom related his evening at the Goose and Gall, describing the pamphleteers who joined him and Thomas Nashe at their table. At the mention of Oliver Oatmeale, Francis laughed out loud, causing his horse's ears to twitch. "I thought Oatmeale was a bookseller's invention."

"So did I," Tom said, "and I doubt Dando was born with his name either. They're scoffers and jesters, but I like them both. They're men who keep their eyes open and their wits engaged."

"Good qualities, especially for witnesses. But they don't seem to know anything of use to us."

"Not yet, but everyone's keen to see Martin's minion locked up."

"Martin's minion?" An apt term, with the added twist of being certain to offend the individual so designated.

"That's what they're calling the strangler. They all swear the anti-Martinists' true identities aren't general knowledge. I believe them. These writers form a somewhat tightly knit company, in their own fashion. Not like a guild — not formally constituted — but there aren't that many of them. They come from everywhere too. Dando spoke like a gentleman, fallen on hard times, perhaps. Oatmeale spoke like a man who learned to talk like a gentlemen from John Dando. Many are university men, like Nashe and Greene. And Christopher Marlowe."

Francis nodded. Pamphleteers and playwrights were near the bottom of the literary scale, a rung or two above balladeers. Most books with any claim to more than ephemeral interest were written by scholars and gentlemen of leisure. Pamphlets might relate news about affairs in Europe or press some point of view. This sort were often commissioned by the Privy Council. Francis had written several such things himself, although he didn't publish them. His were meant for a very select audience.

But catch-as-catch-can writers like Dando and Oatmeale were a different breed, a new breed, unique to London. Their frivolous accounts of strange occurrences, sightings of ghosts, and unsolved murders were published cheaply and quickly to feed the hunger for entertainment of the middling sort. For whatever reason, these writers had chosen to inhabit the shadowland between gentility and trade, scraping out a precarious living, but one lived on their own terms.

"What did you think of Anthony Munday?" Francis asked. "Canon Bancroft mentioned him. He's the one who arrested that pitiful gadfly Giles Wigginton — a sorry substitute for Martin Marprelate."

"Nobody likes Munday. They told me as much. I didn't like him either. My gut tells me he's one to watch out for."

"Hmm." Francis knew his assistant had a great respect for the opinions of that organ. And in truth, it had proved itself worthy of respect on more than one occasion.

Tom added, "They all agreed that Munday enjoyed his work too much, as a pursuivant of Catholics, that is. He liked watching his victims hang. He even bragged about it."

"Canon Bancroft said he'd been recommended by Sir Richard Topcliffe." They traded grimaces, remembering the things they'd learned about that gentleman last year.

"Well," Tom said, "that tells us a lot about Munday's qualities, doesn't it? I like him for Martin's minion. He fits what we know so far."

They paused their conversation while a pair of doubly burdened horses trotted past them. Each horse was ridden by a well-dressed man with a better-dressed woman behind him, each woman wearing a vizard to protect her face from the dust and sun. The strange-looking masks seemed ill-omened, if one believed in such things.

After they'd passed, Tom said, "It's obvious Martin's minion is someone who knows that tight circle of pamphleteers intimately."

"It's obvious that he does not," Francis said, "since he managed to confuse John Lyly, a well-known favorite of the court, with this John Little, who sounds like the meanest sort of writer, spinning homilies out of exaggerated rumors of unnatural weather."

"The poor man was strangled, Mr. Bacon."

"And may God rest his immortal soul. I only meant to underscore the difference between the actual and purportedly intended victims. John Lyly is also a very small man, shorter even than my cousin Robert. The murderer must have only heard — or rather, misheard — the name. And then what? How would he find him?"

"He might have asked for John Lyly in the tavern and been pointed at Little, then followed him home. That does suggest someone who knows which tavern to ask in."

"Or someone who got the names from one who really does know. You said your friend Nashe is a prattler."

"True." Tom lifted his hat to wipe the sweat from his brow. The day grew warmer as the sun rose above the tree line.

Francis added, "We must not ignore the possibility that these murders have nothing to do with Martin Marprelate, even if the intended victims happen to be anti-Martinists. Greene and Lyly are the most popular writers of the day. You say your friend Nashe also has talent. Perhaps the killer fears another strong competitor and wants to stop him before he can get fairly started."

"And here comes sour-faced Anthony Munday again. Dando thought he was envious that the others were hired to write anti-Martin counterstrikes when he was not. He fancies himself a rival to Robert Greene."

That motive made more sense than any of the rest so far.

They rode in silence for a little while, separating to ride around a cart loaded with hay — a cart large enough to transport a disassembled printing press. They both studied it as they passed, plainly wondering the same thing.

Tom said, "Munday's the best we've got. Everything seems to fit."

"Only the most trivial elements. You're forgetting the most important thing we've learned about Anthony Munday."

"What's that?"

"He's working for Canon Bancroft. He wants to catch Martin, not protect him. If he's the strangler, he must be playing a very complicated game, working for both Martin and the anti-Martins."

"Oatmeale thought of that too, except he was casting Nashe as Martin's minion."

Francis didn't want to hear an account of that absurd proposal. But was it really so absurd? Not that Nashe would pretend to be trying to murder himself; the other part. "Now that I think of it, it's not impossible Martin should have a spy inside the enemy camp. He hasn't been caught in spite of the best efforts of the Church authorities."

"You would do it," Tom said. "If you were Martin, I mean. You'd want to stay one step ahead of the hounds. Martin's minion must feel sorely threatened by Nashe's snooping. One false move now and the whole delicate deception collapses. It's good."

"No, it isn't. It's too complicated. People are rarely so bold in actuality. The fox runs and hides; he doesn't dress himself in a hound's skin and join the pursuing pack."

They came in sight of the outskirts of Barnet and let the discussion drop. Martin Marprelate had sympathizers everywhere. They couldn't risk being overheard.

They stopped at the Mitre Inn and engaged a private room for two hours. They made a small meal, not wanting to overstuff, and then stretched out for a nap. At least, Francis napped. Tom pulled out a pamphlet by Anthony Munday, displaying it with the air of a man whose work was never done. Since the piece was entitled *A View of Sundry Examples Reporting Many Strange Murders*, Francis felt justified in ignoring the implied reproach.

The horses were fed and rested as well. They set out again, this time riding into the heat of the day with the sun beating down on them. Francis wished he'd worn a hat with a wider brim, however undignified it might look. Those glimmering fields of oats now glared whitely, and the frolicking horses stood listlessly in whatever shade they could find.

Ah, well. Last leg. After an hour or so, Francis noticed Tom muttering under his breath and counting on his fingers. "What are you calculating?"

Tom glanced at him as if he'd forgotten he wasn't alone. "I'm adding up fees for my suit of general livery, trying to figure out how long it will take me to get to the end."

"Too long," Francis said. "The odds of your agents achieving a survey of your lands accurate enough to satisfy a feodary of the Court of Wards are nearly nil. They have a vested interest in finding errors, and find them they will."

"That doesn't seem fair."

"It isn't. The whole notion of wardship is unfair. And ultimately harmful to the Crown's interests. People conceal lands owing feudal duties, so the queen gains nothing when they're passed on. Then the feodaries hire agents to search out concealed wards. Neighbors must either inform on their neighbors or lie to government officials. Worse, sometimes the agent or the feodary exacts a bribe to wink at the concealment. That encourages people to view the whole system as corrupt, which of course it is. Even if all the laws are followed to the letter, the court's procedures have grown so bloated the queen ends up with a mere fraction of the total fees."

"How can that be allowed to go on?" Tom asked, indignant. "That court should be abolished."

Francis chuckled. "It's difficult to abolish an institution that provides comfortable livings to so many lawyers."

Tom shot him a black look, as if it were his fault.

"You might as well save your pennies," Francis advised. "Suits of general livery are doomed to failure. You should borrow the money to pay the fine for special livery and get it over with minimum fuss. That's what everyone else in your position does."

"My father didn't approve of debt, especially for such large sums. It drags out the agony and ties your hands in the future."

A naive view. Francis couldn't remember a time when he hadn't owed money to someone, except for the brief period after Tom's father had paid off his creditors in exchange for taking his son under his wing. Francis had resented the imposition at first, but things had turned out well enough.

"If you're thrifty," he said, "you should be able to pay it off by the time you pass the bar. Meanwhile, nothing will teach you thrift better than my aunt's guardianship. You're flourishing under her care. Frame your mind toward contentment, Tom. You have many years of study and hard work ahead of you. Why not leave your estate in my aunt's capable hands in the meantime?"

That excellent counsel — free of charge — won him another black look. Tom nudged his horse to trot ahead, leaving Francis alone with his own thoughts, which were beginning to focus on the soreness of his bottom and the aching of his head.

They skirted the west side of St. Albans and took a grassy lane leading to Gorhambury House, entering the estate where Francis and his brother Anthony had grown up. The boys had explored every brook, pond, and burrow and known which birds nested in which favorite trees. These days, Francis did little more than stroll around the well-tended paths near the house, but he liked to imagine the landscape still contained those boyhood wonders.

He slowed as they approached the break in the trees deliberately created to frame the first view of the house, smiling as he heard the soft "God's bollocks!" as Tom caught sight of it. They stopped by mutual consent to admire the prospect.

"Home," Francis said.

"It's like a palace."

"Her Majesty did grace us with her presence a time or two."

The house had been enlarged in 1568 in anticipation of such a visit. Three stories surrounded a central courtyard with a chapel and a long gallery on the west side. The walls were built of flint for strength, hidden by pale pink plaster tooled to resemble bricks. The crowning element was the central front porch that rose the full height of the building. Sir Nicholas had designed it himself, sparing no expense. Doric columns flanked the arched entrance on the ground floor. Ionic columns stood atop those to frame the upper windows. The columns were faced with gleaming white clunch trimmed in the costliest limestone. Atop the whole, outside the small windows of the attic, stood a pair of painted wooden angels, which Lady Bacon had nicknamed Anthony and Francis, admonishing her sons to look up at them and be guided by their better natures.

"Magnificent," Tom said. "I look forward to seeing your mother again."

"She'll be glad to see you, here where you can't escape her. She'll question you about me, about Gray's, our chaplain, Sunday services, the food. No need to go into any detail; in fact, say as little as possible. I'll tell her about our commission. You can simply answer that I've asked you not to discuss it with anyone."

"I understand." Tom chuckled. "She corners me every time she comes to visit her sister."

"Then you've had practice. After supper, if you would, make an excuse to leave us alone. I want to speak with her in private."

"Gladly. It won't be dark for a couple of hours yet. I'd love a walk to stretch my legs."

"If you should happen to notice anything to suggest a printing press has been installed anywhere . . ."

Tom tapped his nose. "If there is one, I'll smell it out. I'll poke in everywhere, chat with the servants, see if there've been any visitors lately. Especially anyone holed up in a chamber writing."

"Be subtle about it. Most of my mother's servants grew up under her care. They're as devout as she is and loyal to the core." Francis drew in a deep breath and let it out, fortifying himself.

They clucked their horses into motion, rode down the curving lane to the yard, and dismounted. They were met at once by servants eager to help the young master and his guest. Lady Bacon came out to greet them, kissing Francis on both cheeks and extending a hand for Tom to bow over. Francis felt his petty discomforts — the prickling heat, his aching bottom — dissipate as he let himself be tended by those who knew him best.

Stablemen led the horses away while a man led Francis and Tom to their respective rooms to change their shoes and stockings and wash their hands and faces. Then Francis led Tom down to his mother's favorite parlor, which faced west onto the orchard. They found supper ready laid on a round table in the center of the room. A fire had been lit since here in the country, where the winds blew unobstructed, even July evenings could be chilly.

Francis took his usual chair by the fire, noting with gratitude the soft pillow that had been placed for him. Tom waited until his hostess had seated herself, then took the remaining chair. They both ate with good appetite, savoring the fresh food, prepared just for them rather than a hall full of hungry lawyers. Everything but the wine, the flour, and the spices had been produced on the estate: partridge pie with mushrooms, a warm spinach salad, and a cheese tart liberally dotted with fresh strawberries. Francis took pride in both the food and its presentation on pewter plates with wine served in Venetian glasses.

He ate in silence while his mother catechized their guest, testing his knowledge of the Bible and Calvinist theology. Tom acquitted himself well enough. After supper, Tom offered his thanks for the meal and begged to be excused, as planned. The dishes were cleared away and Lady Bacon's armchair moved to the fire. The servant set her embroidery frame ready to hand along with the workbasket filled with silk threads. The piece in the frame had the shape of a collar band and was already partly covered with intricate blackwork. Francis looked forward to receiving another handsome shirt.

He poured himself a second glass of wine, knowing his mother wouldn't want one. He turned his chair toward the fire as well and leaned back with a sigh composed of a deep physical contentment mingled with the anticipation of a challenging conversation. His mother had been his first and best teacher in every subject from Latin grammar to natural philosophy. Her memory seemed to be playing tricks on her lately, but her powers of ratiocination had not diminished one whit.

Lady Bacon picked up her needle and began to ply it, glancing from her youngest son to her work as she queried him about his health, his diet, and his associates, moving from those absorbing topics to her standard lecture about his inadequate disciplining of Pinnock, whom she judged inadequately schooled in Christian principles.

Francis approved of discipline in the abstract but didn't like to exercise it himself. When at last she began repeating her favorite recipes for sleeping draughts, he interrupted her. "Mother," he said, meeting the hazel eyes that had supplied the mold for his own. "I have something rather delicate to discuss with you."

"Oh?"

The steeply rising tone of that short question told him her mind had leapt in the wrong direction.

"Delicate in the political sense."

"Ah." She stabbed her needle into the fabric, folded her hands, and said, "Tell me."

"I suppose you know about Martin Marprelate?"

"*About* him? I've read every word he's written. I fully support his aims, if not entirely his methods. But of course you know that."

Francis nodded. "I wanted to begin at the beginning. I have a new commission from my Lord Burghley."

"God's mercy, Frank! Does he expect *you* to catch Martin Marprelate when the whole episcopacy has failed to find so much as discarded page of misprints?" Her eyes sparkled as she gave Francis a look of mock outrage. "Or does he suspect I'm keeping Martin *here?*"

She'd jumped straight into the heart of the matter, as he'd known she would. None of the Cooke sisters ever needed lengthy explanations. She seemed delighted by the idea, however, which was not the attitude Francis would prefer.

"If he thinks it, he hasn't confided as much to me," he said. "But I have spoken in the past few days to both Canon Bancroft and Archbishop Whitgift, each of whom made a point of implying that they considered you among those likely to be sheltering Martin or his minions."

"Don't say *minions*, Frank. It smacks of the French court and has ugly connotations."

"That isn't an answer, Mother."

"Did you ask me a question?" She beamed at him, enjoying herself. "What is your commission, if I may pry into my son's affairs to such an extent?"

"Someone murdered two pamphleteers in London a week ago, which would not be remarkable except that they appear to have been mistaken for two of the men posing as Mar-Martin, writing the popular anti-Martinist works that have been appearing since June."

"I've heard of Mar-Martin. I refuse to read such vulgarities. But I must admit Martin did supply the provocation. He ought to have left out the insolence and confined himself to the plain truth."

Which is what she would have done. At least Francis could be confident that Martin Marprelate was not an alias for his own mother.

"He would have lost three-quarters of his audience in that case," Francis said. "The most appealing aspects of Martin's works are his irreverent witticisms."

"That could be debated, but not now since you only grant me one night of your company."

"I have a commission, Mother. I can't keep my lord uncle waiting. You wouldn't want more men to die while I sit here eating strawberry tarts."

"Certainly not." She gave him that wiser-than-thou look, the one that said she knew perfectly well that he was making excuses. "What makes you think Martin has anything to do with your murders? I assume that's the weighty matter my Lord Burghley has asked you to investigate." She wrinkled her nose as at a bitter odor. "I don't like it, Francis. He uses you as a mere thief catcher, slightly glorified by some vague political dimension to the crimes. It isn't dignified. It isn't worthy of your talents."

Francis shrugged. He'd thought the same thoughts, but what use was it to complain? These tasks seemed to be the best he could get. Until this year, they had at least afforded him the occasional private conversation with his most powerful relation. "If I could identify Martin Marprelate, I'd lay up a very great store of political capital."

"A dubious antecedent, dearest. Martin could be anyone. Indeed, why should you assume Martin is singular? We have a Martin Junior. Soon no doubt we'll hear from Martin Senior. And if Martin has a son, why not a daughter? If a father, why not an uncle? A mother, an aunt, a cousin, a godparent? Or all of them together, writing as one devoted family."

"That has occurred to me as well, although the works are written in a consistent voice. His style is distinctive. But whether the author of Martin's works is one man or many, he must have confederates to operate that secret press. There can only be one of those."

"Not so. Many skilled tradesmen and women share our religious views."

Francis didn't correct that *our.* "But printers serve apprenticeships with members of the Stationers' Company. There aren't an infinite number of them. And presses are expensive. I don't know what a full set of type costs, but it must be a substantial investment."

His mother shrugged at that. "There are many wealthy persons among our number, all of whom would willingly lend Martin and his pressmen a hand, if needed. We are legion, my son. Our truth can not be denied."

Francis repressed a sigh, taking a sip of wine instead. "Perhaps. Happily, I am only tasked with stopping one individual. My best conjecture at present is that the pamphleteers were murdered to prevent them from discovering Martin's press. One of the anti-Martinists has been scouting around, picking up rumors and bits of gossip. My clerk says the man has a talent for teasing confidences out of people."

"Ah, well, then. Your work is half done." Her tone dripped with irony.

"I know. But my man Clarady is also good at teasing out confidences. And I can gain access to depositions and whatever official records have been collected. There may be a clue hidden in them that has hitherto gone unregarded."

"At least you'll be safe inside the library at Lambeth. I don't like the idea of you consorting with these scoffing pamphleteers. Their kind attracts violence, the way they live."

Francis couldn't imagine how his mother — gently bred and tended every day of her life — could know anything about the dread satirist and others of his ilk. She'd dined at respectable establishments like the Antelope Inn, where the redoubtable Widows Guild held their monthly meetings, but in her mind that would be nothing like the Sodoms and Gomorrahs where playwrights and poets squandered their idle hours.

He gazed out the window, where the day had almost disappeared, leaving only a thin band of ruddy light atop the orchard wall. "That isn't what I wanted to discuss with you, Mother. Although I am glad to know you don't have Martin Marprelate living in your gatehouse."

"Not now." Lady Bacon gave him a saucy smile, revealing the ghost of the lively young woman she once was. "If Martin asked me for house-room, I might provide it."

"Mother!"

She shrugged one slender, black-clad shoulder. "I haven't been asked. I merely share with my own son, in the privacy of my home, the opinion that the *Theses Martinianae* are precisely what I would have written myself." She smiled again. "Although I did not."

Francis gave her a dry look. "Who do you think Martin is?"

Her playful expression turned Sphinx-like, giving the distinct impression that she knew more than she let on. "An educated person. A devout student of Calvin's teachings. A passionate advocate for a full Reformation — a true Reformation. Beyond that, I wouldn't care to speculate."

Why speculate about something she already knew? Francis doubted he'd ever get a better answer. "Some people think he may be a member of one of the Inns of Court."

"Do they? Which one?"

"Does it matter? The four inns together must have over a thousand members."

"You'll never find him that way, then." She sounded amused.

"Many people think Martin is a member of the House of Commons."

Lady Bacon smiled her Sphinx smile again. Confirmation? Or dismissal of an absurd notion? She used that smile when she wanted him to solve a problem — a tricky translation, a moral argument — for himself. She could be frustratingly opaque.

Francis took a sip of wine, savoring its fruity sweetness as it glided down his throat. "I had a curious thought as we were riding today. I wonder what you might think of it."

Lady Bacon raised her thin eyebrows, ready to listen.

"I should note first that I haven't actually spoken with my lord uncle."

"I thought he gave you this hazardous, undignified, and doubtless unpaid commission."

Francis couldn't fault that description. "The excuse given to me, when I answered his summons, was that he hasn't recovered from my aunt's death."

"We all miss her," Lady Bacon said. "I am comforted to know that Mildred is in heaven now, freed from pain and care."

Francis nodded. "My uncle is shifting many burdens onto my cousin's shoulders. He's given Robert charge of his stable of intelligencers."

Her nostrils flared. "A category in which he includes you, I suppose."

"Not quite, I hope. But it was Robert to whom I spoke, relaying his father's wishes, ostensibly. I'll have Clarady deliver reports and ask for money for expenses."

"Good. He'll be more difficult to refuse, especially since dipping into his purse would mean negotiating with my sister Elizabeth." Her eyes flashed. "I'm surprised she allows her ward to engage in such unsavory activities."

"She doesn't know. And please don't tell her." Francis let a small pause develop while he organized his central point. "I don't see Robert very often, you know. Only on occasions when we both happen to be attending upon the queen, and then there are always so many others present."

"You were never close friends," she observed. "You always went your separate ways, even when you three appeared to be playing together. Anthony is headstrong. No one can tell him what to do, nor does he wait to see if he's being followed. You have that preternatural capacity for intense focus. You could kneel beside the fish pond for an hour, enraptured by the little world under the water, while other children ran and shouted all around you. Robert wasn't interested in the secret life of ponds. He prefers the secrets of people. He loves to find them out and store them up, waiting for that moment of best advantage. I could well believe that he's discovered who

Martin is and is holding that secret close to his chest until its revelation serves his purposes."

"That's a perspective I hadn't thought of." Francis well remembered days like the ones his mother described. "But Robert and I have never been rivals, not explicitly. And you know, Mother, he fits the general assumptions about Martin's background."

"Ha!" Lady Bacon's eyes twinkled. "Is *that* where you're headed?"

"I know, it's absurd at first blush, but consider it. He's educated, well versed in Calvinist principles. He spent several months in Switzerland in Theodore Beza's own house. He's never lived at Gray's, although he is a member. He has served as a member of Parliament."

"Apart from the travel and the residence at Gray's, all that could be said of you."

"I know, but I have no motive to play Martin Marprelate. It would be a terrible risk with nothing to gain."

"You might do it to please your mother." She batted her lashes at him.

"It would not please you to see me hanged for treason, Mother. And we both know I'm not Martin, so that is not a helpful observation."

She clucked her tongue. "It would be as great a risk for Robert as anyone else."

"No one would ever prosecute Lord Burghley's son for writing pamphlets," Francis said with a touch of bitterness. "That's one of the best arguments in favor. Hear me out. Martin Marprelate has dominated Archbishop Whitgift's every waking moment for the better part of a year. All he can think about is catching Martin, silencing him, punishing him, and drowning out his ideas with a cacophony of rebuttals. But Martin isn't the only man in England who wishes the archbishop wielded less power and had less influence with the queen. A member of the

Privy Council might foster such a character in order to distract the archbishop from other business. This councilor could easily protect his creation from discovery and fund the whole venture from his own purse."

Lady Bacon clapped a hand to her breast and said, "Oh, my Lord and Savior, Frank! You do possess the most extraordinary mind."

He laughed at the praise, glad she hadn't scoffed at his convoluted proposal. "Then you don't think it's completely beyond the pale?"

"Far beyond, if it were true, which I very much doubt. Although . . ." She picked up her needle and took a few more stitches. Francis waited, giving her time to consider the ramifications of his proposal. After a few moments, she put down her needle. "I assume you've cast your uncle in the role of Machiavelli, with Robert as his instrument."

Francis nodded. "They would never have intended murder to result from their stratagem, of course. Although it would amuse Robert to set me on the trail, daring me to catch them out. But the archbishop isn't fond of Robert. He said as much to me on Tuesday. He doesn't like him being slid onto the Privy Council without discussion. But my uncle wouldn't want to provoke a direct confrontation with him and risk raising the queen's ire." Francis traced his moustache with his index finger, frowning. "No. Now that I've said it all aloud, I can see that it's too intricate. Too indirect."

"I'm not so sure. Your uncle is a deep strategist, willing to set small things in motion and step back to allow them to develop with only an occasional nudge to keep them moving in the desired direction. And your cousin Robert has always been a sly one. He's willing to allow his desired ends to justify his means."

"I expected you to tear my mad little notion into pieces."

"Your aged mother has a few surprises left." She smiled fondly at him. "You and Robert have much in common, but you were brought up quite differently. I don't think either of you realizes it. By the time you boys were born, the long, dark days of Queen Mary were past."

Francis grew still. She rarely spoke of that time, now thirty years past. While others of their religious beliefs fled for the safety of the Protestant Low Countries, Sir Nicholas and his new wife, Anne, remained in England, offering their services to the Catholic queen. Lady Anne obtained an appointment as a gentlewoman of the queen's Privy Chamber, tending the monarch's personal needs, swallowing her faith and her fears to help her husband keep his job — and his head. Francis admired her for that more than any other of her many achievements.

She spoke in her storytelling voice. "When our good Queen Elizabeth succeeded to the throne, your father and I chose to put those days behind us, not wanting to burden our children with past troubles. But your uncle William, now my Lord Burghley —" She broke off with a sniff. She'd never reconciled herself to the fact that her brother-in-law had been elevated to the peerage while her husband had not. "Your uncle could never stop gnawing over old battles, mumbling out which stratagems succeeded and which failed. That persistence makes him an extraordinary councilor and works to the good of the realm. But I believe he infected his son with that sense of pervasive intrigue and the need for constant, sometimes ruthless, defensive action."

"But my uncle hates turmoil and disruption. That's one of his best-known qualities."

"Yes," Lady Bacon said, "but he hates and fears religious persecution even more. And that is what Whitgift has come close to with his wicked oaths, forcing men to choose between their God and their queen. They must perjure themselves in this world and the next to satisfy him or face the severest punishment. That makes men desperate, my son, and desperate men are not moderate. They are not calm. They do not work steadily and contentedly toward the betterment of all mankind."

The great goal of the humanists, whose philosophy Francis had absorbed at his father's knee. "But my uncle wouldn't invent Martin Marprelate just to stop Whitgift from exacting those oaths, using mockery to add insult to the injury."

His mother waited, watching him with that expectant gleam in her eyes that said she was waiting for him to work the problem out by himself.

"My uncle wouldn't do it," Francis said slowly, "but Robert might. He would enjoy the deception and the cleverness. Having spent his life, as I have, under the shelter of Her Majesty's long peace, he doesn't share his father's fears of religious upheaval. He would consider Martin a calculated risk, a reasonable gamble. Nothing that couldn't be charged to a few well-paid servants who could be whisked abroad if things got too sticky." He frowned at his mother. "I wouldn't allow myself to think about it, but now that you've helped work it all through, I believe it may be possible that my cousin Robert is behind this whole controversy."

Lady Bacon's lips curved in the satisfied smile that said he'd done well. He'd arrived at the desired solution.

ELEVEN

Trumpet and Catalina dressed in their street clothes, eager for their Thursday afternoon out. They were ostensibly bound to visit Trumpet's maternal aunt, Lady Chadwick, at her home in Bishopsgate, a destination approved by Lady Russell. And they meant to stop there, but only to change clothes again. Once disguised as young gentlemen, they meant to enjoy their liberty in a tavern near the theaters in Shoreditch.

At the moment, however, they looked the very portrait of a pious noblewoman with her equally pious maidservant, clothed in black from the long veils draped over their heads to the leather slippers protected from the dirty streets by thick wooden pattens. They pulled on their black gloves and Trumpet collected the latest Martin manuscript, snugly wrapped in canvas soaked in linseed oil. They would deliver it to the printer on their way.

Vautrollier's print shop, now owned by Richard Field and his new wife, Vautrollier's widow, stood just around the corner from Lady Russell's house. The new couple continued to specialize in the works that had earned the shop its sober reputation: Protestant theology and high church music, a curious combination. Most of their books were printed on behalf of booksellers with shops in St. Paul's yard. They kept only a few samples in the shallow front room of their Blackfriars establishment, the bulk of the house being given over to the print shop, the acrid smells of which permeated the house.

Trumpet rang the bell on the narrow counter. A tall apprentice poked his head through the rear door, held up a finger, and disappeared. He returned in a moment, tying a clean apron around his slender waist. "Good afternoon, my lady. Another package for me? Already?"

"We've been inspired."

The apprentice, whose name was Wat Whyting, nodded uncertainly. He obviously hadn't expected another manuscript so soon and had to figure out how to cope. He must need to send a message to someone, though Trumpet had never been able to intercept any such. There were always boys coming and going from the back of the shop, running messages between the busy printer and his customers. Carts stopped to load up barrels of new books or unload barrels of paper. Any one of them might be employed to take a note to the next conspirator in the chain.

Trumpet watched his long face with its new-sprung beard and sparse moustache. He must be about her age, nineteen or a little younger. She supposed Lady Russell had roped him into the task of delivering Martin's works to the intermediary who delivered them to the hidden press. This young man might know the other party to the exchange.

She didn't believe the pamphlets were printed here. Field's print shop was too close to home and Lady Russell was far too canny a cat to be so obvious. Trumpet had wheedled and hinted, trying her best to find out where the manuscripts went after the apprentice took them, but had only learned that they were left in a secret place to be collected when no one was watching. Some place out of the rain, presumably. She wouldn't trust this oiled cloth to withstand a summer storm. Also some place not too far away, since Whyting came to work at the usual time the day after a delivery. She and Catalina had kept watch twice to be certain.

Whyting offered her a sheepish smile. "You needn't wait, my lady. The package is safe with me."

"I believe you." Trumpet met his brown eyes, laden with poorly concealed admiration. She batted her thick black lashes and treated him to her best cupid's-bow smile. "*Won't* you tell me where it goes from here? I want to count the days until I can hold a printed copy in my hands." She placed her hands on her breast, emphasizing that feature.

"I understand, my lady, but I honestly can't tell you."

"You must know where you take it!"

His wide mouth turned down. "Lady Russell made me promise never to tell anyone, not even you, my lady. I beg you not to ask me again. I daren't risk her displeasure."

Trumpet's eyes narrowed. "Do you not fear *my* displeasure?"

A swift quirk of his lips betrayed the true answer, forcing Trumpet once again to lament her short stature and lack of any other source of intimidation. No husband to charge in with a gang of retainers; no money to withdraw from the business; no credibility even to make the withholding of recommendations a viable threat.

She drew in a long breath through flaring nostrils, tilting up her pointed chin. "I can be very ill-tempered, you know. And I am known to hold grudges."

Again, that quirk of amusement. "I have no doubt of that, my lady."

"I will find out who receives these manuscripts and where they go to be printed."

"I have no doubt of that either, my lady." Whyting picked up the package and began to walk backward in very small steps. When he reached the wall, he added, "But not from me," and slipped through the door.

Trumpet pounded both fists on the counter in frustration. As they walked back onto the street, she said to her maidservant, "We'll have to find a way to follow him."

Catalina nodded. "We may pay a boy to do it." Her English had improved by leaps and bounds, but she still left out bits and pieces and retained the accent of her native Spanish.

"We can at least find out when he leaves each day. Then perhaps we can manage to deliver the next one on a day when my Lady Russell is bedridden or entertaining guests."

They walked around the corner to enter Lady Russell's stable, where two grooms waited with horses to convey them to Bishopsgate. Men helped them up, seating each woman sideways behind a groom. Trumpet hated riding this way, with her feet resting on a little shelf and one arm awkwardly gripping the sweaty groom's waist. It made her feel like a sack of corn. She rode astride at home with long drawers under her skirts and her own hands on the reins.

The requirements of rank were often ridiculous. Lady Chadwick's house lay less than a mile from Blackfriars, across some of the most densely populated wards in the city. She, Tom, and Ben had never bothered with horses when they went out to explore the city or run errands for Mr. Bacon. It was faster to walk, even now when she wore skirts, with the added benefit that you didn't need a groom, who owed allegiance to another, to tend to the horse. But Lady Russell wouldn't hear of it, and so Trumpet had to jolt and sway, helpless, if dignified, through the crowded streets.

They eventually gained the stable behind Trumpet's aunt's house and were helped to the ground. She sent the grooms straight back, telling them Lady Chadwick's men would see them home. Which they wouldn't since she wouldn't ask them. She liked walking; it was simple and anonymous. She'd gotten used to coming and going on her own during her wonderful year pretending to be a young gentleman of Gray's Inn.

Those had been glorious days! She'd spent nearly every waking minute in Tom's company, forming a bond of friendship even her startling change of gender hadn't broken. Now she rarely saw him apart from Sunday dinners under Lady Russell's gimlet eye, and her adventures were limited to these precious Thursday afternoons.

Her aunt, Lady Chadwick, decided long ago to turn a blind eye to Trumpet's play-acting, as she termed her niece's taste for dressing like a boy. Her uncle, Lady Chadwick's younger brother, was a barrister who had flexible notions of acceptable behavior himself and was more likely to assist his wayward niece than chastise her. He was the one who had given her Catalina Luna, the servant of her dreams.

They skipped up the stairs to the bedchamber reserved for Trumpet's use, greeting the housekeeper with a wave of the hand. Lady Chadwick's servants loved bribes and owed nothing to Lady Russell. Lady Chadwick was seldom home at this hour, spending the warm summer afternoons drinking and gossiping in a friend's pleasure garden in Shoreditch.

Trumpet and Catalina helped each other out of their dull gowns and into suits of doublets and hose. Catalina liked short, round hose, well-puffed to hide her womanly hips. Trumpet preferred pleated galligaskins that reached almost to her knees. She would have liked brighter colors, like scarlet and canary, but duller shades attracted less attention.

Catalina darkened their chins with a charcoal pencil and pasted false moustaches to their upper lips. They itched more when not worn every day, but there was nothing like a moustache to fool the casual eye. Trumpet donned a tall hat with a short feather. Catalina preferred a squashy velvet cap with a small brim to shade her eyes.

They gave each other a quick inspection, making sure all laces were tied and no traces of girlishness lingered anywhere about their persons, and then simply walked out the front door onto Bishopsgate Street.

Free! Trumpet relished every minute spent walking with her stride unencumbered by skirts and her view unobstructed by veils. She'd trained herself to notice as much as possible without staring, which might attract notice. She marveled at how little ordinary people appreciated the freedom to simply walk down a street, fast or slow as the traffic allowed, even when the summer sun rotted peelings and horse dung faster than the sweepers could collect it.

They strolled under the arch at Bishopsgate, taking their time, surveying the customers in each tavern they passed, not ready to leave the sunny street until they reached their favorite Thursday afternoon haunt — the Black Bull, a coaching inn where plays were often performed. There they got mugs of ale at the counter and stood waiting for good seats at a table looking into the central courtyard.

They sat in silence for a while, listening to the talk around them. Trumpet wanted to hear what people were saying about Martin and Mar-Martin, greedy for reviews of her work. There was plenty of chatter, but nothing caught her interest.

Then a pair of clowns bounced out into the yard, turning somersaults, heralded by a roll of drums and a tantara of horns being blown from the balcony. One was dressed in plain brown fustian and carried a whip; the other was dressed like an ape in shaggy black stuff with his face smudged black. People came out of rooms on all three floors of the inn, jostling for good spots along the railing to watch.

The ape and the whip-man began to chase each other around, spouting insults and pleading with the audience for

105

aid. They got laughter and a splatter of nutshells. The whip-man paused in the center of the yard and shouted out a few verses from *A Whip for an Ape*, winning a smattering of applause. He seemed disappointed at the weak response. That was one of Mar-Martin's early works and had been a great favorite for several weeks.

"The Mar-Martins need new material," Trumpet murmured to Catalina. "People are cheering for the ape now as much as the gaoler."

"The ape-man, he is more funny than the other." Catalina was a severe critic of such entertainments, thanks to her years in the commedia dell'arte.

The chase began again, with the gaoler cracking his whip loudly and the ape shrieking and gabbling, frolicking and rolling around the yard. He was exceptionally agile, even for a professional clown. His antics made everyone laugh, including Trumpet. Even Catalina gave up a few grudging chuckles.

Then the ape leapt onto an overturned crate, placed one hand on his chest, and raised the other high, pointing up to the heavens. He proclaimed in stentorian tones, "I am Martin Junior! The bishops can neither catch me nor refute me! I expose their monstrous corruptions, their slandering, and their lying. Fire and faggot, shackles and blows — these are the tools of their holy profession!"

Trumpet, caught by surprise, spat out a mouthful of ale. She'd written those very words! She'd meant them to be mildly funny, but this — this was hilarious! No wonder men became so addicted to writing for the stage. She should try something more ambitious some fine day.

"Lady Alice?" a soft voice murmured, close to her ear.

Trumpet leapt up, drawing her knife. At the same moment, Catalina jumped to her feet and grabbed the interloper, shoving him facedown onto the table. Trumpet set the edge of her knife against the man's cheek and demanded, "What do you want?"

"Nothing! It's only me! Tom Nashe!"

She used her free hand to grab a hank of hair and jerk his face sideways so she could see it. He grinned at her, showing his crooked tooth and his pug nose. She expelled a breath and nodded at Catalina, who released him. Trumpet shot a glare at the men at the nearest table and growled, "A misunderstanding." They shrugged, not caring, and turned back to the clowns.

Nashe righted himself and collected his hat. Then he picked up Trumpet's overturned stool and set it in place for her with a bow. She sat down and grumbled, "Don't bow, you idiot!" She saw words forming on his lips and added, "If you call me 'my lady,' I'll cut off your ear."

Nashe audibly choked back the words. He looked about and found another stool, which he placed between the two women, sitting with his hands in his lap and an air of not-quite-mocking submission. "What should I call you?"

Trumpet drummed her fingers on the table, thinking. "You may call me Mr. Trumpet." She tried that on in her mind and added a caveat. "Unless Tom is around, in which case, you may omit the *Master*."

"Yes, Mr. Trumpet," Nashe said, so meekly it forced a giggle from her throat, which had to be covered with a cough and very fake-sounding low-pitched laugh.

"I'm surprised Clarady isn't here with you," Nashe said, "assuming that's the Tom you mean. Doesn't he escort you when you go out, ah . . ."

"We don't need an escort. We're quite capable of handling ourselves in any situation."

"I gladly attest to that fact." Nashe acknowledged Catalina with a short nod. "Mr. Luna, you're looking very well. Extremely well, if I may say so without causing offense."

She grinned at him, her dark eyes flashing. She made a strikingly handsome gentleman with her silky black moustache and her naturally thick eyebrows.

Nashe turned back to Trumpet. "Casting no aspersions on your competence in any arena, I'm still surprised Tom isn't here. I assume he enlisted your help in resolving my perilous predicament."

"Tom can't do anything without me." Trumpet strove to maintain a neutral expression, though her ears felt as if they'd grown to twice their size. This must be the new commission he'd refused to tell her about. What a fool to think he could keep a secret from her! She'd have the whole story in no time.

She smiled benignly at her new informant and beckoned the wench to bring a jug of dragon's milk, a doubly strong variety of ale. She shot a quick wink at Catalina as she passed her a cup, getting an acknowledging flick of the eyebrows in return. They'd pretend to sip while keeping Nashe's cup full.

"We divide our efforts," Trumpet said, "now that my movements are somewhat restricted."

"Tom told me you were living with his guardian."

She nodded. "I chose to accept a loss of freedom in exchange for invaluable training in the art of widowhood. My Lady Russell is a model well worth emulating."

Nashe's freckled face grew somber. "I heard about your loss, my — Mr. Trumpet. Please accept my condolences. I'm sure the Viscount What-d'ye-call-him was an honorable man."

She waved that off. Viscount Surdeval had possessed that quality and more, but she'd barely known him. The main things she'd lost were her pride and her confidence, and those had been largely restored. "I suppose you read about it in the pamphlets."

"I guessed it might be you underneath the hyperbole. 'Hair as black as night and eyes as green as a tiger's' and so forth. The castle on the coast, in which the murderess learned her dark trade, gave it away for anyone familiar with that desolate stretch of Suffolk."

Several pamphlets had appeared in the wake of Viscount Surdeval's murder, most of them assigning the guilt to her, thinly disguising her identity as a French countess. None of them bothered to explain how the Frenchwoman found herself in Suffolk. Once the real murderer was identified, a fresh outpouring of ballads and illustrated reports had appeared, driving the first round into oblivion, but the stench had clung to her like the smell of dead fish on the hair of a wet dog.

"I suppose you're watching the crowd here," Nashe said in a low voice. "Keeping an eye out for anyone with an especially hostile interest in the whip-man."

"You mean the ape."

Nashe shrugged. "Either way, I suppose. Someone who applauds the ape and boos the whipper. A Martinist among us, spying out the opposition."

So Tom was searching for Martinists. *God's death!* Trumpet's heart leapt into her throat. Had Lord Burghley charged Francis Bacon with identifying Martin Marprelate? This was news indeed. The archbishop and his churchmen had proved hopelessly inadequate to the task. But Bacon was a far more potent adversary. She had the utmost respect for his ability to see through all manner of obfuscations and deceits to arrive at the ultimate truth.

She took a swig of the strong ale, which burned on the way down, but calmed her beating heart. Even clever Mr. Bacon would never suspect his own aunt. And now she, Martin Junior, was forewarned. If only she could think of a way to alert Lady Russell to the danger without divulging her source.

But Nashe had said "*my* perilous problem." What peril? What did he have to do with any of this?

She refilled his cup. "I must confess I haven't learned anything useful yet. These people show more favor to the ape than the gaoler. But the gaoler has nothing new to say. Mar-Martin's falling behind. He's getting dull."

"Now, now, Mr. Trumpet! Be kind." Nashe's hand wobbled a little as he lifted his full cup to his lips. He let out a little gasp after gulping the fiery liquid. "Genius takes time, you know. And we have to send every piece we write to the canon for approval before it goes to the printer."

Trumpet turned her head to face him, studying his freckled features with new interest. She'd bet an angel Nashe was Pasquill Caviliero, the adventuring anti-Martinist. She should have guessed it at first reading. It had that mad Nashean flavor. "I knew *Martin's Mirror* was yours! Your style is unmistakable."

"Thank you." Nashe's face lit up but then sank along with the rest of his body. "Alas, in my quest to make a mark, I've marked myself. Now I hardly know where to turn. I don't suppose your lady has a spare tuft of straw in her stable for me to sleep in?"

"Don't you care for your current lodgings? I forget what Tom told me . . ."

"Under other circumstances, I'd be happy as a lark with Robert Greene, Master of the Mar-Martins, most worthy tutor in the practice of prolific pamphleteering. I sit at his feet — until he kicks me. But wherever I lay my head, another man turns up dead. If we don't catch Martin's minion soon, I'll be forced to flee back to my father's house in Norfolk, where I'll find nothing to sustain me but cold pottage and stale homilies."

Trumpet ignored the last part. She remembered that Nashe's father was a vicar, but she doubted he was as poor as that, though what a witty wag like Nashe would find to do in rural Norfolk, she could not imagine. But she could see the whole plan of Tom's commission laid out before her. "It's grossly unjust, but you can hardly blame yourself."

Nashe cast her a woeful glance as comical as the ape-clown's dour grimaces. He drank a deep draught of his dragon's milk and burped, covering his mouth with a muffled apology. "If only I knew what it is that I know."

"How's that?"

"What have I learned?" he asked the dregs of his drink. "A month of rambling, trying to pick up Martin's trail, sleeping in haystacks, begging scraps of food and tidbits of gossip from stablemen and dairymaids. Somewhere, somehow, I must have crossed paths with one of Martin's minions and come too close his hiding place." He turned toward Trumpet, his eyes wide. "I must have just missed the man. I might have come this close to Martin himself!" He measured a scant inch with thumb and forefinger, his hand wobbling as he tried to hold it up for her to see.

"Or even closer," Trumpet said, repressing a grin. *Secrets, pah!* "Why don't you tell me all about it? I know the broad outlines, of course, but perhaps I'll spot something you and Tom have missed."

Nashe proceeded to tell her everything about the two poor pamphleteers who were strangled in his stead and the stories the writers had concocted to lay the guilt on the man they liked the least, a churl named Anthony Munday. Tom's gut reportedly voted for Munday as the murdering minion. Trumpet respected Tom's gut — to a point.

She felt confident that she'd gotten everything Nashe knew, which wouldn't be all of it. Bacon always kept something back. And now she had a commission of her own. She'd have to stop Martin's minion before Francis Bacon could unmask Martin herself.

TWELVE

Tom found Nashe peering through the arched gate at Gray's Inn's front entrance, with one eye on the watchful gatekeeper. The satirist had sent in a note saying they could catch Robert Greene at home if they dawdled and arrived sometime between noon and night. This commission took precedence over fair copies, so he stuck his quill in the holder and went down to change into his hunting clothes, a comfortable brown suit made of tough fabric. The term applied whether his prey was rabbits in the fields behind Gray's or villains in the suburbs north of the City walls.

"I'm at liberty, more or less, until we catch our man." He clapped his friend on the shoulder as he strode through the gate.

"I'm always at liberty," Nashe said. "In poverty, for my sins, but always liberty. And how not? I live in a liberty — the liberty of Norton Folgate."

They walked up to Clerkenwell Road and headed east past Charterhouse and Garter House, names that delighted Nashe. Tom enjoyed afresh the familiar route through London's northern sprawl in the company of this witty newcomer. They paused for a while to watch the archers practicing in Finsbury Fields. Tom hadn't touched a bow since his friend Benjamin Whitt had gone home. Ben's father, an old-fashioned gentleman, had exhorted him to regular practice, insisting that the long bow might still prove itself to be England's best defense.

Tom's father, by way of contrast, had sent him a pair of ornamented wheel-lock pistols that he took from a Spanish grandee along with the rest of his ship. Less strain on the back, if a good deal more costly to keep in working order.

They soon found themselves in a dense pocket of ill-assorted houses that had sprung up like mushrooms in the past decade or two, built without regard for the health or convenience of the inhabitants. Alleys narrow enough for Tom to span with open arms branched off one another like the tangled canes of berry bushes. Jettied upper stories sometimes leaned so close together an agile man could jump from room to room. Housewives had strung lines across the way, where gray linens hung limply, waiting for the five daily minutes when the sun would pass directly overhead. They'd missed it today already. The sky was turning dark.

Trees had thrashed in the freshening wind as they crossed Finsbury Fields, but no such breath entered into this dank precinct. Tom kept his eyes on the street, not to enjoy the rich array of rotting materials strewn thereon, but to avoid getting garbage on his shoes.

"Ugh! I don't think much of the beadles in this liberty. Or don't these parishioners believe in sweeping?"

Nashe shrugged. "You get used to it." He shot Tom a grin. "I'm in London with a roof over my head. What more can a man want? Especially a man who means to find his living with his pen."

"I wonder that you ever left the university. You seemed at home there."

"It was my home for many years. But every chick must leave the nest sometime. And it wasn't any fun after Kit left. God's bollocks!" He stopped abruptly, turned around, and walked back a few paces. "I miss it every time. Here we are. Welcome to my new abode. I'm sure you'll be suitably impressed by the amenities."

"Ooohhrrr! Ain't you a pretty one!" A feminine howl greeted them from overhead.

They stepped back out from under the overhang and looked up. A full-figured woman in an overstuffed bodice leaned her plump elbows on the windowsill to peer down.

"Now that's more like it, Nashey!" She ogled Tom, winking and grinning widely enough to show the gaps in her teeth. "You never brought me nothing so lovely as this one before. Wherever did ye find 'im?"

"Shhh!" Nashe held a finger to his lips, although everyone on the little lane must have heard her yowling. "If I tell you, you'll rush off and get another one for yourself." Several faces had appeared at windows to gape at Tom. Most of them turned right around again.

He rolled his eyes and took a bow. So much for conducting a quiet investigation. How could a man be strangled among these crowded houses without anyone raising an alarm? They must be used to odd noises during the night and know better than to poke their noses out. And if you didn't see it, you couldn't be summoned to testify about it.

"Well, bring 'im in! Bring 'im in!" The woman beckoned vigorously, shaking her bounteous bosom for Tom's appreciation.

He grinned at her, partly to gain favor for the questioning to come, but also because such frankly willing women ought to be encouraged on general principles, especially now that his guardian made sure he no longer had money to pay for their favors. He preferred fair and willowy damsels with a melancholy air, or he had before he learned Trumpet was a girl. Now his dreams were filled with short, curvy, dark-haired tigresses with glowing green eyes.

Failing that, he'd take what he could get.

The front door opened onto a room that spanned the narrow house and ran about twenty feet back. The air inside was cool, though the windows were shut tight, and redolent with the aroma of fish pottage. The smell rose from a cauldron hanging on a hook in the wide hearth against the far wall. The remains of dinner still lay strewn across the long table standing in the center of the room. The diners had finished their meals and moved on.

Apart from crumbs and dirty dishes, the place was cleaner than Tom expected given the condition of the streets. The well-packed rushes were muddy by the door, but clean enough farther in. The scent of tansy puffed up as he walked across them. The whitewashed walls looked in good repair, as did the long sideboard and the motley collection of chairs, stools, and short benches. A busy lodging house, but a well-kept one.

A woman almost as wide as the stairs descended, holding her skirts up with both hands and huffing in short breaths as she came. "Who's your new friend, Mr. Nashe?"

"Not new," Nashe said. "This is Thomas Clarady, an old friend from Cambridge. Mr. Clarady, meet the finest landlady between here and the house next door, Mrs. Emma Ball."

She offered him a plump hand ornamented with two silver rings. Tom bowed over it and said, "My pleasure, Mrs. Ball."

"Oooohhhh! What lovely manners! We don't see such fine gentlemen as you hereabouts. Not often. Although Mr. Greene, my principal lodger, has friends in all stations. He's a gentleman himself, is Mr. Greene." She measured Tom from head to toe, her pink tongue poked between her lips. "Are ye in need of lodgings, Mr. Clarady? I could put Nashe in with my other poet. It's a smallish room on the third floor, but you'll get three meals a day. Tasty ones too, if I say so myself."

She licked her lips slowly to show how tasty a meal Tom could find in her house, if he chose to. She was a ripe one, all right. She wore a dark red gown with a bright pink apron. Tom couldn't tell if she wore an extra-large bum roll to bell out her skirts or if her own lush shape performed that service. The latter, most like, judging by the breasts overflowing her bodice. Her cheeks were pink and smooth, though a fine spray of wrinkles spread from the corner of her pale blue eyes, now twinkling with good humor. Neither young nor old, with plenty of fun left in her.

"The soup smells delicious," Tom said, "but I'd hate to budge out old Nashe. Besides, I'm well enough fixed for now, thanks."

Nashe said, "Mr. Clarady's doing me a favor, seeing what he can find out about John Little's death. He wanted to ask you a few questions."

A favor? That wasn't the agreement. That point would have to be revisited when they left this house.

"Oh, poor, poor Mr. Little!" Mrs. Bell patted her bosom as if to calm the heart which beat deep underneath. "My gentlemen tell me his death may not have been an accident."

"I fear it was not," Tom said gravely.

Nashe nodded with equal gravity. "Strangulations seldom are." Then he grinned and said, "Although that reminds me of a time in —"

Tom gave him a quelling look. "Didn't your neighbors see or hear anything that night, Mrs. Bell?"

"Most would deny it even if they did. They don't want the strangler to come after them!" Mrs. Ball crossed her hands over her stomach and leaned toward Tom, lowering her voice. "But Mrs. Aldertwitch across the way, whose bedchamber overhangs the very spot where Little met his untimely end, swears she heard a lurking sound outside, just after the last echo of St. Leonard's midnight bell died away."

"A lurking sound." Tom struggled to maintain his grave expression, even when Nashe unhelpfully took several shuffling steps, scuffing his feet under the rushes and making a soft *clop, clop, clop* with his tongue.

Tom didn't bother trying to quell him again. Nothing short of a cuff on the head would serve that turn. He nodded at Mrs. Ball to thank her for that vital piece of evidence. "Perhaps we should look at this the other way around. We're supposing the strangler meant to attack John Lyly, but somehow got the wrong name and thus the wrong man. How could that have come about?"

"Oh my, aren't you the crafty one? Let me give it a think." Mrs. Ball clasped her hands under her bosom and screwed up her round face, lips pressed together with the effort. Finally, she said, "Well, if you were to visit one of the taverns where these poetical gentlemen go to refresh themselves after their solitary labors and ask for a knave named John Lyly, and if you said it a little bit off, perhaps not quite as clearly as you ought . . ."

Nashe offered a few variations on the name Lyly, mimicking different dialects and ending with a babbling, "Lit-ly, lit-ly, lee lee lee."

"But would it be unusual for a man to ask for someone like Lyly in such a place?"

"Not at all," Nashe said in his normal voice. "It's the usual way to find us, if I may be so bold as to add myself to that illustrious company."

"You're the wittiest lodger I've ever had," Mrs. Ball said kindly, "if not the prettiest. I love to hear you read your latest here by my fire. There's nothing I like better than an educated gentleman." She batted her pale lashes at Tom. "Unless it's a gentleman who's both educated and comely."

He smiled. "How would the strangler know where to ask? There must be a hundred taverns in the city and twice that many alehouses."

"He knows us," Nashe said. "He knows the places we frequent, like the Goose and Gall on Ivy Lane. Or he

117

might've asked one of Lyly's printers. They know where to find us — or avoid us — when it's time to pay up."

"It wouldn't be difficult," Mrs. Ball said. "Writers don't want their names kept secret; more the other way around. And once that dastard had Mr. Little's name, it wouldn't take much to learn he lived in Norton Folgate. He might guess that much on his own; so many writers and actors and suchlike favor this quarter. Close to the theaters, you understand, which pays your poetical gentlemen better than most anything else."

"A play's the thing," Nashe agreed, "if you can pester someone in a company to give you a chance."

"Once you're in the liberty," Mrs. Ball said, "it's nothing to find out he lived in Emma Ball's house. That'd be anyone's first guess. I only have poetical gentlemen in my house. Poets, playwrights, pamphleteers. It's my specialty."

"How many lodgers do you have?" Tom asked, wondering if they were all at risk.

"Four at present, with Mr. Nashe now instead of Mr. Little. Another pamphleteer and a playwright — six months and four. Mr. Greene's the longest." She caught the word and tipped Tom a saucy wink. "Though not in all parts."

Nashe giggled. Tom grinned through clenched teeth.

Mrs. Ball gave a little shrug. "Can't read a word, you see, but I love the beauty of a fine-turned phrase. I just can't help myself, though I know it's a weakness."

"Ale! Bring me ale, you swag-bellied strumpet!" a deep voice roared from over their heads.

"I've got company, you tottering mouldwarp!" Mrs. Ball screeched at the ceiling. Then she turned to Tom and batted her lashes.

Nashe laughed. "Sounds like Greene's awake. You should talk to him as long as you're here. He had an accident last night at the White Hart that may not have been an accident."

"I want breakfast! Do you mean to starve me, you heartless quean?" the voice upstairs shouted.

"Get your own poxy breakfast, you great lolling pumpion!" Mrs. Ball shouted back. But she found a tray and began loading it with the best of what was left on the table.

Tom followed Nashe up the stairs to a bare landing with two doors. The one at the back was firmly shut, but the other one stood wide open. They entered a room that looked like a whirlwind had blown through it, with clothes and papers and other oddments strewn from one end to the other.

A small pillow flew past Tom's nose and he understood how the disaster had occurred. A man was struggling out of a bed that was the source and center of the chaos, with sheets and blankets moiled and tossed, like froth beaten up on the waves of a stormy sea. At first, Tom thought the man had tangled himself in his own bedclothes, but as more of him emerged, he realized the figure was bandaged from head to toe. Or rather, one leg was thickly wrapped and one shoulder likewise shrouded and further suspended in a sling. His head had a vast handkerchief tied around it from chin to crown, causing his long, pointed red beard to jut forward like a hairy spear point. A crosswise bandage held a thick patch of something yellowish on his brow.

"What do you mean trying to get up, you feeble-minded old fool?" Mrs. Ball thrust her tray at Nashe and pushed the bandaged man back into his bed just as he'd managed to get one foot on the ground.

He howled in pain and a florid exchange of curses erupted between the two. The bandages did nothing to inhibit the man's capacity for speech.

"Robert Greene," Nashe said, walking around to balance the tray on the other side of the bed. He seemed unaffected by their battle of words, which held little real heat. He lifted a piece of cheese from the tray and nibbled on it while he ambled back to Tom's side.

Greene cast a last scowl at his landlady, hoisted himself into better position with many grunts and groans, then grabbed at the cup on the tray and gulped down half its contents. At last, he looked at Tom and said, "A man could die of thirst," as if that was the message Tom had come to collect. "Who are you, then?" Greene asked when Tom failed to comment.

"The one I told you about," Nashe said. "Thomas Clarady, my friend from Cambridge."

"Also a friend of Christopher Marlowe's," Tom said, hoping that would help. He was a great admirer of Greene's work, especially his romances, which were guaranteed to make young women swoon if you read them in a dusky voice by candlelight. Now his wits were boggling under the strain of connecting those eloquent passages with this shipwreck of a man.

"Marlowe!" Greene roared. "That charlatan? That mammering, clay-brained coxcomb?"

Nashe whispered loudly at Tom, "Not one of his favorites. Kit earns twice as much from the Admiral's Men, who'll drop whatever they had in hand for a chance at his next play."

"I scarcely know the man," Tom said to Greene. "And I don't trust him." Which was true enough, in some situations.

Greene grunted and glugged more of whatever was in his cup.

Tom took that for acceptance. "What happened to you, Mr. Greene?"

"I took a tumble down the stairs last night at the tavern. Three men had to carry me home."

"Which floor were you on?" Mrs. Ball asked, setting her hands on her hips. "I didn't get to hear that part. The

120

surgeon kept me running up and down the stairs as if I were a serving girl, wanting this and that and then some more. As if you deserved it! Should've rolled you back into the street and left you there."

Mrs. Ball busied herself shaking out clothes and draping them over a drying rack that stood near the windows. Greene's eyes followed her as she bent over, displaying a fine expanse of backside. He tipped Tom a wink and said, "I went upstairs to look at a cat. Marvel of the world, that cat. He sits in a chair and plays primero, day and night."

"I've heard of him," Nashe said. "He always wins too. He's set down the canniest players everywhere from Bishopsgate Within to Bishopsgate Without." He shot Tom a wink. "Alas, I hear the pussy cheats."

Tom shook his head. Getting information out of these comedians was harder than teaching a cat to play cards. "Who was there besides the cat?"

"There were men playing cards," Greene said. His eyes slid toward Mrs. Ball. "There may have been women watching."

Nashe supplied the rest. "The stairs open straight into another big room with tables where people like to play cards or stand around watching other people play cards. There's as much betting on the betting as there is on the cards."

Tom nodded. "It was crowded, then. Do you remember anyone in particular?"

"Munday was there," Greene said. "Nashe said you've met him. He'd push me down the stairs just to take my place with my publishers, as if they'd have him. I have more talent in my little finger." He held up the finger on the unbandaged hand. "I remember a couple of gentlemen in fine clothes — Inns of Court men, perhaps. They come to rub shoulders with actors. Other that than, I couldn't say exactly who was where, being somewhat under —"

121

"Being drunk as a drowned mouse, he means," Mrs. Ball said.

"A man takes a sip or two, just to be polite, and she calls it drunk." Greene growled at her. "I have a memory, but not a clear one, of Munday coming up behind me. I couldn't swear to it. I wish I could. I was standing near the stairs, deciding whether to go back down or join the game or go up —" He shot a glance at his landlady. "I think I felt a hand on my back, but I couldn't swear to that either. Maybe one of the men watching the game took a step back, making me take a step back . . ." He shook his head, then groaned at the motion. "I went down with enough force to crack my head on the bannister and roll right on down to the bottom."

"Didn't you recognize anyone else?" Tom could go back to the tavern and ask the servers if they remembered anything, but it would help to have another name or two.

"Dando was there," Greene said. "At the table, facing the stairs. Ask him." He slapped at Mrs. Ball's hand as she tried to straighten his nightshirt. Then he narrowed his eyes at Tom. "I'll bet Nashe promised to pay you."

"He did."

"He won't. But I will. I can't live cooped up in this room for the rest of my life. You'll have to play clerk, Nashey. I've got to get *The Spanish Masquerado* to the printers by the end of the week or I'll lose my fee."

Mrs. Ball pulled a pillow out from under him, plumped it roughly, and stuffed it back into place. "If you miss your deadline, don't think I'll forgive your rent, you old pinchpenny. You're no good to me like this. You can barely lift yourself up enough to piss in the chamber pot. If you can't pay in kind, you'll have to pay in coin, same as the others."

She gave Tom another measuring look, this time performing for Greene. "Or perhaps you could borrow the rent from your friend here."

122

Nashe's eyes flashed. "I have plenty of that particular coin, Mistress." She beamed at him in a way that told Tom he'd already filled Greene's role in that establishment at least once.

Tom had been tempted earlier, a little. His guardian kept him on very short rations, not understanding a young man's needs. But Mrs. Ball shared her favors a bit too generously for his taste. One thing Lady Russell couldn't possibly know — and he could never tell her — was that it was better to pay more for your lightskirts than less. Your higher-priced whores held themselves in higher regard and thus were fussier about their clients. Free was not always the better bargain.

"I'll give you your rent," Greene shouted, "you dizzy-eyed Jezebel!" She roared back at him and their battle began anew.

Nashe cocked his head toward the stairs, and Tom followed him down. They barely reached the bottom before the ropes of the bed upstairs began to creak in a familiar rhythm.

"Ah, love!" Nashe said with a grin that swiftly disappeared. "Whatever Greene says, I think he was pushed. The villain's getting bolder."

"Or more desperate. What do you know? What did you learn out there on your hunt for Martin's minions?"

"I can't remember. I learned a hundred details about all manner of things." Nashe looked miserable. "Now I'm afraid to go back to the Goose even when it's full of people."

"Don't give up yet. Martin's minion doesn't know about me, and it's a safe bet he doesn't know Francis Bacon is on his trail. We'll catch him." Tom scratched his beard, staring out the window at the parlor across the street, where three women sat sewing and talking at a seemingly breathless pace, while casting frequent glances at the two men across the way.

"We've got to get you out of here," he said. "That much seems clear. Today, for a preference."

"I don't have any money. I lied about that fee. Or rather, I figured someone else would come up with it."

"I know. And someone has." Tom studied him for a moment, then heaved a sigh. "All right, then. You're coming home with me."

Nashe clapped his hands together. "Clarady, you are a true friend. Let me grab my notebooks and my other shirts."

He left Tom to run back upstairs. Tom planted himself before the window, folded his arms, and stared at the women in the opposite house. They set down their sewing and stared back at him, mouths working in a barrage of chatter he mercifully couldn't hear. Nashe jogged back down with a canvas sack over his shoulders and Tom waved at the women across the street as they walked past.

He eyed the sack, which wasn't large, although it probably contained the man's entire estate. He had to credit Nashe's courage, leaving the safe harbor of the university and moving to London with nothing but a quick tongue and a ready eye. He was following Marlowe's trail, but Kit had already sold a play before he made the leap, and he had his intelligencing to keep him in funds when the theaters were closed.

They walked back the way they'd come without loitering this time, going west until they were well past Gray's Inn so they could cut across the fields and come in the back. Tom slipped his knife into the jamb to flip up the latch and swung the window open. It was an easy hop over the sill for him, but a bit of a climb for his guest. He stood in the center of the room, holding out both hands. "It isn't much, but it's home."

The room was half the size of the bedchamber he'd shared with Ben last year, but he had it to himself, and he didn't spend many of his waking hours here. His lute and rapier hung on one wall and his rarely used bow and quiver of arrows on another. A cloak hung on a peg near the door. The rest of his things were kept in chests pushed against the walls. He had a desk in one corner with a stool tucked under it, but he preferred to read on the bed, which was narrow but warmly curtained and well furnished with pillows and blankets.

"A cupboard at an Inn of Court is worth a house in Norton Folgate." Nashe flung his sack into a corner and leapt onto Tom's bed, stretching out full length and folding his arms behind his head.

"Oh, no you don't!" Tom yanked the pillow away and rolled him off, letting him thump into the rushes. "You sleep on the floor. Don't worry, there's plenty of blankets. And here." He dug into a large chest and pulled out a set of old black student robes. "You can wear these coming and going. They're torn at the hem, but that won't matter. Take them off the minute you're out of sight of Gray's. Only go through the window, never the door, and duck down by the wall until you're well past. Don't make any noise. Don't touch any of my belongings. And do *not* piss out the window or we'll have to smell your stink all night. And don't go back to Greene's house or St. Paul's or any taverns where you might be recognized. In fact, don't go into the City at all."

Nashe sat up to lean against the bed, grinning while he listened to the lecture, his delight at his good fortune undimmed by the list of constraints. Tom had thought this small, low chamber a mark of lost status after his father's death. He'd spent many a disgruntled evening plucking laments on his lute and grousing about his lot. The glow in Nashe's eyes now gave him a twinge of guilt for despising his good fortune. That twinge made him all the more irritated with his unwanted guest.

"I eat in the hall. You don't. Do not go out this door or into the yard for any reason. I have to appear for supper tonight or my absence will be noted. But afterward we'll slip down to Holborn to the Antelope Inn. Mrs. Sprye, the proprietress, is a friend."

Nashe's face lit up. "Innkeepers adore me."

"She's nothing like Emma Ball, so mind your manners. She'll give you your meals, but don't be greedy. In fact, it might be better —"

Two raps sounded on the door. "Tom?"

"Hssst! It's Mr. Bacon!" Tom pointed under the bed and Nashe rolled underneath.

Bacon half opened the door and was peering around before Nashe got his left leg out of sight. Tom stepped in front of the bed, trying to act like he'd jumped up from taking a nap. He stretched and yawned. "Do you need me for something, Mr. Bacon?"

"No, no. Not now. I just wanted to let you know I'll be dining with you at my aunt's house tomorrow. I invited myself and just received her reply."

"Good," Tom said. "Good."

"Since you have Sunday mornings free, I wanted you to know before you left the house. We'll want to leave in plenty of time, what with the traffic on the river these days."

"Good thought," Tom said. "I'll wait for you here."

"Good." Bacon glanced around the room as if reminding himself of its proportions. He nodded as if satisfied and turned to go. Then he paused and looked over Tom's shoulder the way he did when lost in thought or feeling awkward. "Ah, Tom. A word of advice. Don't talk to yourself, even when you're alone. You'll fall into the habit and start doing it everywhere. People don't like it, I've found. They'll think you're a little odd."

THIRTEEN

Francis spent Saturday recovering from Friday's twenty-mile return trip from Gorhambury, mostly sitting up in bed mulling over the conjectures he'd discussed with his mother, his most trusted confidante. He wouldn't so much as hint at the idea to Tom. The risk of being wrong far outweighed any putative benefits from being right. Robert Cecil, the engineer behind Martin Marprelate, constructing the whole controversy to obstruct Archbishop Whitgift? The mere thought of explaining that to anyone new made his neck prickle as if encircled by a rough hemp noose.

He shouldn't think about it. He mustn't think about it. But the more he scolded himself, the more his mind refused to let it go. He needed to discuss the idea with someone else, someone discreet, who knew his uncle and cousin as well as he did. Someone like his Aunt Elizabeth.

He wrote her a note inviting himself to Sunday dinner with Tom and felt better for having taken that step. Saturday afternoon, he went out for a good long walk and then added three drops of poppy juice to his bedtime cup of spiced wine. He managed to fall asleep sometime after midnight, but even in his dreams he wrestled with his doubts.

The sermon on Sunday morning helped soothe his mind by virtue of its sheer inconsequence. The chaplain never exerted himself between terms. But Francis left the pew feeling more settled, having arrived at a viable compromise. He could not in good conscience ignore the possibility that his own cousin might be party to the greatest deception perpetrated on the English people in his lifetime.

Well, that was an exaggeration. Martin wasn't plotting against Her Majesty's life; on the contrary, he repeatedly claimed to love her as much as any loyal Englishman. Although that could be construed as another point in favor of the Cecils as conspirators.

Francis couldn't ignore it, but neither could he investigate it directly. For one thing, he wouldn't know where to begin. He could hardly have Robert followed day and night, and even if he could, it wouldn't help. How many persons must visit his office at Burghley House on any given day? Men and women of all stations, one presumed, if he'd taken over the Lord Treasurer's intelligencers. Any one of them might carry a slim octavo tucked into his doublet to pass on along the chain to Martin's printer.

His uncle had asked him to catch a murderer, not Martin Marprelate. In fact, Robert had said it in so many words. "Leave Martin alone." A suggestion or a command?

Francis determined to focus his attention — or rather Tom's attention — on the circle of pamphleteers and whatever scraps of he could glean from the depositions taken from the sad fools Canon Bancroft had interrogated so far.

He might risk one more very delicate exploration of Robert's potential criminality, the attractive axiom on which his theory rested. At dinner today, he would lead his aunt into a discussion of Robert's character and elicit her opinion of his taking on so many new functions. It would be only natural to ask her who she thought Martin Marprelate might be. Lady Russell was every bit as quick-witted as the other Cooke sisters. She'd grasp the connection between those topics at once.

He dressed in his second-best suit, the lightweight black with gray silk linings. While Pinnock laced doublet to hose, Francis advised the boy to spend the afternoon practicing his catechism so as to be better prepared next time Lady Bacon came to town. A waste of breath. The minute he left the house, Pinnock would curl up on his bed with the latest pamphlet about monstrous births and fearsome beasts, sucking sweets and sipping his master's beer.

Francis jogged down the stairs and rapped on Tom's door. So convenient to have his assistant living in the same house. Tom had dressed in his best suit, as he always did on Sundays, and combed his curly blond locks into some degree of submission. He'd made a special effort to look his best today in the vain hope of charming Lady Elizabeth Russell into releasing three hundred pounds from his estates to pay for his special livery.

Francis couldn't blame him for trying, though he couldn't remember a case in which his aunt had surrendered any particle of lands or rents.

As they walked through the alley that ran between the rows of new houses in Fulwood's Rents and on across Holborn to the river, Tom told him about his visit to Robert Greene's house. They agreed that the tumble downstairs could well be Martin's minion's latest attempt to silence his opponents and that their mission was all the more urgent. But they despaired of getting a useable identification from the witnesses Tom had met so far.

"We could try setting a trap," Tom suggested, "using Nashe as bait."

"In an alley at midnight?" Francis dismissed the idea, partly because he couldn't see how they could control the situation, but mainly because Robert had suggested it too.

As they approached the wharf where they would find a wherry to take them down to Blackfriars, Francis said, "Remember that we must keep our new commission a secret, even from Lady Russell and Lady Alice. Especially Lady Alice."

"I said I would, and I keep my word."

"I meant no offense. I'm reminding myself as much as you. I intend to ask my aunt what she thinks of Martin Marprelate, especially now that he's begun publishing again."

"Ha! She must be one of his greatest admirers. He's probably living large at Bisham Abbey even as we speak."

"I sincerely hope not. Although, I concede the possibility." Francis could think of half a dozen well-placed widows who might be sheltering Martin or his press. "We mustn't imply that we suspect her of that."

"She'd take it as a compliment. One thing I like about my guardian — she isn't afraid to express her opinions." Tom laughed, more pacifically this time. "She'll refuse me, won't she?"

"I would be astonished if she didn't."

"Well, a man must struggle to reach his dreams, else what's the point of having them?"

An intriguing notion, if awkwardly expressed.

They made the short trip downriver in companionable silence, enjoying the breeze skimming over the water. Lady Alice welcomed them as they entered the house, inviting Francis to visit the orchard with her while Lady Russell gave an audience to her ward.

Little had changed since Francis's last tour of his aunt's walled gardens, although they always afforded a pleasing respite from the city's grime and grayness, even in winter. The orchard, though small, supplied enough fruit for the household as well as occasional gifts for Francis and Tom.

They strolled slowly around the paths, examining each detail of the gardener's efforts and their effects. As Lady Alice pointed to this mounding herb or that flowering vine, Francis appreciated the newfound mildness of her manner. She had grown calmer and more womanly under his aunt's tutelage. She'd kicked and flailed against her lot for a time, under the unwholesome influence of her uncle, but seemed at last to have reconciled herself with the necessary truths of life.

She was the better for it, by appearances. This observation affirmed Francis's conviction that Tom was also better off under Lady Russell's guidance. True, the lad had attained the ripe old age of twenty-one, but he was newly hatched as a gentleman and had a lot to learn. They should both be grateful for his aunt's generosity.

A servant came out to call them in for dinner. They gathered around the table, with Lady Russell at the head. Francis sat on her right and Tom on his. Lady Alice sat on the other side of the table. Tom took his seat with tight lips and a set jaw. He met Lady Alice's raised eyebrows with a slight lift of his shoulders. She frowned prettily and his expression relaxed. It would appear those two continued to communicate in spite of their rigorous separation. Happily, policing that relationship was not Francis's job.

As the first course was served and wine cups filled, Lady Russell engaged Francis in talk about Gray's Inn. She liked to be kept abreast of the benchers' meetings as a matter of general interest. There was little to report in this dull season between legal terms. Some men lived there year round, as he did, but the majority went to their homes in other counties and wouldn't come back until Michaelmas term began in late September.

The light conversation did not interfere with their enjoyment of the artfully prepared meal. The principal dish in the first course was a beautiful turbot pie, accompanied by fresh salmon, eggs in mustard, and green pottage flavored with herbs from the garden. After a desultory review of that week's weather, Francis asked his aunt, as if only mildly interested, "Have you happened upon a copy of Martin Marprelate's latest effort, my lady? I refer to the one entitled *Theses Martinianae*."

"Martin's works have been banned, Nephew. You don't expect me to have copies here in my house!" She frowned at Lady Alice, who mirrored the expression.

"Of course not. But they do circulate in spite of the Stationers' Company's best efforts. I thought you might have caught a glimpse of it somewhere."

"Well, perhaps a glimpse. And since you ask, I may observe that the *Theses* are the most comprehensive, full-throated expression of the faults in the English church, and the remedies thereunto, that I have ever read. Martin has outdone even himself."

"He makes his points clearly, in plain language anyone can understand," Lady Alice added. "He speaks with authority. I find it most compelling."

They must possess a copy which they had both been studying.

Tom said, "His prose is sprightly too, alive with character. It holds your interest."

"Too much character," Francis said. "He's grossly insulting toward the bishops. 'Master John Kankerbury'? How can he expect to be taken seriously?"

Lady Russell sniffed. "None of Her Majesty's prelates should consider himself above criticism. Are they demigods, to be worshipped? Or servants of the Lord, their congregations, and the queen?"

Francis raised up a pacifying palm. "I didn't mean to embark on a debate about the prelacy. Everyone agrees on some of Martin's points, such as that our priests ought to be better educated and more fairly paid. I am curious about what stimulated Martin to renew his attacks though. He seemed to have given up in March."

"Never," Lady Russell said, setting her fist onto the white cloth. "Not until our church is fully reformed."

Their plates were removed and the second course served. Tom tasted his smothered rabbit and said, "This is delicious, my lady. I'll store up the flavors in my mind to remember during our simple supper at the inn *later tonight.*" His gaze shifted to Lady Alice as he spoke.

An awkward compliment for either lady, especially with the curious emphasis on the last two words. Francis echoed the sentiment in more conventional terms, then asked his now-standard question. "Who do you think Martin Marprelate is, my lady?"

She gave a short laugh, a single musical note. "If I knew, would I tell you? You'd run straight to your lord uncle to deliver the good news."

"I would have a positive obligation to do so."

"Nor would I fault you for it." She raised her pewter cup and took a sip, then held it while she tilted her head and regarded him with a twinkle in her eye — the same twinkle that appeared in his mother's eyes when she meant to tease him or pose him some perplexing question. "Besides, Nephew, what makes you think Martin is a singular person? Martin Junior, author of the work we were just discussing, claims to be another soldier rising up to aid his father."

"The styles are very similar though, aren't they?" Francis asked. "But then I haven't studied the complete works with sufficient attention to make that claim with confidence."

"There you are." His aunt seemed to feel she had made her point. "Martin could be many people, by which I mean many individuals might be Martin, or Martin might be the name of a group. Martin might be a woman, for all you know." She winked at Lady Alice, who seemed startled by the idea. Everyone laughed.

"A woman might be sheltering Martin," Francis said. "I was worried enough about my mother to ride up to Gorhambury on Thursday."

"I trust my sister was able to dispel your fears."

"More or less." He licked his lips and asked the necessary question. "You're not harboring Martin or his accomplices at Bisham Abbey, are you, my lady?"

"I am not, Nephew. In fact, I haven't been there in months." She caught his gaze and held it. "And I further assure you my servants are not harboring Martin or anyone else for any illicit purpose. You may rest content on that score. But the simple truth is that Martin is legion. Cut down one and a hundred others spring up in his place."

"Heaven forfend!" Francis smiled in genuine relief at the direct answer. He'd expected more of the evasive teasing he'd received from his mother. "We have enough stir and tumult with only one."

"The tumult is caused by those disrespectful, reprobrious pamphleteers who were set on by that irritable simpleton, Canon Bancroft. How anyone could imagine buffoonery to be an appropriate response to a religious debate escapes all understanding!" Pink spots flared on Lady Russell's pale cheeks.

"That is not supposed to be general knowledge, Aunt. How did you find out?"

She clucked her tongue at the foolish question. "My neighbor, Lord Cobham, told me after church a few weeks ago."

"Ah." Baron Cobham was a member of the Privy Council and Robert Cecil's new father-in-law. Francis envisioned the web of connections growing around his cousin, sitting like a hunched spider in his chamber at the front of Burghley House, where everyone eventually entered. How easy it would be to control the webs of rumor being spun about Martin Marprelate from such a vantage!

"The tumult has become lethal," Lady Alice said. "Perhaps you haven't heard, my lady. Two pamphleteers were murdered. Some believe they were mistaken for Mar-Martin."

Francis frowned. This struck a little too close to the topic he wanted to keep secret. His gaze drifted from Lady Alice's somber face to her plate, where she had arranged the bones of her rabbit in what looked vaguely like the letter A. *A for Alice*, he supposed, surprised at the self-absorption.

Fortunately, Lady Russell took the conversation in a different direction. "That assumption is unwarranted, Lady Alice. You can have no conception of the rough-and-tumble life such writers lead. They spend their days in the lowest sort of taverns, drinking and gambling and engaging in other unsavory acts. I have not the slightest doubt that those 'murders,' as you term them, were the result of the mindless violence that permeates their existence."

"That's a little harsh," Tom said. "There are respectable writers, like John Lyly, for example."

"An exception which throws the rule into stark relief," Lady Russell said in a tone that brooked no further objection.

Francis had none to offer. Every day he wrestled with the probability that his commission was a fool's errand and that the pamphleteers had been the victims of their individual circumstances. If it weren't for Tom's report about the near-escape of Robert Greene, he would almost be ready to abandon the whole enterprise. But three attempts against the Mar-Martins in a single week made too many to be mere coincidence.

Tom's foot abruptly collided with Francis's shin, causing him to glare at his clerk. "My apologies," Tom said. He had also been playing with his food. He usually devoured everything the instant it fell upon his plate. Now he had shaped his piece of spinach flan into an upside-down seven, or a right-side up sickle.

A final course of fruits and sweetmeats was served and their cups refreshed. Time to broach the main topic. "I hope my Lord Cobham and his wife are getting on well with the new addition to their family. My cousin Robert, I mean."

"As well as can be expected," Lady Russell said. "By all accounts, he works as much as his father. He spares precious little time for his bride."

"The press of work," Francis said. "Were you aware, Aunt, that Robert has been placed in charge of my lord uncle's intelligencers this past month?"

"I was not." Lady Russell dismissed that with a shake of her head. "He's far too young. That position demands a seasoned man with a breadth of experience."

"I tend to agree." Francis sensed a shuffling under the table as Tom adjusted his restless legs again. "It is a great charge for a man who's barely turned twenty-six."

"Too great," Lady Russell said. "Although he has a very able secretary. From Northamptonshire, I believe. A Mr. Holiday or . . ." She wiggled her finger as if summoning the name.

Tom supplied it. "Peter Hollowell. I've met him."

Francis coughed, then hid a slight shake of his head with his napkin.

Lady Russell seemed not to notice. "Hollowell, that's right. A personable young man and a skillful assistant. I write to my nephew frequently, as you might imagine, offering him my counsel of matters of current interest. This Hollowell answers me as often as not, but he's very polite and, I suspect, more candid than Robert would be."

"Robert is seldom candid," Francis said wryly, though he'd been accused of the same fault.

Tom said, "Mr. Hollowell has been kind enough to explain some of the finer legal points of wardship to me." He apologized to his guardian with a humble grimace. "There isn't much written, as you know, and since he's also Mr. Cecil's assistant in the Court of Wards —"

"Why should Robert need such assistance?" Lady Russell asked.

Francis said, "He seems to be moving inexorably into all of my lord uncle's posts. He'll doubtless become Master of the Court of Wards in due course." He failed to keep the bitterness from his voice.

That would be an ideal position for him, since one might reasonably expect a thorough knowledge of the law to be a prerequisite. The office was breathtakingly lucrative. The regular fees, combined with the less openly acknowledged bribes, had built his uncle's palace in Lincolnshire as well as Burghley House.

Lady Russell scowled into her cup, then she cocked her head toward Francis. "Your cousin Robert has always been a sly boy. I've always thought so, though of course I never said it to Mildred. But you know, Francis, if you looked only at the political effects of Martin Marprelate's work, you might discover a different motivation underlying the whole affair."

Francis smiled. This was the topic he'd been working toward. It would be better discussed in private, but if he tried to send the young people into the garden, Tom would leap to the conclusion that they were talking about his wardship behind his back and be even more cross-tempered than usual.

They would simply have to be oblique. "I had a similar conversation with my mother."

"So she told me in yesterday's letter."

They smiled at one another. They were reading from the same page.

Francis glanced at young persons, who seemed fully occupied with sorting the nuts and candied fruits on their plates. He turned slightly away from them to speak quietly to his aunt. "My mother and I discussed the changes taking place on a certain advisory body."

"Oh? What sorts of changes?"

"Young non-members attending meetings without comment from an older member, who is being distracted by complaints from unidentified sources."

Lady Russell nodded. "All people grow old, Nephew, but they do not all grow wise. Some old people, sensing a waning of their power, try to tighten their grip by exacting impossible oaths. Other old people might object but fear ruffling more important feathers, or may no longer have the vigor to act."

"You may be right, my lady. A loyal son, seeing a father in such straits, might move to loosen such a grip by encouraging still louder complaints."

"Thus frustrating the first old person all the more." Lady Russell smiled. "He might go farther, this loyal son, if he has the foresight to promote the inevitable remedy. A reformation, if you like. He might encourage those complaints to spread by protecting the complainers until their voices grow so numerous and so loud their demands can no longer be denied."

"If he shouts too loudly," Francis said, "he can expect to be roughly silenced."

"Not if he reforms the advisory body, replacing that fearful old person and the rest of his party." Lady Russell's hazel eyes gleamed as she held Francis's gaze.

He blinked and looked away. He'd gotten more than he bargained for here. His mother had suggested, or led him to suggest, that Robert Cecil was fostering Martin Marprelate in order to push back against Archbishop Whitgift's aggressive oaths of compliance, which were designed to expose nonconformists lurking within the priesthood. That pushing would anger the queen, but not many others. Lawyers hated those oaths on legal grounds since they obliged a man to bear witness against himself. Under this theory, Robert and his father were acting to forestall religious conflict by means of a counterbalance that entertained the masses.

138

But Lady Russell seemed to be suggesting something more far-reaching: that Robert had created Martin for the purpose of fomenting conflict, inflaming public opinion to demand the dissolution of the prelacy. Not to limit the archbishop, but to eliminate him, and all the hierarchy of bishops and canons along with him. That was nothing short of rebellion and a treasonable offense.

Francis shook his head. "It's too much. It can't be true. It's too uncertain, too dangerous."

"I'm not so sure." Lady Russell echoed her sister's answer to the same question. She set her elbows on the table and rubbed her slender hands together. She gave him a half smile with a conspiratorial gleam in her eye. "Many people, both young and old, are unhappy with the current state of affairs. It would be well for you to bear that in mind, Nephew, while you pursue your present pursuits."

FOURTEEN

Trumpet paused, a grape seed poised on her tongue, and counted the bells ringing from St. Andrews. Seven o'clock. She spat the seed at the copper chamber pot near her chair, only missing by an inch this time.

"Tom's late," she said to Catalina, who sat by the window, wrapping wooden buttons in black silk thread.

"Only that he is not early, my lady."

Trumpet grunted. She would willingly wait an hour, though she would never let Tom know that. But this small dining room on the first floor of the Antelope Inn in Holborn had come to feel like her private parlor, a sort of sanctuary. She and Tom, with Catalina as chaperone, often met here on Sunday evenings after Lady Russell went to bed. They talked and played cards, sometimes even venturing into the public room to chat with the proprietress, Mrs. Sprye. In this slow season between legal terms, there was little risk of Trumpet being recognized from her year at Gray's in the guise of Alan Trumpington, her imaginary cousin.

Mrs. Sprye had been Trumpet's second-best ally in that deception, after her uncle, with whom she had lodged. The innkeeper had given Trumpet a place to change clothes when necessary. The Antelope Inn was a favorite retreat for members of the Inns of Court. Mrs. Sprye had learned a great deal of the law from her patrons, especially concerning its injustices toward women. She generally chose to make her own rules. She and Trumpet had found natural allies in one another.

Mrs. Sprye trusted her young conspirators to behave within the bounds she defined, and so they did, restricting themselves to opposite sides of the table. It wasn't enough, but they had learned that they could not merely kiss and hold hands and be content. Anything further courted disaster. Trumpet must be a virgin when she married, especially after last year's near-catastrophe.

She chewed another grape and spat the seed, winning a satisfying *clink* to reward her improving aim. A handful of grapes later, a knock sounded on the door, which opened to reveal Tom's cheerful face, grinning directly at the seat he knew she'd be in.

She threw a grape at him but caught the shorter man who followed him instead. Still, she'd hit a mark, square on the forehead. And no one deserved it more.

"Nashe!" she cried. "I wasn't expecting you."

"Do you remember each other?" Tom asked, sliding into his customary seat.

"Who could forget so beauteous a lady?" Nashe said.

Trumpet waved that away. "We met Thursday afternoon, at the Black Bull in Shoreditch."

"This Thursday?" Tom asked.

Trumpet enjoyed the procession of emotions marching across his beloved features. First, confusion, as he tried to put people in places three days past. Second, outrage, that a secret had been kept from him. Third, a narrow-eyed suspicion of collusion between two friends. Finally, his shifting glance settled on Trumpet's face, and the angry lines smoothed away like wrinkles fleeing a warm iron. He rolled his eyes and grinned, rueful, surrendering with a shrug.

"He's told me everything," Trumpet said. "All about your great new commission from Lord Burghley."

"From *who?*" Nashe's mouth opened wide in surprise.

"He can't have told you everything," Tom said. "He doesn't know everything."

"Only because he doesn't know Mr. Bacon, which I do." Trumpet smirked. "I filled in the gaps."

"She's implacable," Nashe said by way of apology. He swept off his hat and made a courtly bow to Catalina, earning pleased smiles from both servant and mistress, then helped himself to a seat near the window. He licked his lips as he surveyed the dishes scattered about the table.

"Have you supped?" Trumpet asked. "Please help yourselves. There's wine in the red jug and beer in the green one." She waved a hand invitingly toward the small feast. Her uncle had taught her that generosity in such small things often paid for itself with loyalty in larger ones.

"I had a few bowls of pottage," Tom said, pouring wine for himself and Nashe. "But this is better than what we get at Gray's."

The men heaped plates with cheese, slices of cold ham, olives, boiled carrots, and pickle sauce, tearing chunks of warm bread to go with the rest. Sliced fruit and sweetmeats waited their turn. Catalina rose and poured another cup of beer for herself and her mistress and then returned to her work. Two candles had been lit and two others were set ready, but for now the soft evening light slanting through the windows was enough.

"How much did this clatterfart tell you about our investigation so far?" Tom asked.

"Next to nothing," Nashe said.

"Practically everything," Trumpet said, "but I'd rather hear it from you. He was vague about the wheres and whens."

Tom summarized the details of the two murders. "Both strangled in alleys in Norton Folgate in the dark of the night."

"I don't think so," Trumpet said. "It couldn't have been all that dark. There was a full moon last week."

Tom paused with a hunk of bread stuffed with cheese and ham halfway to his mouth. "That's right, it was. But faces look much alike by moonlight, especially under any kind of hat. Both men were about the same height as Nashe, and they were caught almost on their doorsteps. I assume the villain followed them from a tavern or someplace to be sure they were going into the right house before making his attack."

"Why does he want to kill you?" Trumpet asked Nashe.

"He wants to stop the Mar-Martins before they reveal too much," Tom said. "Why else? I imagine he's also furious with what they're publishing."

"In the latter case," Trumpet argued, "why haven't we seen a general slaughter of clowns? This fiend would have to strangle half the population of Shoreditch to achieve that aim."

"Both specious and an exaggeration," Tom said, his blue eyes sparkling. Their friendship had begun in just this way, taking opposite sides of some legal question or, more often, something absurd, like the putative charms of a barmaid or the relative merits of vendors of hot pies. "No one thinks the anti-Martinists are being murdered to stop them writing doggerel. Martin's minion must be afraid that Nashe learned something that can point the finger at the secret press. Enough hints were given in *Martin's Mirror* to raise the alarm."

"Pasquill's latest should be out tomorrow," Nashe said, "though since I'm in captivity, I suppose I won't get to see it. It's called *A Countercuffe Given to Martin Junior.*"

"More of the same?" Tom asked.

"Worse, from Martin's point of view. I gave more details about the villages where Martin could be hiding, or his press anyway."

"That sounds vague," Trumpet said.

"Not if you're Martin's minion," Tom said.

143

"If I were Martin," Trumpet said, "I'd pack up and move. I wouldn't send my minion to London to strangle men at random."

"It isn't random," Tom said. "We've established that. Mr. Bacon believes it."

Trumpet grunted her acceptance of that proof. "But according to Nashe, your best suspect is one of the canon's pursuivants, Anthony Munday."

"He's an unpleasant, scowling sort of rascal," Nashe said.

Tom caught her gaze. "He used to chase Catholics for Sir Richard Topcliffe."

She grimaced. Neither of them wanted any further dealings with that odious gentleman. "Unpleasant, I agree, but that association is purely circumstantial as evidence."

"It's the strongest argument against him, for my money." Tom dusted crumbs from his hands and leaned forward, setting an elbow on the table to wag his finger at her. "The leopard doesn't change his spots."

Trumpet chuffed at that response. "Which one is the leopard? Martin or his pursuivant?"

"Both," Tom said, grinning. "From what I've heard, this Munday is a slippery sort of eel."

"Eels don't have spots," Nashe said.

"Nor are leopards slippery," Trumpet added. They grinned at each other, in perfect accord, and turned skeptical faces toward Tom.

"Fair enough," Tom said. "My metaphors are not of the best. But hear me out. Munday is a clever cat. Peace!" He flapped his hand at them. "Although a leopard is a kind of cat. But leave out the animals. Munday is sly enough to play both sides. He hates Catholics enough to hunt them down and send them to the gallows. Well, nobody hates Catholics more than a Puritan. They can't even stomach the faint whiff of incense on old robes found in

Grandmama's garret. Munday is more likely to support Martin than oppose him."

Trumpet had started shaking her head halfway through that weak argument. "My Lady Russell supports Martin too, in a general sense, but she doesn't prowl the liberties outside the wall hoping to get her long white hands around a pamphleteer's neck."

That image was too much for everyone, including Catalina, who bleated a small laugh.

"Of course not," Tom said. "But if I were Martin, I'd do my uttermost to get an informant into the opposing camp. What simpler way than to bribe one of the archbishop's pursuivants? You'll notice no one's been caught who knows anything about anything. What better way to ensure that than to have your own man directing the pursuit?"

That silenced her next objection. Tom's idea was not beyond the bounds of the possible. Lady Russell had loyal friends and servants of all stations in every county in which she owned land, which was most of them. She earned that loyalty not just with the generosity of small things, but also by defending her tenants' rights almost as hotly as her children's. And she was devious enough to nudge Canon Bancroft toward hiring the man of her choice, indirectly, of course, through a chain of acquaintances. She would never countenance murder, but she hadn't known about them at dinner on Sunday. Maybe they'd stop, now that she did.

Trumpet chewed on her lip while thinking this through, noticing after a few moments the look in Tom's eyes as he watched her mouth working. She stopped abruptly, pressing her lips together. He gave her an audible sigh.

"What does Mr. Bacon think of your idea?" she snapped, pushing thoughts of lips and their uses out of her mind.

145

"He thinks it's too complicated."

"Hmm."

"It makes sense to me, my — Mr. Trumpet," Nashe said.

Tom mouthed the words *Mr. Trumpet* with a comical expression on his face.

Trumpet clicked her tongue at him. "He has to call me something." She turned politely toward Nashe. "Please tell me what you think of this deranged and convoluted notion."

"I'm not sure it's too convoluted," Nashe said. "There's only one twist, or rather, a turning back. Munday pursues himself, as it were. I don't know him well, but my friends Dando and Oatmeale do. They think he's capable of small deceptions. Laying claim to another man's work or bragging about offers from publishers that far outshine the usual fees, which fall through at the last minute owing to someone else's fault. That sort of thing."

"So he's a braggart and a liar," Trumpet said. "That's a far cry from a murderer."

"It shows the man's character," Tom said, "which supports my idea. But leave Munday aside and let's look at it from another angle." He pointed his cup at Nashe. "You must have learned something vital, something more than a list of villages in Northamptonshire with Puritan-leaning churches."

"Alas, I don't know what I know."

"You haven't found anything in your notebooks?" Tom asked. "You've had nothing else to do during the day, unless you've been plucking at my lute, which I forbade you."

"He's staying in your room?" Trumpet asked, a flame of jealousy licking at her heart. "Does Mr. Bacon know?"

Tom shook his head. "He doesn't notice things like that. He doesn't hear anything when he's reading or writing. If I stood on my desk and danced a sailor's jig, I'd bet you a shilling it would take him a full half minute to look up."

"I won't take that bet," Trumpet said. She'd witnessed Bacon's powers of concentration at first hand.

Tom sighed. "I'll be glad when term starts. Then I'll be in the hall or in court or anywhere but Bacon's chambers most of the day."

Trumpet hummed in false sympathy for his plight. He could walk out the door and go anywhere he liked during his free hours. She couldn't even do that small thing without careful planning and subterfuge.

"I have another question," she said, turning back to Nashe. "Munday can't be the only pursuivant. They've been chasing Martin and his accomplices for nearly a year. How could you learn something in one month that they failed to discover in all that time?"

Nashe grinned. "I have my ways, Mr. Trumpet. People take pity on me; I'm a peculiar sort of fellow. I make people laugh, which they like. They buy me drinks to keep me talking and then tell me their own stories in return. I'm not an official of any kind, you see. Not a pursuivant, a feodary, a constable . . . not even an assistant to the deputy clerk of the deputy sheriff." He laughed at his own wit. "I'm too shabby, for one thing. Anyone can see at a glance that I'm harmless. So they tell me things they would never tell a man like Munday, with his royal writs and his glowering glare."

"I can see that," Tom said. "I can't imagine anyone telling Munday anything. You saw the way all conversation stopped whenever he walked up to a table at the Goose."

Nashe said, "You don't have to be likable to find Catholics. You don't eavesdrop in alehouses or charm the village gossips. You pay a visit to the local vicar or the justice of the peace and show him your writ. You say, 'I'm from the queen's appointed somebody-something' and demand a list of families who aren't attending church."

147

"That wouldn't help you find Martin's minions," Tom said. "Protestant hotheads go to church Sunday morning and then on to their Bible study groups at home. The more church, the merrier, if I can use that word for those unmerry folks." He shuddered.

Trumpet shuddered with him. He'd come very close to joining their ranks in truth during his months in Cambridge. She and Ben had brought him back to himself with great effort, dragging him out to taverns every night, plying him with drinks and dancing until he stopped spouting Bible verses in answer to everything.

Nashe nodded at his objection. "That's probably why the bishops haven't found anything. They need a fresh approach. They can't study old court records either, like feodaries and their agents who spy out orphans and widows with lands owing feudal duties." He pointed at Tom. "That's probably what happened to you."

"No," Tom said. "I brought my misery on myself. I remember bragging, more than once, about my father's lands after supper in the hall, trying to prove that I belong at Gray's as much as the men whose fathers are real gentlemen. Stupid!"

"Lots of us bragged about lots of things," Trumpet said. "Everyone was trying to prove something. You couldn't know how it would turn out."

"They'd have found you out anyway," Nashe said. "It's a miracle anyone escapes, the game is so profitable. I bumped into one of them in Northamptonshire. A clerkish-looking cove who said he'd been straining his poor eyes studying ancient deeds of sale, searching for parcels that once belonged to a church or a great lord. He said he could earn ten pounds for one good find."

Trumpet and Tom gawked at him. Tom said, with a touch of awe in his voice, "That's an enormous sum of money."

"Tempting, isn't it?" Nashe said. "He caught my interest, I'll warrant you. I asked him how a man could make so much for doing so little. He scoffed at the 'little' and admitted that he'd only earned that sum once, for a widow with an estate worth a thousand per annum. He was nice enough to throw me one crumb. He said even a quick note sent to your county feodary could earn you a pound or two. They're always on the alert. Or you could get your pound directly from the widow by warning her about what you'd discovered. It would be worth it to her to buy your silence."

"That's blackmail," Trumpet said with authority. A useful tool in its place, but not to be used for trivial purposes. "And low, in this case. Lower than informing on recusant Catholics."

"I agree," Nashe said, "in spite of my empty purse. I did let the churl pay for my supper."

Tom's eyes narrowed, doubtless imagining some varlet making such an offer to his mother. "Who would inform on a widow and her children in their darkest hour of grief? If that had happened to us, I would've hunted the bastard down and strangled him myself."

"No, you wouldn't," Trumpet said.

"I might." Tom squared his jaw. The yellow light of the nearest candle caught the ruddy tints in his beard, making them glow like polished bronze.

Trumpet loved that brushy rill. He'd never grow it an inch longer if she had anything to say about it. Which she did. "I meant you would never strangle anyone. You would challenge the knave to a fair fight with his choice of weapon and then trounce him justly."

"True. And thanks." Tom treated her to a full-dimple grin. Then he turned back to Nashe. "I'll grant that your clerk was a scoundrel, but you won't find lists of radical Presbyterians in old land records either."

"No," Nashe agreed, "which is why your average pursuivant will get nowhere in your average village. Those folks won't betray their masters to any passing stranger. You can't dance jiggery-joggery into the local alehouse and start asking questions. You have to tell stories, the funnier the better, especially ones that hint at scandals in the neighboring parish. Then you'll be treated to their stories in return. Lots of stories, endless stories, stories utterly bereft of wit or purpose." He rolled his eyes to heaven. "But eventually someone says something about the new men up at the manor who never come to town. Once I heard that one such unknown varlet had been seen hanging small sheets in the barn."

"Sheets of paper?" Tom asked.

"That was my guess," Nashe said, "though I kept it to myself. The simpleton who told me thought it was a nefarious plot to frighten the washerwomen."

"That's very interesting," Tom said, refilling Nashe's cup.

"And very vague," Trumpet said. "Unless your simpleton also gave you a description of the paper-hanger detailed enough to pick him out of a crowd. That might be enough to alarm our villain, but it doesn't help us identify him. We need more. We need something definitive."

"We should set a trap," Tom said. "Like we did last time, remember?"

Trumpet whistled. "You nearly lost that gamble."

"It was close, I'll grant you," Tom said, "but the result was definitely definitive. And frankly, I can't think of another play. I'll keep looking for witnesses, but I'll bet you the next round of spiced wine that the best I'll get is" — he shifted into a falsetto — "welladay, my good sir, all I can tell you is he was a tall man with a black hat and a hook instead of a hand."

They laughed, but not for long. Trumpet pointed her chin at Nashe, who was stuffing bread and cheese into his pockets. "I suppose we'll use this one as bait."

"He's all we've got," Tom said.

"Wait!" Nashe cried. "Can't we steal a scarecrow from a field or a tailor's form? I'm too young for such a fate."

"Don't worry," Trumpet said. "We'll be watching. At worst, you'll have a sore throat for a few days." She winked at Tom. "I suppose you have a plan?"

"I do. I've been thinking about this since we got here. We were so unconscionably late" — he gave Trumpet a wry look — "because we stopped to make arrangements with Mrs. Sprye for Nashe's meals. He can't eat in commons, of course, and neither one of us has any money. She agreed to feed him twice a day in exchange for some fair-copying and sorting out some old accounts. It'll only be for a few days, if my plan works."

"Let's hear it." Trumpet popped a dried cherry into her mouth and chewed it with a saucy snap.

"It's simple," Tom said. "Nothing can go wrong. Our strangler likes to grab his victims in a narrow alley close to their destination. Our friend Nashe will be walking from the Antelope here to my room at Gray's every evening. He can't pass through the gatehouse and walk across the central yard to the front door, so he has to take the shortcut through Fulwood's Rents and climb in the back window. I'm thinking the most likely point of attack will be at the end of that passage. It's like a bottleneck. After that there's a short, open stretch to get to my window."

Trumpet walked the familiar route in her mind. Fulwood's hadn't been completely built in her year, but she knew the general lay of the land. "That should work. We three" — she nodded toward Catalina to include her in the plan — "can hide before and aft, so to speak. When the villain strikes, we leap out and grab him. The three of us should be able to overpower him easily enough."

Tom grinned, but did not utter so much as a chuckle. He knew her qualities. "The moon was full last week, which might be why our strangler chose to strike then. If this weather holds, it should be bright enough for the next few nights to tempt him out again."

Nashe's face still held a pained expression, but he seemed reconciled to his role. The others were either too tall, too small, or too curvy. "How will we lure our prey into this trap?"

"We'll have to put the word out," Tom said. "We must make sure Anthony Munday hears about it, which should be easy enough. From what I saw at the Goose and Gall the other night, all you have to do, Nashey, is spend an hour or two at your regular table gossiping with your blabber-mates, Dando and Oatmeale."

"*John* Dando and *Oliver* Oatmeale?" Trumpet cried. "You didn't tell me you'd met them. They're Ben's favorites! I buy everything they write to send to him so he can keep up with their doings."

"I haven't had much chance to tell you anything," Tom said. They traded forlorn looks. What kind of cruel world kept friends like them apart? The rank injustice nagged at each of them, all day, like a hole in a stocking that rubbed blisters on your foot.

"There's no trick to meeting those muddy rascals," Nashe said, oblivious to the undercurrents. "I'll take you there next Thursday afternoon, if you like."

Tom opened his mouth, but Trumpet talked right over his predictable objection. "I accept. This strangler business may be over by then."

"If we're lucky," Tom said. He met her eyes. "Do you think I should tell Mr. Bacon first?"

"I don't know," she answered. "What do you think he'd say?"

He laughed and she nodded. "We have a plan. We each have our role to play. We have a moon."

"When should I start spreading rumors?" Nashe said.

"Why wait?" Trumpet answered before Tom could come up with another objection. "Let's do it tomorrow."

FIFTEEN

Tom stuck close to his desk all day Monday, partly to get caught up on his fair-copying, which Bacon had unreasonably scolded him about once he'd managed to drag himself out of bed. He'd been abstracted, then peevish when interrupted, unwilling to discuss the investigation so far. He seemed to find any question on the subject impertinent. Then he'd been summoned to a day-long meeting of the benchers. On his way out, he'd admonished Tom not to go running around the town spreading rumors.

That choice of phrase would have been disturbing from a more alert master since Nashe had sneaked out shortly before noon to go to the Goose and Gall to spread their carefully crafted rumor to their carefully selected audience.

Tom was glad for the excuse to stay in. He didn't want to risk disturbing the bait Nashe was setting out by accidentally contradicting some minor embellishment. The trail through the back streets of Norton Folgate would grow a few day's colder, but it was already fairly cool. It might even be an advantage to let the strangler think they'd given up.

He considered telling Bacon about the trap for almost a minute before deciding it would do more harm than good. First, there was no point in suggesting anything to a man in such an ill humor. Second, the whole thing might be over before anyone at Gray's noticed Nashe climbing through his window. And third, Bacon would surely note that the plan required more than one lookout and ask about the other members of the party. Tom hadn't broken his promise not to tell Trumpet about this commission, but that nicety might be buried under the other objections to her involvement.

On Tuesday, Bacon refused to emerge from his bedchamber before ten o'clock. He greeted Tom with a grunt as he settled into the commodious chair behind his spacious desk, surveying the documents laid thereon with a disgruntled curl of the lip. He acted like a man with an unresolvable problem weighing on his mind.

It didn't take a genius to figure out what that problem was. Tom was neither witless nor deaf. Bacon and Lady Russell had been talking about Robert Cecil and his father, Lord Burghley, after dinner on Sunday with all their "old persons" and "advisory bodies." They'd come within a hair's-breadth of accusing the most powerful man in the kingdom of perpetrating a year-long masquerade aimed at dismantling the established church.

The wisest course would be to make some excuse and bow out of this commission, but what excuse? The courts were adjourned for another six weeks, so Bacon could hardly plead press of business. He could throw himself down the stairs, hoping to break a leg or an arm, but Tom would have to do the same. How plausible would that be?

Somehow Bacon had to think of a way to catch a villain without identifying the villain's master. Ticklish, any way you looked at it.

Bacon heaved a weary sigh, then dipped his quill and began to write. Whatever he was working on seemed to settle his inner turmoil. Tom could see the lines on his brow smoothing and the tightness around his mouth relaxing. Then the chapel bell tolled the quarter hour. Bacon returned his pen to its holder and asked, "Have you finished a complete copy of the *Maxims*?"

155

"One more and this is done."

"Good. Go ahead and finish it up. Then after dinner I'd like you to go to the Stationers' Hall and examine their record books. Make a list of every master printer still living, noting his place of origin and current place of employment, if that can be determined."

"What!" Where had that come from? Tom's heart sank at the prospect of spending a hot afternoon in a stuffy closet at the Stationers' Hall. "There must hundreds of printers, not to mention journeymen."

"Not so many as that," Bacon said, unruffled by the heated response. "There are only about fifty presses in all of London. Add a few for Cambridge and Oxford. I doubt you'll find more than a hundred men still young enough to work. It seems the logical place to start when searching for an illegal press, but no one else seems to have though of it. Although I didn't ask." He frowned out the window. "Perhaps I ought to."

He wrote a short note. "Before you go into the city, take this note across to Lambeth Palace for Canon Bancroft. I'm asking for permission to spend an hour or two in the library this evening, but what I really want is an invitation to supper. I might learn more after a good meal and a few glasses of wine. Tell whoever takes your message that I would be honored to invite the canon to supper at Gray's. Tell him that even between terms, we usually manage to set a respectable table. Frown when you say that, so the footman understands that any guest can expect day-old pottage with the odd lump of mutton."

Tom chuckled. "I understand. I'll make it clear that you desire a private, informal meeting but that dining at Gray's would be the worst way to accomplish the goals of both conversation and nourishment."

"Precisely." Bacon petted his moustache with his index finger, gazing down at his manuscript, then looked up again with a smile. "That's enough for today. We'll see what we learn. One cautious step at a time, that's the safest procedure."

The door swung open and Pinnock bounded in, holding a square letter with a large red seal on his flat palm as if bearing a plate of jelly. Bacon took it and scowled at the seal.

"Oh, this is *really* too much!" He waved Pinnock out and waited until the door closed before showing the page to Tom. "It's from the pygmy — my cousin. He wants me to drop whatever I'm doing and rush down to his house to deliver a report. He's confusing me with one of his servants!"

Tom rose to accept the letter, then sat down again to read it. He bit his lip to keep from laughing. Mr. Cecil's note seemed scrupulously polite to him, merely suggesting that his cousin pay a visit, at his convenience, to discuss the progress of his commission, if he should be inclined to do so.

But Bacon wouldn't hear it. Cecil's mere name seemed to prickle him like a coarse shirt on sunburnt skin. He spread his hands wide to indicate the two or three unanswered letters neatly squared on the corner of his largely empty desk. "It's impossible! Anyone can see that I'm overwhelmed with work!"

"I'll go," Tom said. "It's my job, after all. I can stop at Burghley House after taking your note to Lambeth." With luck, they'd keep him waiting long enough to rule out a visit to the Stationers' Hall that day. With more luck, something else would turn up tomorrow. Or their trap might be sprung tonight.

"Tell him as little as possible," Bacon said, eyes flashing. "No, he'll see through that. Tell him about your man Munday. He's plausible; play that up. Make it clear that we're searching high and low, which happens to be the literal truth. He can't complain about the truth, I shouldn't think."

* * *

Tom set out on his errands shortly after dinner. Sure enough, he returned from his jaunt across the river with an invitation to supper for Mr. Bacon and the warm assurance that the barrister was most welcome to avail himself of Lambeth's library at his pleasure.

He had the foresight to equip himself with a copy of Robert Greene's *Pandosto,* a romance featuring an adventurous princess — the sort of tale Trumpet favored. She'd want to meet Greene too, presumably, now that she knew Tom knew him. Things would be easier if she had her own house with a dead or absent husband, but that dream wasn't likely to come true. Sooner than he could bear to think about, she would marry a handsome young lord, move off to some enormous manor miles from London, have half a dozen babies, and forget all about her old friend at Gray's Inn.

But that hadn't happened yet, and the gallery on the first floor of Burghley House was a pleasant place to read, cool and shady with a rosemary-scented breeze rising from the interior courtyard. He read a couple of dozen pages, envisioning Princess Fawnia as a black-haired, green-eyed beauty in a filmy, one-shouldered gown, before Peter Hollowell poked his head out of a nearby door and crooked his finger at him. "Mr. Cecil can see you now."

Bacon had sent a crisp note acknowledging the summons, advising the summoner that Tom would be performing the duty in his place.

Tom had seen Robert Cecil once or twice when he'd accompanied Bacon to court, but he had never been introduced. Now he swept off his hat and made a half bow to show his respect and hopefully mollify any offense that might have resulted from his master's ill-tempered note.

No offense appeared to have been taken. Cecil smiled and gestured him to a chair not far from Hollowell's tiny desk, barely sufficient for note-taking, but then he had his own decently sized and well-appointed office nearby.

Cecil remained seated, as was his prerogative. His stature appeared almost normal behind his desk. His chair had probably been specially built to create that illusion. His coloring was much like Bacon's, pale skin and brown hair, but his eyes were darker and his chin longer, an effect exaggerated by his pointed beard. Still, his expression seemed mild and welcoming.

"Have you any news?" he asked. "I know it's early days, but we like to stay abreast of developments as they occur."

"Mr. Bacon understands that." Tom had already rejected the idea of apologizing for Bacon's non-appearance. These men were cousins. They knew each other well enough. "We haven't identified the murderer yet. Naturally, we would have communicated that to you at once. We've barely had time to take our bearings, so to speak, but we have determined some promising directions of inquiry."

"Such as?" Cecil asked, raising his thin eyebrows.

"As you know," Tom said, "Mr. Bacon is nothing if not thorough. He began by visiting Archbishop Whitgift and Canon Bancroft to acquaint himself with the progress they have made in identifying Martin Marprelate's accomplices."

"Which is none," Cecil said. "I could have told him that. In fact, I think I did. But it is the logical first step. What then?"

"Well," Tom said, "I myself have questioned the anti-Martinist pamphleteers. I don't know if you're aware of this yet, but there was another assault, this time on Robert Greene. He was pushed down the stairs at a tavern favored by writers."

159

"I heard," Cecil said, flicking an amused glance at his secretary. "Although what I heard was that he fell down the stairs in a state of extreme inebriation."

"That's possible," Tom said, "but it's a striking coincidence under the current circumstances, and we would be remiss not to investigate it."

"Fair enough," Cecil said. "Did Greene remember who pushed him?"

"No. But I am pursuing the matter. Never fear. If anyone saw anyone push or crowd against Robert Greene that night, I'll find them."

Cecil smiled slightly, nodding as he regarded Tom with interest. "My cousin told me you were a lively lad. That's the sort I like to employ."

"Thank you." Tom blinked, realizing he'd just been complimented twice. He stood a little straighter, squaring his shoulders. "My investigation among the pamphleteers has borne some early fruits, in the form of one strong suspect."

"Who?" Cecil asked.

"A man named Anthony Munday."

Cecil cut a glance at his secretary, then shook his head at Tom. "You don't mean Munday, the pursuivant? The one Archbishop Whitgift has employed to locate Martin's press? The man recommended by Sir Richard Topcliffe as a most effective discoverer of hidden Catholics?"

Tom grinned. "That's the man. His pursuit of Catholics is one of the arguments in his favor — as a suspect, I mean. Nobody hates Catholics more than a nonconformist Protestant, I can tell you that with complete assurance."

"Yes, I've heard about your exploits in Cambridge. But if he's pursuing Martin Marprelate, why would he want to hinder others working toward the same objective?"

"By all accounts," Tom said, "this Munday is a crafty one. Suppose that he's one of Martin's min — er,

160

accomplices. He might have gotten himself hired by the archbishop in order to be able to warn Martin about impending searches."

Cecil's eyes cut toward Hollowell, his mouth twisted with suppressed mirth. The explanation now sounded hopelessly light-witted in Tom's ears too. He should have listened to Mr. Bacon.

"That would be crafty," Cecil said drily. "And Martin has managed to stay a step — or a league — ahead of the bishops." He wagged a finger at Tom. "You may have something there, Clarady. Perhaps I should bring Munday in and question him myself." He turned a frown toward Hollowell, as if asking him to consider that option.

Heat rose in Tom's cheeks. He scrambled for something more impressive to report. "Not yet, if it please you, Mr. Cecil. We have a plan in place to expose the strangler. If he really is Anthony Munday, you'd give our game away."

"We wouldn't want to do that," Cecil said. "Please tell me about this plan, if it isn't too secret. I know my cousin likes to keep such things in the dark as long as possible."

"That's only good sense," Tom answered. "Although of course he wants you to know about it. If we're successful, we'll need a man taken into immediate custody." He paused to gather his thoughts. He had now crawled all the way out on a very shaky limb. What if Mr. Cecil met Mr. Bacon somewhere before the trap was sprung? He couldn't fail to mention it.

Too late now. Tom asked, "Are you familiar with Holborn Road and the area between it and Gray's Inn at all?"

"Somewhat," Cecil allowed.

"There's an excellent inn on the high street," Hollowell put in, "called the Antelope. A favorite haunt of the legal community, I believe."

161

"Yes," Tom said, smiling at him with more gratitude than the comment merited. "That's the starting point." He sketched the route they'd planned, describing the bottle opening that broached into the court behind Bacon's house. "That's where we'll close the trap and catch our villain." He clapped his palms together with a soft *pop*.

"Ah, the trap!" Cecil traded another amused glance with Hollowell. "I've been waiting for this. My cousin has made traps something of a specialty. No doubt he'll be watching the action from the safety of his bedroom window. Do let me know at once how it works out." He tilted his chin at his secretary, who rose, causing Tom to rise as well.

The interview was over. It had not gone the way Tom had imagined; quite the opposite, in fact. Now he'd laid something of a trap for Mr. Bacon. They'd have to solve this case quickly to forestall serious embarrassment.

Hollowell bowed him out of the office, not bothering to accompany him to the stairs this time. As the door closed behind him, Tom turned to walk down the gallery, but stopped in his tracks. Anthony Munday was sitting on the very bench Tom had recently occupied, apparently waiting for an audience with Robert Cecil.

Shock ran through Tom's body, like stepping on a hot coal with a bare foot. That had only happened to him once, but it wasn't something you forgot.

They glared at one another in mutually hostile recognition. Then Tom turned his back, taking the long way around to the staircase. He walked slowly down the marble steps, his mind churning up possible outcomes of that surprise encounter. Munday knew Tom was a friend of Thomas Nashe and might easily have learned already that he'd been asking questions about the murders. Now he could assume Tom was in the employ of Mr. Cecil. It would be only natural to connect those two things.

Did he know enough about Robert Cecil's family to link him to Francis Bacon? If he'd heard Nashe's rumors today, he could readily draw a line from Nashe to Gray's Inn. Mr. Bacon's membership in that society was widely known, thanks to his late father's position as Lord Keeper of the Great Seal.

Tom's spirits sank with the weight of the ever-expanding ramifications of this already complicated case. He'd succeeded in trapping himself too.

SIXTEEN

Francis Bacon put down his fork and pushed his plate away, smiling as if replete, although the supper laid out by Canon Bancroft had been meager, if of excellent quality. He couldn't complain. It wasn't wise to eat a large meal in the evening, as his mother reminded him on a weekly basis.

He accepted another glass of the French claret, which was too tart for his tastes, although he knew it had been chosen to honor him. The meal had succeeded in establishing a comfortable accord between him and his host. They'd spoken little while eating, another sensible habit. They smiled now at one another over their cups in mutual recognition that the time had come for serious conversation.

"Have you made any progress?" Bancroft asked.

"A little," Francis said. It wasn't entirely an untruth. "My assistant has made inroads among the denizens of the ward where the murders took place. He's quite expert at turning up witnesses where others have failed."

"Good. The villain must be stopped. I predicted that Martin's accomplices would turn to violence eventually. Privately, of course. No need to stir things up."

"No, indeed," Francis said. He refrained from noting that "things" could hardly be more thoroughly stirred up, thanks to the canon's rash decision to unleash a team of satirists into the controversy.

"Are you receiving the support you need from Mr. Cecil's office?"

Francis shrugged. "No more than one would expect."

Bancroft grunted a bitter laugh.

Francis said, "I don't know much about the pursuit of Martin's co-conspirators, but as an impartial observer, I must say the Privy Council seems to have done little to support the effort."

Another bitter grunt. "They've all but obstructed us. If it weren't for the queen, we'd get no help whatsoever."

"There are many members of the Council who sympathize with Martin's philosophy, if not specifically with his tactics."

Bancroft nodded, his dark eyes glittering. "It has been a constant battle since John Whitgift was made archbishop. You'll remember the opposition he faced from Lord Burghley over his Articles of Religion a few years ago."

"I do," Francis said. Who could forget? Whitgift had demanded that every clergyman in England swear to uphold his three articles, blatantly designed to be offensive to nonconformists. He expected them to swear not to use anything other than the Book of Common Prayer in their services, an unnecessarily severe limitation that served no useful purpose. Many otherwise law-abiding ministers had refused and been forced thereby into open opposition, when before they had presented only a mild deviation from established practice. Lord Burghley had objected, standing up for common practice and tolerance.

Francis added, "Lord Burghley had allies on the Council during that conflict, as I recall."

"Too many. And more of that breed in Parliament. If it weren't for the stalwart support of Her Majesty, England's church would be in a state of chaos even as we speak." Bancroft's monkey-like features twisted fearfully, as if he could smell the torches of rioters at the gate.

"A disaster that must be prevented at all costs," Francis said. But not by fomenting greater hostilities. "You still have a majority on the Council, do you not? The archbishop, Lord Chancellor Hatton . . ."

Bancroft shook his head. "Too narrow a margin and likely to tilt the other way in the near future, if I read the changes in the wind aright."

"You refer to the possibility of Robert Cecil being appointed to the Privy Council."

"Possibility! A certainty, in my view. He attends every meeting, did you know that?"

"I've heard." Envy increased the acidic aftertaste of the wine in Francis's throat.

"He could, of course, be counted upon to echo his father's voice in response to every question. And Cecil isn't the only one."

"How so?" Francis frowned. Lord Burghley had another son, who had never shown any interest in politics.

"The Earl of Essex," Bancroft said, as if the name were too obvious to mention. "The queen's favorite. And, need I add, one of Lord Burghley's wards."

"He's only twenty-four," Francis said. "Surely he's far too young?"

"Pah! Youth is no obstacle. Your cousin is only twenty-six. Sweep aside the old generation, all the men who remember what life was like in England before our righteous queen ascended to the throne. These young blades care less than that" — he snapped his fingers — "for religious unity or the stability of a proper hierarchy of prelates."

Francis counted himself among the "young blades," but he cared greatly for stability. Enforcing rigid conformity by oaths and threats, however, was not the method he recommended for achieving that goal. But his opinions weren't relevant here. "Regardless of their private beliefs, my Lord Burghley and Mr. Cecil are wise enough to see the harm that Martin Marprelate is doing to the body politic. Enough is enough. I should think they'd be as eager as anyone to see him caught and the whole controversy laid to rest."

"You and I may think that. We see the harm all too clearly." Bancroft shook his head. "Alas, we are in the minority, struggling with such poor tools as we can muster for ourselves. You can't have failed to notice that the three best-staffed intelligence services have chosen not to supply a single man to assist us in tracking Martin's press. Not one!"

Francis had not noticed that, although he ought to have. The three services in question must be those of Sir Francis Walsingham, the Earl of Essex, and Lord Burghley, now in the hands of Robert Cecil. "Didn't Anthony Munday come to you from Sir Francis Walsingham?"

"Bah! He's next to useless. The only offender he has apprehended is that idiot Giles Wigginton. No trick there. That profane noisemaker thrusts himself into every controversy. I think he's happier in gaol than out."

"Sir Francis must have considered him capable, or he wouldn't have recommended him. Or did he come to you from Lord Burghley's service?"

Bancroft wrinkled his small nose. "Perhaps he did. I don't remember." He took a long drink from his silver cup, then shook a thin finger at Francis. "It wouldn't surprise me. What better way to hinder our pursuit than to send us an incompetent pursuivant?"

* * *

Francis turned that question over in his mind while he stood on the Lambeth wharf, waiting for a ferry. The river was crowded with small craft this evening, their shaded lanterns bobbing above and below, reflected in the darkening waters. They would soon be outshone by the half moon rising over the broken spire of St. Paul's. Music in many strains and voices, plucked from lutes or bleated through reeds, echoed across the water, blending pleasantly into a musical mist. Half of London must be afloat, taking advantage of the cooler breezes on a summer night.

He had no desire to join them. Damp air filled his chest with catarrhs. But he wasn't quite ready for bed, with so many questions to ponder. He decided to stop at the Antelope for a slice of Mrs. Sprye's incomparable almond tart and a cup of something sweet to chase away the lingering taste of the canon's astringent claret.

His favorite small table in the nook behind the hearth was available. He sat with his back to the room, as usual, although it was nearly empty with the courts in recess. Mrs. Sprye knew him well enough not to take offense at his unsociability. She would understand that he wanted to think.

He gazed absently out the window onto the high street, where lengthening shadows threw the doorways under overhanging jetties into total darkness. As he savored a mouthful of the lightly sweetened tart, he chided himself for not noticing the absence of effort on the part of Sir Francis Walsingham in the hunt for Martin Marprelate. The Secretary of State had been in the vanguard in the search for English Catholics who might be colluding with Spain or Rome. But then, Sir Francis had been one of the Marian exiles, like so many of the older generation of Protestants. He'd spent those years among the Calvinists in Switzerland. His sympathies lay with Martin and his adherents.

Sir Francis had also been increasingly unwell in recent years. Perhaps he simply hadn't the strength to pursue an overreaching Protestant whom he would regard as merely improvident.

Even so, he had years of experience on the Privy Council and enjoyed the confidence of the queen. He would have insights into the Marprelate controversy and the futile attempts to resolve it. He had always been kind to Francis, in honor of Sir Nicholas Bacon and respect for Lady Anne. The men and women of that generation understood each other in ways the rising generation never could, thanks to the shared extremity of danger during the Marian years.

Francis didn't need an elaborate excuse to visit so good a friend. He would send a letter in the morning begging a few minutes of counsel on a confidential matter. Simplicity itself.

The Earl of Essex, now; that was more delicate. No one would reasonably expect the young nobleman to know anything pertinent to the Marprelate problem. In fact, he'd been suspected of being Martin, briefly, jokingly, after an incident in court. Her Majesty had just declared in no uncertain terms that possession of one of Martin's tracts would be made a punishable offense. The earl had promptly incriminated himself by pulling a copy of the *Epitome* out of his pocket. He had apologized prettily, winning an exasperated swat from the queen, but his point had been made. Martin's pamphlets were everywhere.

The earl would not know anything about Martin *per se*, but he had been building up his stable of intelligencers, positioning himself to rival Lord Burghley. He might know something about the pursuit or the interrogations last autumn that Francis hadn't heard. Furthermore, he would be flattered to be consulted, and any excuse to flatter the young nobleman should be acted upon.

Francis swallowed the last bite of his tart, pleased to have satisfied both his physical and intellectual lacks. Now he had letters to write and questions to ask. He need speculate no further until he'd gathered those expert opinions.

Another glance out the window told him he had better hurry on home. Evening had almost transformed into night, the little remaining light more likely to confuse his path.

He rose, tipped his hat to Mrs. Sprye, and went out to hurry across the empty street. He took the shortcut through Fulwood's Rents, grateful for his father's prescience in building his house on the corner closest to Holborn. When he'd built it many years ago, there had been cows grazing almost all the way down to where he now walked.

As he neared the end of the almost pitch-black passageway, he saw a young man climb out of Tom's window, clearly outlined in the open field behind his house. The figure stood there for a moment and then climbed back in.

What now? He knew Tom employed that means of egress from time to time, but this figure was too small.

Not — surely not Lady Alice! Even if she'd dressed in man's clothing, she and Tom were treading on very thin ice. They'd bring disaster down upon them all. This dangerous foolery must be nipped in the bud at once.

Francis quickened his pace, then a sudden rush of motion startled him. Before he could say, "Who's there?" a sinewy arm crooked around his neck and tightened. He thrashed and flung himself about, loosening the grip enough to shout, "Help! Help!"

His assailant threw him hard against the wall, pressing him back with his body. Two strong hands wormed under his ruff, wrapping around his bare throat, pressing inward, choking him, strangling . . .

"Mr. Bacon?" Tom's voice sounded from somewhere. Francis nearly fainted in relief.

"Is that you?" Tom shouted. "Hoi! You there! Stop that!"

"Bacon?" The strangler's hot hands released their grasp, but then one clutched his ruff to drag his ear toward panting breath and a growling murmur. "Take this as a

warning, *Frank*. Don't stick your neck out where it might get wrung." The villain threw him to the ground and ran thundering down the alley.

SEVENTEEN

Tom stood outside Bacon's chambers with his hands on his hips, glaring for all he was worth at Pinnock, who had opened the door barely wide enough to show his face. The black-eyed imp had just turned fifteen and was nearly as tall as Trumpet. He'd spent the past three years fetching, cleaning, and running errands for Francis Bacon, who had about as much skill in managing servants as he had in sword-fighting.

"Five minutes," Tom said. "That's all I ask."

Bacon had taken to his bed after his attack and had not emerged since. Worse, he wouldn't allow anyone to enter his chambers but Pinnock. Tom couldn't even get to his desk. It had been two days and he was going mad with restlessness and indecision. What should he do? Were they giving up the case?

"Master says no," Pinnock said, a touch of impudence in his voice. "Nobody but me."

They locked eyes in a silent contest, which was lost before it began. Pinnock was less afraid of Tom than he was of Bacon, whom he feared not one jot. In merchant's terms, that would make Tom the debtor, in which case he ought to fear Pinnock — a pure impossibility.

"Two minutes," Tom begged.

Pinnock shook his head.

"One."

Pinnock's eyes danced at the idea of anyone holding a one-minute conversation with Francis Bacon.

Tom frowned deeply to make his displeasure clear, tapped his foot on the oak floor a few times, then gave up. "Tell me the *very minute* he's ready to —"

"Yes, yes. The very minute." Pinnock flashed a cheeky grin and swung shut the door.

Tom plodded back down to his own room and slumped behind his second desk. Never in all his active boyhood had he ever imagined he would end up spending his days shifting between two cramped desks. Or worse — *wanting* to sit at the lesser of the said desks.

He rested his cheek on one fist, gazing out the window at the glorious summer day. He couldn't sit here twiddling his thumbs until Bacon chose to rejoin the living. That could be days, or even weeks, even though he hadn't been much injured in the attack.

They'd verified that much on the spot. As soon as they knew he was all right, Trumpet and Catalina melted away. Nashe had just come through the shadowed passage, reaching Tom's window without incident. When Bacon shouted, "Help," he rushed to join what was left of the fray. Then he helped Tom carry Bacon up to his bedchamber, bringing him in through Tom's window to avoid the curious gaze of men in the yard. They removed his ruff and doublet, unlacing the collar of his shirt. Dark bruises marked the pale skin of his throat and his voice was hoarse, but nothing worse. The hoarseness was much soothed by the warm, honeyed wine Pinnock tearfully fixed for him.

Of course, the insult to his system had been tremendous. Anyone would feel out of balance for a while, especially a pacific sort like Bacon. He never engaged in physical pursuits like fencing, dancing, or shooting. As far as Tom knew, he had never cultivated any of the manly arts; contrarily, he tended toward frailty, easily falling ill from rich foods or chilly draughts. Being nearly strangled could be expected to take a toll.

173

Even so, he'd left Tom to shift for himself, and he wasn't sure what he ought to do. He needed a consultation with his collaborators, which he could accomplish. Today was Thursday. Trumpet would be out and about this afternoon.

He jotted a note asking her to meet him and Nashe at the Antelope at her earliest convenience. He selected a small rock from the supply he kept in a pot near his desk for this purpose and wrapped the note around it, securing it with a scrap of string. Then he put on his hat and walked out the front door, crossing the yard to go through the gatehouse onto Gray's Inn Road, calling a cheery greeting to the gatekeeper as he passed. The window was more convenient, but he had to be seen occasionally or people would begin to wonder.

When he got to Blackfriars, he circled around to Trumpet's window, which stood open, as expected. He checked to be sure no one was watching, whistled a little of "The Sweet and Merry Month of May," and tossed the note-wrapped rock inside. Then he strode briskly off toward Holborn without a backward glance.

He found Thomas Nashe sitting at the most undesirable table in the tavern, way at the back, closest to the privy. The small, clouded window admitted some light but was kept firmly shut to keep out the faintest whiff of air. The table was covered with neat stacks of paper, presumably the bills and letters Nashe had been hired to sort.

As Tom approached, Nashe looked up and grinned his gag-toothed grin, running inky fingers through his straw-colored hair. "We should marry innkeepers, Clarady. This place produces more coin than the Royal Mint."

"I've proposed to Mrs. Sprye at least twice," Tom said, grabbing a stool. "She says I'm too young for her."

Nashe studied him with a critical eye. "Hmph. Perhaps she prefers wit to beauty."

"Sorry, old chum. You have to be at least a serjeant-at-law to get her attention."

"Ah, well. Another dream shattered." Nashe pretended to wipe a tear from his eye. "Anything yet from Mr. Bacon?"

"Not a word."

"I didn't think he was so badly injured."

"He wasn't, he's just —" Tom turned around to follow Nashe's gaze, which had shifted toward something behind him, which turned out to be Trumpet and Catalina, dressed as tradesmen's wives in simple gowns with dark veils to protect their faces from the sun and the dusty streets. They could be anyone, male or female, in that garb. How easy it was for women of the middling sort to walk about anonymously!

They drew off their veils as they sat down, revealing neat white coifs tied under their chins. The costume made Trumpet look like a diligent housewife, a disguise more deceptive than galligaskins and a false moustache.

"How's Mr. Bacon?" she asked.

Tom shrugged. "I can't even get in to ask."

She clucked her tongue sympathetically, comprehending the situation without further explanation.

Nashe, however, was unschooled in Bacon's ways. "How long is this going to go on?"

Tom and Trumpet shrugged in unison. She answered, "Several days, probably. A week or more, possibly. He doesn't fare well in the face of strong affronts of any kind. A scolding from the queen, a set-down at court, a tumble down the stairs . . ."

"But why won't he let Clarady in?" Nashe asked. "Doesn't he trust you?"

"Of course he trusts me. It isn't that. He won't leave his room until he's recovered from the fright. Refusing to see me is something else again." He met Trumpet's eyes with a look laden with meaning. She narrowed her eyes and gave him a short nod to show she understood.

Tom threw Nashe a crumb. "He's thought of something he doesn't want to talk about, not even to me."

"But how can you catch the man who attacked him if he won't tell you everything he knows?" Nashe asked.

"He never does that," Trumpet said, flashing a grin. "Trust me, you don't want him to. But this . . ." She shook her head, pursing her cupid's-bow lips in a way that made Tom pinch his leg under the table to keep from kissing them, public house be damned.

He looked at Nashe instead. "I think he may have stumbled onto a link to someone too great to touch and he hasn't decided how to handle it."

He and Trumpet shared another knowing look. They had both been at dinner on Sunday during that oblique conversation between Bacon and Lady Russell, which Trumpet could interpret equally well. Granted, they'd been engaged in a little covert dalliance, trying to catch each other's feet beneath the table and forming messages with their food, but you can do that and listen to the grown-ups' conversation at the same time.

Bacon suspected his cousin Robert Cecil of creating or managing or sustaining Martin Marprelate, with or without his father's approval. But now one of Martin's subordinates had turned deadly, with or without their consent, and they'd tasked Bacon with cleaning up the mess because they thought they could control him.

"He can't just quit and leave a murderer at large," Trumpet explained to Nashe, "especially not one bold enough to attack a man at the edge of a compound filled with lawyers."

"A half-empty compound," Tom said, "but your point is well taken. Mr. Bacon has a moral obligation to stop the killing, but he'll want to tread *very* lightly around the great one, whoever it may be." A thorny problem, to say the least. Tom didn't wonder that Bacon had taken to his bed. "The question is, should we wait until he makes up his mind?"

"I vote nay," Nashe said. "I can't spend the rest of my life in hiding, the span of which promises to be small if the strangler is left at large. Two minutes slower and my neck would've been the one being crushed between his hands." He shuddered.

"I wonder about that," Tom said. "We did everything right. We were in position well before dark. Nashe walked the gauntlet at a normal pace, in his usual gait."

"That takes courage," Trumpet said, pointing at Nashe. He ducked his head at the praise.

Tom didn't think he deserved special acclaim. The man had walked down an alley — he hadn't fended off a pack of wild dogs. "What possessed you to come back out of my room?"

Nashe shrugged. "Once I got inside and looked out, it seemed so light still that I thought perhaps I ought to go back to Holborn Road and try again. But then when I climbed out and looked into the alley, I realized it was too late."

"I don't think that made any difference," Trumpet said. "I doubt the strangler even saw him."

"Still, it was sloppy," Tom said. "But it's done, and we won't be trying this trick again. Did anyone see the villain? I couldn't see into the bottleneck from my post, though I was the closest. I didn't hear anything but Nashe's footsteps before Mr. Bacon cried out for help."

"I was looking straight into darkness," Trumpet said. "I didn't see Nashe until he was three steps into the yard."

"I saw someone enter the alley after we all hide," Catalina said. "He stop and hide also."

"That's lucky," Tom said. "Your sighting him, I mean. What did he look like?"

"I do not see much," Catalina said. "Only his shape. I saw him grab Mr. Bacon. He was a little taller and more broad in the shoulder. He wore a cap, puffy on top, and long hose like my lady's favorite."

"Galligaskins," Trumpet said. "Anything else? A short cloak? Boots?"

Catalina shook her head, frowning, her dark eyes sad. "It is my fault poor Mr. Bacon is hurt. I saw the villain. I saw him let Mr. Nashe pass him, but I said nothing. I should cry out, call the alarm."

"No, you were right," Tom said. "You couldn't warn us without spoiling the game. But that supports my suspicion, that the killer let Nashe go to wait for Mr. Bacon."

"That makes no sense," Trumpet said. "How could he know that Mr. Bacon would walk down that alley at that very moment?"

"He could have seen him sitting in the window, right over there." Tom pointed toward the front of the tavern. "He told us, as we were putting him to bed, that he'd stopped in for a slice of almond tart. He always sits at that little table at the front. The killer would have passed right by him, sitting there staring at nothing the way he does, and guessed that he'd be taking the shortcut home."

"A likely enough guess," Trumpet said, conceding the possibility, "since it's three times as far by Gray's Inn Road. He wouldn't know how long he'd have to wait, but he'd catch a bigger prize if he knew —"

"And another thing," Tom said, talking over her. "Mr. Bacon has a beard. A short one, like mine, but even in the dark, a strangler would feel it and know he'd grabbed the wrong man."

The others winced at that vivid description of Bacon's ordeal.

Tom tapped his finger on the table to help him sort the thoughts tumbling through his head. "Beards are a key to

this locked box; I can feel it in my gut. You are beardless."
He pointed at Nashe.

"It adds to my boyish charm," Nashe said, trying to look winsome.

"Edgar Stoke, also beardless," Tom went on. "John Little's beard is irrelevant, since he was falsely identified by his name, not his appearance."

"But Bacon's beard is like yours, close to the jaw," Trumpet said. "Inns of Court regulation. No beard of more than three weeks' growth allowed, tuppence penalty for noncompliance." She held out a hand for an imaginary payment, grinning.

Tom ignored her game, mentally reviewing all the beards he'd seen in the course of this commission.

"I will make beards for us, my lady," Catalina said. "But long is more easy, to hide the wire. We are too old to be boyish."

"Speak for yourself," Trumpet said. "Do we hook the wire over our ears? That sounds uncomfortable."

"Could we please stick to the subject at hand?" Tom demanded, glaring at the women. "All right, then. We've accounted for the victims, beard-wise. Now for the villain. Mr. Bacon said he felt the man's beard brush against his cheek as he murmured those last threatening words."

"What threatening words?" Trumpet asked. "I haven't heard about that."

Tom held up his palm. "Later. First, the beards. If you can feel a beard brushing against your cheek, it must be longish, don't you think? Longer than mine." He rubbed his jaw with the back of his fingers, testing.

Nashe and Trumpet shrugged. Trumpet said, "How could he tell the difference between a beard and a lace-edged ruff?"

"Very different," Catalina said. She was the only person at the table with any relevant experience. "And a short beard very different from a long. Short is brushy, stiff, like a painter's brush. Long is like hair, only not so fine."

"So, a short beard," Tom said. "Brush-like, not long and straggling. Our favorite suspect so far, Anthony Munday, has a short beard." He snapped his fingers at Nashe, making him jump. "Munday! I saw him outside Mr. Cecil's office on Tuesday afternoon. I forgot all about it."

"What was he doing there?" Nashe asked.

"How should I know? Waiting to see Mr. Cecil, same as I had been a few minutes before." Tom frowned. "That doesn't bode well, does it?" He caught Trumpet's eyes for another worried look.

"They think I can't see them," Nashe remarked to Catalina. "That I can't tell they have some dire notion about this person in a high place they suspect Mr. Bacon suspects. I suppose it's my smallishness or my boyishness, but —"

Trumpet clucked her tongue to silence him. "Let's go back to the beards. Short, brush-like, pointed or rounded. Who do we know? Anthony Munday, for one. Anyone else?"

Nashe held up his hand. "John Dando has a roundishly pointed short beard. He's about the same height as Munday as well."

"And I got the feeling he was jealous of you and Greene being hired by Canon Bancroft instead of him," Tom said.

"Who would hire him for that?" Nashe asked, incredulous.

"Who wouldn't? He's popular enough. Not like Greene, but he must envy Greene, now that I think of it. And he's the one who put envy on the table as a motive for Munday."

"I like Dando and Oatmeale," Nashe said sadly. "I see them nearly every day. I don't want to think either one of them would try to kill me, not even for a guaranteed run of a thousand copies."

"I don't want to think it either," Tom said, "but we have to keep an open mind. Apart from a general description, these men don't look anything alike. Dando's nose is long and narrow. Munday's plumps out at the end. His face is square and coarse, while Dando's is longer, more oval, less brutish."

Trumpet shook her finger at him. "You're letting your likes and dislikes color your observations. Mr. Bacon warned us about that."

"True," Tom said. "I retract the word 'brutish.' But you'd never confuse the two men."

"Not in daylight," Nashe said. "But at night? Or from a distance?"

They fell silent. Tom had no idea what occupied the others' minds, but a third man who fit the general description arose in his: Peter Hollowell, Mr. Cecil's secretary. He also knew about their trap. In fact, he knew nearly everything Bacon knew, thanks to Tom's garrulous reports. But in fairness, he'd had no reason to hold back and every reason not to — until now.

He couldn't share his new candidate with the others, especially not babbling Nashe. It veered too close to the dangerous waters keeping Mr. Bacon below deck. He'd think of a subtle way to test the wind first. For all he knew, Hollowell had been playing cards with sixteen worthy gentlemen on the nights Stokes and Little had been murdered.

"Tell me about those last threatening words," Trumpet said.

"Ah yes," Tom said. "It was while we were helping him into his nightshirt, after he'd drunk off his cup of wine with poppy juice. It hurt to speak, but he wanted to tell us everything before he fell asleep. Let's see. When he heard me shouting, the strangler loosened his grip, but before he let go, he said, 'Take this as a warning, Frank. Don't stick your neck out where it might get wrung.'"

"Ugh! Poor Mr. Bacon!" Trumpet shuddered. "No wonder he's locked himself in his chambers. But that changes everything." Her tone changed from sympathetic to disgruntled in the blink of an eye. "I've been thinking about it the wrong way for two whole days." She crossed her arms and glared green daggers at him.

"How is that my fault?" Tom asked. "This is the first chance I've had to tell you anything. You could have sent a note, you know, asking how he was. You don't have to throw pebbles in the window and whistle like a fool. You can just send a messenger, like everyone else. I suppose you were too busy weighing marriage proposals to trouble yourself."

"It isn't as easy as you seem to think. I can't just walk out the door and *whistle* for a boy. I have to —"

Nashe cleared his throat. "Returning to the problem of my imminent demise. Even if the strangler did catch his intended victim this time, I don't think he's going to give up. He'll try again. He'll come for me or Robert Greene sooner rather than later. Or you, either of you, or Mr. Luna here, which would be a great loss to all lovers of womanly beauty."

Catalina laughed, surprised, then gave him a measuring look. He grinned encouragingly.

"We can't stop," Tom said, ignoring their byplay. "We can't wait for Mr. Bacon either."

"What's your plan, then?" Trumpet asked, still indignant.

Tom ignored that too. He had enough balls to juggle. "Nashe, you had better keep out of sight. Stay here or in my chambers, coming and going only in broad daylight. No wandering around, no going home, and absolutely no popping in to the Goose and Gall."

Nashe grumbled, but didn't argue. It was his neck at risk, after all.

Tom went on, "I'll keep trying to scare up a witness. We have a better description now — slightly better anyway. It might be enough to prick someone's memory. I need a name."

"What about hats?" Nashe asked. "Munday usually wears a tall hat, but Mr. Luna says our man wore a cap Tuesday night."

"It's easier to keep a cap on in a scuffle," Trumpet said. Her ruffled feathers had smoothed. Now she seemed eager to add her bit of expertise to the discussion. She'd loved getting into scuffles during her year as a boy, which Tom had always had to pull her out of.

The memory made him sad. They'd had so much fun together, but those days would never come back. He gave her a tight smile, letting the sadness show in his eyes. She smiled, nodding to show she remembered too.

Tom sighed. They were together here and now, and that was something. He said, "I'll do what I can to track Munday's movements on Tuesday," then winced as the others laughed.

"What can I do?" Trumpet said.

"Nothing," Tom said, then raised both hands to appeal for mercy at her outraged glare. "I don't have anything for you. Try to think of something better. You have an advantage, you know."

"What?" She sounded suspicious, for no earthly reason.

"Your advisor, Lady Russell. She knows all sorts of people, high and low, here, there, and everywhere. You might ask her who she thinks Martin is, for a start."

"Oh. All right." Trumpet's delicate black eyebrows furled at that suggestion. "What did Mr. Bacon have planned before the attack? Anything?"

"He wanted me to go to the Stationers' Hall to study their records, to try to identify Martin's printer. He must be a master printer; Martin's works are good quality. And he must not be employed in a known shop."

"That's a clever idea," Nashe said. "Why hasn't anyone else thought of it?"

"Because they're not Francis Bacon." Tom shrugged at the obvious answer. "But I don't relish the prospect of spending who knows how many hours in some stuffy back room poring over a pile of dusty books."

"Why would they show them to you?" Trumpet asked. "You can't stroll into a guild hall and poke your nose into their records, can you?"

"Why not?" Tom grinned. "I can go almost anywhere. I tell them I'm on an errand for Francis Bacon — you know, the late Lord Keeper's son — and they dust off a chair and offer me extra quills."

"Huh." Trumpet seemed impressed. He would have thought she knew that already.

"I could do that job," Nashe said. "In fact, I'm a better man for it since I know more about printers and booksellers than you do."

"No, no, and no again," Tom said. "You stay out of the City. No Stationers' Hall, no Goose and Gall. You stick within the narrow space bounded by Gray's and the Antelope." He drew an oval shape on the table top, tapped the center of it, and pointed at Nashe.

"I could go," Trumpet said.

"Don't be silly." Tom softened it with a grin. "It isn't likely to do much good. I'll go, when Mr. Bacon sends me. Best you just stay home and wait for further news."

EIGHTEEN

The next day, Trumpet and Catalina left the house in Blackfriars to go shopping on London Bridge, or so they told Lady Russell. She sent a groom to accompany them, but he was happy to accept an angel and be sent to the Old Bell instead. Over the course of her months of penitential semi-captivity, Trumpet had learned which of Her Ladyship's servants could be bribed and which could not.

Their first stop was Field's print shop around the corner. She had spent the past week writing another short pamphlet, unbeknownst to Lady Russell, cobbling together bits and pieces from their earlier works. She didn't expect it to be published. This one was intended as bait.

She handed the package to Wat Whyting with a great batting of lashes, winning a sigh of longing. She did not ask any questions. She merely said, "Thank you for being so trustworthy a soldier in our godly campaign." Then she turned and walked calmly out the door.

As soon as they turned the corner, she put her thumb and forefinger between her lips and blew a shrill whistle. Two small boys trotted up — Jack and his brother, roundabout ten or eleven years old. She and Catalina had been interviewing urchins since their last manuscript delivery, stopping to talk with those who danced around them begging for a coin. Jack was far and away the brightest of the lot and had the added advantage of a ready assistant.

She took a penny from her purse and held it up. "He'll go after work, if he goes. You know who I mean."

Jack nodded. "The tall one with the spots. We know 'im."

"Good. It might not be tonight or even tomorrow, but he lives with his master above the shop. If he goes anywhere, follow him. Don't let him see you."

Jack scoffed at that improbability.

"Mark where he goes and what he does. He should be carrying a package about so big." She measured a thin book with both hands. "Mark what he does with it. He'll leave it somewhere or give it to someone. Mark the spot where he leaves it if you can and then come running, quick as a wink, to find me. Understood?"

Jack nodded, his eyes on the penny. She flipped it to him with a grin. "You'll get another one just like it when you come back with my news."

"Two," Jack said, pointing at his brother.

"One. Plus another farthing for every day you have to wait."

Jack nodded, grabbed his brother's arm, and scampered off, no doubt to buy food to munch on while they lurked about Field's shop. Trumpet didn't worry about their being noticed. Boys like that were ubiquitous, anonymous, and nigh invisible in their dirty clothes, which appeared to be dirt-colored to begin with.

She hoped they would succeed, and soon. This was her last idea.

She and Catalina hurried on to Lady Chadwick's house to change into their gentlemen's garb and then walked back past St. Paul's toward the Stationers' Hall. Trumpet planned to do Tom's job for him, using Mr. Bacon's name to get inside.

Nice of Tom to hand her that excuse, even while telling her to go home and sit on her hands like a good little girl. They'd be sacrificing their Thursday afternoon of tavern-hopping, but times of crisis demanded sacrifice. Let it never be said that Alice Trumpington failed to rise when the call for action sounded!

She couldn't allow Tom and Mr. Bacon to solve this case, not completely. She couldn't even let them get too close to Martin's minion, who must be the man who collected her oilcloth packages. There couldn't be more than one person delivering manuscripts to the printer and bringing printed copies back. Each visitor to that hiding place brought new risk.

She had an advantage, all right. She held one end of the string leading from Martin to his accomplices in her hands. If she could pull hard enough, she could draw out the murdering minion and somehow persuade him to stop before Bacon shifted his attention from his uncle to his aunt.

But she couldn't do brain work with a grumbling tummy. So they popped into a fishmonger's to slurp up a dish of scallops minced with pepper and cumin. Trumpet ate like a fastidious courtier under Lady Russell's critical eye but couldn't resist the savory aromas wafting from the stalls of the food vendors dotting the city. She and Tom had competed with each other to try them all during her glorious year at Gray's. Yet another pleasure denied to her on account of her sex and status. A tradesman's daughter could eat spicy fish standing in a pocket-sized shop. A gentle*man* could do it. But she, in her own persona, could not.

They leaned at the rough counter and accepted the wooden plates and spoons from the fishmonger's wife. The food was delicious and they ate in silence at first, listening to the fishmonger and his wife bicker placidly about whether the mackerels should be displayed noses out or tails out.

"When I am mistress of my own house," Trumpet said, "we'll eat whatever we want whenever we want it."

Catalina nodded, but added in a low voice, "Until you become pregnant. Then you will eat what you want and throw it right back up again."

Trumpet grimaced. "Don't tell me things like that. I have enough problems facing me right now. I'll cope with the future when it gets here."

"A new proposal today?" Catalina asked in the same low murmur. "I saw a letter came and you spoke an hour with my lady in her *estudio*."

"Another bad one." Trumpet picked out a piece of shell and flicked it out the window into the street. "Some baron in Lancashire with two sons already. He doesn't need me to supply a third, so he doesn't care about my rumored lack of virtue. He just wants his eldest to be an earl."

"Where is Lancashire?"

Trumpet shrugged. "Far away. Don't worry, we won't go there. Lady Russell was more offended than me." She sighed. "We still have the other one."

"It is good enough, the other one. He is young, Mr. Trumpet. I think he will be not so bad. I think he may be gallant and handsome and jolly for you."

Trumpet gave her a weary look. "He will be none of those things. Most importantly, he won't be Tom."

"Only one there is of Tom. But he will still be here. He must study his law."

Trumpet surveyed her empty plate, wondering whether to order another. Best not. "He may be here, but he won't be free either. Lady Russell has compiled a list of marriage prospects for him. She asked me if I knew any of them, which of course I don't. Merchant's daughters, mostly."

"Mr. Tom is too young to marry."

"He's the same age as my one acceptable suitor. But if Lady Russell can arrange a match for him, she'll get a nice fat fee from the bride's family. What's more, if she presents him with a plausible match and he refuses it, she gets to hold on to his estates until she extracts twice the value of the match from the rents."

Catalina shook her head. "You English have more ways to take money from each other with your law than any other peoples, I think."

Trumpet nodded. "Never become a ward of the state, my friend. It is a fate to be avoided at all costs."

The sole reasonable proposal she'd received hung over her head like the fabled sword of Damocles. She'd have to accept it soon, like it or not.

She paid for their food, and they went on to the Stationers' Hall. Bacon's name worked like a charm. In a matter of minutes, they were ensconced in a room as small and breathless as Tom had predicted.

No matter. Trumpet didn't have to study all the membership records for the past twenty years. She only wanted to look up two names: Richard Field and Walter Whyting.

Catalina sat on a stool on the far side of the small square table. She pulled a book at random from the shelf, opened it, and began sounding out words under her breath. Trumpet had taught her to read, but she could always use more practice, especially with handwritten documents.

Trumpet set to work, humming the song she'd been practicing at the music master's that morning: *Can she excuse my wrongs?* The singer lamented the injustice of his lover, but he addressed her plaint to Dame Fortune. *Shall I call her good when she proves unkind?* She intended to have it played at her wedding supper, as a subtle complaint about the injustice of her limited marital options.

She tilted her head sidewise to read the labels on atlas-sized volumes stacked three or four high. Richard Field had taken over the Blackfriars shop not long ago. Two years? Three? She found the volume for the past five years and wrestled it onto the tabletop.

She'd forgotten how much these things weighed. She'd done most of her studying at Gray's with Tom and Ben, strong young men who had done the labor of reaching and lifting fat law books without a second thought. She sorely missed those days. Benjamin Whitt continued to serve as her principal legal advisor, although now they communicated only in writing. And Tom — well, she'd have to get through many years and at least one husband before she could spend a tranquil afternoon reading in a library with Thomas Clarady again.

She banished the might-have-beens from her mind. She unpacked her writing instruments from the small leather case she'd used as a law student, then got Catalina to help her put two more volumes on her stool to raise her to a more comfortable writing height. Another useful trick she'd learned at Gray's. When she'd first proposed her scheme to her uncle — her terms for keeping a treasonable secret she'd stumbled onto — he'd warned her she'd be spending most of her waking hours trapped indoors studying. She and Tom had both had trouble adjusting to that regimen, but she'd discovered she had both an aptitude and an appetite for the work.

Even apart from the basic grounding in the common law, she'd learned a host of useful things that year. The secret life of boys and men, for example, hidden from most women, especially young ones. Martial arts, scaled to her size and strength. No need to list gambling, drinking, brawling, burping, and rambling about the city just to see what could be seen.

And she'd met Tom, whom she'd banished from her thoughts once already. It must be the smell of the ink, which she still bought from the same stationer. Would writing tools forever remind her of him? Now there was fitting punishment for her youthful folly.

She scolded herself again and turned her full attention to the task at hand. It didn't take long to find Richard

Field's name in the register. He had taken ownership of the Blackfriars shop along with his former master's widow this past year. He came from a town in Warwickshire with the grandiose name of Stratford-upon-Avon. It was probably little more than a damp patch on the banks of a muddy river. Lady Russell owned land in Warwickshire, but Trumpet didn't need to go that far to find a connection to the shop around the corner.

On the same page, however, she found something potentially more interesting. Field had two apprentices. One she'd never met and didn't care about, but here was the entry for Walter Whyting, the lovelorn youth who took charge of her special packages. He came from Northampton, the principal town of Northamptonshire, the county where Nashe had turned up his best hints about Martin Marprelate.

Now that was something. She noted the particulars in her commonplace book. Then she sat nibbling on the end of her quill, wondering what else she could look for while she was here. She wished there were a registry of writers, but they were too motley a group by their nature. However, licensed works were registered, presumably with the author's name along with the publisher's.

She hopped up and found another volume on a different shelf, labeled "Works, 1589. January – June." She had Catalina help her get the beast onto the table and began at the first page, looking for any of the writers involved in this affair.

She found Robert Greene and John Dando at once, in many entries. Greene published at a breathtaking rate. He must write faster than Thomas Nashe could spout nonsense. Most of the entries just paired authors and titles. Only a few added the printer or publisher. Frustrating!

She turned the page to scan the entries for the month of March, and Fortune's wheel took a turn in her favor at last. Here, in the record of yet another of John Dando's silly fables about the bay horse, she found the line, "alias Barnaby Snorscombe, gent., Northamptonshire."

Barnaby Snorscombe. No wonder he'd changed his name. That line had been written in a different hand and a slightly different color. Perhaps a clerk with a grudge against the successful Mr. Snorscombe?

Although a laughable name wasn't the only reason a pamphleteer might want to conceal his identity. Gentlemen didn't publish popular tripe, and they didn't publish for money either. They wrote short books expounding the secrets of fishing or growing fruit, religious meditations, or small books of poetry. They published to share their wisdom or flatter a superior.

Dando might be the black sheep of his family, fallen into dissolution and disgrace, condemned to scrape a living with his quill. Or more likely, a brother or cousin paid him a monthly sum to keep his bad habits away from home. Trumpet didn't care about that, although she wanted to meet the man more than ever. His family lived in Northamptonshire. She had no idea how large that county was, but it couldn't be pure coincidence that it kept appearing wherever they looked for Martin's minion.

She'd bet a shiny new angel Tom didn't know anything about Mr. Snorscombe and his Northamptonshire connection. She would move heaven and earth — and Lady Russell — to be there when he found out. She giggled while she scribbled the new tidbits into her book.

"You have found your name?" Catalina had been fanning herself with a sheaf of paper that had been left on the table. "May we go soon, Mr. Trumpet? It is hot in here." A light sheen of sweat gleamed on her forehead.

"I have." Trumpet closed the heavy registry book with a thump and packed up her writing materials, casting a glance around to make sure she hadn't left anything. They'd leave the books for the Stationers' clerk to put away.

She was close, very close. She could feel the tingling on the back of her neck that she trusted the way Tom trusted his gut. She knew more than he did, that much was certain. Another piece or two and it would all come together.

She cocked her head at her faithful servant. "Let's go get a drink. Let's have a look at that Goose and Gall we've heard so much about."

NINETEEN

The Monday morning after the incident, Tom made his usual attempt to gain entry to Bacon's chambers and received the usual rebuff. Pinnock had embraced his new role as King of the Castle, taking it upon himself to wad up the note Tom tried to thrust through the crack in the door and pitch it down the stairs.

"I give up," Tom said. "Tell him I intend to spend the whole day, today and every day henceforward, boozing and playing cards at the Antelope."

Pinnock shrugged. "Anyone could guess that."

Offended at that gross injustice, Tom dusted his hands together. "So be it." He gathered his dignity and stalked down the stairs.

He had no desire to spend the day squandering money he didn't have. He couldn't enjoy himself while wondering which poor scribbler would next be found dead in an alley with finger marks around his throat. Martin's minion had to be stopped and if Francis Bacon wouldn't do it, he would.

He could kill two birds with one stone, after a fashion, by sending a letter to Peter Hollowell inviting him to supper at the Antelope. In fact, he'd be killing three birds, or even four. If Hollowell were guilty, Tom ought to be able to catch a whiff of it — a hesitation, an overly hearty laugh, a shifting of the eyes. Better yet, an inability to account for his whereabouts on any of the crucial dates, which would be suggestive, if not definitive.

If Hollowell were innocent, which he most likely was, Tom stood to gain a new friend who happened to know a great deal about the Court of Wards. He had every reason to cultivate the man's acquaintance. Similar age, similar circumstances. Both bachelors. Both clerks in the service of influential courtiers. Well, not Bacon so much, but he sometimes had the ear of persons with influence. Forming a cordial alliance with Mr. Hollowell made sense given their mutual concerns and interests.

Furthermore, if Hollowell were innocent, or even if he weren't, sooner or later Tom would be obliged to report the attack on Mr. Bacon. In fact, Mr. Cecil might already know and be angry that he hadn't dashed straight over on Wednesday morning to inform him.

That had not occurred to Tom until this very moment. Now that it had, the need to correct the fault possessed him with a powerful urgency and an even greater reason to request a meeting away from Burghley House. Tom considered his phrasing for a moment, then wrote the invitation. He kept it short — less chance of offending — only hinting at news to be delivered.

He had his reply by midafternoon. He dressed with almost as much care as he would for an afternoon at the theater with Trumpet. At the last minute, he remembered that he had two things to discuss with his supper guest, assuming he turned out not to be a murderer. He ruffled through the box in which he kept everything pertaining to his wardship and stuffed the scroll with his proofs of age into the deep pocket of his hose.

He found Nashe at his usual table, even inkier than before, and hustled him out to spruce himself up in the scullery. He refrained from mentioning his suspicions. Let Nashe provide an objective view in the forthcoming conversation.

Mrs. Sprye willingly provided a handsome repast in her smallest private dining room. "Your friend Mr. Nashe has saved me a pretty penny, I don't mind telling you. He's caught two errors in bills from tradesmen and discovered four unpaid bills from lawyers who stayed in my rooms during Trinity term. Those varlets! See if I'll let them into my house again!"

Nashe returned with fresh cuffs and neatly combed hair. He entertained Tom with his adventures in innkeeping until Dolly, the serving wench, opened the door to announce their guest. Peter Hollowell strode in with a smile on his face and his hand already extended to shake Tom's. He'd trimmed his beard to a slightly sharper point and wore the dark red suit again. That was a useful color that ought to be allowed by Gray's Inn's restrictive dress regulations. Now that Lady Russell enforced his compliance, Tom was limited to "sad colors," meaning black, brown, gray, and puke.

When Nashe rose to be introduced, Hollowell's genial expression transformed into one of delight. He clasped Nashe's hand in both of his, exclaiming, "So *you're* the famous Thomas Nashe! The cause of all our toil and strife!"

He winked broadly at Tom, who couldn't help but chuckle at the man's infectious enthusiasm. He would swear before the Lord Chancellor and the Archbishop of Canterbury together that Hollowell had never laid eyes on Thomas Nashe before this moment.

They sat around the table and Tom poured wine, passing the water jug and sugar bowl around so each could adjust it to his taste. Hollowell shoveled in a heaping spoonful and stirred it in vigorously, grinning happily at Nashe all the while.

"I am a great admirer of your work, Mr. Nashe."

"I haven't got much to admire," Nashe said, pink-eared with pleasure. "I haven't found a publisher for my *Anatomy*, but I'm still hopeful. There's a few who haven't yet had a chance to turn me down."

"I can't imagine any bookseller worth his salt turning down a sample of your lively wit. If only you could tell them you were the author of *Martin's Mirror Mar'd*. That would change their tune, I'll wager." Hollowell sampled his wine and added more sugar. "Anatomy of what, if I may ask?"

"It's an *Anatomy of Absurdity*," Nashe said. "I wrote it at Cambridge, but I've freshened it up quite a bit."

"Absurdity!" Hollowell crowed. "I can't wait. But I hope that won't prevent you writing another one of your delicious Mar-Martin pamphlets? They're so engaging, and you know, I agree with my master. I think they've helped turned the tide of public opinion against that pernicious troublemaker."

Bacon had implied the opposite, that Cecil had agreed with him. Reckless and irresponsible were the actual words he'd used, but Tom kept that to himself. Hollowell was probably just being polite.

Nashe shrugged. "I suppose we'll stop when Martin is caught or, if that never happens, whenever Canon Bancroft gives up and closes his purse."

"Oh, he'll be caught eventually," Hollowell said. "Though I must confess I've enjoyed the 'battle of the wits,' if I may so declare it. It's all the more fun when you know the true names of some of the contenders, isn't it, Mr. Clarady?" He nodded at Tom to include him in the conversation. "One of the advantages of posts like ours, inside the halls of power. We're privy to secrets other men can only speculate about."

"That is an advantage," Tom said. "I'll confess to you in my turn that I've had a bit of fun lately in commons, when people start guessing about Mar-Martin's identity. I like to hint at someone untouchable, like Sir Walter Raleigh."

They all laughed at that idea. "He would do it for the mischief alone," Hollowell said. "Although of course he's far too honorable a gentleman."

"Of course," Tom agreed.

Dolly came back with another server to unload trays of food. A third servant set out a bowl where the men could wash their hands, handing them towels embroidered with a row of prancing antelopes. Once the other men were seated again, Tom carved the joint of lamb, doing an expert job. Lady Russell had insisted he learn the art, one of the essential skills of a gentleman and hard to practice at Gray's Inn.

The talk revolved around the food as they passed around plates of lamb, mackerel pie, and other dishes, friends among equals. Once they'd taken the edge off their appetites, the conversation expanded again into matters of greater concern.

"I understand you spent a fair amount of time in Northamptonshire, Mr. Nashe," Hollowell said. "I myself hail from that fair county, though I live in London now. I have part of a house in Blackfriars, convenient to the wharf. But my family's still in Northampton, and I know the county well."

"Do you?" Nashe said, casting a questioning glance at Tom, who merely smiled blandly. The place name had pricked his ears as well, but he didn't want to lead the discussion in any way. Let it go where it would, then he'd see where it brought him.

"Oh yes," Hollowell said. "My late wife was from a village called Little Everdon. Did you happen to pass that way in your ramblings?"

"Little Everdon? That's near Fawsley, isn't it?"

"It is." Hollowell nodded slowly, his expression turning grave. "I'm sure you remember that name. You mentioned it in your *Countercuffe*. Which I enjoyed at breakfast this morning, thank you very much."

Again, Nashe glanced at Tom before answering, but Tom happened — not by accident — to be lifting his cup to his lips.

Nashe kept the topic rolling. "I heard some gossip about a rumor about someone saying they'd heard of a printing press hidden in an outbuilding at Fawsley Manor a year ago, or perhaps longer."

Hollowell whistled noiselessly. "Vague."

"You never mentioned that before," Tom said. "It may be vague, but it could be worth following up on. If it had been a three-horned devil in the road, no, but people don't go around having visions of printing presses."

"I told you about that before," Nashe said. Then he cocked an eye at the ceiling. "Didn't I?"

"No, you didn't," Tom said.

Hollowell chuckled. "You couldn't possibly remember everything you heard or everyone you met. A lot of wild stories circulate in those country alehouses. It's the only form of entertainment people have, apart from reading month-old broadsides. You must have been a popular man, Mr. Nashe, with your lively wit and your friendly manner."

"People do tend to tell me things," Nashe said. "But by the time I get back to my little nest in the worst room at the top of the oldest house, I've had too many ales and heard too many tales to get it all written down."

"Then you kept a notebook," Hollowell said. "Wise man. Tell me, do you ever use a pencil?"

Nashe blinked at the sudden shift in topic. "Do you mean those little sticks of black lead?"

"I use them," Tom said. "Mr. Bacon told me about them. Very handy for writing standing up or in tight spots where you can't set out your inkpot."

Nashe wrinkled his nose. "I know the things you mean. But you get black stuff all over your fingers, and next thing you know it's on your nose and your cuffs . . ."

199

Tom and Hollowell laughed together. "You use a little holder made of wood," Hollowell said. "I'll send you one, as a gift in thanks for the pleasure you've brought me. And for the service you're doing for our queen."

"That's very kind of you," Nashe said.

Tom had to agree. Would a murderer send small gifts to a victim he'd failed to murder three times now? His suspicions had fairly well evaporated.

Hollowell's smile faded as he leaned in toward the others and lowered his voice. "But you know, Mr. Nashe, between you and me and Mr. Clarady here, I believe that particular rumor is worth pursuing. I don't personally know anything about printing presses at Fawsley Hall, or I would have spoken up long ago, but I can tell you that Sir Richard Knightley, the master of that hall, is one of the most outspoken Puritans in Parliament." He gave Tom a knowing look. "Your Mr. Bacon will know all about him. He's a hot one, I can tell you that much. He's been censured on more than one occasion. I'm not sure how these things are managed, but now that you put Fawsley Hall on the table, perhaps someone ought to give it a closer look."

"Sir Richard Knightley of Fawsley Hall," Tom said, committing the name to memory. "I'll keep my ears open. You know, everyone I've spoken to thinks Martin Marprelate is a member of Parliament. Sir Richard might just be our man. And if that's so, then Martin's minion will probably turn out to be one of his retainers or workmen. You don't have to be educated to run packages back and forth."

"Or to lurk in an alley waiting for your victim," Hollowell added darkly. "Let us both pass our suspicions on to our masters. As for Mr. Nashe, I didn't mean to suggest that you should rush right back out into harm's way. I pray that you are keeping yourself under Mr.

Clarady's watchful eye and not exposing yourself to any more risks."

"Speaking of risks," Tom said with a stab of guilt, "you'll think me the most unfeeling of monsters, but we've been so amiable here this evening, I completely forgot. I have some news that might distress you, though now I must hasten to assure you that all is well, more or less."

He told Hollowell about the trap and its unexpected result. The man's eyes and mouth rounded in horror at the description of the attack on frail Francis Bacon. At the end, he let out a great sigh of relief. "God's mercy, what a narrow escape! I don't blame him for staying in bed. Such frights are a serious hazard, very unbalancing to the humors, very dangerous. Has he consulted a physician?"

"I don't think so," Tom said. "He hasn't chosen to confide in me. Although I did accompany his servant to the apothecary on Wednesday morning." In truth, he'd followed Pinnock there and back, nagging him fruitlessly for details all the way.

"Good, good, good," Hollowell said. "I hope he'll be back on his feet soon."

They traded frowns, establishing their mutual concern for Francis Bacon's health and well-being. Tom refilled cups and pushed a dish of sweetmeats toward his guest. "I had an ulterior motive for inviting you this evening, Mr. Hollowell, if I may be so bold now as to declare it."

"How so?" Hollowell paused in the act of popping a sugared almond into his mouth.

"I did as you suggested and asked my guardian if she would find the money from my rents this year to pay my special livery. She refused, as you predicted. She said it would be too great a drain on the estate and that I ought to be grateful to have a wise head managing my lands while I complete my education."

Hollowell hummed sympathetically, then turned to Nashe. "I'm the feodary of Northamptonshire, did Tom tell you that?"

Nashe blinked, caught off guard. "He doesn't tell me much of anything."

"Well, that *is* the first requirement of a confidential secretary," Hollowell said, casting a wink at Tom. "You can expect him to ask more questions than he answers." He tilted his head and asked, "Do you know what a feodary is?"

"Of course." Nashe pointed his thumb at Tom. "He's not reticent on that subject, I can assure you. The feodary is the officer of the Court of Wards responsible for squeezing every last farthing out of the poor widows and orphans in his county."

Hollowell winced and held his side, pretending to be deeply wounded. "A hit! And a most feeling one. We squeeze only the rich widows, I promise you. The queen must have her penny, you know, and someone has to collect it. Then she locks it up in her treasure chest and is loath to let it out again. My Lord Burghley has many demands on his purse, as I'm sure you can imagine, with little help from the state." He leaned forward again, lowering his voice. "Confidentially, the Court of Wards supports everything in Burghley House, from the pot boys to the secretaries' salaries. Including mine" — he grinned — "which is why my master granted me the office. I try to be fair, but the law's the law."

"I don't blame *you*," Tom said. "In fact, I see it as something to aspire to somewhere down the road. I'm certainly learning a lot about wardship from the orphan's side of the coin."

"That's a healthy attitude," Hollowell said. "No sense in wallowing. Will you try for the general livery, then? A piecemeal suit, as it were?"

"What else can I do? I have my proofs of age, if you wouldn't mind . . ." He pulled the scroll out of his pocket and shoved it across the table.

"Let's have a look." Hollowell took the roll of paper and read it, unrolling a few inches at the bottom with one hand while re-rolling the top with the other in the practiced manner of a man who spent his days handling such documents. He hummed here and there as he read, finishing with a final, "Hmm."

Nashe flicked his fingers eagerly for a turn. "May I?" Hollowell glanced at Tom, who shrugged. Nashe might play the fool, but his magpie mind contained any number of odd facts. He might have something useful to offer.

Hollowell spoke to Tom, though his eyes remained on the scroll in Nashe's hands. "That might serve, Mr. Clarady. It just might."

"Might? Why only might?" Tom asked, dismayed. He thought he'd cleared this first hurdle with room to spare. "What's wrong with it?"

Nashe had been blurting out small bursts of laughter as he read. Now he rolled the scroll up again and tossed it to Tom, shaking his head, a wide grin on his face. "Ah, Mr. Clarady, my good friend! It must be gratifying to discover how well-loved you are amongst the residents of your birthplace."

"How not?"

"Well, let's see." Nashe held up two fingers. "Two of your witnesses remember the day of your baptism because each one had a sister die on the same day." He added two more, counting them off with his other hand. "One of those along with two others marked the day because they both broke their arms falling out of a cart. The same cart, one feels compelled to ask? Perchance the very cart in which the bodies of the fallen sisters were being carried to the churchyard?"

Tom narrowed his eyes to slits, pressing his lips together tightly.

"Last and most convincing," Nashe said, but in a kindlier tone, "four of your witnesses said they saw a great comet blaze across the sky on the day of your birth, confusing you, perhaps, with our Lord and Savior, although I fail to see the resemblance myself."

Tom groaned, defeated. "I paid nearly two pounds for that document, all things considered."

"It's a problem for everyone, Mr. Clarady," Hollowell said, "unless your parish church keeps extraordinary records, which few of them do. Special livery is the only sure course. You'll just have to find the money somehow."

"How?" Tom asked without hope of an answer. He took a long drink of wine, which tasted more bitter than it had before.

"Well," Hollowell said, still smiling that congenial smile in spite of dashing Tom's plans to pieces, "have you thought about marriage?"

Tom choked on his drink. Nashe laughed, wagging his finger. "An innkeeper, Clarady! What was I telling you?"

"I think you can look a little higher than that," Hollowell said. "You have a handsome income and a handsome face, if you don't mind my saying it."

Nashe rolled his eyes. "He hears it everywhere he goes. Women stand on rooftops crooning to him, like the sirens of Ulysses."

"I'm not ready to marry," Tom said. "I plan to wait until I pass the bar."

"That's sensible," Hollowell said, "although your guardian may have other plans. And your wardship problem could be solved without cost to you if she arranges a good match. You have friends in the legal profession. They could insist that a portion of your bride's dowry be paid in cash, sufficient to obtain your livery. That's especially likely if your wife is a merchant's daughter, for instance, with her wealth in goods and money rather than lands, although I should think a young man with your prospects could look as high as a knight's youngest daughter, assuming there's enough money there to satisfy your needs."

Tom slumped in his chair, hiding his face behind his cup, stunned by the whole unreasonable, unlooked-for prospect of acquiring a wife. *Who*, for the love of a merciful God? He didn't know many women, unless you counted whores and Trumpet, who was as far above him as the strumpets were beneath.

Trumpet or a strumpet? That would make a clever sonnet . . . but one he would have to burn the minute after he wrote it for fear that it would somehow fall into her hands.

Nashe and Hollowell chatted cheerfully about the sorts of women a man like Tom could expect to wed. They agreed on the virtues of widows with property and without children, if any such could be found who were young enough. Tom ignored them, lost in his own turbulent thoughts on the subject.

A server came in to ask if they wanted more wine. Only Nashe said yes, but there was enough left in the second bottle to satisfy him. The server removed a few plates and left.

Hollowell glanced out the small window. "I'd best be going home soon if I want to get there before dark. There's such a crowd on the river every evening; I'll have to wait forever for a wherry." He gazed across the table at Tom, plainly wanting to broach another topic. Then he cocked his head and said, "You haven't asked me . . . Well, if it were me, after what happened to Mr. Bacon on Tuesday night . . ." He waved his hand to erase that. "I'll simply be direct. You must have asked yourselves who knew about your plans? About that trap?" He pointed at Nashe. "The men you wanted to know, the ones you told, yes, but there is another." He turned his finger toward himself. "Me. And Mr. Cecil, of course, but you wouldn't dream of suspecting him."

Tom pointed at him too, shaking his finger as if at a slightly naughty joke. "Since you mention it, Mr. Hollowell, I did wonder. And now that you bring it up, I suppose I'd better go ahead and ask. Where you were on Tuesday night?"

Hollowell nodded like a schoolmaster pleased with a bright pupil. "That would be about nightfall, didn't you say?"

"Right on the cusp between day and night," Tom said.

"Well, I was at home, in my library, with my feet on a cushion and a book in my lap. Tacitus's *Histories,* if you care to know, though I'm afraid he can't vouch for me." He laughed, but broke it off. "Not a laughing matter. Unfortunately, I only have one servant, and I had sent him off to bed. But —" He shifted onto one buttock to reach into his pocket and drew out a small commonplace book, which he held up as if displaying a piece of evidence. "I keep a diary of daily events, important matters at work, anything noteworthy. I recommend the practice. You have no idea how impressed your master will be when you can conjure up the precise date and time of something that happened weeks ago."

"Did you note the dates of the other attacks?" Tom asked. "Stokes and Little?"

"And Greene's tumble down the stairs," Nashe put in.

Hollowell frowned at him. "Well, I didn't note that one since it wasn't clear whether it was an accident or not. But the others, yes, certainly. Let's see." He flipped a few pages. "Yes, here's Edgar Stokes, murdered on the twenty-second of July, under a waxing half-moon. That was a Friday. I noted the murder in its place when we learned of it. But I can prove where I was that night." He licked his lips and glanced at the two other men. "If I can rely on your absolute discretion."

"Absolutely," Tom said. "And I'll warrant Nashe's discretion as well."

Hollowell's gaze wandered a little, then settled on the tabletop. "I was with a woman. A — well, you know the sort of woman I mean."

Tom shot a quelling glance at Nashe and nodded somberly. "We understand, Mr. Hollowell. There's no need to explain. A man in your circumstances . . . Can you tell us her name?"

"Of course! I mean, I wouldn't want you to think I didn't know the woman's *name!*" Hollowell shook himself a little. "Well. You're men of the world, and I'm being overly nice. Her name is Moll Tiploft. She has a room in a house not far from the one where Edgar Stokes — where you used to live, Mr. Nashe. Your landlady may know her. She's a striking woman, Moll is. Red hair, round figure." He sketched her shape with his hands. "Find her. Ask her. She'll remember me. She's squeezed more than a few coins out of this old feodary, I don't mind telling you!"

They all laughed.

Tom had to ask one more question. "Do you really note your, ah, assignations in your diary?"

"Not as such," Hollowell said with an embarrassed grimace. "I make a little dot, large enough for me to know, but no one else would notice it. To be honest, I'm not sure why. I mark the phases of the moon too. Things to keep track of, I suppose."

Tom promised to find the redheaded whore and verify Hollowell's story when he went to question Stokes's landlady, which he ought to do tomorrow. Hollowell rose, declaring it time to venture downriver toward home. The others rose and shook hands all around, although Tom and Nashe were in no hurry to leave since they could walk home together tonight.

Hollowell paused on the threshold to cast a speculative look at Tom. "Speaking of women, Mr. Clarady, if you'll excuse my boldness. You really ought to be looking about you for a wife. Better to choose your own than wait for your guardian to do it for you. If she offers you a suitable match who doesn't happen to suit your tastes, you'll owe her twice the value of the marriage, meaning the girl's dowry, and be stuck in wardship until that sum is paid."

TWENTY

Francis Bacon sat on a silk-covered bench in the anteroom at Leicester House, waiting for the Earl of Essex, who was now at least thirty minutes late for their ten o'clock appointment. The delay must be caused by some vital business. Essex wasn't the sort of nobleman who kept one waiting simply to demonstrate that he could.

Francis had written to ask for the meeting yesterday. Though not quite ready to face the world — and Tom's questions — he knew it was time to get up and return to the fray. He'd been closeted in his chambers for a full week. Picking up the reins he'd dropped in that dark alley, he had also written to Sir Francis Walsingham, whose secretary had offered him a tentative appointment for Wednesday.

Francis had hidden under his covers for two days and nights after that hideous assault, indulging himself with poppy juice and merciful sleep. Gradually, the terrifying certainty that long-fingered assassins lurked within every shadow subsided, and his wits recovered their function. He sat up on a mound of pillows and managed to eat a solid meal.

It made no sense for his cousin to send an assassin to murder him. None whatsoever. He was no threat to anyone, having neither wealth nor position. No retainers, other than Tom and Pinnock. Not even a party in Parliament, where he always voted his conscience, often to his own disadvantage. No one would benefit from his death; rather a sad thought.

No. If the Cecils wanted to prevent him from gaining some measure of power, they need only continue on the course they'd already established: holding him at arm's length, quietly obstructing his advancement, granting him only the undignified chore of investigating murders with subtle entanglements.

As his terror melted away like a layer of lost wax, the note of surprise in his assailant's voice rang more clearly in his mind's ear. *"Bacon?"* he had said, a sharp uplift at the end of the word, suggesting he'd been surprised to learn the name. Francis had not been the intended victim. He'd walked unwitting into a trap set by his inventive assistant.

The trap was not entirely a bad idea. It nearly worked. It would have, if Thomas Nashe had lingered a few minutes longer at the Antelope. Francis had seen him there, jesting with the barmaid. He remembered that odd tooth and the tittering laugh. But he had never met the man until afterward, when he looked up from his bed and saw a stranger removing his shoes.

Tom should have introduced his guest the day he brought him into the house. He also should have told him about the trap. But Francis would have objected to both expedients, in which case poor Mr. Nashe might be lying in his grave by now.

He sighed. He hated this tortured case with its unpredictable hazards, both physical and political. He wanted it over and done with. He didn't think his cousin wanted to kill him, but he couldn't shake off the idea that Robert, with or without his father's collusion, was the spirit behind the whole Martin Marprelate controversy. Like a sore tooth, he'd have to keep worrying at it until the pain subsided, proving itself a fleeting irk, or the whole rotten structure was dragged out into the light.

A bustle sounded from the rear of the house. It resolved into a brisk clapping of feet across the marble floor. Then the young earl appeared in the anteroom, slowing but not stopping as he neared the bench. "Sorry to keep you waiting, Mr. Bacon." He crooked a finger. "Follow me."

"Yes, my lord." Francis hopped to his feet and followed. They entered the library, which seemed to be the earl's favorite room for receiving visitors, their footfalls abruptly hushed by the thick rush matting covering most of the floor.

The earl flapped a hand to indicate a chair, but Francis waited until he plumped himself down on a cushioned couch before sitting. The earl granted him a friendly smile, then sighed loudly as he stretched out his legs. He was dressed for riding in a kidskin jerkin and boots that reached to mid-thigh, leaving only an inch or two of silk stocking visible beneath his round hose. "I've been riding with the queen, and you know she obeys no clock beyond her own desires."

"Nor should she," Francis said. "Our duty is to await her pleasure, as mine is to await yours. A duty most gladly performed, my lord. I am grateful you could find time for me."

"I value your counsel, Mr. Bacon. I will always make time for you."

Essex leaned back and held out each foot in turn so his manservant could pull off the riding boots, replacing them with velvet slippers.

Francis waited until that task was done, then asked, "How fares Her Majesty?"

"Fit as a fiddle, thanks be to God. She'll live forever."

Francis caught a wry note in that prayer. "Would that it could be so, my lord."

The earl flexed his feet in the soft slippers. "Ah. That's better. By the way, Mr. Bacon. Have you heard that the Earl of Dorchester died? Out riding, it seems. He reportedly dropped down dead after a strenuous gallop. He hadn't been well and shouldn't have gone out, or so they say. A willful man, by all accounts."

Unlike every other earl in England, then. "I hadn't heard. But I believe I know his eldest son, or knew him. Stephen Delabere."

"Oh? I must have met him, but I can't recall his face."

"He isn't particularly memorable, my lord. He's about two years older than you are. He was at Gray's for a term, and one of my pupils. My assistant, Thomas Clarady, whom you've met, came along in Lord Stephen's train."

"And now your former pupil is the eighth Earl of Dorchester." Essex, only the second of that title, wrinkled his nose. "You should renew your acquaintance. Her Majesty suggested I might befriend him. She thinks he needs guidance."

"He does," Francis said. "I would echo her wise suggestion, my lord. The new Lord Dorchester lacks your sense of purpose and is quite malleable. He'll emulate whoever first attaches him. Better it should be a peer of your discipline and dedication to service."

Essex absorbed the compliments like a man drinking in fresh sea air. "I'll do it, then. I appreciate your advice, Mr. Bacon."

"I am always at your service, my lord."

"Now what can I do for you? Your note said you had a confidential matter to discuss."

"Yes, my lord. The utmost discretion is advisable."

Essex flicked his fingers at his servant, who bowed and left the room. "I'm listening."

Francis told him about his commission to identify the murderer of Canon Bancroft's anti-Martinist pamphleteers. The earl asked probing questions. They engaged in the usual speculation about the identity of Martin Marprelate, agreeing on the usual characteristics: educated, a barrister or a member of Parliament, protected by a person of influence with considerable resources; in particular, an estate large enough to conceal a printing press somewhere within its private bounds.

Francis led the young earl step by step toward the abyss into which he had been staring for more than a week. Then he waited, but not for long.

"Martin is obviously being protected by someone powerful enough to brave the risks," Essex said. "Someone who favors the Puritan cause. A man bold enough to harbor nonconformists who have been ejected from their livings or their colleges." He paused, an impish smile curving on his lips. "We say 'a man,' but this person of influence might well be a woman. Someone like your own mother, Mr. Bacon."

Francis smiled sheepishly. "It isn't her, thank God. I went home and looked."

"Did you? Ha-ha!" Essex shook his head, chuckling. "Mothers like ours are not to be underestimated, are they?" Then his expression grew serious. "We might look to another branch in your family tree for Martin's protector though, mightn't we? We know Martin has friends in high places. Perhaps those friends are high enough to be *privy* to the archbishop's *counsels* in advance."

A knot loosened in Francis's stomach at those words. The earl had leapt unassisted to the same frightful conclusion. "That thought had occurred to me also, my lord. Indeed, it is what brought me here. I wanted to take counsel with someone who would grasp all the implications and on whose discretion I could rely absolutely."

"I'm glad you came to me." Essex teased the curls in his long ruddy beard with his thumb and forefinger. "Martin has created a tremendous distraction, hasn't he? Like a clown dancing atop a wall taunting the soldiers beneath him while the opposing forces sneak through the postern gate."

"A very apt image, my lord."

"But what is Martin distracting us from?" the earl continued. "What is his protector trying to hide?"

"Hide or merely color? Changes of some sort, perhaps. Something, or someone, whose introduction might arouse comment in quieter times."

Essex met Francis's eyes. "I have noticed that very thing. A person now always sitting by the wall at Privy Council meetings, to which even I am not invited."

Francis nodded. "Were you aware that my lord uncle has shifted the burden of managing his intelligencers onto my cousin's shoulders?"

"A crooked base for so weighty a burden. I suspected as much when my secretary began to receive responses from Cecil's secretary instead of Lord Burghley's." Essex's brown eyes narrowed. "And that suggests another reason for supporting, if not fomenting, Martin's distracting antics."

"What reason, my lord?" Francis almost held his breath.

"We know who sits at the right hand of the queen. Our good Lord Treasurer, who has done more than anyone to foster peace and prosperity. But who sits at Her Majesty's left?"

"Archbishop Whitgift," Francis answered.

"Just so. And the Church answers to no one but the queen, not even the Privy Council. Whether or not the father is troubled by that imbalance, the son will see the established church, with its loyal hierarchy of prelates and its army of priests, as a rival center of power. Your cousin has little interest in the details of religious doctrine. His faith, in my perception, is of a cooler, more intellectual nature. Like yours, Mr. Bacon."

"I believe God created us to be good," Francis said, "and to use His gifts to better ourselves, not to wrangle about robes and incense."

"Nor to debate theology with one's monarch." Essex smiled. "Your cousin is wise enough to avoid that heresy, but he is exquisitely sensitive to subtle shifts in the balance of power. I know him better than you do, having grown up under the same roof."

The Earl of Essex had lost his father at the age of eleven, becoming a ward of the queen. Burghley, Master of the Court of Wards, skimmed off the noble orphans, rearing them in his own home while enjoying the fruits of their vast estates.

"That's true, my lord," Francis said. "I had forgotten. Your observation is very astute. Robert has always been alert to nuances, to signs that this one or that is guarding some secret."

"Whitgift's three articles — those insufferable oaths — have created far more disruption than Martin Marprelate."

"Martin is an answer to the oath," Francis said. "If the archbishop hadn't pushed so hard, Martin wouldn't have been inspired to push back."

"I believe you're right, Mr. Bacon. But college chaplains are not the only ones who want to give old Whitgift a shove. Whether your cousin created Martin or not, he wouldn't hesitate to make use of him to weaken the archbishop's authority. Partly because a weaker church means a stronger Council, but also to distract the Church faction on the Council until Cecil is firmly seated among them."

"I suspected that," Francis said. "But to be honest, my lord, I feared my own ancient resentments might have tainted my opinion."

"I have no such resentments," Essex said airily, "and I see the same contrivance. In fact, now I think of it, I see more than an opportunity to give old Whitgift a slap in the face. I see a scheme to disrupt an opposing power base. Martin is like a rising windstorm, blowing sharp seeds of rebellion across the landscape. Some will take root, but even a few scattered sprouts of sedition are enough to justify gathering more power into the Privy Council's hands — a Council unbalanced by a superfluity of Cecils."

"There are nineteen good men on the Council," Francis said, somewhat alarmed by the earl's active imagination. "And my cousin is scarcely even an apprentice at this time."

Essex waved that off. "Cecil is content to play a long game. He always has been. A word here, another word there, and a minor rift becomes a breach. Likewise, Martin may be a short-lived tempest, but he leaves his opponent battered in his wake. Cecil sees the old guard waning. None of them will last another decade. He's positioning himself to be in the seat closest to the throne when the time comes."

Francis frowned, even further alarmed, but before he could frame a suitably courteous objection, the earl continued, warming to his theme.

"Close to the throne and thus able to influence the choice of its next occupant." Essex sat back against the brocade cushions as if he'd just experienced a profound revelation. "I don't doubt that's what the clever rogue is plotting. He must be opposed, now, before he's able to establish himself too securely."

"That seed has barely touched the soil, my lord," Francis said, picking up the earl's metaphor. He must curtail this line of thought before it grew even farther out of proportion. "Harsh winds or untimely rains may yet prevent it from flourishing. And the royal gardener, as you yourself have said, is in perfect health with many years yet to choose her own plantings."

The earl acknowledged that truth with a tilt of his head. "Even so. I would far rather see you on the Privy Council, Mr. Bacon, than that pygmy."

Francis made a droll face at the nickname. He rarely used it himself, but he liked hearing it. "I thank you for your confidence, my lord, but it is unlikely in the extreme. Besides, I have set my feet to climb the winding stair of the legal profession."

"Then I will do my utmost to help you climb it swiftly."

"Your Lordship is most generous. I hope I may never disappoint you."

Essex nodded, then quirked an eyebrow at Francis. "He won't help you, you know. Your uncle. He fears your brilliance would cast his son into the shadows. He'll keep you dangling for as long as you allow it, but he'll never give you any real power."

"Wise advice, my lord." The same advice his mother had been giving him for years.

Francis took his leave. He crossed the Strand with a spring in his step, buoyed by the earl's encouragement. "I will do my utmost." The words rang in Francis's ears like celebratory bells while clerkships in important courts and even greater possibilities danced through his mind.

The earl was young, and his utmost wasn't much as yet, but he would grow in power and influence as the years went by. The queen regarded him almost like a son. As they both grew older, she would undoubtedly lean on him more in matters of state.

Most of her old supports, like Lord Burghley and Archbishop Whitgift, were older than she. Whitgift had no child to advance, but Burghley had and seemed to have decided the time was ripe to give Robert a strong push forward. Whether the Cecils had started the Martin commotion or not, they did seem to be taking advantage of it.

And of him. His uncle had given him the dirty job of catching whichever of Martin's accomplices had acted beyond his writ. His Lordship knew Francis could be trusted to keep whatever sensitive secrets he might stumble across in doing that unsavory job. His Lordship knew he could count on Francis's loyalty, and how not? He was family, and since his father had died, he had no other advocate. Or hadn't, until today.

Francis had spent years knocking on a door that had always been barred to him, though he hadn't been willing to see it. Now the scales had fallen from his eyes, and another door had opened. The possibilities filled his mind again. He had multiple talents, many skills. He was fitted for many different posts. Think of the things he could achieve, the good he could do, with sufficient scope and an understanding patron!

He fairly bounced on his toes as he walked across Holborn, but when he turned up Gray's Inn Road, his steps slowed again. The earl had taken his speculations about the Cecils' involvement with Martin Marprelate farther than Francis might have wished. Too far? Had he created a conflict where none had been?

Essex and Cecil had grown up under the same roof and had never liked each other. Conflict lay between them, quiescent, like a dish of oil in a cool place. Had he just set a match to it?

Essex had no role in the Marprelate controversy. His opinion had not been sought by anyone else. Francis had violated the confidentiality of his commission — implied, but binding nevertheless— in discussing it with him. But if he hadn't gone today, he wouldn't have heard those wonderful words: "I will do my utmost to help you climb."

The branching and re-branching ramifications of that short conversation tangled in Francis's head, creasing his brow, roiling his tummy. He nearly tripped on the threshold stepping into his own house. He climbed the stairs to his chambers and walked right past Tom's question-filled face to his bedchamber, where he turned the key in the lock. He stripped down to his shirt, added three drops of poppy juice to a cup of wine, and climbed right back into bed.

TWENTY-ONE

A middling boy in a gardener's straw hat tugged at Tom's sleeve as he left the hall after dinner on Saturday and handed him a folded letter bearing Trumpet's seal. He bid the boy follow him to his chamber to wait for a reply.

The note said that Trumpet was sneaking out that afternoon and wanted him to meet her at the Goose and Gall at two o'clock, whence they would go forth to scour up witnesses to the two murders. Tom considered refusing the peremptory command, but in truth, he liked nothing better than prowling London's streets with his best friend at his side. That the said friend was also the most beautiful woman he had ever known only added spice to their adventures.

Besides, how many more adventures would they have? Their days together were numbered, and that number got smaller every day. He dashed off his agreement and gave the gardener's boy a ha'penny for his trouble.

He made sure to get to the Goose early and was pleased see the place half-empty. Not even writers could bury themselves in a dim tavern on such a balmy summer day. Tom got a jug of ale and two cups and sat at Nashe's favorite table, in the same spot as before, where he could watch the street. The serving wench brought him a dish of cobnuts and lingered, trying to stimulate other appetites, but he shook his head and turned back to the window. Trumpet, even in men's clothes — even with that silly little false moustache — outshone other women as the moon outshone the stars.

In the event, he almost failed to recognize her, striding along behind a group of nobodies. She was alone, for one thing. She'd grown a beard, for another. A short black one with a rounded point. Catalina must have made it from trimmings of her mistress's hair.

"That beard is an affront to all mankind," he said before she even got her round arse planted on a stool.

"I like it."

"You always go one step too far, Trumpet. Both good taste and successful deception require restraint."

"Easy for you to say. Catalina thinks my face is getting more womanly, so I need more concealment. I can't wear muddy smudges if I'm dressed like a gentleman."

Tom studied her face. Or rather, he drank in her features like a camel storing up water for a trek across a sandy waste. "It's ridiculous. It won't stay on. And it makes you turn your head stiffly, like you're afraid to jostle whatever it is that's keeping it in place."

"I'll get used to it. I can't take it off now." She fiddled with something behind her ear, pretending to scratch an itch. Then she flashed him that dazzling smile that made his heart stop for a moment. "Enough about my cursed beard. What's afoot? Has Bacon poked his delicate nose out of his room yet?"

"Briefly." Tom shared what little Bacon had told him about his visit to Lord Essex, which wasn't much more than the bare fact that he had entered the house and found the earl in good health. She didn't seem surprised about the one real piece of news, that Stephen Delabere had succeeded to the earldom of Dorchester.

She merely shrugged. "My Lady Russell must have mentioned it."

"Easily forgotten with so many noblemen crowding outside your door." Tom hated the jealousy in his tone, but he couldn't help it. No matter how hard he studied, how loyally he served, or how bravely he performed each and every difficult task set before him, he could never aspire to Trumpet's hand. One of these days, very, very soon, another man would take that hand and lead her to his bed. On that day, Tom intended to get very, very drunk.

"A line from here to Dover," Trumpet said. She didn't sound very happy about it. Their eyes met and skittered apart.

"Where's your trusty comrade?" Tom drew his knife from the sheath at the small of his back and used the haft to crack a couple of nuts. He pushed one toward Trumpet and cracked a few more, glad to have something to do.

"Guarding the door to my bedchamber, pretending that I'm ill and need solitude."

"Will Lady Russell believe that?" Trumpet had the constitution of a Dartmoor pony. She was never sick.

"She spends many days in bed herself. You know how bad her back is. She won't pry."

Tom found another fault. "You shouldn't walk around the city by yourself."

She gave him a weary look from under arched black eyebrows and took another cracked nut, picking out the meat to nibble. "What else is new? It's been nearly a week since Mr. Bacon's attack. Haven't you learned anything?"

"Not much." Tom told her about his short-lived suspicion of Peter Hollowell and the supper they'd enjoyed at the Antelope.

"Why wasn't I invited?"

Tom shrugged, holding up both hands. He couldn't include her in everything. Besides, her presence often made things more complicated. She knew that. She also knew that he knew that she knew, so why fuss?

To add to his misery, presumably. "I wanted to talk to the man in an informal setting. I had thought about asking him out to supper before I suspected him. He's Robert

Cecil's principal secretary, you know. And a feodary in the Court of Wards. Also a wifeless man with an exacting taskmaster, not much older than I am. He could be a friend — a useful one."

"Nice to make new friends." Her tone dripped acid like a pierced lemon.

"You could make new friends. You should be at court right now, living with the other daughters of lords, making friends with people of importance."

"I don't like people of importance."

"Then don't marry one." Tom cracked a few more nuts with more force than necessary, sending shards of shell flying.

She gave him an inscrutable look from beneath lush black lashes. "Maybe I won't." She picked the best piece of nut out of the wreckage and studied it before popping it into her mouth. "This useful secretary of yours. You must have suspected him because he knew about our trap. What made you decide he wasn't the one?"

"I like him." Tom shrugged. "He was so forthcoming about the whore he was with the night Stokes was murdered." He pointed his finger at her. "We should visit her today. And he gave us probably the best bit of information we've gotten so far, about a village in Northamptonshire called Fawsley. One of the ones Nashe visited."

"What about it?"

"It turns out to be the seat of a well-known Puritan, the hottest one in Parliament, according to Hollowell. Sir Richard Knightley." Tom snapped his fingers. "Mr. Bacon will know him. Now that he's talking to me again, maybe it will make him think of something I can go find out or someone else I can talk to."

"Maybe he'll leap up and shout, 'God's bollocks! Sir Richard So-and-So is the real Martin Marprelate. How could I fail to see it before!'" Trumpet sounded disdainful, for reasons of her own not worth pursuing.

"He might," Tom said, "although without the leaping and the cursing. But Sir Richard has all the qualities everyone thinks Martin has. He's rich, he has influence, he has a big estate. He's an outspoken leader of the Puritan party in the House of Commons. And Nashe picked up something that pricked his ears."

"About Knightley?"

"Not the man, but his village. Fawsley."

"Hmm."

"It isn't much, I grant you. But Hollowell offered to sit down with Nashe after we catch the strangler and put together what they both know about Northamptonshire — all the bits and pieces. Would Martin's minion do that? My gut says no."

"The gut has spoken." Trumpet smiled. She trusted his gut too. She turned to survey the low-ceilinged room. "I can't say I think much of this place. Who would want to spend — What ho! I spy a roundishly pointed beard, borne by a man of average height, coming in from the back."

Tom looked in the direction of her pointing chin. "Ha. John Dando. Let's see if we can get him to confess to strangling Mr. Bacon on Tuesday night."

Trumpet grinned. "I'll wring it out of him." She could do it too, with Tom's help.

Dando walked up to their table, looming over them. "Mr. Clarady, what a pleasant surprise. I assumed you'd gone into hiding with your friend Nashe."

"No one's trying to strangle *me*. Join us. We've stolen your favorite table."

"It is *a* table," Dando said, taking a stool and turning to Trumpet with a courteous smile.

Tom made the introductions. "Mr. Trumpet is helping me with my inquiries since Nashe is unavailable."

Anna Castle

"Pleased to meet you, Mr. Snors — er, Dando," Trumpet said in her man's voice, a couple of notes lower than normal. "I'm an *enormous* admirer of your work. I can't wait to read the next adventure of Bankes's bay horse." She tilted her head back and brayed.

Whatever she was up to, she was overplaying it. Dando's eyes had taken on a hard gleam, and his upper lip quivered as if she'd offered him a ball of fresh horse dung.

"How is old Nashey?" he asked Tom. "Still breathing, one hopes?"

"I haven't seen him," Tom said. "He's in hiding, you know."

Dando rolled his eyes. "All of London knows. He was in here Monday afternoon telling anyone who would listen, which wasn't many, that he had found work sorting papers at some hole in Holborn, where he also met a kindhearted gentleman of Gray's Inn who offered him a place to lay his head. Scribbling for food is within Nashe's scope, but that last part is hard to swallow."

"Nashe has his charms," Tom said. He signaled to the serving wench to bring another cup and poured a drink for the pamphleteer.

"Charms invisible to the average eye." Dando accepted the cup with a nod. He wore a large gold ring on his right hand. "An inquiring sort of man, such as myself, might wonder why a person going into hiding would boast so loudly of that secret location. Asking for trouble, an observant man might note."

"A man such as yourself," Trumpet said, nodding. "A man of experience, a man who has walked many paths in his life, both high and low." A mischievous light glimmered in her green eyes, but Tom could not fathom what inspired it.

Dando, however, seemed to follow her drift. His lip twitched in that semi-snarl again. "If you ask me, Nashe has been tempting fate since he arrived in this city. Who is

224

he? Nobody. What has he achieved? Nothing. And yet he's managed to make himself the center of attention with this supposed plot against his life. He'd best beware. Such plots have a way of misfiring."

That almost sounded like a threat. Tom cracked another nut with the haft of his knife, noting the way Dando's eyes shifted toward the blade. Tom used the blade to push the small treat toward the other man. "Are you familiar with Holborn and environs, Mr. Dando?"

"I've been there." Dando picked out a nut meat and chewed it. "Rare good fortune, don't you think, for Nashe to meet an Inns of Court man at the very hour of his need."

"What are you suggesting?"

"Not suggesting, Mr. Clarady. Merely observing. I'm the observant sort, remember?"

"He's the sociable sort, our Nashe. He makes friends everywhere."

"Even places you wouldn't think he'd go." Dando turned his sneering smile toward Trumpet. "Do you have friends at the Inns of Court, Mr. Trumpet?"

"Doesn't everyone?" Trumpet leaned on one elbow, shifting her glittering gaze from Tom to Dando and back. "Nashe's problem will be solved in a matter of days. We did learn one thing before he went into hiding. He is certain he crossed paths with Martin's minion somewhere near Fawsley in Northamptonshire. Do you know anyone in that locality, Mr. Dando?"

Dando's expression hardened. "Doesn't everyone?"

* * *

"What was that all about?" Tom demanded as soon as they were out of earshot of the tavern's open windows. Dando had gotten up and walked away with the feeblest of excuses. Tom had tossed a few coins on the table and herded Trumpet out the door. She'd spoiled what chance

225

they had of learning anything from that source. They might as well move on.

"Just testing the man's temper," Trumpet said. "That question about Northamptonshire made him angry. Did you see that?"

"You angered him from the start with that obvious fumble over his name. What did you call him? Mr. Snores? You won't gain favor with a writer by telling him his work is boring."

"Snores. That's funny!" Trumpet giggled. "I never said that."

"Yes, you did, and you did it on purpose. What's your game, *camarade*?"

She gave him that little toss of her head and shoulder that made him want to— He grabbed her arm and pressed her against the plaster wall of whatever house they were passing. He looked down at her, struggling to maintain a stern expression — an impossible feat with that absurd fringe draped around her chin.

"Tell me," he growled. Then he gave her a half smile that showed his full dimple. She loved the dimple. And the growl.

She bit her lip and sighed deeply, her chest rising and falling. The challenge in her tiger's eyes helped in nowise to temper his frustration. He had to kiss her to stop that ruby smirk, but he couldn't risk kissing a bearded man on a public street. People gawked out of windows and burst suddenly around corners.

He stepped back and held up both hands in surrender. "Just tell me what you're up to, Trumplekin. We're partners, aren't we?"

"For today, anyway." She drew in a long breath and let out another sigh with a different meaning. "It's nothing. Just having fun."

They locked eyes, understanding and not understanding each other in equal, maddening measure.

Tom broke first. "Let's go see Edgar Stokes's landlady. She won't know anything, but it has to be done."

They started walking again, not bothering to talk, which made a restful change. Tom focused on finding the right house in this maze of closely packed tenements. He'd gotten directions from Nashe but still had to ask for help several times. One of the gossips standing in a doorway cackling at another across the alley scanned Tom from head to toe, smacking her lips. "That room's bad luck, sweetikins. Why'n't ye come in and try what I've got to offer?" Her cackle followed them around the next corner.

Mrs. Darby was not one of that breed. She was a thin, pinch-faced woman in a patched kirtle and dirty apron. She let them up to see a pocket-sized room at the top of her house, empty but for the flea-jumping rushes on the floor, a sagging cot pushed against the wall, and a cracked chamber pot in the corner.

"I can't get another lodger," she said fretfully. "Folks think my house is cursed. Why me and not the other, I don't know. How'm I supposed to get by? Catch that man, good sirs, if it *was* a man and not a devil."

"It was a man," Tom said, "and he'll hang, I promise. Did you see or hear anything that night?"

"No, nor any of the neighbors. People around here don't stick their heads out their windows every time they hear a bit of noise at night."

Tom nodded. He'd expected no more.

"But you know, remembering back, I think I saw a man skulking around just before nightfall. A gentleman, by his clothes." She looked from Tom to Trumpet and back again. "Not so tall as you, sir, nor yet so small as you, sir, if you'll forgive me. He wore a beard too. Not so long as to call it a long beard, good sirs, nor yet so short as yours, sir." Another nod at Tom.

"I see," Tom said, edging toward the front door.

She clutched his sleeve. "He had brownish hair, I should say. Not as dark as this gentleman here, sir, but nothing like as fair as yours, sir." She folded her hands across her belly and beamed at them. "Look for that one, good sirs. You can't mistake him."

Tom muttered vague courtesies until the door closed behind them. He avoided Trumpet's eyes until they were well away, then they both collapsed in howling laughter, holding on to a wall for support. As the laughter spent itself, Tom wiped his eyes with a knuckle. "I hope I can remember all that for my report to Mr. Bacon."

Trumpet grinned at him. "At least we can be certain we didn't do it. We have a witness."

Tom turned around twice, not sure which way they'd come. "God's breath! I forgot to ask her where Moll Tiploft lives. It's around here somewhere."

"We'll find her." She looked up the street and pointed at a man hanging out a window, smoking a long pipe.

"Everyone knows Moll Tiploft," the man said with a broad wink. He gave them directions to a house one street over, opposite an alehouse. A slate-faced woman opened that door and pointed them up the stairs. "First floor."

Upstairs, they found the door wide open, so they walked in and found a redheaded woman with a lush figure displayed by a loosely laced bodice and low-cut shirt. She sat on a rumpled bed with a jug and a single cup on the floor by her bare foot. Several wooden crates stood about the floor, half-filled with jumbled garments.

"No business today," she said, clearly more than a little drunk. "I don't do threesomes anyway."

"We're not here for that," Tom said. He walked in to stand near the stone hearth that looked too clean ever to have held a fire.

She looked him up and down with a crooked smile. "Send the little one away and I might change my mind."

"We want to ask you two questions," Trumpet said, standing halfway between Tom and the harlot with her hands on her hips. "Do you know a man named Peter Hollowell?"

"Long Pete? He's my best customer."

"Was he here on Friday night, two weeks ago? There was a half-moon?"

"When that man was murdered, you mean. I heard about that." She picked up her cup and took a deep drink, coughing a little as she set it back down. "Yes, Peter was here. I remember the night well. He's my best in more ways than one." She winked at Tom. "And we had the full moon shining in the window, adding to the pleasure. White skin under silver light is any gentleman's delight." Her words were enticing, but her tone and her eyes were flat.

"Did he stay all night?" Tom asked.

"He spends the night when he likes, though he's out and gone at the crack of dawn."

That wasn't exactly an answer. "Did you hear or see anything in the street that night?"

"I was working, I told you. They don't pay me to look out the window." She bent to refill her cup, making sure Tom got a good look at her breasts. But when she sat back up, she said, "Don't bother to come back. I'm moving to Rye, where I'm from. I've got enough to buy my own house now, and I'm tired of London."

Tom followed Trumpet down the stairs. The slate-faced woman rose from a chair near the window, where she'd been mending stockings. Tom asked if she had seen or heard anything on the night the man had been murdered nearby.

"I'm deaf after dark," she said, opening the door to let them out and closing it on their heels.

"Where now?" Trumpet asked. "We aren't getting very far."

"We're getting nowhere. Let's go to the White Hart and find out if anyone saw Robert Greene being pushed down the stairs last Saturday night."

They pressed on eastward toward the inn on Bishopsgate and asked the barman if he remembered the night Robert Greene took a tumble down the stairs.

"I remember it. That drunken whoreson owes me for two cracked bannisters." He glared at them. "Unless you can prove someone really did push him and make *that* whoreson pay me the cost of repairs."

"I'll do my best," Tom promised.

They walked over to examine the grand oak staircase in the center of the large room, which was divided into sections by massy oak beams. They found the bannisters in question on the landing. Sure enough, two had long cracks running up from the base. That must have hurt.

Tom gave one of the uncracked bannisters a tentative tug. It didn't budge. He'd have to put his back into it even to loosen one of these well-made supports. These stairs had been built by a master carpenter out of quality materials and then aged in place for a hundred years.

Tom continued on up while Trumpet lingered on the landing, looking up and down to assess the distance. As he reached the top, Anthony Munday loomed out of nowhere, going down. They stopped and glared at one another. Tom scrambled for something to say, but before a word could escape his lips, Munday pushed past him with a loud grunt.

"Nice fellow," Trumpet said, climbing up to join him. "A new friend?"

Tom murmured, "That was Anthony Munday."

"Him?" Trumpet craned her neck to catch a glimpse as the man reached the bottom of the stairs and crossed toward the front door. "What did he say to you?"

"Nothing. He just grunted at me like a hog with a burr up its arse." He shook his head at Trumpet as they ambled into the public room. "You know, I don't believe that man likes me."

"That must be a novel sensation for you, Tomkin," a familiar voice sounded nearby.

Tom whirled around. "Kit!"

Christopher Marlowe sat at a table by the fireplace, leaning against the wall, balancing his chair on two legs. He tilted forward and rose to his feet in a well-practiced movement, walking over to clasp Tom in a hearty hug.

Tom clapped his old friend's shoulders, then stood back to see how time had treated him. They'd come through a period of mutual suspicion during Tom's months as a spy in Cambridge, but a night together in a small cell and the discovery of some mutual enemies had created a lasting bond.

Still the same old Marlowe, mostly. He still wore his brown hair cut bluntly above his ruff. His brown eyes still had that gleam in their depths — part mockery, part secret knowledge. He'd grown a short beard, slightly rounded under the chin. Still lean, still rangy, but somehow looking better fed. Certainly better dressed than the shabby robes he'd worn at Cambridge.

"You haven't changed," Tom said.

"Nor you." Kit turned toward Trumpet and pointed his finger, a curious smile playing on his lips. "But you . . . you're different, unless you're not who I think you are."

"I'm the same," Trumpet said in her normal woman's voice. Nobody sat close enough to hear them or seemed to care about them in the least. She tilted up her chin. "I have a new beard."

"So I see." Marlowe shot a droll glance at Tom. "It's different, Lady, er . . ."

"Mr. Trumpet," Tom informed him.

Marlowe chuckled and waved at his table. "Join me."

They sat around the table. Tom pushed the remains of a meal — a plate with a heel of bread and a heap of small

231

bones — into the center and pointed at the book lying open, facedown. "Same old Kit, sitting next to the fire, even when it's not lit, and reading while you eat. And still on college time. I thought famous playwrights supped at a later hour, in the company of ardent admirers."

"My admirers don't know I'm back yet."

"Back from where?" Tom asked, not expecting a straight answer.

He didn't get one. "Here and there. Doing this and that. I'm off again in a day or two."

"I *loved* both *Tamburlaines.*" Trumpet put her elbows on the table and grinned at Kit with sparkling eyes. Tom would be eaten with jealousy by her expression if Kit were a man who liked women. "I must have seen them three times each."

She and Kit had discovered themselves to be kindred spirits when they'd met in Cambridge. She picked up his small jug and peered into it. "Ale? That's not good enough for this reunion." She hopped up to bellow down the stairs, "A bottle of sack and three cups! Best in the house!"

"It's good to see you both," Kit said. "And still together, against all odds. I'm surprised we haven't bumped into one another more often if you've been haunting this tavern."

"We don't get out much," Tom said. "Neither of us." He told Kit about the events of last autumn and the scandal that had tarnished both their reputations. And about his father's death.

"I am truly sorry, Tom. That's a grievous loss."

A wench came up with their wine, setting the bottle and cups on the table, collecting the bread crusts and greasy plate. Tom asked her if she'd been here the night Greene had fallen down the stairs. She was here, but hadn't seen anything other than a crowd of hard-drinking gentlemen and an unruly lot of poets.

After she left, Kit said, "I've heard about Nashe's stalker."

"I thought you'd only been back for one day," Tom said.

Kit shrugged. "I hear things. And Old Nashey has a way of making himself known. How did this come to be your concern?"

Tom told him about that as well, skipping over anything touching on Bacon's undiscussed worries.

Kit laughed. "More Puritans! That's becoming a specialty for you, Tomkin." He raised a cup. "May you rid us of that troublesome breed altogether!"

"Hear, hear!" Trumpet raised hers in enthusiastic reply. Tom joined them but felt compelled to add, "They're not all equally bad."

"Yes, they are," Kit said. "Although Nashe does have a knack for making enemies. People either love him or hate him. I'm one of the former. I miss the old ragabash. I should walk down to Holborn this evening and leap out at him as he's walking home."

"I beg you not to," Tom said. "He's staying in my room, remember. He thrashes around and snorts in his sleep. It's like living with a pig who has nightmares. The sooner we hang Martin's minion, the sooner Nashe can go home."

Kit said, "I'm putting my money on Leicester's ghost. But you undoubtedly have a list of plausible suspects and are slowly but inexorably drawing the noose around the best one's neck."

"Not yet," Tom said. "Maybe you can help. You know these writers better than I do."

"Try me," Kit said. "Though Robert Greene's no friend of mine."

"He's a victim, not a villain," Trumpet said. "Although I wish I could meet him before —" She shot Tom an inscrutable look. "Before this is all over. Do you know a pamphleteer who goes by the name of John Dando?"

Kit laughed out loud. "The prop and mainstay of the Goose and Gall? He lives upstairs. He may own a share in the place, come to think of it. He can't be supporting himself by publishing the idle farts of a wayward mule or whatever's his latest fancy." He shook his head. "You don't think Dando has anything to do with any of this? I've heard the man can carry a grudge, but he's too idle to try again after missing his man the first time, and he's no more a Puritan than I am."

"I don't believe he's Martin's minion," Tom said. "But he's plainly envious of Nashe and Greene for being chosen to play Mar-Martin when he wasn't. That rankles."

"Rankles," Kit said. "A faint motive for strangling two men."

"He has a secret to protect," Trumpet said. She gave Tom a lip-biting look that made him want to — that made him bury his face in his cup for a long draught of surprisingly good wine.

Kit chuckled softly. "I don't wonder your minders are trying to keep you two apart. What's the secret, Mr. Trumpet?"

"Tom told us that Mr. Bacon wanted him to look up printers in the Stationers' Registry. So I went and looked."

Tom nearly choked on his drink. Once again, she'd caught him completely off guard. Where would he ever find another such surprising, infuriating, intoxicating rarity?

"I went to the Stationers' Hall," she said pertly. "I told them Francis Bacon sent me and just like you said, they let me in and left me to it. I spent half an hour in their records room, which was every bit as stuffy as you thought it would be. I was looking for — not anything in particular, starting with this year and hoping something would jump out and something did. John Dando's real name." She stopped and beamed at them, waggling her eyebrows.

"And the name is . . . ?" Tom obliged.

"Barnaby Snorscombe, gentleman of Northamptonshire."

"Snorscombe?" Tom and Kit echoed, trading amused looks.

"Do you mean Barnaby *Snors*combe?" Tom repeated, his horse's voice winning a delicious giggle. He stored that up in his camel's hump too.

Even Kit chuckled. "I'll grant that's worth killing for, though you'd think the poor churl would go after his parents first."

"On the other hand," Tom said, "if that name is in the Stationers' book, other people must know it. It could be one of those not-so-secret secrets, if you follow me."

Kit nodded. "Ask Greene if he knew. He loves to root around in other writers' dirty laundry. I can say that it fits the little I know of Mr. *Snors*combe." He imitated Tom's horse voice and got a round of chuckles. "I'm not surprised to learn that he's the black sheep of a good family. He talks like a gent."

"The question is, how black is he?" Trumpet asked. "Black enough to strangle Thomas Nashe?"

"It's still not enough for me," Kit said. "While I admire your initiative, I must give Dando the thumbs-down. Who's next?"

"What do you think about Anthony Munday?" Tom asked.

"Munday? He was just here."

"I saw him. He's another one who's jealous of Greene and Nashe."

"Oh, that goes back a while," Kit said. "Not Nashe. He couldn't care less about him. But Greene's the most prolific writer in England today. I think he's the only one of us who actually makes a living at it. The rest need something else to keep the wolf from the door. If you're the competitive type, he's the one you'll want to beat."

"That's only an added motivation for Munday," Tom said. "He's also working for Canon Bancroft as an intelligencer, searching the counties for Martin Marprelate."

"Not an intelligencer," Kit said. "That's what I am. I know you guessed it, but it's all you'll ever know, so it doesn't matter. But no one would hire Munday for that work. You have to have courteous manners, a pleasant appearance, and an ability to mingle with people, get them to talk to you."

"Like Nashe has been doing," Trumpet said.

"More or less, although he's not much good at melting into the background and not presentable enough for every occasion."

Tom had a vision of Marlowe, handsome and well-groomed in his best doublet, standing at the back of some nobleman's audience chamber, conversing articulately about poetry and art in Latin, listening more than he spoke. Nashe would be a disaster in that role, but Tom would be good at it. Better than Marlowe, maybe. He could tease secrets from the ladies, who had teased them from their lords.

Since his father's death, he often thought about packing a bag and going — where? Marlowe had a master, whose name he never even hinted at. If Tom ever decided to leave Gray's, perhaps he'd ask him for a reference.

"Munday's a pursuivant," Kit said. "That's a horse of a different color. He has a warrant from the archbishop or some kind of writ. He goes around visiting local justices, sheriffs, other authorities. He shows them his writ and tells them what he wants. They don't have to like him to share what they know; they just have to fear the wrath of the writ-writer. Part of his job is to make them feel that fear. If they have something, or someone, they'll give it up. He's not a nice man, is Munday. He's disagreeable, not trustworthy. Retainers playing dice while waiting for their lords and the like aren't going to tell him anything."

"That's an interesting distinction," Tom said, "of which I was not aware, but it doesn't disprove my conjecture. He's playing some kind of game." He told Kit about seeing him waiting on the bench at Burghley House.

Kit burst into laughter. "Let me get this straight. You think Anthony Munday is Canon Bancroft's pursuivant" — he held up one finger —"Martin's minion"— he held up another —"*and* an agent of Robert Cecil?" He laughed some more, shaking his head and refilling all their cups. "Tom, Tom. You've missed your calling! Add a jilted mistress and you've got the makings of a passable play."

"You have to admit his presence on that bench was suspicious."

"No, I don't. He was undoubtedly bringing a message from the canon to Mr. Cecil."

"Then why did he glare at me?"

"He glares at everybody. He has neither gift, craft, nor wit, but for some reason, he's decided he wants to be Robert Greene. And no, I don't believe he'd strangle Nashe to make that dream come true. It wouldn't help, for one thing. You can't squeeze a man's talent out of his throat."

Tom glowered into his cup, but had to admit the truth of that last observation. Kit hadn't finished demolishing his ideas. "Here's another count against Martin's minion as the strangler. Religious extremists don't murder to keep from being discovered. They might assassinate the opposition's leaders, I suppose, but ultimately they *want* to be discovered. They long to be recognized by the other zealots as courageous defenders of the faith."

"There is a hidden press somewhere," Tom insisted. "Which means there are men hiding along with it. They'll probably hang when they're caught. I should think they'd do whatever they could to postpone that eventuality."

"They could pack up and run," Kit said. "I have one more count against both Dando and Munday. They knew those two victims, Stokes and Little. Neither Dando nor Munday would mistake them for anyone else, not even at night. They have voices as well as beards, you know."

Tom growled under his breath. He'd forgotten about voices. "Assuming they had a chance to cry out."

Kit smiled like a patient tutor. "Any others?"

Trumpet said, "Only one — Peter Hollowell, Mr. Cecil's secretary. He claims to have been with a whore on the night Stokes was murdered. She backed him up, but I don't believe her."

"She's come into a sum of money recently," Tom said, nodding. "Where'd she get it?"

Trumpet added, "I saw yellow marks along her cheek, under her straggling hair. Like old bruises."

Kit's eyes flicked from one to the other as they spoke, a weary expression on his face. "Robert Cecil's secretary. The Lord Treasurer's son. The one who asked your Mr. Bacon — who happens to be his cousin, as I recall — to look into these murders in the first place."

"That's right," Tom said. "But I don't believe it was Hollowell. It's the same problem as Munday, isn't it? He'd have to be working for both Martin and the people who are trying to put Martin in prison. Still, someone gave that whore enough money to buy a house in Rye."

Kit laughed heartily, pressing a hand to his breast. "Perhaps she's a thrifty soul and skilled at her profession. Let's wish her a *rousing* success among the smugglers in her new establishment!" He raised his cup and kept it raised until they joined him. "Come on now, Tom. I know you. You've been saving the best for last, haven't you?"

Tom traded defeated frowns with Trumpet. "Well, there has been talk about the Earl of Leicester's ghost."

TWENTY-TWO

The wherryman helped Francis step onto the wharf at the Custom House, solicitous of his gentleman passenger for an extra ha'penny. Francis didn't need the helping hand. He was feeling like his usual self again, meaning slightly dyspeptic and pricked by the horns of a moral dilemma. He felt as if his soul had aged ten years last night, tossing and turning, fearing he had stimulated a conflict that could ultimately prove far more damaging to the body politic than Martin's ill-advised antics. But his body was still only twenty-eight years old. He could climb out of a flat boat held steady without mishap.

Sir Francis Walsingham could free him from those horns of self-doubt if anyone could. He had been a member of Her Majesty's Privy Council for twenty years and more, serving also as her Secretary of State and leading spymaster. He had uncovered numerous assassination plots, including the one that led to the execution of Mary, Queen of Scots. He'd fled to the Continent during the Marian years, returning on Elizabeth's accession to rise in her service with other equally committed Protestants. A close ally of Lord Burghley's since those early days, Walsingham would nevertheless be able to consider Francis's dangerous conjecture with an unbiased mind.

The large house on Seething Lane, not far from the Tower, had once included a handsome garden with vine-covered arbors, plots of herbs, and fruit trees trained against the walls. Francis remembered racing his brother

Anthony around the mazed paths on summer afternoons long ago while the adults sat conversing inside the hall. Robert must have been there on some of those days, though he wouldn't have raced with them. He didn't like games that exposed the deformity of his crooked shoulder.

The garden had been reduced to the merest patch of green, kept to ease the aching eyes of clerks toiling inside the house. An enormous stable, larger than the one at Gray's, now occupied the lion's share of the property, with a partially covered yard where messengers could wait out of the weather. As he was admitted, Francis saw two men stride toward saddled horses and sling themselves up, guiding the steeds toward the postern gate. They would pick their way through the crowds on London Bridge and then canter south to Dover, or wherever they were being sent. To Paris, perhaps, or even farther.

Francis had spent three years in France in his youth, learning the civil law and perfecting his French. It had been a worthy experience, but not one he cared to repeat.

He found Walsingham in the front room on the first floor. Peering between a gap in the tall houses across the lane, he could see the white stones of the Tower looming watchfully over the Thames. A potent view, but one to which the Privy Councilor had turned his back. Walsingham sat in a high-backed armchair near the fireplace, where coals glowed red in spite of the season.

"Come in, Mr. Bacon," Walsingham said with a wave of his hand that both beckoned him in and instructed his servant to close the door behind him.

"Thank you for seeing me, Sir Francis." Francis bowed slightly, noticing how frail the older man looked with a coverlet tucked around his legs and black woolen coif covering his head. Deep lines drawing from nose to chin made his long face seem longer. "You should be at your house in Surrey. It would be quieter, with sweeter air."

"The bustle in the yard is the same there, only less convenient for Her Majesty." Walsingham smiled. He seemed resigned to his declining health. He would keep working until the last breath. "What can I do for you?"

"I have a thorny problem. A tangle of opposing ideas that I cannot find a way through."

"That must be quite a tangle. Sit down and tell me about it."

Francis drew up a padded stool, a little too close to the fire for his comfort but positioned so Walsingham wouldn't be obliged to turn his head. "Do you know about my latest commission for my Lord Burghley?"

"Identifying the murderer stalking the anti-Martinists?" Walsingham smiled thinly. "I've heard. It won't be easy."

"It hasn't been. The murders must be stopped, but I may not be able to do it. All I have so far are hints, conjectures, and suppositions."

He told Walsingham everything he'd learned thus far, about the mistaken identities, the open secret of Nashe's involvement in Mar-Martin's works — even the matter of the beards, which Tom had related to him with great earnestness that morning. More pertinently, he'd also told him about the convergence of Thomas Nashe's ramblings and rumors of a secret press at Sir Richard Knightley's home in Fawsley.

Walsingham listened in silence, his gaze slightly averted. He raised his head at the sound of Knightley's name. "That's plausible. He would shield Martin's pressmen if asked, I warrant. Has he been questioned?"

"Not yet, as far as I know. He does fit the general thinking about Martin, and Northamptonshire is the perfect distance from London, in my judgment. Far enough to avoid notice but near enough to stay abreast of the anti-Martin publications and catch news of pursuivants."

"I don't think we can make any assumptions about where Martin is. He could be across the lane for all we know." Walsingham pointed his chin toward the windows. "If I were Martin Marprelate, I'd stay as far away from that illegal press as possible. Consider it, Mr. Bacon. A gentleman sits in his library every day" — he gestured toward his desk — "writing this and that. Letters to friends, a speech for a dinner or the next meeting of Parliament, notes about his readings dutifully entered into his commonplace book. If one day he shapes a fresh quill and writes an epistle or a hundred and ten theses, who's to notice? Not his wife. Nor even his manservant. A gentleman's papers are his own business. But a press, now — a press reeks of ink and potash. It's noisy, squeaking and thumping, with men grunting and calling out to one another. Don't forget those men need meals and clean linens. They won't like hiding in a cellar month after month either. Sooner or later they'll come out, go to the local tavern for a mug of ale and a change of fare, where someone will notice them. Someone like this Thomas Nashe, who sounds interesting."

"He wouldn't do for your purposes, I don't think," Francis said. "He has a prattling, agitated manner and an unattractive appearance. But I thank you for the correction. I won't exclude London from my thoughts about Martin."

"He isn't on the Continent either," Walsingham said. "That's one good effect of Bancroft's otherwise ill-advised strategy. Martin responded too quickly to *Martin's Mirror Mar'd* to be overseas." He grunted. "We'll catch the printers sooner or later. The word is out, and people are watching. But I'm not certain we'll ever know who Martin really is."

"Thankfully, that's not my job," Francis said. "Although I keep being drawn toward that question because we have so little else to go on. There's only one

Martin, presumably, but there could be any number of accomplices fearful enough to kill to protect their secrets."

"True. And they won't be so distinctive. There are many more men with dark suits and short beards than there are members of Parliament."

Francis winced. "Put like that, it seems impossible. We did make one attempt to draw the murderer out, or rather, my assistant, Thomas Clarady did." He related the story of the misfired trap, emphasizing the reasoning behind it and minimizing the actual attack.

But Walsingham's pale face grew paler. "Thank God you survived! You mustn't put yourself in such danger."

"I merely walked home from my favorite inn," Francis said, smiling. "I wasn't hurt at all. And I have fully recovered from the fright. It wasn't a bad idea, given how unproductive everything we've tried has been. And it did give us another question to ask, at least: Who could have known about that trap?"

"Every writer in London, from what you tell me about Thomas Nashe."

"In fairness, not quite all of them. My assistant believes Nashe kept the details within the narrow circle of our interest. But Clarady told my cousin all about it, in the presence of his secretary." He recounted Tom's short-lived doubts about Peter Hollowell.

Now a light danced in Walsingham's black eyes. "Robert Cecil's secretary? You have been struggling, Mr. Bacon."

"My assistant is nothing if not thorough. If anything can be found among the writers' haunts and lodgings, he'll find it. But the secretary was a shrewder guess than he knew, I think."

"How so?" Walsingham folded his fingers together in his lap.

Francis stroked his moustache. He'd come to the core of his dilemma. "I can't help wondering why Martin

Marprelate is so difficult to catch — his team of accomplices, if not the man himself. Surely the combined forces of the Church and the Privy Council could turn up one very active printing press!"

"Our forces are nowhere near as all-powerful as people imagine."

"Even so. Even so. It makes me wonder if perhaps not all those forces are genuinely searching, or if they're being diverted by someone who doesn't want the press found."

A single one of Walsingham's dark eyebrows rose.

"Bear with me, Sir Francis, if you will." Francis outlined his theory of the Cecils as Martin's master, devising and directing the whole affair as a ruse to distract Archbishop Whitgift and lessen his influence on the Privy Council. He did not include any of the Earl of Essex's far-reaching speculations about fomenting rebellion as an excuse to consolidate power. That whole branch of conjecture must be sawed off and burned.

Sir Francis was that rare sort of listener who gave his full attention to the speaker without inserting his opinions or visibly planning his rebuttal. But as Francis faltered to the close of his argument, which now sounded absurd in his own ears, a wry yet tolerant smile curved on the old man's lips. The smile grew into a chuckle, abruptly halted by a cough. Walsingham clutched his lower belly with a wince, but a smile still played about his lips.

"Ah, Francis! What a fine Machiavelli you would make! I understand the wisdom of the queen, keeping you trammeled within the precincts of the law. You're far too inventive for politics. It's an intriguing notion, and I can understand how compelling it must be for you especially, but no, my dear, young friend. No. Your cousin is not Martin Marprelate, and neither is his father. Nor do I think either of them created Martin for any purpose."

"In my heart, I knew that, I think, but once the idea took hold of my thoughts, I couldn't shake it out. I had to hear someone with your authority do it for me. Although now I feel the veriest fool."

"Not at all. It's not beyond the realm of the possible for your cousin, not in my estimation of his character. He is a cunning fellow. But he is still wholly under the guidance of his father, who would never approve anything so disruptive. Lord Burghley is like the queen in that regard. They hate turmoil above all things." Walsingham smiled at him fondly, though he seemed to be growing tired. He'd enjoyed his little laugh, but it had hurt him.

"I should leave you to rest," Francis said, rising. "Thank you for untangling my knot."

"My special gift." Walsingham nodded at something in his own thoughts. Then he held up a finger to stay his guest a moment longer. "I'm not among those pursuing Martin, as you've noticed. I share his views, even if I deplore his methods. But if I wanted to find him, I'd look for someone on the fringes of power. Someone like Sir Richard Knightley, or more plausible still, a widow of some great person, virtual queen of her own estate with friends in high places and a passion for reform."

Walsingham's wise eyes held a glimmer of unspoken meaning that Francis easily interpreted: someone like his mother. He'd come full circle.

Worse, he had succumbed to one of the most fundamental intellectual errors: he had allowed his own prejudices to direct his search for truth. He had watched his cousin receive favors from his uncle and the queen for years while he was overlooked and pushed aside with sweet words and comforting promises. Bitterness had turned to envy, the most malignant of the affections. Unable to rise to his cousin's level by his merits and hard work, Francis had sought to pull him down by weighting him with this foul conspiracy.

All he'd achieved was the tarnishing of his own soul — or he hoped that was the only ill effect of his descent into delusion. He'd have to think of a way to distract the Earl of Essex before he took any steps to confirm or contest his new interpretation of Robert Cecil's motives. That shouldn't be too hard. Essex was full of plans for new campaigns against Spain this year. Francis could come up with another excuse for a visit and turn the conversation in that direction.

How many days had he wasted in his fevered dreams of corruption and collusion? Too many, with the result that he'd done nothing to fulfill his commission. He must go back to the starting point and begin again.

TWENTY-THREE

On Wednesday afternoon, Lady Russell retired to her bedchamber after dinner to ease her aching back. Trumpet offered to leave her in peace, deciding to spend the afternoon attending upon her aunt. Then she and Catalina went out to the stables and submitted to the indignity of being perched behind grooms to make the treacherous journey into the wilds of Bishopsgate.

As they plodded up St. Andrew's Hill, she considered her options for this unexpected afternoon of liberty. First thing, she'd send a note to Tom. They should go back and talk to that whore again. Something about her story smelled false. Catalina had a good nose for the lies of whores, having been one herself, more or less. If there was anything to get, she'd get it.

Any fresh tidbit would help cheer Tom up. He'd been dismally cast down by Marlowe's shredding of his precious conjectures. But that was Kit, not truth. The man lived to throw stones at established beliefs. What was *Tamburlaine* if not a stone cast at God Himself?

Kit knew nothing. But Trumpet felt that tingling at the back of her neck when she thought about John Dando. He had something to do with all this. He might be Martin's minion, collecting her packages and trotting them up to Sir Richard of Fawsley. She had nothing certain, but she'd keep plucking at that thread until she pulled something loose.

They had to wait at Cheapside for a coach to pass with an entourage of mounted retainers. The Earl of Oxford, by the arms painted on the door. She gave thanks once again that she wouldn't have to marry him since he was already married to the Lord Treasurer's daughter. Unhappily, by all accounts. He had a dire reputation, which of course did no harm to a man's prospects. Still, another arrow dodged.

They resumed their plodding course northward, edging pedestrians aside. A boy with a jaunty manner caught Trumpet's eye — her new minion, Jack. He must have followed them from Blackfriars. When their horses plodded into her aunt's stable, she spoke to the groom before he had even landed her feet onto the hard-packed floor. "You may both return to Lady Russell's house at once. My aunt's men will bring us home. Tell the housekeeper not to expect us for supper."

She pretended to let Catalina dust her skirts until the men had remounted and ridden away, then she went back out into the alley, where Jack appeared out of nowhere.

"News?" she asked.

"Yes, my lady. He left, like you said, only at dinnertime. Good thing we were watching!" He cocked an eye at her, but she wasn't that easily swayed.

"Not a groat until I hear it all."

He told her, with much elaboration, the tale of following the printer's apprentice to a brick wall alongside a pleasure garden in Shoreditch, where he had removed a loose brick and stuffed the oilcloth package inside the hole. Jack had left his brother to find that loose brick and followed the apprentice back to Blackfriars.

"Well done," Trumpet said. "If we can find that loose brick, you'll get a whole extra penny."

"We'll find it, my lady."

Jack led them north through Bishopsgate into the sprawling liberties north of the City wall, where labyrinths of three- and four-story tenements had replaced small farms. The new buildings were chiefly inhabited by the lesser sort, but a few great estates had been divided into a patchwork of pleasure gardens where the well-breeched could while away a summer afternoon drinking sweet wine in a breezy banquet house or challenging their friends to a game of bowls.

Trumpet's aunt, Lady Chadwick, spent her afternoons in that fashion with her friend Lady Fulburne, who owned one of these Shoreditch parcels. So Trumpet was well familiar with the narrow passages running through the area.

They spotted Jack's brother sitting in the middle of a brick-lined alley with his back against the wall, in the shade of an overhanging lime tree, munching on a handful of plums. He jumped up when he saw them and pointed at a brick higher than his head. Trumpet started toward him, but Catalina caught her arm. "Don't go in, my lady! Someone may be watching."

Trumpet gestured at the nine-foot walls. "Where could they be?"

Catalina treated her to a full Iberian shrug, both arms slowly rising with open palms. "A tree, a window. Why choose such a place if not to watch? He may see us now."

"Then we should stop clustering here at the entrance and march on through." She shook her arm free and nodded at Jack. "Pretend to drop something when we get to that spot."

He did as she bade him, but no one could see them in the middle of the alley — unless there was another hole in the bricks in just the right place for peering.

That was an ugly thought. Trumpet shook it off. It was broad daylight, with people within screaming distance of both ends of the passage. They had nothing to fear — but best be quick.

Jack's brother had marked his brick with a strip of sticky plum skin. The brick slid out easily enough, spilling grains of loose mortar onto her skirt. If this hole had been used since the beginning, it had now been removed and replaced twice times six manuscripts. The last one, her cobbled-up bait, now lay inside the hole, which was just wide enough to house a wrapped pamphlet. She replaced the brick and nodded at her band of intelligencers. "Let's go. Walk out the other end at a normal pace and turn left, back toward Folgate. Wait there."

They did as she instructed. Trumpet paid the boys a penny apiece and bade them watch each entrance of that alley. She considered asking them to follow whoever collected her package, but they couldn't very well travel all the way to Northamptonshire or even know for certain that the collector hadn't passed the thing on to someone else inside a crowded inn. The best they could do was to watch and remember. She promised an extra farthing to the boy who noticed the most telling detail.

They scampered off to their posts, leaving the two women at loose ends. "You know," Trumpet said, "I'm not certain, but I think that wall might belong to the property next door to Lady Fulburne's. Let's walk back past it and see."

Which they did, and which it was, the last in a row of six walled gardens laid out side by side with shared walls running between the middle properties. They rang the bell at Lady Fulburne's and were admitted by her manservant — a slender, gray-haired man with a sprightly manner. He clapped his hands with joy to see them, inquired solicitously after their health, and led them briskly past square flowerbeds to the banqueting house, which was a small, octagonal building with large windows and a fancifully crenellated roof. It was raised up some seven or eight feet from the ground to catch breezes otherwise trapped between the walls.

The two senior ladies reclined on couches like Roman senators, both facing the same pair of open windows. "My dearest, darling Alice!" Lady Chadwick crooned. "What a delightful surprise!"

Her delight was echoed in still fruitier tones by Lady Fulburne. Judging by the expansiveness of their welcome, the women were more than a little drunk and getting bored with each other's company.

"Sit, sit, sit!" Lady Fulburne sang, waving her hand as if to summon more couches from the aether. Her servant drew up two ordinary armchairs, placing Trumpet's where both ladies could speak to her comfortably without blocking the view through the windows. He seated Catalina by the wall, where only Trumpet could see her. He poured tall cups of wine for everyone, assessed the supply of sweets and pastries, and bowed himself out.

"We were just talking about you," Lady Chadwick said. "Any new offers?"

"Not good ones." Trumpet told them about the rude baron in Lancashire.

"Unacceptable!" Lady Fulburne declared. "What did Lady Russell say?"

"She agreed with you," Trumpet said, "although at greater length."

"Ah. Then he must not be one of *her* kind," Lady Fulburne said. The two ladies traded meaningful looks. "You know what I mean. One of those" — she dropped her voice to a hoarse whisper — "Presbyterians."

More dark looks, followed by deep draughts. These pleasure-loving ladies had no patience with Puritans.

"What else are you about this afternoon, Niece? I doubt you'd give up an afternoon at the theater to visit a couple of old gossips." The ladies giggled at one another.

"It's too hot for the theater," Trumpet said. "The groundlings smell like composting socks. I wanted a walk. We've been all around this little district here, peeking through gates at everyone's pretty gardens. Yours is by far the nicest, Lady Fulburne."

"Why, thank you, Lady Alice! Isn't that kind of you?"

Trumpet smiled sweetly. "What sorts of people do you have as neighbors here, my lady?"

"Only the best, I assure you. These six gardens were created all at once by Lord Hoxton, oh, twenty years or so ago. His Lordship was *very* particular about *whom* should be allowed to acquire them. He's descended from Edward the Third, you know."

"I did not know that." Trumpet nodded as if this were a most valuable bit of news. "So is *my* father." That descent was very indirect, but it didn't hurt to underscore the fact that, while she was younger than the other women, she outranked them. These ladies were the widows of mere barons.

They possessed that most desirable of estates, however: a well-endowed widowhood. They had everything Trumpet wanted, but they chose to squander their freedom in the pursuit of pleasure — a very lazy pursuit at that. She would do more with her time and wealth when she had them in her power. She didn't know what yet, but she had plenty of time to discover it.

She asked, "Did Lord Hoxton's ancestor owe knight service to King Edward?"

Lady Fulburne blinked at her. "Why, I suppose he must have. That was rather the purpose of the nobility in those days, wasn't it?"

"She's thinking of her friend, Lady Russell's ward," Lady Chadwick put in with a swift frown at Trumpet. Her refusal to cut off all contact with Tom was a bone of constant contention.

"Oh," Lady Fulburne said. "That poor boy! Well, then, yes, my dear, I suppose these gardens would fall under the aegis of the Court of Wards — the greedy beasts. If anyone in your family tree has ever owned so much as a *toothpick* that once belonged to a monastery, you had better be careful to stay alive until your heir reaches his majority!"

"Or hers," Lady Chadwick said. "Thank God you're safe in that regard, Alice."

"My father is hale and hearty, thanks be to God." Also fearless, reckless, and addicted to the most dangerous sport in the world — privateering. But she'd inherited her sturdy constitution from his side of the family. "Are your neighbors friendly people?" she persisted. "Do you meet them?"

"Not often. The place on the right is owned by the Earl of Huntington's wife's favorite nephew, but he spends summers in the country. The one on the left is owned by Sir Richard Knightley of Northamptonshire. His wife is the youngest daughter of the late Duke of Somerset, you know. Unfortunately, Sir Richard is one of *those*." She traded disapproving grimaces with Lady Chadwick.

"One of the worst," Lady Chadwick said, "according to my son, who likes to attend debates in the House of Commons when he's in town. Every bit as intolerant as your Lady Russell — not that she isn't the ideal guide and advisor for you in this difficult year, Alice."

"Thankfully, he never comes here." Lady Fulburne smirked at her friend. "Sir Richard doesn't approve of *pleasure*."

"Or leisure," Lady Chadwick quipped, sending them both into bubbling gusts of laughter.

Trumpet was grateful for their besotted condition because that name had startled her so much she might actually have jumped a little. Catalina had noticed, but the ladies hadn't.

So Sir Richard Knightley owned the wall with the loose brick, behind which Martin's last masterpiece now waited to be taken to — Fawsley, it would seem. By whom?

She trilled a short laugh, catching up with the others as they wound down. "It seems a shame to waste such a lovely property. Doesn't anyone *ever* go there?"

"Oh, it isn't *wasted*, my darling girl." Lady Chadwick winked broadly at her friend. "Sir Richard has a cousin, or is it a nephew? A *very* pleasant young man named John Snorscombe, who has the most *charming* gentlemen friends."

"Charming in every way," Lady Fulburne said, and they both giggled.

"As a matter of fact," Lady Chadwick said, craning her neck to look through the window into the neighboring garden, "it ought to be about time, oughtn't it?"

"Here they come," Lady Fulburne sang out, hoisting herself into a more upright position and fastening her gaze on the window overlooking the next garden.

Trumpet twisted around on her hard chair and saw two young men with excellent legs, fashionably dressed in closely fitted doublets, thin silk stockings, and very short melon hose, pace across the long strip of grass next door, setting up jacks for a game of bowls. When the shorter one turned in their direction, she ducked, though he wasn't looking at her.

There, as close to her manuscript as she was to Catalina, stood John Dando, weighing a ball in his right hand, preparing to take the first turn.

TWENTY-FOUR

"Marlowe effectively slashed, shredded, and put to the torch every idea I've had about Martin's minion," Tom said. "All I've got now are ashes."

Mr. Bacon nodded. "My one substantial conjecture about Martin's identity has also been definitively refuted, to my everlasting relief."

He had never mentioned this great and terrible conjecture, so Tom pretended to know nothing about it. Let him think that conversation with Lady Russell had been completely confidential, in spite of Tom and Trumpet sitting right there with four fully functional ears and native graps of the English language. "What do we do now? I can't think of anyone new to talk to."

"I'm not ready to discard what you've achieved so far on the casual word of a playwright, however popular his works may be. Martin's minion is either someone we haven't caught a whisper about with all our poking and prying — in which case, we'll never find him — or he's one of the men your friend Marlowe so imperiously ruled out. I choose to believe the latter."

"I'm willing," Tom said. "But what more can we do?"

"I have one last avenue to explore. Everyone I've spoken to shares the same general conception of the kind of man Martin must be, judging by his works. But no one seems to have studied those works with an eye toward discovering the man who wrote them."

Tom frowned. "How's that?"

Bacon smiled. "All writers have habits. Vices, you might say. Favorite turns of phrase, long sentences or short ones. They return over and again to the same works for illustrative examples. There are also curiously indefinable but recognizable qualities of style. One man writes well; another simply doesn't."

Tom was staggered. "You can figure out who Martin is by reading what he's written?" This was why, at the end of the day, he didn't mind serving this fussy, irritating, sometimes incomprehensible man.

Bacon shrugged. "I should at least be able to determine who he is not. Your new discovery, Sir Richard Knightley — well done, by the way — might be involved with the Martin business, but I don't believe he wrote any of the works. I've heard him speak in the House several times. He is not a gifted orator, to put it kindly. He is passionate but earnest. His style lacks wit. I say that without judgment, you understand, purely as an objective description."

"I understand." Tom had been on the receiving end of Bacon's "purely objective descriptions" more than once. He was never wrong, but never spared the recipient's feelings either.

"In fact," Bacon went on, "his speeches could be fairly characterized as ponderous, bombastic, and repetitive. Martin, on the other hand, is a gifted writer. He switches deftly from the playful to the serious. He can be thrilling, convincing, picturesque, sometimes even droll. His works are popular for good reason."

"I see your point. What's the plan, then? Shall I go out and buy up the bookshops?"

"Not you," Bacon said. "This task requires my judgment. I expect it will keep me engaged for several days at least." He folded his hands on his desk with a self-satisfied smile.

Tom couldn't fault his cleverness, coming up with a vital task that obliged him to spend a week reading in bed.

He made a note to tell Pinnock to lay in a supply of nuts, dried fruits, and other tidbits so the genius could maintain his strength without going down to the hall for food.

"While you're reading, I could go back to the people I've met so far and try to shake a little more out of them, which isn't likely to be much." Tom pursed his lips and tapped one finger on his desktop until he noticed Bacon's brow furling in annoyance. "All I can come up with is to try setting another trap."

Bacon flinched, grabbed his penknife, and shrank into his oversized chair, staring out the window as if expecting an imminent attack.

"Not here!" Tom hastily added. "Nowhere near here." He watched with concern as his master recovered from his fright, not even slightly tempted to laugh. Bacon had brain, not brawn. The man couldn't defend himself from a disgruntled blackbird. Nor should he have to. Tom couldn't identify people by reading their pamphlets. "I don't have a plan yet, but whatever it is, it will unfold in Norton Folgate, around where the murders were committed. I'll have to use Nashe as bait again. He's all I've got."

"He's a clever fellow," Bacon said. "He knows these pamphleteers and their favorite haunts. Perhaps he can think of something."

Tom snapped his fingers, making Bacon jump again. "Not Nashe. His ideas are too far-fetched. But Robert Greene can craft a plot better than any man alive. I doubt he's dared set foot outside his house all week. He must be half-mad to get out again. Let the man who wrote *Pandosto* set our next trap!"

* * *

Tom went downstairs to change into his intelligencer garb, as he now thought of his hunting clothes. He didn't plan on getting dirty, but he'd represented himself as a fellow scribbler on the prowl for opportunities and he didn't want to muddle that impression. People might be less forthcoming to an Inns of Court gentleman.

He swung past the Antelope Inn to pick up Thomas Nashe, whence they walked on to pass through Aldersgate and cut across the northern part of the city. They weren't in any particular hurry, which was good because Nashe was a truly irksome walking companion.

He was endlessly distractible. First, he'd lag behind to peer into an open door or examine the wares on some shopkeeper's folded-down shutter; then he'd skip — up and down, up and down — to catch up. Sometimes he'd stop short and spin full around to gawk at someone wearing an unusual hat or speaking a foreign language. Tom kept to the course he'd set, maintaining a steady pace, refusing to be diverted.

"Have you decided who to marry?" Nashe said, popping up at his side again.

"I'm not marrying anyone."

"A rich innkeeper, Clarady, I'm telling you. It's the best of all worlds. Mrs. Sprye's a gentlewoman, you know. Her father was a barrister, well respected in the county and the courts. Her late husband was a gentleman too, with a fine estate near Falmouth in Cornwall. A lovely place, she said. She still misses it sometimes, but she fell out with the local gentry after her husband died. Land grabbing. You know the sort of thing."

Tom frowned. "She never told me any of that and I've known her nigh on three years."

"Didn't ask, did you?" Nashe shrugged. "If you can't find a woman with a thriving business like the Antelope, you should look for a pretty merchant's daughter. A rich one."

"I'm not marrying anyone."

"Better yet, a rich merchant's *widow*." Nashe tilted his head to grin straight up into Tom's face. "Virginity is vastly overrated, if you ask me. You want a bedmate who's —"

"*Not* a rich merchant's widow!" Tom almost shouted it. He glared so fiercely at a passerby who somewhat fitted that description that the poor woman startled and hastened away from him, patting her chest.

Nashe stepped in front of him now, walking backward, grinning. "I know what your trouble is, my friend. You're in love with Mr. Trumpet. Well, who wouldn't be? You think she's too far above you, and so she is, for now. But that might not always be the case."

"What do you mean?"

"Dolly told me. You know Dolly." Nashe leered. "The maid of all works and all wonders, she of the lush and bounteous —"

"Nashe!" Tom put a threat in his tone.

"Sorry! The delectable Dolly told me about Mr. Trumpet's difficulties. The aftermath of the events of last August. The irreparable harm done to her reputation and near-universal lack of trust. People wondering if Lord Surdeval's death mightn't have been just a trifle too convenient for his very young widow . . ." He shrugged, raising both hands.

Wrath bubbled in Tom's gut at these unwarranted insults, but he kept a lid on it. "What's your point, if by some remote, improbable chance there actually is one?"

"Well, she's fallen, hasn't she? Unfairly, unfairly! I fully agree. Still, there it is. Her status is not as high as it once was. If she could hold out for a little longer, or fall a little farther, and you could pass the bar a little quicker —"

Tom's wrath boiled over, filling his chest with steam and fury. He grabbed Nashe by the front of his doublet and thrust him against the nearest wall, forcing him up onto his toes, and snarled straight into his face. "You listen to me, you tickle-brained ninny! Trumpet will never lower herself to the level of a commoner like me. *Never!* She has lost nothing. Not status, not honor, not trust. *Nothing!* She is going to marry an earl or a prince or maybe even the king of a small country. He will be handsome, wealthy, educated, even-tempered, and generous. He will *treasure* her and cosset her. He will grant her every wish the moment she — no, the moment *before* she knows she wants it. He will treat her with *unflagging* tenderness and respect every minute of her life henceforward, because if he fails to do so, even once, however briefly, I will hunt him down and slaughter him in the street like a rabid dog. Do you understand me?"

"I do," Nashe said, nodding vigorously. "I do. Unequivocally. Every word."

"Good." His fury spent, Tom felt drained. A little wan-witted. "Good." He loosened his grip, allowing Nashe to land both feet on the ground. He dusted both of the smaller man's shoulders and teased open a couple of crushed pleats in his ruff. Then he took a step or two back, opening a space between them. "I just wanted to make that clear."

"You're clarity itself." Nashe burst into a giggle. "Clarity, Clarady. Get it?"

Tom rolled his eyes. The man was irrepressible. The only cure was to catch the murderer so Nashe could go home and spew his foolery at a broader audience. Much broader.

Tom gestured for the fool to lead on. They wanted to cut through a narrow passage to angle across a churchyard instead of going around on the busy street.

"As a general note of consideration," Tom said, speaking to his friend's back, "I'm not overly fond of jests involving my — Nashe? What ho?"

The man had taken an odd jerking step off the main path, then yelped and disappeared behind a mossy tomb. Tom moved in that direction too, head turning to see what had attracted Nashe's attention. Movement — too close — on his left lifted the short hairs on his neck. A heavy hand gripped his shoulder, pulling him backward, off balance, while an iron band of an arm wrapped around his neck.

The strangler!

Fear pumped blazing fire through Tom's sinews. He wrapped his left hand around his right fist, close to his chest, and drove his right elbow into his attacker's belly. The man grunted, released his grip, and fell back. Tom pivoted on his left heel, swinging his right fist up and around as he turned, driving it into a face whose features he now recognized as those of John Dando.

"Dando! What the devil?"

The pamphleteer had been knocked back a pace by Tom's blow, but he kept his feet. Now he stood with his head lowered like a war-minded bull, fists clenched and ready, his mouth twisted into a scowl. "I mean to teach you a lesson, you craven, dog-hearted varlet!"

Craven! Tom didn't need to hear another word. The man hadn't drawn a knife or tried to get his fingers around Tom's throat. Whatever was biting him, he wasn't the killer.

If he wanted a brawl, Tom was more than willing to supply it. He was no spindly barrister. No scrawny satirist. He was a tall man trained in the arts of combat by London's most expert masters. Moreover, he'd spent a year on his father's ship acquiring the quite different skills of extemporaneous brawling from a crew of salt-hardened sailors.

"Come on, then, scribbler, if you've got the stomach to try me!"

They adopted fighting stances, knees flexed, fists up, and circled, assessing one another. Tom had the reach, but Dando was no flabby blowhard. He had a quickness in his step and the advantage of a purpose in starting this fight, whatever it might be. A cry sounded across the churchyard. Nashe, most like, coping with his own assailant, probably Oliver Oatmeale. The noise broke the tension holding Tom and Dando apart, flinging them at one another like dogs slipped from taut leashes.

They rained blows on one another, punching and parrying, ranging across the yard, seeking any small advantage in the terrain. Tom had his man at his mercy for a few satisfying moments, trapping him against a tomb and pummeling his midsection, pounding out a series of short grunts that told him his fists were taking their toll.

Dando got away, and they chased each other around the churchyard, dodging and ducking, each trying to land that quelling blow, but mostly missing. Then Dando got Tom backed up against a headstone to repay the belly-pounding. Tom flailed away at his head and shoulders, trying to get a knee up into Dando's gut. His foot kicked back against the headstone, which had had as much as it could take of this unexpected assault. It tilted abruptly back and jammed for a moment, in which Dando pushed against Tom in an effort to right himself, then fell flat on the ground, taking both men down with it.

Tom rolled out from under and scrabbled away on hands and knees, too spent to get onto his feet. He aimed a feeble kick at Dando, who had staggered upright and was following him on wobbly legs. He missed, but he managed to rise up on his knees and raise his fists. Then Dando swung at him and missed by a mile, carrying himself off balance in the wake of his swing and falling flat on the ground. Tom, meanwhile, had launched his own mighty punch, which drove through the empty air where Dando had been, landing on his face in the muddy grass.

There they lay, panting, a couple of feet apart. When Tom's breath returned to something like normal, he rolled over onto his back and stared up at the sky, where dark clouds seemed to be gathering. "Looks like rain," he remarked. He chuckled at the stupidity of that remark, then winced at the bruises on his chest and belly. They would hurt like the very devil tomorrow.

Dando groaned and rolled over. "Best get inside, eh? We wouldn't want to get wet." He chuckled, groaned, and chuckled again, making Tom laugh, which made Dando laugh, which made them both groan.

"What," Tom said, turning his head so he could see his erstwhile opponent, "if I may be so bold as to inquire, was that all about?"

"You've been lying to us."

"About what?"

"You're not plain Tom Clarady, lately down from Cambridge, scouring about for a way to earn your bread with your pen. You're Mr. Thomas Clarady of Gray's Inn, which means you must have a purseful of money tucked into those hose and more where it came from. Worse, you're clerk to none other than Mr. Francis 'I know more than everyone about everything' Bacon."

Tom couldn't fault that description of his master. "How'd you find out?"

"An old friend told me when I happened to mention your name. I was at Gray's, you know, some years back. Not for long. Your Mr. Bacon didn't approve of me."

"He doesn't approve of me either, some days. But the benchers don't listen to him. If you were expelled, it must've been from another cause."

Dando grunted. Not a topic for sharing, it would seem.

"Who's the friend?" Tom asked.

"A barrister. Well respected. Man named Welbeck. Do you know him?"

"I know him." Nathaniel Welbeck was Trumpet's uncle, the same uncle who had helped her deceive the whole population of Gray's Inn for the better part of a year. Not from the goodness of his heart, which organ seemed lacking in that quality. She'd used blackmail to

263

persuade him to play his part and provide her with a trundle bed in his chambers. He'd never been caught on the wrong side of the law, as far as Tom knew, but he always seemed to turn up when trouble was afoot.

"Here's a thought," Tom said. "You don't suppose Welbeck could be involved in this Martin business?"

Dando's burst of laughter died with a groan. "Stop making me laugh, will you? It hurts. No, I don't suppose that at all. Welbeck's more likely to take the other side. Catholics are richer. Puritans prefer poverty."

"Except for the ones that don't. There are lots of wealthy Puritans. Say, now I think of it. You're from Northamptonshire, aren't you?"

"Who says I am?"

"It's a simple question."

"It's a curious question that comes out of nowhere. What if I am?"

"Do you happen to know a man called Sir Richard Knightley? He's a Puritan, I'm told, and a hot one too."

Dando struggled up onto one elbow. "That fault-finding, hypocritical, soul-crushing, tight-fisted whoreson Sir Richard Knightley? Is that the man you mean?"

Tom chuckled. "That's the one."

"He's my uncle, as it happens," Dando said. "Not that I get much good of it, or wouldn't if my brother weren't so careful to lick the man's knightly boots on every occasion."

"No love lost, I take it?"

"None."

"Huh. That suggests you're not likely to be Martin's minion either."

"Is that what you thought? You thought I was the strangler? That's an outrage. I ought to beat you senseless." Dando fell back with a groan. "Just as soon as I can get up again."

Tom, still prone, raised his fists into fighting position. "I'm ready for you."

Nashe's face loomed into view. "Are you two planning to lie there chatting all afternoon?"

"Help me up." Tom held out a hand, which Oliver Oatmeale grasped to heave him onto his feet and lead him to perch on the edge of the tomb. Then he and Nashe performed the same service for the other fallen warrior, setting the two combatants side by side.

Dando shot a sidelong glance at Tom. "What, pray tell, possessed you to cast me in the role of Martin's minion? I hate the Puritans more than most, having greater cause."

Tom shrugged. "You were only one of three possibilities and never my favorite. My colleague, Mr. Trumpet, discovered your true name and place of origin in a record at the Stationers' Hall. We thought the name *Barnaby Snorscombe* might be worth protecting by any means necessary."

"Barnaby Snorscombe." Nashe echoed the name in hallowed tones, as if he'd been handed the Holy Grail.

Dando snarled at him, showing him a fist. "That name never leaves this graveyard." He turned his head stiffly to catch Tom's eyes. "I remember your colleague, *Mr. Trumpet*. A slight, slender fellow with lush black lashes and cheeks like newly washed handkerchiefs."

Nashe nodded. "Like sun-whitened peaches, dewy and tender, with a ripening bloom —"

"Enough!" Tom glared from one man to the other, shooting a hostile glance at Oliver Oatmeale for good measure. Then he pointed at Dando. "You will never mention that name again, do you hear me?"

"I hear you clearly and understand you well. I also have a name I prefer never to be mentioned."

They locked eyes, then Tom nodded. "Understood." He turned to his friend. "Do you understand too, Nashe?"

"I may be the only one who fully understands every aspect of this multifaceted and fascinating exchange of changing identities."

"Silence is what we're looking for here, Nashe," Dando said.

"I won't tell a soul." Nashe mimed locking his lips with a key. "Not even Christopher Marlowe."

"Kit already knows," Tom said.

Dando shrugged. "I don't mind Kit knowing. That man can keep a secret. In fact, Nashey, I think you should discuss all this with Kit at your earliest opportunity, to get it off your chest."

Tom flexed his neck and shoulders gingerly, making sure they still worked. He caught Dando doing the same, and they grinned at one another. Nothing like a good brawl to sort things out between gentlemen.

"I thought you suspected Anthony Munday of being Martin's minion," Oatmeale said. He and Nashe had muddied each other up a bit, but neither seemed the least bit damaged.

"I still do," Tom said. "In fact, he's the only suspect I've got left."

"What's his motive supposed to be?" Oatmeale asked.

"Envy, partly, like Dando said the other night. It must eat at his gut not to have been picked as one of the Mar-Martins."

"I don't buy it," Oatmeale said, shaking his round head. "It's not plausible. You can't tell me anyone would strangle the wrong man — twice— on account of hurt feelings. It won't work, Clarady, not even in a revenge tragedy."

"Not even in a revenge tragedy written by Anthony Munday," Dando added, winning a laugh.

"All right, then," Tom said. "I withdraw my motion of envy and submit a motion of self-preservation."

He explained his idea that Munday might be working both as Canon Bancroft's pursuivant and as Martin's minion, running pamphlets to the printers along with reports on the canon's plans. He hadn't gotten very far before bleats of laughter started bursting from his listeners' lips. As he wound up his articulate and well-paced argument, the chuckles exploded into howls. Dando clutched helplessly at his belly while Oatmeale gripped his friend's shoulder for support, tilting his head toward the sky. Even Nashe, who had heard it before, laughed so hard he rolled off the tomb where he'd been sitting.

Tom waited with lips pressed tightly together while they emptied themselves of merriment at his expense. Oatmeale recovered first. "It was well argued, Clarady, I'll give you that. You'll make a fine barrister one day. And while I don't believe your lunatic notion in the sense of a thing that might actually happen here in the world, I believe it could make for a popular play. The audience would roar with excitement when that second twist is revealed."

"You should write it," Dando said.

"Not my sort of thing," Oatmeale said. "But I might get a few shillings for the idea. Marlowe's too haughty these days, but Thomas Kyd seems to be in a dry patch . . ."

Tom surrendered to the judgment of his three-man jury. "All right, I rest my case. But I need something more substantial for Mr. Bacon than your opinion of how well my story would work on the stage."

Dando clapped his hands together. "Munday's bound to be at the Goose. Let's go shake it out of him."

* * *

They found their man upstairs at a table in the corner, busily writing, with his squat inkpot near his right hand and a clay mug near his left.

"Stand up, Anthony Munday!" Dando called as they marched up the stairs. "It's your reckoning day!"

Seeing the quartet of mud-smeared men approaching, Munday jumped up and drew his knife, kicking his stool over so it rolled out of his way. "What do you lot want with me?"

267

"Answers," Tom said. He grinned at Dando. "Who draws a knife when he sees his comrades coming?"

"Cowards," Dando said, "and fools."

The two new friends gripped the edge of the round table and shoved it hard against Munday's midsection, forcing him against the wall and making it impossible for him to reach anyone with his slashing blade.

"We only want to ask you a few questions," Tom said. He reached out and pushed the wad of wool into the top of the inkpot in case Munday chose to overturn the table instead of answering. Ink made such a mess, and Tom had no quarrel with the tavern people.

Munday grumbled and growled and tossed out a few idle threats but mumbled out a confession in the end. He had pushed Robert Greene down the stairs, enraged by an unwarranted spate of boasting, which the four interrogators allowed was one of Greene's most irritating habits. Munday swore he hadn't meant the man any serious harm. It was pure bad luck that the stairs happened to be free of customers at that precise moment to break his fall.

Munday further swore, in terms Tom would hesitate to share with his late father's crew, that he would sooner roast himself in the fires of hell than give the slightest aid to that monstrous, scheming, whoreson traitor Martin Marprelate.

Satisfied, the table was pulled back and bottles of wine were shouted for. When the wench came, Tom asked for platters of cheese and meat and anything else that was fast and tasty. He was hungry, having risked life and limb in pursuit of this commission. And he trusted Peter Hollowell to let him charge this small reward to Mr. Cecil's purse.

TWENTY-FIVE

Francis Bacon entered the shop of his favorite bookseller on Paternoster Row and stood for a moment, adjusting to the dim light, savoring the intoxicating perfumes of ink and paper. Oliver Brocksby, printer and proprietor, looked up from the counter at the back where he stood leafing through an elephant folio. "Good afternoon, Mr. Bacon! What do you lack today?"

"Everything," Francis said, walking back through the narrow aisles of stacked books. "And nothing." They both chuckled at the philosophical witticism.

Brocksby gave him a friendly smile. His thinning brown hair moved a little farther back from his forehead every year, but his wiry frame kept its spring and the strength to port even stacks of big Genevan Bibles from barrel to shelf.

"I need an assortment of pamphlets," Francis said, explaining the types of authors he had in mind. "And I have a question or two about Martin Marprelate."

"I don't know who he is," Brocksby hastened to say.

"I never imagined you did. But you must have ideas about what sort of man he is."

"Only the usual. He's educated; that much is obvious. He's clever at disputation as well. Note how well he parries these recent counterstrikes. Quick-thinking and light on his feet, rhetorically speaking. I shouldn't be surprised to learn he was a barrister, to be honest with you."

"Nor should I," Francis said. "Or a member of Parliament. That seems to be the common view." He drummed his fingers lightly on the counter, trying to read the title of Brocksby's new book from the corner of his eye.

Brocksby helpfully turned it toward him. *The Voyage and Travaile of M. Caesar Frederick, Merchant of Venice, into the East India,* translated by T.H. "Fascinating," Francis said, stroking the leather cover. "Is this new?"

"Last year, but still popular, I hope. People do love these travel accounts."

"Mmm." People like Francis, though his bill in this shop had already risen to the delicate level. Their eyes met briefly, and Brocksby shifted the book to a shelf beneath the counter.

Never mind. That wasn't what he'd come for. "I wonder about Martin's printer," Francis said. "He must be a member of the Stationers' Company, mustn't he?"

"One would assume so, though he could be retired. Or he might be on the Continent. Or merely a journeyman, although the quality of the books suggest a master craftsman to me."

"I think so too," Francis said. "Where do you suppose Martin would find such a man? He couldn't very well walk into a workshop and ask if anyone would like to spend a year dodging the authorities to produce copies of illegal tracts."

"Mercy, no!" Brocksby pulled a grayish handkerchief out of his sleeve and mopped his narrow forehead at the mere thought. "I've thought about that too. Wondering if it could be anyone I know — which I very much doubt. Educated gentlemen and printers only meet in a few places, when you think about it. Martin could have recruited his printer at church."

"At church. Of course." A few pieces fell into place somewhere in the back of Francis's mind, like imaginary pieces of lead type. Not a readable message — not yet — but tantalizingly close. "They would know from long attendance where each other stood in such matters. Moreover, it's one of the few places where men of different stations do meet and get to know one another enough to establish trust."

"They would have chosen that church for its preacher," Brocksby said. "You wouldn't meet Martin in my church, for example. St. Bride's conforms with established practice without qualm or quibble."

"That's an important consideration. It would tend to rule out Inns of Court members too. Each inn has its own chapel, attended solely by members. Although —" Francis's thoughts were racing ahead of his speech. "Many men, especially the married ones, have their own houses in town and would normally attend the church in that parish."

"Your hotter churches are mostly in the city. You won't find radical nonconformity being preached from a pulpit in Westminster."

"No, you wouldn't." Francis laughed. But what delicious irony, if Martin had met his co-conspirators at a church down the street from Whitehall Palace. "How many men would Martin's printer need? A typesetter, I suppose. Although you sometimes set type, don't you?"

"Only for very special editions. Or in a pinch. I like to keep my hand in." And his teeth, judging by their grayness. Typesetters tended to tuck pieces into their mouths while they were working.

"Could two men produce Martin's works?"

Brocksby shook his head. "I very much doubt it. They're well made, for pamphlets. I'll bet he's got a second man helping to operate the press and hang the pages to dry. And you don't want your typesetter proofreading his own pages if you can help it."

"That makes sense." Francis stroked his moustache with his forefinger, searching for another question and not finding one. He'd have to consider that hint about recruiting at church. His aunt, Lady Russell, could probably give him a list of the most radical churches in London, if she were inclined to assist him, which he rather doubted. She might not shelter Martin in her own home, but she wouldn't help to apprehend him either.

Brocksby placed his hands flat on the countertop. "Do you have specific authors in mind, or are you just wanting Puritan-leaning tracts in general?"

"Let me try an assortment. If you have anything written by members of Parliament, that's where I'd like to start."

"What will you be looking for, if you don't mind my asking?"

"I don't know," Francis admitted. "A sense of style. Martin is witty, unlike every Presbyterian or Calvinist I've ever read."

Brocksby nodded. "If you don't mind my making a suggestion, take a close look at the type as well. If you've got a pair of spectacles, try those. Martin's printers won't find it easy to replace a damaged piece, so you might find a crack in the *W*'s or a missing bit from the down stroke of an *S*."

"That's an excellent suggestion. Thank you!" Francis kept a pair of spectacles in his writing box for studying illustrations. He loved using them. They made him feel that he could peer into the very heart of the book itself. This promised to be a most enjoyable couple of days, even if he didn't find any answers.

* * *

By Saturday afternoon, Francis had exhausted his stock of pamphlets, his eyes, and Tom's patience. He'd sent him out on Friday afternoon to knock on doors in Gray's Inn asking to borrow commonplace books with notes from speeches made by the Puritan party in Parliament, especially from the seventies, when the battles over the Book of Common Prayer had raged the loudest. Francis had stayed up until the wee hours, so entranced by this extraordinary glimpse into those debates that he often forgot why he had embarked on the study in the first place.

Otherwise, the effort had not been successful, other than in the negative sense. He could rule out Sir Richard Knightley as the author of Martin's witty tracts; also John Penry, another name often bandied about in that context. He'd never read such stultifying speeches in his life. A detailed transcript of a speech Job Throckmorton gave in favor of the execution of Mary, Queen of Scots, tickled Francis's rhetorical instincts, but it lacked the peppery sauce of Martin's prose. Close, but not quite.

He had set Thomas Nashe, who was no fool in spite of his manner, to studying the minutiae of the printed pages, comparing Martin's works to every printed book, pamphlet, or broadside in the house. The satirist had been able to identify several quirks unique to Martin's texts, but could not find similar flaws anywhere else. Those characters must have been damaged in transit, after Martin's gang of printers had been assembled.

Those errata would testify against those men once they were caught, but wouldn't help locate them.

Francis clambered off his high bed and went to the stand by the mirror where Pinnock had left a basin, a jug, and a spray of herbs. He frisked a sprig of rosemary in a splash of water and dabbed it about his cheeks and temples to revive his wits. Then he wrapped a shawl around his shoulders and went into his study chamber to slump in his big chair and stare at the spines of books laid in tidy stacks on the shelves. Something tugged at his memory, something connected to something in Martin Junior's *Theses*, which he'd just finished reading again. Something, therefore, specifically Presbyterian.

He didn't collect such works, although his mother and his aunt owned them all. Francis held the sprig of rosemary under his nose, inhaling the inspirative scent. The book he wanted undoubtedly reposed in his mother's library at Gorhambury. No good to him now. Or . . .

His gaze shifted to the ebony chest where he kept personal letters worth reading again, mostly words of advice from his uncle and aunts about pursuing or ceasing to pursue some post or honor. He read more than books and pamphlets, didn't he? He must read four letters a day on an average day, most of them written by his well-educated, Reformation-minded relations.

He hopped up and got the chest, setting it on his desk and opening the carved lid, releasing the scent of the lavender his mother used to ward off plague. He began unfolding letters, reading just enough to remember their contents, then folding them back up, setting the visited ones aside. Halfway down, he found the one he sought: a letter from his Aunt Elizabeth written several years ago, when Gray's had been searching for a new chaplain.

She'd been outraged by some remarks made by one of the benchers that Francis had passed along as a conversational tidbit over Sunday dinner. She must have fumed about it all night because the next morning brought this tart missive, including, word for word, Martin Junior's thesis number seventy-five: "That by the doctrine of the Church of England it is popery to translate the word *presbyteros* into priests, and so to call the ministers of the gospel, priests." This word means 'elder,' Nephew. Cleave closely to the original source and language in any translation, lest you stray down false paths laid by lesser interpreters."

Nothing irritated the Cooke sisters more than a mangled Bible translation.

He dug through the chest, searching out all his aunt's letters, including three with poems she'd written commemorating events in her life. She was an accomplished poet; he'd forgotten that. Reading them all together like this revealed the distinctive qualities of her style — the very elements of Martin's prose that had been tickling his memory all this time. Aunt Elizabeth had Martin's erudition, rich vocabulary, and passionate conviction, but more — she shared his inimitable energy of expression and a capacity for vivid characterization.

He jumped up to retrieve his copies of Martin's pamphlets, sitting back down to shift between those and the letters. *Yes, yes!* It was so clear once the key had turned to unlock the fundamental secret. His aunt had surpassed herself in her guise as Martin Marprelate, achieving a sprightly, challenging, gleeful tone not to be found in her letters. But then, Martin wrote for a larger audience.

He had it. He heaved a great sigh and leaned back in his chair, holding the letter limply in his hand while the pieces fell into place in his mind, like metal letters snicking into a typesetter's composition stick. Only now the message was complete. Martin Marprelate's true name was Lady Elizabeth Russell, formerly Elizabeth Cooke, self-styled Dowager Countess of Bedford.

At last, he understood how Martin had been able to evade the combined efforts of the Church and the Privy Council. *He* was in fact a *she*! Not a member of Parliament, though Lady Russell would make a formidable one. Archbishop Whitgift had come the closest with his veiled accusation of Francis's mother. He'd aimed in the right direction, but struck at the wrong sister.

Francis laughed out loud, alone in his chambers, but his exhilaration swiftly faded. He had solved the greatest mystery of the day all by himself. But who could he tell? He pictured himself visiting his aunt in her house in Blackfriars, scolding her soundly, forbidding her ever to write anything other than a personal letter again. Her imaginary laughter burned his ears. He had as much authority over his aunt as he did over his mother, and his authority over his mother was exactly nil.

TWENTY-SIX

Trumpet listened to the sermon on Sunday morning with only half an ear. In the past, she'd gotten some of Martin's best ideas from St. Ann's fervent — sometimes frenetical — preacher. But Martin's days would soon be over. She trusted her urchins to spot the man who collected her last opus. Even if they failed to describe him well enough for her to identify him, the printer would surely recognize the falseness of the text. At least, she hoped he would. Anonymous or not, she took pride in Martin's work and the recognition it had achieved. She would hate to see that reputation marred by her ill-made decoy.

She wouldn't have to spend many more Sunday mornings in this ill-made substitute for a church either. The space had been squeezed out of some prelate's lodgings by Henry the Eighth's Master of Revels, to whom the old Blackfriars monastery had been granted after the Dissolution. He'd been obliged to provide his new residents with a parish church, but he'd turned the old chapel into a pair of profitable tennis courts. He satisfied the letter, if not the spirit, of the law with this cramped upstairs parlor.

The present congregation doubtless preferred the lack of aesthetic qualities. Puritans loved plainness. As Lady Russell had once said, with her nose in the air, "We come to hear the word, not gawk at objects of idolatry." Fair enough. But Trumpet would use all her wiles to prevent her future husband from purchasing a house in Blackfriars so as to avoid this miserable church.

In fact, she'd add that to the list of desiderata she was compiling for her marriage contract. She'd come home from visiting her aunt and informed Lady Russell that she was ready to accept her single non-insulting proposal. She intended to prolong the negotiations as far as possible, but even so, her life had now entered a new phase. She would pass out of Lady Russell's tutelage within the coming year.

The past year had been a hard one, with all the praying and the Calvinist tracts and the endless sea of black filling her clothing chests. She had only partially succeeded in restoring her reputation, though that would no longer matter once she married. But she had achieved her other goal, of learning the role of a woman of importance, by dint of surrendering herself wholly to Lady Russell's requirements.

It had been a hard year, but worth the sacrifice. As Tom liked to say, the best way to learn the ropes was to get right on board and start swinging.

She could abandon this ship of righteousness and rectitude whenever she liked now. She might move back to her aunt's, or better yet, petition for another chance as one of Queen Elizabeth's maids of honor. She'd have to surrender every last scrap of freedom, even her music lessons and her Thursday afternoons, but she'd be in the best position to curry favors and forge connections for her new husband. His power would be hers, after all.

The congregation rose and began to file out of the pews. The service must have ended. Thank God for that! She wanted a gulp of fresh air and a cup of well-watered wine. But Lady Russell remained planted at the end of their row, offering her hand or a supercilious smile to fellow worshippers who swam against the prevailing tide to greet her.

One of these was a gentleman in a dark red suit. Trumpet had seen him here before but had never met him. Now Her Ladyship chose to introduce them. "Lady Alice. Have you met our neighbor, Mr. Hollowell?"

"I have not yet had the pleasure." Trumpet held out a hand for him to bow over.

"The honor is mine."

"Mr. Hollowell is the secretary of my nephew, Robert Cecil," Lady Russell said.

"That must keep you busy," Trumpet said.

Her lips mirrored the shape of her advisor's cool smile as she took in the secretary's medium stature, his hair — the color of wet sand — and his bluntly pointed beard. Tom had suspected him for a while but changed his mind after their friendly supper, to which Trumpet had not been invited.

She wouldn't mind asking this courteous gentleman a few questions of her own, but where? Not here, certainly. Hollowell murmured a few polite words about paying a visit, bowed again, and left.

Trumpet gathered her skirts to press through to the aisle, but Lady Russell continued to sit, now chatting with some old buzzard about rose clippings. He left, to be replaced by a pinch-faced young woman who attended St. Ann's every Sunday. Her father was a goldsmith or a locksmith — some sort of smith.

"It is *so* kind of you to invite me to dinner, my lady," Ms. Pinch gushed. "Such a *gracious* way to meet a prospective husband, don't you agree? Oh! But of course you must since you arranged it, didn't you?" She shrilled a laugh which swiftly rose to a pitch only dogs could hear.

Trumpet's wandering mind snapped into focus. *Dinner, today?* The only prospective husband she might meet at their house today was a fair-haired, dimple-cheeked, long-legged law student named Thomas Clarady. When did all this arranging take place?

"*Far* less formal than sitting around a cold table with a band of sour-faced attorneys." The simpering twit burst into another shrieking laugh, covering its pale lips with a limp hand. "But I mustn't object to that, must I? My prospective will soon be a barrister himself, won't he?"

Why did she phrase every utterance as a question? Could she possibly imagine anyone would respond to such trite remarks?

Trumpet bit the inside of her lip. Ms. Pinch's face wasn't the only thing about her that was narrow. She was slender and tall, with that lithe, fragile quality Tom liked. Worse, her hair was the color of the sunshine streaming in the east-facing window — a clear, pale yellow. It went without saying that her eyes, though placed too close to her long nose, were an equally clear, pale blue.

She had a long neck too, rising whitely out of her lace-trimmed ruff. Trumpet's eyes narrowed. What would it take to place that goose-like neck in the path of Martin's strangler?

* * *

Trumpet was climbing the stairs in the Blackfriars house to go up, lie on her bed, and stare at the underside of the canopy until dinnertime. She didn't truly wish Constance Golding to be strangled, but a tumble down a hard staircase, like this one, would not be displeasing.

The housekeeper's voice rose from the entry hall. "Good morning, Mr. Hollowell. Her Ladyship is in the library."

Trumpet peered over the bannister and caught a glimpse of Hollowell being led to the ground-floor library, Lady Russell's favorite room for doing the morning's correspondence and receiving visitors. Tom may have stricken this man from his list of suspects, but Trumpet had her doubts. That redheaded whore had been lying about something, and there had only been one topic on the table.

She waited until the door to the library closed and the housekeeper's coifed head passed by, going in the direction of the kitchen. Then she slipped as quietly as a stalking cat out the rear door to the garden, lifting her skirts and ducking low to take up a listening post beneath the windows. No one would see her. The gardener and his boy had Sunday mornings free, which they usually spent sleeping off their Saturday night in their room above the stable. The rest of the staff would be busy in the kitchen and dining hall.

She crouched behind a rounded boxwood, leaning a shoulder against the wall for balance. She could hear the conversation in the library quite clearly.

Hollowell had a pleasant voice, warm and masculine. "I fear it will take me longer to deliver the latest work, my lady. Our friends have been obliged to move again. They're in Manchester now, over a week's ride each way. I'll be gone for more than a fortnight."

"That's much too far," Lady Russell objected in her clarion tones. "And also unwise, to set up in a small town. They'll be noticed in a matter of days. If you want to do something in secret, you must do it in the heart of the city or on your private estate. Why couldn't they stay in Northamptonshire? We were so well settled there under Sir Richard's protection."

"I'm afraid that infernal pest Thomas Nashe picked up our scent. He came perilously close to the truth."

A silence fell. Trumpet could imagine Lady Russell's eyes narrowing and her lips thinning as she framed her next question. "You wouldn't know anything about these murdered pamphleteers, would you, Mr. Hollowell?"

"God's mercy, my lady, I do not! I would have come to you at once."

That was a brazen lie. He knew everything Tom and Mr. Bacon knew. Although he couldn't reveal that knowledge since Lady Russell didn't know about their commission. Trumpet bit her lip. How could she judge anyone's truthfulness with so many secrets crisscrossing one another like threads in a tapestry?

At least one thing was now certain: Peter Hollowell was the link between Martin Marprelate and Sir Richard Knightley. And Knightley was linked to Dando, also known as Snorscombe, whose role in all this had yet to be explained. The disparate threads began to form a picture, if still an incomplete one.

Lady Russell hummed, a neutral sound. "Do you think those murders have anything to do with our work?"

"I do not, my lady. Not for one minute. I'm sure those tragic deaths resulted from some private quarrel. You don't know these men, my lady — these writers. They're an unruly lot. They dress like gentlemen, but they're rogues at heart, living in those ungovernable liberties where they can do as they please. They love trouble. Scandal sells copies. Idleness and dissolution are the seedbeds of violence."

"Whoever is slack in his work is a brother to him who destroys," Lady Russell quoted.

Trumpet shifted onto her knees, padding them with the hem of her skirt, letting the bands of her farthingale collapse in a circle around her. Catalina would be unhappy about the dew soaking into the black taffeta, but it couldn't be helped. As she settled onto the folds of fabric behind her knees, she glimpsed a reflection of Peter Hollowell in the half-open window.

The image wavered where the lines between the diamond-shaped panes transected it, but it was clear enough to see the pious expression on his face. Another strike against him. Trumpet hated that expression on any face.

"How long will it be before our latest work appears in London?" Lady Russell asked.

"If all goes well, about three weeks. But my lady, all is not well. I am informed that the printer and his men are growing fearful and chafing at their confinement. Restless, fretful men are not reliable keepers of secrets. It may be time to bring this phase of our great project to a close."

"I'm afraid I must agree. It's just as well. I have said all that I have to say in this form."

"And said it well, my lady. Martin Marprelate's works will live forever."

Lady Russell sighed. "Is that all, Mr. Hollowell? I have guests for dinner today."

"I have everything I need, my lady." Hollowell's reflection met Trumpet's eyes, startling her and making her duck.

Silly goose! It was only an image, a semblance, like a portrait with a knowing gaze. The portrait couldn't see you, however real it felt.

* * *

Two hours later, Trumpet conducted Tom and the Golding creature into the walled orchard behind the house, leaving Mr. Bacon and Lady Russell conversing in the library. Tom had evidently been warned about the additional guest. He'd taken extra pains with his appearance, adding another stupid hawk feather to his hat, as if anyone would believe a mere clerk had the time or money to go hawking. The Golding didn't seem to notice, but what woman would look at feathers when Tom's face was in view?

He treated her with courtesy, which was only just and to be expected. The creature hadn't asked to be given a duck's bill for a nose and beady eyes placed too close together. But his courtesy had that extra touch of charm he reserved for women he liked. He was considering her as a possible wife, Trumpet could sense it, like an elusive fragrance wafting from him that only she could smell.

Tom stopped beside a plum tree laden with red fruit that had been artfully trained against the red-brick wall. "These plums look delicious. I hope we'll find some on the table today."

An obvious sally, to which everyone ought to reply, "Oh yes. Quite lovely."

But the Golding sniffed, tilting up her sharp little chin. "Plums are all very well, I suppose, but they can't compare with *peaches*. We have peaches at our house in Sussex, Mr. Clarady. Two different varieties, brought all the way from Italy."

"Italy, you say?" Tom's tone was polite, but his lips had twitched, and a little furrow had formed briefly between his eyes. Nobody liked a braggart, especially from the issue of a mere tradesman. A goldsmith was a smith. Gold, black, it made no difference — the man still hammered bits of metal together to earn his bread.

Trumpet wrenched a plum from the tree and bit into it, bending abruptly forward to keep the juice from dripping onto her skirt. She tossed the thing into a patch of blooming mint and drew a handkerchief from her sleeve to wrap around her sticky hand. "Delicious! My favorite fruit."

Tom barked a laugh, knowing her favorite fruit was raspberry, but recognizing that the Golding's boast demanded some sort of set-down. He turned away from the smith's offspring to speak directly to Trumpet. "I met our friend John Dando yesterday."

"Oh? What did he have to —"

"Dando?" the Golding's nasal voice cut in. "I don't believe I know that name."

"He's a pamphleteer," Trumpet said. "Quite a famous one."

The Golding frowned, her thin lips turned down like a carp. "Ugh! I wouldn't care to know *that* sort of person."

"Don't worry," Tom said. "I wouldn't introduce you." He shot a wink at Trumpet and passed behind his future bride so the two old friends could stroll together along the path, walking away from the intruder. He bent his head and murmured, "Dando's clear. He didn't do it."

"How do you know?"

"I fought with him." Tom rubbed his chin gingerly and gave her a grin that made her heart skip two beats. "There's nothing like a good brawl to get the measure of a man."

"So true," Trumpet said. "I hear Sir Richard Topcliffe has added fisticuffs to his roster of interrogation methods."

"Brawling?" The Golding had crept up behind them. "I cannot believe *you* would engage in such disorderly acts, Mr. Clarady."

"It was all in good fun," Tom said, smiling tightly as he stopped and turned to face her.

"Oh, you naughty, naughty man!" The Golding shook her finger at him, her face twisted into what she probably thought was a charming pretense at admonishment.

Tom's eyebrows furled in alarm. Trumpet choked back a laugh, slipped her arm through his, and turned him away from the intruder, continuing on around the garden. "What about Munday?"

"Monday is impossible." The Golding had cut across on one of the diagonal paths and now stood in front of them again. "I must not see you again so soon, Mr. Clarady. I wouldn't wish to appear too *eager.*" She batted her lashes, lips pursed in a simpering smile.

This time Tom's upper lip curled as he took a hasty step back. Trumpet's heart danced a merry jig. This day was turning out to be rather pleasant after all.

"Munday's out too," Tom said, meeting Trumpet's eyes with a quelling glare. She might have emitted the tiniest of giggles.

285

"What's next, then?"

He shrugged. "Another trap, I guess. What else can we do?"

"Traps?" The Golding peered from Tom to Trumpet, clasping her bony hands to her flat chest. "Traps? What sort of traps?"

"Traps for rats," Trumpet said, putting a growl into the word.

"*Rats!*" the Golding shrieked in a voice so shrill Tom actually recoiled from her, backing into the brick wall. The look on his face was beyond rubies — wide-eyed, open-mouthed horror.

Trumpet heaved a satisfied sigh. Her work here was done. "Shall we go in for dinner?"

* * *

More treacherous undercurrents flowed around the dinner table that Sunday than raced under London Bridge during a rising tide. Each word seemed laden with hidden hazards. Trumpet enjoyed parts of it, especially the hastily covered grimaces with which Tom responded to the Golding's attempts at conversation. She'd speak, he'd twitch, then stretch a polite smile across his lips while shooting a panicky glance at Lady Russell. That august person's eyes turned too often toward Trumpet with a thoughtful expression, as if calculating the days since her last Martin manuscript and wondering why it had taken so long for it to be collected.

Mr. Bacon's eyes were hollowed by dark shadows. He looked as if he hadn't slept for days. He kept casting anxious glances at his aunt, as if he expected her to leap up and strike him. Any question put to him, however bland, was answered by a babbling exegesis of some obscure work of Roman classical literature which must have borne some relevance in his complicated mind, but no one else could divine the vaguest connection.

Trumpet watched him surreptitiously, though he sometimes seemed to sense her gaze and flinch away from it. She knew everyone else's secrets here today, or was fairly certain she did. But what fresh knowledge did Francis Bacon have hidden up his velvet sleeve?

* * *

Trumpet offered to walk home with the Golding, accompanied by her maidservant, but the offer was refused — as expected. One of the smith's grooms came to collect the spawn. Mr. Bacon clung to Tom's side as they milled toward the entry, preventing anyone from getting a private word in. Frustrated, and determined to avoid being summoned to the library to explain the lag in delivery of Martin's last manuscript, Trumpet simply vanished, running up the rear staircase and hiding ignominiously in her room.

When the housekeeper came up with Her Ladyship's predicted request, she bade Catalina speak through a crack in the door, explaining in heavily accented English that her mistress suffered from the derangement of the head and necessitated much repose. Having nothing better to do and not daring to sneak out, Trumpet let Catalina undress her and tuck her under a coverlet with the latest romance from Robert Greene. In spite of her morning of unpleasant surprises — or perhaps because of it — her eyes closed of their own accord after only a few pages.

The late-afternoon sun cast long stripes across the room when next she opened them. She blinked away the dregs of a dream about sailing to Bohemia with Tom, then yawned and stretched. "What's the clock?"

"After four, my lady."

"Is Her Ladyship in her room?"

"I believe so."

"Good." Trumpet sat up and swung her feet to the floor. The nap had settled her jumbled feelings and left her mind clear, ready to evaluate the new developments and determine on a plan. "Let's go walk in the garden, where can we talk."

Catalina dressed her in a plain woolen dress, not bothering to add sleeves over those of her chemise. The afternoon was warm and they weren't going out. She added a wide straw hat to protect Trumpet's cheeks and collected her sewing basket. They padded quietly through the house, out the rear door, and into the orchard. Catalina sat on her bench in the shade of the arbor and picked up her needle.

Trumpet folded her hands behind her back and began to pace back and forth along the sunny path. "I think I have it all. Every odd piece of this curious case, neatly hemmed and ready to lace together, like the parts of a bodice that can open either front or back."

"Very clear, my lady."

"Peter Hollowell is Martin's minion. I'll wager he's the one who set the whole thing up once my lady asked him if he knew a printer who could keep a secret. She never told me how it all began. I don't suppose it matters now. Hollowell used his knowledge of estates in Northamptonshire, gained through his work as a feodary, to select Sir Richard Knightley."

Catalina echoed the quaint word under her breath. "Fee-oh-dah-ree."

Trumpet nodded at her. "From what my Ladies Fulburne and Chadwick said, on top of what Tom has told me, those feodaries are constantly on the prowl for orphans with lands. I'd bet a golden angel that it was Hollowell's clerk who gossiped with Thomas Nashe in that alehouse near Fawsley. Then here comes Nashe's *Martin's Mirror Mar'd*, naming Fawsley in plain print. Hollowell must have been gnashing his teeth, wondering what others details had been kept back for the next pamphlet."

"He don't sleep now," Catalina said.

"Not well, my friend. Not well. On one of those restless nights, he decides to silence Nashe and the other anti-Martinists once and for all, acting on the time-honored principle that three may keep a secret if two of them are dead."

Catalina chuckled. "This is an old Italian proverb."

"It is?" Trumpet paused to consider it, then shrugged and resumed her pacing. Like any good barrister, she thought better on her feet. "Unfortunately for Edgar Stokes and John Little, Hollowell didn't know what Thomas Nashe looked like. He listened to gossip at the Goose and Gall, the writers' lair, which he could have learned about from any printer or bookseller, I suppose."

Catalina shrugged. She was a little disgruntled about being left out of Trumpet's last adventure with Tom. She especially wanted to meet John Dando, having gotten a glimpse of him from Lady Fulburne's garden.

Trumpet continued her summation. "He's a persistent fellow, our Mr. Hollowell. One failure, even two, don't discourage him, not even after his master, Robert Cecil, engages Francis Bacon to pursue him. Perhaps that inspired him to try even harder, pushing Robert Greene down the stairs and walking right into our trap, intent on catching Thomas Nashe. It must have been quite a surprise to find he'd caught his master's cousin instead. Oh!" She clapped her hands together. "He called him 'Frank'! We wondered about that, but it's only natural for Peter Hollowell, who would have heard his master refer to his own cousin by that name often enough."

"Remember the whore," Catalina said. "You say she lies. I could tell you for certain if I speak with her. No whore may lie with me."

"*To* me," Trumpet corrected. "No, I think we'd better let her go. I'm afraid more attention might get her killed as well. We have the clerk in Northamptonshire, if Nashe can find him again. We have the fact that the wall where the manuscripts are hidden belongs to a parcel of land owing feudal duty. Who would know a thing like that other than a feodary? And that parcel of land is owned by Sir Richard Knightley, who is rumored to possess a private printing press and who has a nephew who is the brother of John Dando, who was my favorite suspect until Tom ruled him out by trading a few blows somewhere. I wish I could have been there."

Trumpet made a full circuit of the garden to give her legs a little stretch. On the return leg, she snatched a sprig from a coriander plant, holding it under her nose. The fragrance reminded her of the minced scallops they'd eaten on the way to the Stationers' Hall, which reminded her of that entry in the record book, which had helpfully supplied Dando's true name and place of origin.

God's light! She'd noticed the difference in ink at the time. What odds Peter Hollowell had added that note before pushing Tom toward Dando? She had to admire the man's thoroughness. Then again, he hadn't been made personal secretary to the son of England's most powerful man on account of his looks.

"Yes, I think I have it all," she said, coming back around to the arbor. "A detail here and there yet to be supplied, but I have sufficient proofs. But toward what end? I can't let anyone find out about any of this."

"But Mr. Nashe! We must not let him die, my lady. He is a sweet one, in his way."

"*Nashe?*"

Catalina shrugged. "A man like him, he is always so grateful. That has appeal, sometimes. A woman likes to be appreciated."

"Hmm." Trumpet wondered if Tom was ever grateful in such circumstances. She didn't know much about them, apart from what Catalina had told her, but she suspected that in Tom's case, the gratitude tended to run the other way. "Of course we won't let Nashe die. The killing must stop. In fact, the whole Martin Marprelate business must stop. My lady agreed to that this morning. It's all become too difficult. The printers were forced to run to Manchester to escape the pursuivants. They're afraid they'll be captured any day."

"Where is Manchester?"

"I have no idea. Someplace far. I'm glad it's over, to be honest. I can't keep playing Martin Junior now that I have a marriage to manage."

Catalina's sallow face brightened. "Let us return to your aunt, my lady. She is so much more jolly and close to the theater. We may go every day."

"We will see every play in London henceforward. We will have supper at the Antelope whenever we like. We will ride there in a coach, which I will demand my new husband provide for me."

"Oh yes, my lady! Much better for the skirts."

Trumpet smiled. She would add that excuse to her demand. The coach might well pay for itself. "First, however, I must deal with Peter Hollowell."

"He knows you and my Lady Russell. He will tell, will he not?"

"To save his neck?" Trumpet nodded. "Of a certainty. Which is why I can't allow him to be arrested and interrogated." She came to a stop in the shade of the arbor and pulled off her big hat, dropping it on the bench beside her maidservant.

"Will they hang her?" Catalina's black eyes widened. "Hang *you*, my lady?"

Trumpet flapped a dismissive hand. "They don't hang the nobility. They cut our heads off." When her servant gasped in horror, she added, "Never fear, it won't come to that. My Lady Russell is too important a personage. She's the sister-in-law of the Lord Treasurer. And I am the daughter of an earl, now betrothed to an earl. Furthermore, all we've done is publish some mildly provocative religious tracts under an assumed name. We'd get off with a slap on the wrists and a stiff fine."

"Then let Mr. Hollowell be captured and put in prison, where he no harm our friends."

"Only as a last resort. The scandal would be utterly fantastical. For one thing, it might cause my suitor to withdraw his offer. Nothing has been signed yet. For another, the queen would be furious. We would hear her roaring all the way from Whitehall. And now that I think of it, she'd undoubtedly put us all in the Tower at her pleasure, which could be many months."

"I no like the Tower, my lady. It is very damp and very boring." They had spent a few nights there after Viscount Surdeval's untimely demise. In the relative comfort of the Lieutenant's own home, but still, a prison.

"I agree," Trumpet said. "But it's better than hanging, which is what Hollowell can expect. So I can threaten to expose the whole affair to extract a promise to stop strangling pamphleteers."

"Do you trust his promise, my lady?"

Trumpet raised her hands, palms up. "I'll have to, won't I? As he must trust me. We both have secrets with undesirable consequences. It's a simple matter of mutual consideration and respect."

Catalina nodded thoughtfully. "This is how you call blackmail, is it not, my lady?"

"Yes, it is!" Trumpet beamed at her. "It's the right answer, I'm certain of it. I understand blackmail. It's a useful tool in negotiations — one that precludes the use of violence, I might add." She started pacing again, counting tasks off on her fingers. "I must send a note to Hollowell

292

first thing in the morning. He must live in Blackfriars, but I don't know which house."

"The stablemen may know."

"Of course they would know! Then I'll send it tonight. Who knows how many letters he finds on his desk every Monday morning at Burghley House? I'll tell him meet me at —" She broke off and stopped in front of her servant. "Where?"

"A big place, my lady. Many people. The Duck and the Dog?"

"No, we can't be seen together. I know! He can meet me inside the Savoy at my music master's house at ten o'clock. I'll send a note to Mr. Lewis telling him . . . something." She'd have to sort that out.

"No, my lady. He will kill you."

"Mr. Lewis?"

"The *estrangulador*, my lady. You must see him in a busy place."

"No, no. There's no danger. Murdering me would cause nothing but trouble for him. I'm not some poor writer, to be cut down in the street and forgotten two days later. I'm a lady. A person of consequence. Besides, I will take the precaution of leaving a letter explaining everything to Lady Russell, who would hang the man with her own hands for harming me."

Catalina frowned, but had no further objections. You'd think a woman who had traveled as widely as she had would have more courage, but breeding mattered when it came down to it. Trumpet's ancestors wouldn't hesitate to treat a loathsome cur like Hollowell as he deserved.

She clapped her hands together briskly. "I believe we have a plan. And I have three somewhat ticklish letters to write."

"Yes, my lady." Catalina stuck her needle into a wad of wool and folded the cuff she'd been embroidering. "You go and write your tickling letters. I leave you in peace. I wish to hang your taffeta gown in the kitchen garden and brush him."

"Brush him to a fare-thee-well," Trumpet said. It always made her happy to cut through a tangled undergrowth of confusion and half-truths and expose a clear path to action.

Catalina rose from her bench and shook out her skirts. "My lady, another thought. If we meet this man in the Savoy, your uncle may help us."

Trumpet's uncle, the barrister Nathaniel Welbeck, had rooms in one of the surviving towers of the old Savoy Palace, at the back of the complex, overlooking the river. "No, he may not and don't try to tell him. He'd try to wring some money out of the deal, which would only make things more difficult. In my experience, blackmail yields the best results for both parties when it establishes a simple *quid pro quo*."

* * *

Tom sat at the desk in his bedchamber, picking his teeth with the end of his quill, trying to devise another trap for Martin's minion. It wasn't easy since he'd had to abandon all his previous ideas about the man. Martin's minion could be anybody tall enough to reach Mr. Bacon's neck. Trumpet could be ruled out, but that was all.

He stared out his window at the westering sun, wracking his weary wits. Then a woman in black with a long black veil loomed into his view, gliding toward him across the grass.

"God save me!" He leapt up, knocking over his desk, spilling ink into the rushes. He fumbled his knife out of the scabbard at his back — thank God he was still wearing it! — and pointed it at the witch, who now laid her black-gloved hands upon the very sills of his windows.

"No affright yourself, Mr. Tom," the apparition said in a familiar Spanish accent.

The air rushed out of Tom like a punch in the gut, taking his terror with it. "Catalina. You startled me."

He stuck his knife back into its scabbard and helped her clamber over the sill. Then he turned the table right-side up and scuffed dry rushes over the spilled ink. He offered her a stool and a cup of small beer, which was all he had, but she shook her head at his courtesies.

"I have no time, Mr. Tom. My lady do not know I am gone and I must tell you a terrible thing."

He gave her his full attention as she told him about Trumpet's plan to meet Peter Hollowell, whom she'd identified as Martin's minion, alone, at her music master's house. She refused to tell him how her mistress had decided Mr. Hollowell was the villain.

"It is no matter, Mr. Tom! This Hollowman, he is the *estrangulador*. He has kill two men and almost Mr. Bacon also. He is too dangerous for my lady. But she say, no, no. Blackmail is useful, she say. He has secret, she has secret, all is secret, all is well. But I am afraid of this man. You must stop her."

"I will, I promise. At least, I'll protect her." Stopping Trumpet was more easily said than done. "What's her secret?" No harm in trying.

Catalina refused to tell him that either. "I have betray enough already."

"You have not betrayed her. You are right to tell me." He scratched his beard, thinking how to manage things. He couldn't reach Trumpet in her Blackfriars redoubt and a mere letter would have no effect whatsoever. "I'll meet you at the gates of the Savoy at ten o'clock. If I'm there, she'll have to take me inside with her."

TWENTY-SEVEN

On Monday morning, a misty drizzle shrouded the streets, keeping indoors anyone with a choice in the matter. Trumpet and Catalina draped themselves in long black veils and sat together in silence for the short trip down the river to the Temple Stairs. They could have gotten off at the Savoy Palace, but Trumpet feared her uncle would recognize her, even looking out the window two floors up, even when she was covered from head to toe in anonymous black.

They walked down the Strand to the Savoy's middle gate and marched quickly into the first alley on the left. That led to a row of small houses snugged up against a high brick wall.

"This would be a good place to hide books," Trumpet said as she nearly tripped on a brick that had fallen out of the wall. "Look at this mess!" When no answer came, she turned around. Catalina was yards behind her, dawdling and casting glances back toward the gate.

"He won't see us," Trumpet said, pitching her voice just loud enough to carry that far. "My uncle hasn't even gotten out of bed yet. We'll pop in and surprise him afterward, if you want."

She didn't wait for an answer. She didn't have time. She'd come half an hour early to get rid of the music master. She'd decided against writing a letter. A brightly polished angel would speak more clearly. She'd offer him the coin in exchange for half an hour alone in his house, encouraging him to believe she was meeting a lover. From what she'd heard, facilitating such assignations was one of the principal functions of a music master.

She marched up to the last door in the row and raised her hand to knock, but it opened before her fist met the oak. A man in a mask grabbed her around the waist, lifted her off her feet, and pulled her inside, clasping her to his chest. The door banged shut behind her, the lock clicked, and a wide hand covered her mouth and nose. "Don't scream and I'll let you breathe." The voice belonged to Peter Hollowell.

His grip loosened enough for her to gasp a breath and answer, "I never scream."

Catalina pounded on the door, shouting. Hollowell answered, loud enough to be heard. "Stop that noise or I'll kill her right now. Be quiet, be patient, and you'll see her soon."

He carried Trumpet farther inside the house, into the front room where she had her lessons. She could barely see the shuttered front windows through her veil. She kicked at him, but her skirts muffled the effect. He squeezed her waist and shook her. "Stop that."

He set her on a hard chair and pressed her down while he wrapped a rope around her chest. He let go then, but pulled the rope tight before she had a chance to wriggle free. Finally, he drew off her veil. "Wouldn't it be awkward if I'd grabbed the wrong woman?"

She glared up at him as he chuckled. Then he took a few steps and offered her a mocking bow. "Martin Junior. At last we meet."

She'd signed that name to the letter she'd written him last night. "How do you know it's me?"

"I saw you in the window, Lady Alice. Don't you remember? It was only yesterday, after we were introduced in church. I was in your house talking to Lady Russell, also known to a select few as Martin Marprelate. One doesn't have to be Francis Bacon to put those pieces together."

Trumpet shook her head. "You couldn't see me. That was only your reflection."

"If you could see me, then I could see you. It's a simple matter of optics."

Trumpet scowled, not only at him. Tom probably knew everything about optics from his classes at the university and had failed to share that useful knowledge with her. "Are there books about optics?"

Hollowell laughed. "This is your first question for me? Of course there are. I'll send you one if I decide not to kill you."

"You won't kill me. It'll cause far too much trouble. But what have you done with poor Mr. Lewis?"

"I've granted his fondest wish. He's been pestering my master for months for an audition with the Chapel Children's company. I sent him an invitation to perform tomorrow in Richmond, with a few shillings for his journey. Then I sent a faster messenger to advise the master to show him every courtesy, as a favor to Lord Burghley. It's wonderful, the things one can accomplish from a seat of real power."

Trumpet grunted softly. "That's better than the bribe I was going offer him."

"I'm not a monster, Lady Alice. I've done what I've done to protect our mutual secret — and the reputation of Lady Russell, whom I hold in the highest regard."

"As do I, Mr. Hollowell. I frankly don't see the need for all this drama. We have a mutual problem, you and I. We should be able to arrive at a mutually satisfactory solution."

"We should, in principle, and yet I have doubts, my lady. You seemed so familiar with Mr. Bacon and his clerk yesterday. Of course I know about your history with Tom

Clarady — how you were discovered half-naked in his arms beside the bed of your murdered husband."

"That is *not* what happened," Trumpet said. "Rumors are always grossly exaggerated, Mr. Hollowell. You know that."

"Even so, I fear you might be tempted to share your new discovery with Clarady, who would trot straight to Francis Bacon with it like the good little dog he is." Hollowell shook his head sadly, as if coming to terms with an unpleasant truth. "No, you can't be trusted, my lady. You'll have to go."

Fear raced up Trumpet's spine at the calmness in his tone, raising the hairs on the back of her neck. She blinked and swallowed, mastering herself. "Catalina is right outside that door. If I fail to appear, unharmed, in a few minutes, she'll summon help. Furthermore, Lady Russell will soon find the letter I left explaining everything. You'll be exposed and she will bring the full wrath of her powerful family down upon your head."

"I don't think so," Hollowell said, although his mouth had tensed at the word "wrath." "Not right away. Your reputation will give her pause. And I can easily lure your servant inside here, where I can silence her as well."

He walked around behind her and untied her ruff, tossing it aside. Then he stroked her bare neck, making her shudder with revulsion. Her stomach roiled with dread.

But she was her father's daughter. Her ancestor had helped Great Harry sack Ravenna. She wouldn't beg and she wouldn't give up either. She would watch this varlet hang and cheer while the rope strangled the life out of him. If she could just loosen these bands . . .

"I'll enjoying strangling you, my lady," Hollowell purred. "This soft white throat, so smooth to the touch. Like well-washed silk. Then I'll strip you naked and toss you into the Thames after dark for the fish to nibble."

299

He was trying to scare her, no doubt from some sick humor. That alone roused her courage. She'd spend eternity in the iciest level of hell before she'd let this frustrated play-actor frighten her. "You'd be seen," she said dismissively. "It's light till nine o'clock these days, and after that the river is crowded with lamp-lit barges filled with merrymakers."

"I'll wait until the wee hours."

"That won't work either. There's no moon. You'd need a lantern and you can't carry that and me both." A shadow passed across the front windows. Catalina must be seeking a way to get in.

Hollowell laughed. "Aren't you a quarrelsome wench? No wonder you're still unmarried at your ripe age. I can carry you over my shoulder with ease. You can't weigh more than seven stone."

She winced as he squeezed her throat — lightly, teasingly, testingly. She couldn't think of another argument and didn't think arguments would do much —

Glass exploded from the windows with a ripping crash and a thundering roar. Bricks flew past Trumpet's head, smashing into the wall. Tom burst through the debris, howling like a barbarian, swarming over the furniture, knocking down tables and lamps, grappling Peter Hollowell in both hands and hurling him bodily into the cold fireplace.

Tears sprang into Trumpet's eyes and rolled down her cheeks as she laughed in sheer relief. Her heart overflowed with gratitude and pure joy for that amazing, powerful, loyal, loving, awe-inspiring man. No wonder she adored him. He was beyond all compare.

Hollowell lay still, crumpled on the stone floor of the hearth. Tom watched him, head cocked, hands on hips. Trumpet could not take her eyes off Tom, though she heard Catalina clambering through the broken window, murmuring something in Spanish.

300

"That was too easy," Tom said, but then Hollowell groaned and stirred and rolled over. He crawled out of the hearth on his hands and knees, shooting a black look at Tom, who laughed and said, "Stand up, you coward, or I'll kick you like the slinking dog you are."

Hollowell used the shallow mantelpiece to haul himself onto his feet. He stretched his shoulders with a little groan, then faced Tom with a sneer. "You'll let me go unharmed, Clarady. That little bitch has secrets she doesn't want shared."

Tom danced forward, slapped him sharply across the face, then danced back. "Language, please. There are ladies present." Then he tilted his head toward Trumpet, whose bonds were being cut by Catalina. "All right, Trumplekin?"

Trumpet nodded. "I had everything under control."

"I know." Tom gave her half a grin. "I'm just helping."

"Mmm. Thrash him soundly, won't you?"

"Gladly. Care to join me?"

She laughed, fresh tears springing into her eyes. "Not in this dress."

He shrugged. "Suit yourself." His eyes were a little shiny as well.

Hollowell moved a few feet from the wall and Tom's attention snapped back to him. "Going somewhere, Pete? I'm not done with you yet."

Hollowell held up his hands. "I'm not your enemy, Tom. She is. She's Martin Junior!" He stabbed his finger at Trumpet.

"She's *what?*" Tom whirled around to gape at Trumpet. "How can that be?"

She gave him a full Iberian shrug. "It was Lady Russell's idea. She's Martin. That varlet is — or was — Martin's minion. We knew nothing about the murders, of course. We didn't even know who — Tom!" she shrieked. "Look out!"

Hollowell had drawn his knife. Now he dropped into a fighting stance, slashing toward Tom, who whirled on his heel and reached out one long arm to slap the man across the face again while the other hand grabbed the wrist beneath the knife. He pressed the man to the wall, holding him with an elbow while he cracked the knife hand hard against the oak mantelpiece.

"Am I short, Mr. Hollowell?" he demanded, cracking the hand again.

Hollowell winced but kept the knife in his grip.

"Am I bookish?" Tom asked, with another crack.

"You do read a lot," Trumpet offered.

Tom grinned but didn't move his gaze from Hollowell's face. "Am I a *woman*, Pete? Caught by surprise?" This time he crushed the wrist so hard the fingers wilted, letting the knife fall to the floor. Catalina swooped in to pick it up.

Tom shifted his stance abruptly to wrap his other hand around Hollowell's throat. "Not as pleasant from the other side, is it, Pete?"

Hollowell gurgled. "Mercy, I beg you."

Tom shook his head, frowning doubtfully. "I'm only a clerk, Mr. Hollowell. Like you. In truth, I'm inclined to let your master decide what to do with you."

Hollowell paled visibly. "No, please."

"But then there's this Martin Junior business to consider." Tom shot Trumpet a glance over his shoulder. "We really must discuss that, but this churl keeps interrupting us."

"He's very rude," Trumpet agreed.

Tom nodded. "And more than a little arrogant." He looked the varlet in the eyes and smiled in a friendly fashion. "Time for a nap, Pete."

"I have money," Hollowell begged. "Lots of money. Enough to pay your special livery."

"Too late for that." Tom let go his throat and took two steps back, pulling his captor with him. Then he drew back his fist and drove it into Hollowell's jaw, smacking his head against the plaster wall with a satisfying thump. Hollowell crumpled to the ground again, this time fully insensate.

"Sweet dreams," Tom said. Then he turned full around and spoke to Catalina. "Would you do the honors?" Leaving her to secure the villain, he walked toward Trumpet, slowly, his intentions burning bright in his blue eyes. He wrapped one strong hand around her waist and smoothed the other up her neck to cup the base of her head. "I'm going to kiss you."

"I know." She tilted up her face. "I'll help."

After a long, long time, in which all her fear was healed as if she'd never been an inch away from death, Catalina's voice sounded somewhere nearby. "My lady?"

"Mmm?"

"Where is Mr. Lewis?"

"Who's he?" Tom murmured, nuzzling under her ear.

She inhaled his special fragrance, that mix of musk, warm wool, and pure Tom. Then she placed her hands on his chest and pushed him away so she could think again. "The music master. He's gone for a few days. Hollowell —" She glanced at the man on the floor, who still hadn't awoken. "He sent him on an errand to get him out of the house."

"That's a relief." Tom laid one last kiss on her cheek and went over to poke their captive with his foot. He bent to place his fingers on the man's neck. "He's alive."

Then he inspected Catalina's bindings. She had tied Hollowell's hands together in front of his body, palms out. Next to impossible to undo. She'd also used Trumpet's veil to lash his ankles together.

"Nice work," Tom said, grinning at her. Trumpet realized only now that Catalina must have warned him about this meeting, the little traitor. For that dirty deed, she deserved a week at a comfortable inn with a very pretty man.

"What should we do with him?" Trumpet asked.

"I'll stay here and guard while you and Catalina run up to Gray's and tell Mr. Bacon." Tom grinned. "He won't be happy."

"Better for him that Martin should be his aunt than his cousin though, don't you think?"

"Trouble either way," Tom said. "But you're probably right." He regarded her with a curious look, as if struggling to reconcile this new quality with what he'd known about her before.

Trumpet held her breath. She trusted him, mostly, but this was big. Almost as big as turning from a boy to a girl in the space of a few minutes.

But no — she knew her man, and her man was true. Tom flashed that dimpled grin that melted her insides and said, "You wily women outfoxed the whole of England, from the queen on down. If I hadn't lost my hat in the scuffle, I'd take it off to you." He bowed, a full court bow, sweeping his arm across his chest. Then he turned and bowed to Catalina too.

"Let's go to Italy," Trumpet said, eyes brimming. "All three of us, today. We'll find that troupe of players Catalina used to travel with."

"I wish we could," Tom said, and the spell was broken.

Trumpet picked her way through the rubble he'd created with his dramatic entrance to a sideboard against the far wall. She poked her nose into jars and jugs, searching for something to drink. She found some wine that smelled fresh enough and poured a cup. Leaning back against the sideboard, she cocked her head and gave him a challenging look. "Are you going to marry that driveling nidget?"

"*La femmina* Golding?" Tom laughed. "No. I sent my refusal to Lady Russell the minute I got home. I'd sooner marry Nashe, though I didn't put it that way."

"You'll be stuck in wardship with her for another year."

"Longer. That Golding girl is *rich*. But it can't be helped, Trumplekin." He tilted his head to meet her eyes. "She doesn't measure up."

Trumpet sighed. Her newly betrothed didn't either. He didn't belong in the same room as Thomas Clarady.

"Have you chosen from among your flock of swains?" Tom's voice held a bitter note.

"I have."

"May I know the name of this fortunate knave?"

"I only got one decent offer, you know." She stopped the protest signaled on Tom's face by adding, "I have my pride, which is worth nothing. In spite of a year of penance with the irreproachable Lady Russell, my reputation remains in tatters. He's the only one who didn't care."

"What's wrong with him?"

"Nothing — much. He wants a wife of the same age and status, which narrows the field considerably. And he used to be friends with my cousin Allen."

"Wait." Tom held up a finger. "Your cousin Allen is you, or he was, during your time at Gray's. A short time, after which Allen vanished into the mist. Not many people would remember him, especially not people of the same age and standing." His eyes narrowed. "No, Trumpet. It can't be. Please tell me your future husband isn't —"

"Stephen Delabere. Alas, *camarade*, it is."

"That mewling, spongy, clay-brained, flap-mouthed witling Stephen Delabere? God's great green and mossy bollocks, Trumpet! You care for him about as much as I do. How can you even think about marrying him?" That last part was almost growled.

"He's the only one who made me a decent offer, Tom. I can't wait any longer. You have no idea what's it like. The constant jabs and nudges, the whispers behind my back, the peck-peck-pecking from every woman I meet. Even my uncle! 'You must marry, Alice. You're getting too old.' I'm nineteen, which is practically ancient by the standards of the nobility."

"You're twice as beautiful as any woman in the world and ten times as smart. A hundred. You must not marry that prattling idiot!"

Trumpet shrugged. "Remember when I said I wanted a man who was old, wealthy, and stupid? Two out of three isn't bad, considering."

"Stephen's not wealthy."

"Oh, he is now. His father kept him on very short rations. And their lands are worth *much* more than they've been getting in rents, according to Ben. Once I get my hands on them, they should produce several thousand a year at a minimum. I could do a lot with that money."

Tom scowled at her. He kicked at some pieces of broken window, then picked one up and punched the last pane of glass out of the twisted mullion. "When's the happy day?"

"Not soon. Ben thinks we can stretch things out for a year, at least. I have a long list of unreasonable demands that will have to be negotiated one by one."

Tom tossed his piece of wreckage aside and showed her a toothy grin. "A lot can happen in a year. For instance, I've learned a great deal about murder since I entered into Mr. Bacon's service. I should be able to cook up a way to get rid of Stephen in that length of time."

"Don't even think about it, Tom, I beg you. This one has to live."

Tom snapped his fingers. "I know! I'll take him out to practice shooting and pass him a pistol rigged to blow up in his hands."

Trumpet blew out a lip fart. "That would just give him a few burns. He's young and healthy. A little salve, he'd heal in a week."

"All right, then." Tom took one thrilling step toward her, his eyes sparking blue fire. "I'll push him into the Thames and watch him drown."

"No good. He's an excellent swimmer. How many stories have you told me about those halcyon days on the River Frome?"

He took another step toward her, and she nearly leapt into his arms. She bit her lip and envisioned the sacking of Ravenna. Smoke, fire, women wailing, men dying . . .

Tom said, "Then I'll push him down a steep flight of stairs."

She trilled a laugh. "That never works! We've seen it fail ourselves twice in as many years."

"Three years, but you've made your point." Now scarcely an arm's-length away, he looked down at her, his face somber, his blue eyes clear and candid, like windows into his heart. She saw the battle raging between sadness, fury, and despair. The same three combatants tore at her heart as well.

He sighed and gave her that dimpled half smile that made the rest of the world disappear. "Has anyone ever told you you're an exasperatingly quarrelsome wench, Lady Alice?"

"Why, yes, Mr. Clarady. More than once."

TWENTY-EIGHT

Francis risked arriving a few minutes late for his appointment with his uncle, even though it was he who had requested the urgent meeting. Lady Alice had arrived at his door with her Spanish maid scarcely an hour ago with a most extraordinary tale. And while Tom was fully capable of guarding a bound man, he couldn't do so indefinitely, especially in a place they did not control. That music master must have other pupils. He might also have an abundance of inquisitive friends and neighbors, for all they knew. Peter Hollowell had to be moved to a more secure location as quickly and as discreetly as possible.

But Francis didn't want to sit waiting in the loggia for any longer than necessary. He didn't want to speak to Robert until after the whole story had been unfolded to Lord Burghley; perhaps not even then. He had suspected his cousin of collusion in treasonous acts for more than a week. Genuinely suspected him! He had allowed himself to believe Robert capable of winking at murder and cynically setting Francis on the trail.

Thanks to Sir Francis Walsingham and some thorough soul-searching, he understood that his suspicion had been wholly crafted out of envy and resentment. Now he was bitterly ashamed of himself and not ready to face the unknowing victim of his ill-motivated sophistry.

In the event, he'd arrived precisely on time and had been ushered straight into his uncle's well-appointed study. This was Francis's favorite room, filled with books, maps, and curiosities from around the world. He didn't envy it — he was innocent of that, at least — but he admired it and hoped one day to achieve such a room for himself.

Lord Burghley sat behind his desk, its polished surface hidden by scrolls and stacks of papers. His Lordship seemed to have aged a year in the four months since his wife's death. He'd become an old man and showed an old man's impatience with the usual courtesies. "You have urgent news for me, Nephew?"

"Yes, my lord." Francis stood before the desk, clasping his hands before him like a student reciting a lesson. "I have identified the murderer of the pamphleteers. My clerk has him under guard in a house in the Savoy. He sent word to me via two reliable messengers who already knew the man's identity and can be trusted to keep it secret. Thus there are only four persons who know the truth. Six, counting Your Lordship now, and the villain himself."

"Why all the hugger-mugger? Who is this man?"

"Peter Hollowell, your son's secretary."

Lord Burghley frowned, drawing deep lines from his nose to the chin concealed by his long gray beard. "How can this be? Do you have proofs?"

"Beyond all doubt. We have the man himself, caught in the act of attempting a third murder. That victim is one of the four who know the secret. Furthermore, this identification pulls together everything I've learned about these murders."

"This is a terrible thing, Francis. I know you wouldn't tell me such a thing if you weren't certain. But I find it very hard to believe."

Francis nodded. He let a silence grow, giving his uncle time to adjust his understanding of Peter Hollowell. When he heard the soft sigh of resignation, he said quietly, "I also know who Martin Marprelate is."

"Who?"

Francis hesitated. He should have rehearsed this part, devised some roundabout way to approach the pronunciation of the improbable name. He met his uncle's dark eyes briefly, then looked away. "He is my Aunt Elizabeth. Your sister-in law, Lady Russell."

Silence met that bald assertion. Francis risked another glance at his uncle's face and saw something he had never before seen written across the familiar features: pure, unadulterated astonishment. His aged uncle gaped at him, wide-eyed and open-mouthed. He huffed a hoarse breath, then pushed out a volley of short laughs that quickly rolled into rumbling laughter, tilting his face toward the painted plaster ceiling and shaking his rounded shoulders.

Francis watched in amazement, grinning in sympathy with the merry sound, but utterly confounded. Finally, his uncle drew in a long breath and let it out in a long sigh, wiping his eyes with his handkerchief. He smiled warmly. "Thank you, Nephew. Since my beloved Mildred left me, I feared I might never laugh again." He grinned, another seldom-seen expression. It took years off his face. "Oh, how she would love this! Elizabeth was always the unruly one — headstrong, unwilling to make any concessions to the exigencies of her sex. Your mother helped, I suppose, although I wouldn't have thought either of them capable of some of Martin's more scurrilous passages."

"I'm fairly certain my mother knew. But I believe the more colorful sections were written by Lady Alice Trumpington."

"The Earl of Orford's daughter? The one who has been living with Elizabeth?"

"The same," Francis said. "She's the one who discovered Hollowell's role in conveying Martin's manuscripts to the printers."

"She's an unusual young woman, from what I understand."

"That she is, my lord."

Lord Burghley grunted, his face composed once again. Back to the business at hand. "This can never be known."

"I agree."

His Lordship tapped a finger on his desk. "I will have to tell Robert. It's only fair. And he has a knack for this sort of thing. He'll think of a way to stop Hollowell's mouth."

"There is only one sure way, my lord." Francis would never forget those long fingers wrapped around his throat — never. "He cannot appear at a trial, not even in the Star Chamber. Any jury in England would vote to hang him."

Lord Burghley made a sour face. "You're right. I agree, though it pains me. But Lady Russell is beyond all punishment, other than a time in the Tower, during which she would only write more of those troublesome pamphlets. They'd inevitably be smuggled out, and she'd become a hero, a rallying cry for the radical nonconformists we're trying to suppress."

"I can't begin to contemplate the queen's response to this news," Francis said.

"No!" Lord Burghley shuddered. "Her Majesty must never know." He nodded at Francis with a grim smile. They'd persuaded each other to take a course neither liked nor would advocate in an ordinary case. But nothing about the Martin Marprelate controversy was ordinary. "I'll invite myself to dinner with my sister-in-law and make the situation clear. Martin must cease to publish from this day and let himself fade quietly into history."

"Very well, my lord. We can trust the others to remain silent. My clerk has proven himself more than once, and Lady Alice has a vested interest in burying Martin's identity."

"Good." Lord Burghley smiled and selected a small scroll from the detritus on his desk. "Now I believe it is my turn to surprise you."

Francis accepted the scroll and unrolled it. He read the few short paragraphs at a glance and let out a sharp, "Ha!" Then he caught himself and bowed his head, saying "Thank you, my lord. This is most welcome."

The document granted Francis the reversion of the office of the Clerk of the Counsel in Star Chamber. That meant that when the present clerk retired or died, the post would go to Francis, without having to compete for it by bribing influential courtiers. The Star Chamber was the nation's court of last appeal, in which exceptional cases — or cases involving exceptional persons — were heard by Privy Councilors along with judges from the other courts, presided over by the Lord Chancellor. The Clerk of the Counsel was vitally important. He managed all the routine business of the court and participated in many of its honors and obligations. Honors aside, the potential for lucrative fees and gifts was enormous. Francis's future was assured.

He grinned, eyes dancing with pleasure at the reward, which must have been prepared before this visit and thus without knowing if Francis would succeed in stopping Martin's minion, much less capturing him and identifying Martin to boot. In truth, Francis had expected nothing beyond the usual bland words of praise and vague promises. He'd given up all belief that his uncle would ever help him in any material way.

But this! This clerkship was beyond his wildest hopes. He thanked his uncle again — perhaps several times — and made his way out of the house and through the gardens, his sight obscured by visions of himself in the clerk's traditional velvet robe, solemnly noting those present at some trial of national importance. His feet barely touched the ground.

To think, he'd been inches away from turning his back on his own uncle, wise and generous, to throw in his lot with the young Earl of Essex. A favorite, yes, but an untried youth. His time had not yet come.

No, the motto his father had chosen for the family coat of arms still spoke the truth. *Mediocria firma* — safety in moderation. The best course, the safest course, was to rely on family. They would come through, in the end.

It wasn't until he was climbing the stairs to his chambers that Francis remembered that the present clerk was only something like thirty-five years old. Worse, he was the wiry, vigorous sort who enjoyed good health and a longer-than-normal span. He'd even boasted once, at some court affair, of following the queen's model in taking only light meals and regular exercise. It might be forty years before he gave up the ghost and the office reverted to Francis. Until then, this "reward" was worth less than the parchment on which it was written.

* * *

Tom sat at the small desk in Bacon's study chamber, making another painstaking copy of the twenty-five legal maxims. All the excitement of the past few weeks had died down. Nashe had gone back to his garret, vowing to write the definitive answer to Martin Marprelate. Tom had egged him on, saying, "You'll tease the rascal out of hiding yet, my friend!"

He had not the slightest inclination of ever revealing the great secret. That blast would knock down everyone in a wide circle around Martins Junior and Senior, and he had close ties to both. He would never tell anyone, but that didn't stop him from enjoying the private knowledge.

He didn't know everything anyway. Like, for example, whether Peter Hollowell still breathed. It had been a full week since two taciturn men had backed a cart up to the house in the Savoy and carried out a heavy, rolled-up carpet. Tom had examined the letter they'd showed him from seal to signature, then stood aside to let them do their job. He hadn't asked where they were taking his prisoner.

313

Mr. Bacon had assured him the matter was now out of their hands and they should leave it at that.

Tom understood. They could never let Peter Hollowell say anything to anyone, not even standing on the platform at Tyburn with the rope around his neck.

The door swung open and Bacon strode in, dropping a small leather sack onto Tom's desk as he passed. It made a cheery clinking sound. "What's this?" Tom untied the strings and peered inside, then upended the sack into his left hand, counting the coins with his right index finger. "God's mercy, Mr. Bacon! This is nearly three pounds!"

"Too much?" Bacon took his usual chair with a wry look on his face.

Tom chuffed at that. "More than I expected. I expected nothing, to be honest, after a whole week's gone by. Who's it from?"

"My cousin."

"Did you get one?"

"I did not."

"Huh. Well, you can't have any of mine." Tom poured the coins back into the purse. "I'm saving up for my suit of special livery. Three pounds, plus one from Robert Greene, if I can collect it. Another hundred jobs like this one and I'll be master of my own estate."

Bacon raised his eyes to heaven. "May we never have another job like this one!" He picked up his quill, dipped it in the inkpot, and returned to writing his *An Advertisement Touching the Controversies of the Church of England.*

Tom had asked him why he bothered since Martin had been silenced forevermore. He answered, "Only five people now living know the truth about Martin Marprelate. Besides, the advice I offer here applies beyond the bounds of that single episode in our history."

Tom couldn't argue with that. Then the words "now living" echoed in his mind. That answered his question about Peter Hollowell. Good riddance! He'd played Tom for a fool, and he'd frightened Trumpet, which wasn't easy and could never be forgiven.

Speaking of Her Ladyship . . . Tom picked an angel out of the purse. He could spare a portion of his new wealth to take her and Catalina to the theater. He had a few ideas about her wedding night he wanted to discuss. They could thrash out the details over supper at the Goose and Gall.

Trumpet loved the theater and always insisted on the best of everything: seats in the middle gallery, bags of roasted hazelnuts, mugs of best ale, and a thick cushion for her noble arse. He added those things up, along with two bottles of sack and supper for three. He fished out another coin and flicked it into the air. They had a few good times left before the day of doom. And with a little clever plotting, that day might not be so black after all.

HISTORICAL NOTES

You can find maps of the places we go in this series at my website on a page called "Maps for the Francis Bacon mystery series:" www.annacastle.com/francis-bacon-series/maps-for-the-francis-bacon-series. Some are downloadable, some are links to maps I don't have rights to, including a delightful interactive map of Elizabethan London.

The Marprelate Controversy was only too real for the government and church officials who struggled to put an end to it. For everyone else, it was a year-long entertainment of the Elizabethans' favorite kind: a witty war of words. The core of the controversy was nothing to scoff at, however. Puritans, the sneer word for Presbyterians and Calvinists, wanted to tear down the hierarchy of the established church. They wanted to replace a religious aristocracy with a religious democracy — tantamount to treason in those days. With the advantage of hindsight, we can understand why the government considered daring propagandists like Martin Marprelate to be serious threats. Puritans played a major role in the conflicts that led to the English Civil War, which began only sixteen years after Francis Bacon's death.

Martin has never been identified, to this day. That's one of the things that attracted me to this controversy. Most of his co-conspirators genuinely didn't know who wrote the works they helped to publish and distribute. Martin really did leave his manuscripts in a secret place to be picked up later. He put his under a hedge, which is why I had to learn about oiled cloth. Hedges are moisty, people. Not a good place to store books!

Martin's last blast, *The Protestatyon,* was published in October, 1589. Thomas Nashe et al. continued to publish anti-Martin pamphlets into the spring of 1590. The most famous of these is *An Almond for a Parrot.* (You give the parrot on your ship an almond to get it to repeat gossip.) I fiddled the publication date of Nashe's *A Countercuffe given to Martin Junior*, moving it up a little to keep up the pressure. I made up *Martin's Mirror Mar'd* — or rather the title — to get the ball rolling earlier. I did not write a whole Martin Marprelate pastiche, although I still feel the tug of a job left undone.

Twenty-two candidates have been proposed for Martin over the 390 years since *The Protestatyon* appeared. The list includes such worthies as Robert Cecil and the Earl of Essex, and is a classic example of what I call male pattern blindness. In spite of the fact that many women, like Lady Bacon and Lady Russell, wrote finely crafted religious works and that two women crucially supported Martin by providing house-room for his printers, no one in all those 390 years ever considered the idea that Martin might be a woman. I feel I have rectified a gross error in the realm of historical speculation.

John Penry, a Welsh preacher, was certainly the organizer of Martin's presses, the role I gave to Peter Hollowell. Penry never murdered anybody, but he was hanged in May, 1591, for writing a different treasonous book, *Reformation No Enemie.* He escaped to Scotland in 1589, where he could have lived a full life, if he'd minded his own business. But no, he kept writing and publishing radical Presbyterian works. Lord Burghley pressured King James into banishing him from Scotland in 1590, after which he apparently lived secretly on the outskirts of Edinburgh, where his wife lived. He popped down to London to engage with other conspirators. When they were arrested, he zipped back up to Scotland in time for the birth of a daughter, aptly named Safety. We can understand why the authorities tried, sentenced, and executed him so quickly once they finally caught the slippery eel. His story is a cautionary tale for those who are inclined to view the Elizabethan period as a police state. In their dreams, maybe.

Penry has been a leading contender for the role of Martin, but Carlson rules him out with an analysis of his prose style. Martin is witty; Penry is dull.

Historian Leland Carlson makes the best case in his book *Martin Marprelate, Gentleman: Master Job Throkmorton Laid Open in His Colors*, (Huntington Library, 1981.) I relied on this excellent and beautifully written book for all the facts of the case but one: my Martin is not Job Throckmorton. Mr. Throckmorton himself denied the charge during his trial for treason in 1590. "I am not Martin. I know not Martin," he said. He was acquitted and lived until 1601.

Some twenty-three people were involved in getting Martin's manuscripts into the hands of the reading public. Penry is the only one who hanged. The lesser folk — the printers and their assistants — spent many months in prison, but were eventually let go. The greater folk were fined and imprisoned for a few months at the queen's pleasure. Sir Richard Knightley was fined £2000. Mrs. Wigston, in whose Warwickshire home both *Martin Junior* and *Martin Senior* were printed, was fined £1000. She declared, under oath before the whole Privy Council, that she alone was responsible, saying her husband "being neither overcurious nor meddlesome," knew nothing about it. They evidently believed her, because they only fined him £333 and let him off with an admonishment about letting his wife dominate him. Mrs. Elizabethan Crane, in whose home Martin's early works were printed, refused to take an oath or engage legal counsel or cooperate in any way whatsoever. She was fined £500 and spent a few months in the Fleet.

If you haven't had enough Martin, read my blog (where I have links to many of the works), read Mr. Carlson's excellent book (interlibrary loan, y'all), and then treat yourself to a little Thomas Nashe. The *Countercuffe* is short and not too bizarre, and *An Almond for a Parrot* contains the most information about Martin. Find Martin's works at archive.org: https://archive.org/details/epistleseptembe00arbegoog.

I made one other little fiddle in time for this book. Bacon wasn't offered the reversion to the office of the Clerk of the Counsel in Star Chamber until October, 1589. The office would have been worth £600 per annum, tripling Bacon's income, but he didn't succeed to it for twenty years, by which time King James I had made him Solicitor General. Bacon described the useless reversion as like having "another man's ground buttailing upon his house; which might mend his prospect but did not fill his barn." Ah, Francis!

On to the real historical persons who appear in this book. It would be shorter to list the ones I made up, because nearly everyone in this book is real. I include the regular cast for completeness.

- Francis Bacon.
- Lady Anne Bacon, Bacon's mother.
- Lady Elizabeth Russell, Bacon's aunt.
- Robert Devereux, 2nd Earl of Essex.
- William Cecil, Lord Burghley.
- Robert Cecil, Bacon's cousin. Robert was knighted by Elizabeth in 1591. A few weeks later, he was appointed to the Privy Council. (Bacon wasn't knighted until 1603, in a mass

ceremony, by the new King James.) Cecil's rivalry with the Earl of Essex grew steadily through the 1590s, during which period Cecil increasingly took over management of the state's intelligence service.

- Sir Francis Walsingham was Elizabeth's Secretary of State. known, then and now, as her principal spymaster. He died in 1590.
- John Whitgift was the Archbishop of Canterbury from 1583 to 1604. He was Francis Bacon's tutor during Bacon's short time at Trinity College, Cambridge University and he really did hate Martin Marprelate with a blistering passion.
- Richard Bancroft was the Canon of Westminster in 1589. He was also a prebendary of St. Paul's Cathedral and probably had an office there, but it was simpler to put him in Lambeth Palace. He became the Archbishop of Canterbury after Whitgift's death in 1604.
- Christopher Marlowe keeps coming back. I can't resist him, but I can't give him much play either, because he's too competent! He was a playwright; in 1589, he was THE playwright, author of the spectacularly successful plays *Tamburlaine the Great, Parts I and II.* He did something in the intelligence line; what, nobody knows. I think he ran important messages to and from the Continent, in the service of Sir Francis Walsingham.
- Thomas Nashe, another irresistible Elizabethan. He didn't write *Martin's Mirror Mar'd,* because I made that one up, but he did write the *Countercuffe.* He came to London during the height of the Marprelate controversy and really was hired by Canon Bancroft to write anti-

Martin tracts. Nashe made a scruffy living with his quill, writing bits and pieces for the government, plays, and pamphlets. He wrote a work that some consider a novel, *The Unfortunate Traveller: or, the Life of Jack Wilton.* It's funny and available for free in all digital formats.

- Robert Greene was the most prolific and popular writer of his day. He was probably the first Englishman to make a living writing. He was notoriously dissolute and loved battling with other writers. He's the one who famously referred to William Shakespeare as "an upstart Crow." He died in 1592.

- Emma Ball was Greene's landlady and mistress. She took care of him when no one else would. She lived in Norton Folgate and had an ill reputation, but I like her.

- John Dando and Oliver Oatmeale. Believe it or not, these knaves were real; at least, those are the real pseudonyms of popular pamphleteers. Nothing is known about them, as far as I could discover, beyond those names and the titles of representative works: Dando's "Banke's Bay Horse in a Trance," and Oatmeale's "A quest of enquirie, by women to know, whether the tripe-wife were trimmed by Doll yea or no." I made up everything else about these characters.

- Anthony Munday worked for Sir Richard Topcliffe catching Catholics and for Canon Bancroft fruitlessly pursuing Martin. History books refer to him as a hack writer — one who would write anything for a fee — but that term didn't come around until the turn of the twentieth century, so I can't use it. He wrote a dozen or so plays, which were appreciated in his time, but not ours. He also wrote poetry and pamphlets on many themes. Thomas Nashe didn't like him, which is good enough for me.

- Giles Wigginton was a fiery, irrepressible, Puritan preacher and a perennial thorn in Archbishop Whitgift's side, going back to their Cambridge days. He was arrested many times, including in the course of the Marprelate Controversy. I badly wanted to give him a whole chapter, but the old rascal had nothing to contribute to the story. He had no idea who Martin was, but loved spouting insults at the Privy Council.

- Richard Field doesn't appear, but I use his name. He had the printshop around the corner from Lady Russell's house in Blackfriars, in reality as well as in this book. He came from Stratford-upon-Avon, where his father was a tanner. He and Shakespeare must have known each other there. Field printed the early editions of three of Shakespeare's poems, including Venus and Adonis.

- John Lyly is mentioned but doesn't appear. He was the inventor of the highly mannered literary style called euphuism, about which I happily know nothing. It was all the rage in court circles in the 1580s.

- Sir Richard Knightley really was involved in the Marprelate Controversy. He housed Martin's printers on his estate in Fawlsey, Northamptonshire. Nashe got onto Martin's trail there somehow, mentioning Fawlsey in his *Countercuffe*. Sir Richard was imprisoned and questioned, but got off with a stiff fine.

On to the places. Francis lived in the house his father built at Gray's Inn on and off for his whole adult life. His mother lived on the family estate in Gorhambury, near St. Albans in Hertfordshire, until her death in 1610, after which the estate passed to Francis. Lady Russell lived in a house in Blackfriars and attended that little church of St. Ann around the corner and upstairs. That building fell down in 1597, after which the church was rebuilt, but then it burned with everything else in 1666. You can still visit the tiny churchyard. Find it by touring London's city gardens; the tour meets at the tourist information office near St. Paul's.

Sir Francis Walsingham did have a house on Seething Lane, which is very near the Tower of London and also close to the Thames. Archbishop Whitgift received visitors at Lambeth Palace, south of the river. The Stationers Hall was near the deanery on Ludgate Hill in 1589, but the company moved to larger quarters on Ave Maria Lane in 1606.

I made up the Goose and Gall and the Antelope Inn, but the Mitre in Barnet and the Angel in Islington were there then and are still there now, if you want to pop in for a mug. The Black Bull and the White Hart outside Bishopsgate were real, but are gone now. The liberty of Norton Folgate really was full of writers and actors, garbage and casual violence. You wouldn't want to live there! Christopher Marlowe, Richard Burbage, actor William Beeston, Thomas Kyd, Thomas Watson, and William Shakespeare all lived in this disreputable district at some time or another. We'll be forced to return there in some future book.

I think that's it for factuality. If you spot something missing or something wrong, please write and let me know: castle@annacastle.com .

ABOUT THE AUTHOR

Anna Castle holds an eclectic set of degrees: BA in the Classics, MS in Computer Science, and a Ph.D. in Linguistics. She has had a correspondingly eclectic series of careers: waitressing, software engineering, grammar-writing, a short stint as an associate professor, and managing a digital archive. Historical fiction combines her lifelong love of stories and learning. She physically resides in Austin, Texas, but mentally counts herself a queen of infinite space.

BOOKS BY ANNA CASTLE

Keep up with all my books and short stories with my newsletter: www.annacastle.com

The Francis Bacon Series

Book 1, Murder by Misrule.

Francis Bacon is charged with investigating the murder of a fellow barrister at Gray's Inn. He recruits his unwanted protégé Thomas Clarady to do the tiresome legwork. The son of a privateer, Clarady will do anything to climb the Elizabethan social ladder. Bacon's powerful uncle Lord Burghley suspects Catholic conspirators of the crime, but other motives quickly emerge. Rival barristers contend for the murdered man's legal honors and wealthy clients. Highly-placed courtiers are implicated as the investigation reaches from Whitehall to the London streets. Bacon does the thinking; Clarady does the fencing. Everyone has something up his pinked and padded sleeve. Even the brilliant Francis Bacon is at a loss — and in danger — until he sees through the disguises of the season of Misrule.

Book 2, Death by Disputation.

Thomas Clarady is recruited to spy on the increasingly rebellious Puritans at Cambridge University. Francis Bacon is his spymaster; his tutor in both tradecraft and religious politics. Their commission gets off to a deadly start when Tom finds his chief informant hanging from the roof beams. Now he must catch a murderer as well as a seditioner. His first suspect is volatile poet Christopher Marlowe, who keeps turning up in the wrong places.

Dogged by unreliable assistants, chased by three lusty women, and harangued daily by the exacting Bacon, Tom risks his very soul to catch the villains and win his reward.

Book 3, The Widow's Guild.

In the summer of 1588, Europe waits with bated breath for King Philip of Spain to launch his mighty armada against England. Everyone except Lady Alice Trumpington, whose father wants her wed to the highest bidder. She doesn't want to be a wife, she wants to be widow; a rich one, and the sooner, the better. So she marries an elderly viscount, gives him a sleeping draught, and spends her wedding night with Thomas Clarady, her best friend and Francis Bacon's assistant. The next morning, they find the viscount murdered in his bed and they're both locked into the Tower.

Lady Alice appeals to the Andromache Society, the widows' guild led by Francis Bacon's formidable aunt, Lady Russell. They charge Bacon with getting the new widow out of prison and identifying the real murderer. He soon learns the viscount wasn't an isolated case. Someone is murdering Catholics in London and taking advantage of armada fever to mask the crimes. The killer seems to have privy information — from someone close to the Privy Council?

The investigation takes Francis from the mansions along the Strand to the rack room under the Tower. Pulled and pecked by a coven of demanding widows, Francis struggles to maintain his reason and his courage to see through the fog of war and catch the killer.

Book 4, Publish and Perish.

It's 1589 and England is embroiled in a furious pamphlet war between an impudent Puritan calling himself Martin Marprelate and London's wittiest writers. The archbishop wants Martin to hang. The Privy Council wants the tumult to end. But nobody knows who Martin is or where he's hiding his illegal press.

Then two writers are strangled, mistaken for Thomas Nashe, the pamphleteer who is hot on Martin's trail. Francis Bacon is tasked with stopping the murders — and catching Martin, while he's about it. But the more he learns, the more he fears Martin may be someone dangerously close to home.

Can Bacon and his band of intelligencers stop the strangler before another writer dies, without stepping on Martin's possibly very important toes?

The Professor & Mrs. Moriarty Series

Book 1, *Moriarty Meets His Match*

Professor James Moriarty has but one desire left in his shattered life: to prevent the man who ruined him from harming anyone else. Then he meets amber-eyed Angelina Gould and his world turns upside down.

At an exhibition of new inventions, an exploding steam engine kills a man. When Moriarty tries to figure out what happened, he comes up against Sherlock Holmes, sent to investigate by Moriarty's old enemy. Holmes collects evidence that points at Moriarty, who realizes he must either solve the crime or swing it for it himself. He soon uncovers trouble among the board members of the engine company and its unscrupulous promoter. Moriarty tries to untangle those relationships, but everywhere he turns, he meets the alluring Angelina. She's playing some game, but what's her goal? And whose side is she on?

Between them, Holmes and Angelina push Moriarty to his limits -- and beyond. He'll have to lose himself to save his life and win the woman he loves.

Book 2, *Moriarty Takes His Medicine*

James and Angelina Moriarty are settling into their new marriage and their fashionable new home — or trying to. But James has too little to occupy his mind and Angelina has too many secrets pressing on her heart. They fear they'll never learn to live together. Then Sherlock Holmes comes to call with a challenging case. He suspects a prominent Harley Street specialist of committing murders for hire, sending patients home from his private hospital with deadly doses or fatal conditions. Holmes intends to investigate, but the doctor's clientele is exclusively female. He needs Angelina's help.

While Moriarty, Holmes, and Watson explore the alarming number of ways a doctor can murder his patients with impunity, Angelina enters into treatment with their primary suspect, posing as a nervous woman who fears her husband wants to be rid of her. Then a hasty conclusion and an ill-considered word drive James and Angelina apart, sending her deep into danger. Now they must find the courage to trust each other as they race the clock to win justice for the murdered women before they become victims themselves.

Book 3, *Moriarty Brings Down the House*

An old friend brings a strange problem to Professor and Mrs. Moriarty: either his theater is being haunted by an angry ghost or someone is trying to drive him into bankruptcy. He wants the Moriartys to make it stop; more, he wants Angelina to play the lead in his Christmas pantomime and James to contribute a large infusion of much-needed cash.

The Moriartys gladly accept the fresh challenges, but the day they arrive at the theater, the stage manager dies. It isn't an accident, and it is most definitely not a ghost. While Angelina works backstage turning up secrets and old grudges, James follows the money in search of a motive. The pranks grow deadlier and more frequent. Then someone sets Sherlock Holmes on the trail, trying to catch our sleuths crossing the line into crime. How far will the Moriartys have to go to keep the show afloat? And will they all make it to opening night in one piece?